THE RECKONING & THE REAPER

THE WITCHES OF SALIX POINTE

BOOK 3

NOELLE VELLA

Copyright © 2023 Noelle Vella
All rights reserved.
Singleton's Press Publishing, LLC

This is a work of fiction. Names, characters, businesses, places, events and incidents are either the products of the author's imagination or used in a fictitious manner. Any resemblance to actual persons, living or dead, or actual events is purely coincidental.

Cover Designer: Maria Spada
Interior Formatting: Authortree

No part of this publication may be reproduced, distributed, or transmitted in any form or by any means, including photocopying, recording, or other electronic or mechanical methods, without the prior written permission of the publisher, except in the case of brief quotations embodied in critical reviews and certain other noncommercial uses permitted by copyright law.

ISBN paperback: 978-1-955916-19-6

PRELUDE
TINASHE

Tinashe opened her front door, not even sure how she'd gotten there. She'd put her daughter to bed and grabbed a glass of wine to relax her mind hours ago. Looking down, she saw she was dressed in a floor-length, red silk gown that she hadn't been wearing before. She smelled as if she had bathed in the finest oils, salts, and soaps. Her kinky, bushy hair had been brushed up into a neat bun, while her lips were lightly glossed.

"Don't be alarmed," the man said. "I come in peace."

Standing well over six feet, the man was built like sin. Carnal sin. He held an air of superiority, like he could have been an aristocrat of some sort. Her heart felt as if it was running around in her chest, but oddly, it wasn't because she was scared.

Was she dreaming?

She'd said all her prayers. Had even burned sage to purify her home. She'd been in her prayer closet day in and day out. This couldn't be happening again. Her mind raced back to weeks ago when imp-like demons had attacked her and her daughter. Had she fallen so far from grace that her prayers now fell on ears that refused to hear her?

She'd been paying attention to the news. Things had been happening all over the world. Weird things. Politicians on both sides were playing with the lives of common folk like her. It didn't matter the race, creed, or ethnicity. Didn't even matter the nation of origin. Men drunk on power and the women who wanted a seat at the table were wreaking havoc all over the globe.

Whole forests were on fire. Oceans were being polluted. Toxic chemicals were being spilled. Banks were collapsing. Children were being harmed in the most nefarious of ways. And women? It felt as if there was a war against the feminine divine.

We're living in the last days, she thought.

The man chuckled slow and easy. It was almost hypnotic. "You have no idea how right you are. What if I told you that no matter what happens in this world, you and your daughter will always be protected? Would that ease your mind? Because I can make that happen."

She didn't know why, but for some reason, his words rang true to her. She couldn't explain it, but she felt an odd sense of peace. Hope even.

The air seemed to move in invisible waves as the man gave her a disarming, but charming smile. She couldn't take her eyes off him. His hair was pulled back into a neat ponytail. Within his skin tone she saw many generations of Blackness. His jaw was square and solid. Persona screamed he was a man's man. His body was so well put together that to call him perfect would be an understatement. It was as if he was the man of her dreams.

His smile widened now like he could read her mind, and she suspected he could.

"I can," he confirmed. "You are very proficient at carnal knowledge and pleasure, even though your body hasn't physically experienced it since your daughter's conception."

Tinashe's eyelids fluttered when the bass of his voice settled in the pit of her stomach then traveled further south.

Her hand squeezed the handle of the doorknob as she tried to keep her wits about her.

"Who are you?"

"I am...the man of your dreams. You summoned me here. Called out to me. Don't you remember?"

Shaking her head, Tinashe said, "No, I didn't..."

"You're a single woman, Tinashe. A woman who's refused to date so that your daughter would be safe and protected. Sometimes...you get lonely and your mind, along with your body, conjures up emotions...images. You've called out to me many times, especially when your hands explore your own body. You never give me a face, but always give me permission to help bring you to completion."

She gasped, clutching at imaginary pearls around her neck. How did he know that she sometimes derived pleasure from touching herself? Was he a Peeping Tom?

"You dare insult me by suggesting I have to sneak around and watch you like some kind of perverted incel?" he asked, and she could tell he was genuinely offended by the brief downturn of his plush lips. "It's your dream, my sweet. You invited me in."

"I...I did?"

"Yes...even now your body is responding to me. Your breasts have swelled...nipples are aching not only because you're ovulating, but because they have pebbled against the fabric of your gown in anticipation of my touch. Your palms are sweating. The creases of your thighs are pulsating. And let's be honest, I can smell your arousal. The beautiful earthy aroma whets my appetite." An amused grin morphed his features when her breathing deepened. "When your fingers part your folds to dip inside your wetness...is it not me who you imagine? The desire...yearning you feel is natural."

Tinashe backed up so fast that she bumped into the table sitting by the door. It was only then that she realized that while she was still in her home, it felt different. The sounds were different. She heard the waterfalls in the distance…felt the spray of the light rainfall against her back and shoulders. Pure sensuality oozed through her.

"Jesus," she whispered, the intensity of it all threatening to knock her over.

The man rolled his eyes. "Not quite…"

For moments, Tinashe and the man regarded one another with curiosity. Her remembering what it felt like when she imagined pleasures beyond what mere men could give her. It had been so long since she'd known the comforts of a man. Too afraid of what would happen if she opened herself up like that once more. Nazila's father had abandoned them while she was still carrying, and she didn't want to run the risk of heartbreak again, nor did she want to put her daughter in danger.

"That's one of the things I like about you so much, Tinashe. You will always put your child before your own selfish needs…even if those needs have your womanhood swelling against the thin fabric of your underwear right now. Invite me in…"

The man was setting her body ablaze and she couldn't think straight. Erotic charges had her pressure points pulsating with desire.

"I…can't…my daughter is—"

"Safe, no? This is a dream… That release you need is just a touch away."

The primal male scent wafting from him made her weak in the knees. It was familiar to her. Closing her eyes, she replayed memories of her…head thrown back, mouth open… Her orgasms had been mind-numbing. And the stranger was right. It was he who she imagined.

By God…why did he smell like that? She found herself inching closer. She wanted to inhale him. Devour him. Wrap him in all of her senses and lose herself. She couldn't help it when she put one foot in front of the other and sauntered over the threshold onto the porch. She could practically taste him on her tongue.

He growled when she was within arm's reach. "Your body called to me, and I must respond, my sweet. It is in my very nature."

She was closer now, hands on his chest as she gazed up at him... His mouth offered her a sly, luscious smile as he snatched her flush against him. She felt the warmth radiating from his skin and before she knew it, they were both naked underneath the waterfall she'd heard earlier.

She was on her back, the waterfall like a liquid curtain, shielding them from the rest of the world. She could be free with him. No inhibitions. No shame. No fear. No guilt. Just pure...unadulterated pleasure. His hands skillfully explored her body. Dallying...fingering...massaging... His mouth was on her next, sucking at her core bud as his tongue dipped in and out of her.

"Give yourself to me in all ways, Tinashe, my sweet. Let me make a home of your body...mind...soul. Invite.me.in..."

Her gut knocked at her mental vortex then. It reminded her she was ovulating, but this was a dream. She couldn't get pregnant in a dream. And as his body blanketed hers, her thighs spread naturally. Her body so ready that she felt herself leaking just as heavily as the waterfall shielding them. Ovulation be damned, when he slid into her body, she didn't care what could happen in the dreamworld. She just never wanted this kind of pleasure to end.

PROLOGUE
PART I
ATTALAH

I waited for a reaction, any kind of joy, sadness, pain... Instead, I got my father staring at me as if he'd seen a dead person. Well, I mean... technically, I *was* dead, but with a twist. The incessant barking of the dogs in the surrounding area threatened to make my ears bleed. My father, Professor Octavian Jerrod, continued gawking at me like I had two heads sprouting out of my neck. Coincidently, it could happen if I tapped into my full powers, but currently I was human.

A loud cackle erupted from the front room. "Y'all should close that door," Aunt Elisa yelled. "Dogs barking like that in our neck of the woods means death is walking the streets!"

She doesn't know just how right she is, I thought then cleared my throat. "Um...I know this comes as a bit of a shock, but..."

My mother eased around my father, her jaw slack and eyes watering. "Is she real?" she asked him, but her eyes were locked on me. "The accent, her eyes...her face...*her*..."

"This has got to be some kind of trick," he assured her. "Perhaps a sort of—"

"I assure you this is no trick of the enemy. I am here. I'm real, and we need to talk, as we don't have that much time to thwart what's coming."

Just then Aunt Elisa came breezing around the corner

with a beautiful smile on her dark face. I hadn't laid eyes on her in this capacity since I'd come to retrieve my cousin Safiya's soul. Back then, when she was sitting on the porch of her small home, rocking silently as tears rolled down her cheeks because she knew her last surviving child was gone, she looked so broken, fragile, and dejected.

Now, she was full of life, her laughter like music to my ears, but just as quickly her face fell. The champagne glass that was in her hand now shattered on the floor. Its loud crash overshadowed by the gasp that erupted from her.

Her mouth agape, left hand gripping my father's arm for dear life, she cried, "Attalah?"

"Good evening, Aunt Elisa," I greeted.

"Octavian...Tasmin, move away from her. No matter what...this thing says, clearly this is dangerous and can't be real," Aunt Elisa espoused.

"*Oh, come on.* I love the three of you very much, but you're not being logical here. Aunt Elisa, you're married to a half demon, half-angel. Mommy, you're married to a full arch, but it is farfetched that I, your daughter could be alive —technically?"

The hairs on the back of my neck stood, and I felt more out of sorts than normal. Being what I was, with the job I had, that was never a good thing. And I really did not want to keep standing out in the open as such.

"I can explain everything—"

Before the words could leave my mouth, Uncle Dafari rounded the corner. He asked in surprise, "Attalah? What are you doing here?"

"Brother, you ask that as if her mere presence shouldn't be something that alarms us," Daddy bellowed, almost incredulously.

"How is this possible?" Aunt Elisa asked.

"It isn't," came a threatening snarl from my mother, causing me to focus my attention solely on her.

As it was since I was thirteen, I was taller than she by at least five inches. We shared the same cinnamon-hued skin tone and mostly the same facial features. Sure, I looked like Daddy, too, but I was my mother's child. While she wore her crown in locs, my kinky, loose curls fell wherever they landed.

It broke my heart to know that even though I still walked this Earth, I couldn't alert my parents to that knowledge. To do so would mean I had to break a sacred covenant. That agreement was something I had been willing to always honor…until now. Since the night my father changed the course of our family's history, I had been chosen for this fate.

Dropping my hooded robe fully now, I quickly ripped my blouse open to show my mother a scar she had placed over my heart many moons ago. Over time, the scar had formed a keloid in the shape of a crescent moon.

Seeing fresh tears cloud her eyes, I pleaded, "It's truly me, Mommy."

"No. Nope." Backing away now, she pointed a stern finger at me while in her left palm, I saw energy forming.

I jutted my left hand forward, extending my pinky from which the tip was missing. "Remember, Mommy. You told me you did this when I was just minutes born. It was so if ever I was stolen or sold away for any reason, you could identify me. Remember? Back then, while we had one supernatural parent, we were still mortal. Even having bad-arse witches for mothers didn't mean we still couldn't suffer the same fate as so many of our kind during that time." I hated like hell that my eyes burned with tears. Freaking maternal link! "It's me, Mommy!"

Mommy took two slow, deliberate steps towards me, a contemplative look on her face, but Daddy stopped her in her tracks, grabbing her arm, his grip firm. "Tasmin, what are you doing? You have no idea who…or *what* you're dealing with!"

His voice sounded…different, deeper and harsher than normal, menacing even. I knew him well and could tell he was in protective mode. He was always extremely vigilant regarding the safety of those he loved, but his emotions seemed to be in overdrive, his words cutting me like a knife. Suddenly, his black eyes turned red, and his body began to bulk in size. This time, it was my mouth that dropped open. Last I remembered an angel's eyes couldn't turn red. Only demons like Uncle Azazel, and half-demons like Uncle Dafari, had crimson orbs. What happened to my father? Since when did he have demon in him? Before I knew it, he was in front of Mommy, his signature weapons materializing in his hands, a light energy sword in one, his bec de corbins in the other. He stepped into a battle stance, forcing me to assume one as well. I instinctively called my scythe to me, silently praying that I would not have to use it.

"Daddy, how could you say that? You once told me that the most blessed day of your life was when Mommy became your wife. You said the second was when I was born. That was why you named me Attalah, which means gift of God. Please, tell me you haven't forgotten, *please*," I begged.

Mommy quickly jumped back in front of him. Reaching out her arms, she placed her slender hands on his chest. "Octavian, please calm down."

"How can you ask me to calm down when you're potentially putting yourself in danger?" he shouted.

It was as if he hadn't heard a word I said. I didn't scare easily, and I had never, ever been afraid of my father, but in this very moment, I was frightened.

Mommy quickly looked back at me, then to Daddy before saying, "My love, we don't know for sure that she is dangerous, and I...my gut is telling me that she isn't." She took one hand off his chest, moving it to caress his face. "You can stand here with your weapons in hand. Heck, Dafari, Elisa," she said, briefly peering in my uncle and aunt's direction, "get yours too." Turning once again to address my father, she continued. "Baby, I need you to trust me, trust that I know what I'm doing. Can you do that for me?" Her words, along with her touch appeared to somewhat quell his rage.

"Only if she discards her weapon." His red eyes remained trained on me in a death stare.

Without hesitation, I allowed my scythe to vanish into the ether.

"Brother, Sissy, stand at the ready," he instructed.

Aunt Elisa simply nodded. I noticed she had a staff in her hand. With all that was going on, I didn't realize that she must have run off to fetch it.

"As you wish, Brother," Uncle Dafari replied, his dark matter sword and one of his Mabo throwing knives now in his hands.

Once everyone was battle-ready, they surrounded me, Auntie to the left of me, Uncle to the right, and Daddy behind me.

Mommy and I were now face-to-face. I gazed at her beautiful countenance. In this time, she was younger than she was when she...when we were murdered in 1855 at the hands of slavers. It was almost like staring into a mirror, the feeling surreal. Anyone looking at us might have even assumed we were sisters, as opposed to mother and daughter.

"Elisa and I have been working on our continually evolving powers, and we've discovered that my dream walking comes with a literal trip down memory lane. I need you to stay perfectly still, okay?"

Although she ended her statement as a question, I knew

her well enough to know that it was a demand. She first took my left hand in hers, examining what remained of my left pinky. Being that she was a healer, I had nary a scar after the partial amputation. While I was confident that she would recognize her own handywork, her facial expression was an enigma to me. She gently touched the burn scar over my heart, running her delicate fingers over the borders of the crescent-shaped mark.

Closing her eyes, she placed her palm over the keloid. When she opened them, they were a ghostly white, a trance-like state overtaking her, her palm becoming warm. The warmth was actually quite soothing. Then I felt it, our mother-daughter bond tugging strongly at me. I saw a memory, one that came through loud and clear. It was of Mommy teaching me how to use herbs for various purposes, drilling me on the properties of each one. The next set of memories were as if I was viewing them through her eyes as an interested observer; Aunt Elisa teaching me how to cook; Daddy teaching me and my cousins, Zafer and Safiya, about the different magickal beings in this world; and Uncle Dafari showing us how to navigate the Underground Railroad without getting caught.

The last memory tore at my heart like nothing else could. It was of the night that those murderous bastards caught Mommy and me as we were attempting to save the Moore family. Those heathens stripped us naked, pawed and fondled us mercilessly, then strung us up to hang. My last remembrance as a living, breathing human was of us telling each other, "I love you." Then my life on the earthly plane was over.

All of a sudden, Mommy pulled her hand away as if she had touched something scalding. Clapping her hands over her mouth, I noticed the tears that began to flow in earnest. Her eyes meeting those of Daddy, Aunt Elisa, and Uncle

Dafari, she said between sobs, "Oh, my gosh. Guys, it's her. It's really Attalah." Shifting her attention back to me, her hands rose to cup my face. "It's you. You're really here. But how? Why?"

"Yes, Mommy, I'm here in the flesh...well, kind of anyway. And to answer your questions as to how and why, it's a very long story. Can we please go in the house? I don't have much time to fill you all in, so let's gets started."

PART II
IZRAIL

Dense black smoke twirled around the elongated fingers of Izrail. As his pale horse neighed and whinnied, he stared ahead at the house in the distance. One of his Level One Messengers had abandoned her post. Two sets of his eyes stared east and west, watching several of his Messengers as they answered his call while another pair of eyes watched the five figures in the front room of the abode.

If he were to show himself in his angelic form, the two women in the house would more than likely try to ward him off out of fear, but his nephews…they would attack to kill because they knew what he represented. And his Messenger…she, too, would fight to the death in defense of her family. Her free will to think was something he had always opposed.

Leaves rustled as the winds blew swiftly, and a faint familiar scent caught his attention. There had been trouble in the heavens. Trouble that had landed in this quaint town. Two of Izrail's fallen brothers were near, but also far…which piqued the being's interest. That would be something he would have to investigate later.

Unfurling eight of his wings, he turned his attention back to the house, where his charge had yanked the curtains closed. She knew he was there. Casually opening his right palm, he studied the markings there, watching the black eye in the center cloud to gray then glow white. Lifting that same hand to face the house, with his thumb, pointing, and ring finger skyward, he made sigils in the air, and then watched his Level three Messengers march ahead. Once done, a thin rip appeared in the air. Izrail pulled one side open and then stepped through it, officially cutting his surveillance short.

Chapter 1
ELISA

"I'm Death," Attalah declared, that same charming smile she always had carried adorning her face.

Tasmin's stunned, "Excuse me?" collided with Octavian's incredulous, "I beg your pardon?"

I was silent. Not because I wasn't excited to see my niece. I just wanted to know what any of this meant for me, Dafari…and our children. My eyes found my husband's only to see his were already waiting for mine. I couldn't read what he was thinking. He had closed his mind off to me. That black door he had up was back; however, his concern for me was palpable.

Is it possible they will return to us, too? I sent telepathically, knowing he could hear me.

Would I get a chance to see my children again? He didn't give me any kind of response, only his gaze, holding me…assuring me that all would be okay. I had always loved that with even just a look, I felt his embrace. He knew me just as I knew him… but that black door alarmed me.

Looking at Attalah brought back all kinds of memories and unhealed trauma. She appeared, for all intents and purposes, the same except for her physique. She had more muscle and was toned in a way that said she was trained by, and had trained with, the best.

"I'm…quite literally Death, Daddy," Attalah said then casually waved the scythe she was holding.

"That is impossible," Octavian roared, chest swelling with rage and anger.

Deftly moving her weapon from one hand to the other, she started to explain, "Well, it should have been, but when I got to Hell with Uncle Da—"

"You were in Hell?" I yelled at the same time as Tasmin and Octavian.

"Why were you in Hell?" Tasmin then asked frantically.

"You were there with Dafari?" came from me.

"The better question is why didn't you, Brother, tell me of this?" Octavian snarled through clenched teeth, turning his anger on his brother.

It was then that I remembered Dafari was the only one not surprised to see that Attalah was alive, well…technically.

"Because it wasn't until I laid eyes on her that I remembered." As I watched him, I could tell his mind was somewhere else. His eyes casually roamed left and right before he settled them back on Octavian. "There was a fight for her soul and Hell won."

"Uncle is correct," Attalah said hurriedly. "And right now, we don't have a lot of time to discuss all of the particulars." She rushed over to the window, surveyed the outside area, then yanked the curtains closed. "As Uncle already disclosed, when I was killed, Heaven and Hell went to war for my soul. Topside, the fight lasted all of twenty minutes. On the other side, the battle raged on for days, and Hell was where I lifted my eyes. Uncle Dafari was able to negotiate my release, but with conditions." She then turned to Dafari. "You…really don't remember, do you?" she asked her uncle.

Clearing his throat, he shook his head. "Not in detail, no. There are bits and pieces. It's like watching a movie but parts of it are blurred out…"

"Have you never thought about your time there?" she asked.

"It's something…that I would rather not revisit."

"How do you know that if you can't remember anything, Uncle?" she asked rather impatiently.

"Because I just know. Like humans have a sixth sense, so do we. I feel that I may not want to remember and had something done to make sure that I didn't."

For several long moments, she only gawked at Dafari, slow blinking as if what he'd said made no sense to her. "Do you not remember the deal you made to get me released?"

I watched my husband run a hand through his thick mane while shaking his head. His eyes darkened when he turned his gaze my way. A plethora of emotion was there, and he was conflicted. The way his eyes studied mine as if he was seeing something that was only visible to him rattled my nerves.

"What is it? What's wrong?" I asked, making my way across the room to him now, only to have him stop me.

"No." The leathal rumble of his voice stopped me in my tracks. "No…I don't remember," was all he said before abruptly leaving the room.

My gaze shot to Tasmin who was staring at Attalah.

"Dafari? Brother, what is going on?" Octavian shouted to his retreating back.

"Let him be, Daddy. Something is terribly wrong. I don't know why Uncle doesn't remember all of his time in Hell, but I left my post to warn you. The Horsemen—" Before she could get her words out, a booming clap of thunder shook the house. "He's here."

"Who's here?" Octavian asked.

"He knows I'm here, too." She spoke even quicker now. "Zafer and Safiya's souls still haven't been found. I've been sent to collect them, but I can't do that because I don't know where they are. I am not the only Messenger to be sent after them though. Something Uncle Dafari negotiated gave me free will to think, unlike the others. They *must* collect cousins' souls and they will not stop until they do. That means killing whoever and whatever gets in the way."

The sound of my voice erupting from me startled my own ears. "What do you mean their souls haven't been found?" I screamed. "Where are they? It's been centuries!"

"Aunt Elisa, I don't know all the answers, but I do know if another Messenger finds them before I do, or even if Granduncle Izrail—"

As soon as the name left her mouth, Dafari came charging back into the room. "Why is he here?" he immediately asked Attalah, voice deadly. She took a careful step back then explained all she had told us again. "Why?" he demanded. "Why is he after them and what does he want with their souls?"

Cutting a quick glance at her father, she said, "He should remember this... Why doesn't he remember anything?"

Octavian, eyes red and breathing matching that of a Brahman bull, looked as if he was ready to go into battle. "How in Heaven's name am I supposed to know? And I don't mean to snap at you, but why is Uncle Izrail here?"

"Daddy, what has happened to you? You...have... demon's blood?"

"Your mother and I will be asking the questions. Now, pray tell, why in God's name is he here?"

"It is exactly in His name that Uncle is here. You know why," Attalah returned just as harshly. "Both of you know why! And from what I've gathered, since this family's inception, every time one of us dies, Heaven and Hell battle it out for our souls. Zafer and Safiya not being claimed has tipped the scales in favor of Hell, and He will stop at nothing to ensure that Heaven is the recipient of said souls."

"What?" both Tasmin and I yelled.

Lightning flashed across the sky, illuminating the shadows in the yard. Before we could blink, Attalah, Dafari, and Octavian were racing out the front door.

"Level three Messengers," she yelled, running full speed ahead at a big burley-looking entity.

That thing was so swollen with muscle, it looked unnaturally ghastly, which didn't seem to frighten my niece at all. She tackled the being in and out of the shadows, swinging fists, elbows, knees, and feet! Scrapping like she was in a street brawl as opposed to fighting an otherworldly beast.

Octavian had battled bulked out of his shirt then caught another figure mid-flight, bringing it down hard. His big hands grabbed the beast by the mouth, pulling its jaws so far apart I heard the bones *snap* and *crack*. Another snuck in from a shadow on the left of him, and for its affront, Octavian slammed a hard fist into its throat dropping the beast quickly.

To my right Dafari appeared as one came charging up the stairs of our porch. Just as fast as it moved, Dafari moved quicker, meeting it head on, landing an anvil-like punch to his face. Then, in a move I wasn't prepared for, he heart-snatched the one bringing up the rear.

"What the hell?" I screamed as a shadow moved then grabbed Tasmin.

Not having time to think, I hopped on its back, digging my nails where eyes should have been. Just as I did so, Tasmin screamed then dropped down to a squat, causing the being to loosen its hold. The move caused the black hood it was wearing to fall open, exposing a heart so bruised and blackened that it couldn't have ever been human.

Powers be damned, Tasmin was swinging and kicking like she was back on the meanest block in Brooklyn, and I was holding on for dear life as if I was wrestling with the biggest hog in the pen. My fingers sank deeper into eye sockets, and in horror, I watched maggots and worms cover my hands and wrists.

The being screeched and roared as I tore the soft tissue from its home, falling to the floor of the porch in the process. The drop knocked the air out of my lungs, but I didn't have time to recover. Another one was on me like stank on shit, dropping a heavy fist in my stomach. Everything I'd consumed came out in a projectile. Choking now, I saw the one on Tasmin grab her locs while the one I was fighting yanked my ankle and started dragging me toward a shadow.

"To your left, Daddy!"

Attalah's warning sent Octavian racing in Tasmin's direction, and I was only able to see that because he ran directly past me, tackling the entity that had a hold of Tasmin to the ground just as she got her footing. She was short, yes, but my cousin had always been a scrapper. So, I wasn't surprised to see her pick up a nearby chair and bring it down on the beast's head.

Something was different about these demons. They were stronger, faster… and they smelled like literal manure. Palms burning, I released the squished eyeballs from my hands, jutting my hands forward to blast the Messenger. Fire orbs the size of tennis balls flew at the entity…only to have nothing happen. Not even a flinch from the thing trying to obviously drag me to Hell. Panic settled into my gut, forcing my fight or flight adrenaline to kick up a notch. Screaming now, I wrestled harder against its hold, kicking at anything my feet could touch.

Mournful howls echoed around the area as dogs barked and growled. Wolf-like cries from some of them confirmed that all of my Elders had been correct. If Attalah was indeed Death, then the dogs were making all who believed in the southern superstitions clutch their pearls.

The pounding of boots running my way scared me even more. Was another beast coming to help his comrade? I had to get his vice grip from around my ankle before he got me to the shadows. My kicking was in vain as the Messenger dragged me from the porch, the back of my head clumsily hitting the steps on the way down.

As soon as my hands touched the ground, I threw dirt in the Messenger's face. Roots from nearby trees shot up to snatch at its ankles and arms. Branches lashed out, slapping and attacking with fervor. A series of barks turned into outright howls as two of the biggest dogs I'd ever seen came rushing from the density of the trees, one attacking the Messenger I'd finally gotten off me. Like a rabid wild animal, the big-ass beast launched itself at the Messenger's throat, ripping it out with ease.

Rushing to get to my feet, I got my wits about me as quickly as I could. I turned to see Octavian's foot crashing down on the head of a Messenger with such force that he caved the thing's head in. Tasmin was behind him, blood covered her face and neck as she moved her hands toward the fallen tree limbs then made a slamming motion, sending them flying into the heart of the Messenger who was running at her.

Frantically, I searched for Dafari and found him running for me. "Move back toward the house, Elisa. Stay in the light from the porch, in any sliver of illumination you can! If they drag you to the shadows, they will be stronger, and your powers diminished!"

I wasted no time following his orders while watching the other beast of a dog rip a Messenger's arm clear from its body. Whoever had sent the Messengers must have known how powerful Tasmin and I were. I was tired. Felt drained in a different kind of way. We'd been in plenty of fights, but I'd never come across anything that strong, menacing, and debilitating. Tasmin must have felt the same way as she rushed down the steps, using her powers of telekinesis to throw a dead Messenger at another who was coming in from my blindside.

"Dafari said to stay in the light," I yelled.

"I know. Octavian told me the same. What the heck are those things?"

"Messengers," I responded.

"I know, but what *are* they? And why doesn't our magick work on them?"

Scrambling to get on the porch, we got directly under the light, back-to-back. Surprise filled me as I watched Attalah fight. Her top had been completely ripped off, revealing a black bra and showcasing a warrior's physique indeed. She was squared up with a Messenger three times her size. Taking a running leap, she hopped in the air then brought her right knee to the entity's face. Then the left knee sunk into its midsection, followed by rapid jabs.

She spun, her left elbow landed in its eye before yelling, "Scythe, to me! Now!"

Her weapon sailed through the air so fast it was like a blur, but once it clapped into her palm, she swung it with the precision of a skilled swordswoman, severing the head from the thing's body.

And just like that, the fight was over, Attalah's heavy breathing causing her chest to rise and fall rapidly. "You cannot use magick against these Messengers. You have to use brute force and strength. It's all they understand, and because they were dispatched by Granduncle Izrail, it can only mean one thing," Attalah spat quickly. She was covered in blood and entrails but acted as if it was no bother to her. "Daddy… Uncle Dafari, you must explain to them what all this means. I have to go—"

"Go where? You just got here. We have questions,"

Tasmin said, her voice heavy with emotion as she walked forward.

"No, Mommy. Stay in the light. I don't know how many he dispatched. But yes, I must go. Only for now. I will be back in three days' time."

"You can't just show up and then run off," Octavian spat, still bulked as he stepped from the porch, shirt gone putting his upper body on display. "We have questions, and we demand answers!"

Dafari, moving toward me with fangs in his mouth and a black maggot-infested heart in his claws, had a look of pure rage in his eyes. "He would dare send Level three Messengers to my land to attack my home? My wife? My family?"

Before Attalah could respond, the two mutant-looking dogs with glowing red eyes and oversized jagged teeth ran to Dafari, barking and aggressively rubbing their heads against his thighs as they ran circles around him.

"He would, and look, they remember you after all this time," she said, pointing her scythe at the animals.

Dafari glared down at the beasts, a growl emanating from his throat, which surprisingly made the dogs sit at attention, one on either side of him. Looking at our niece now, he questioned, "Remember me?"

"Yes. You gifted them to me when you were released from Hell. They were yours. I have to go. Three days! Give me three days!"

And before either of us got another word in, she was gone, swept up in a dark funnel cloud.

"Attalah!" Tasmin yelled to no avail. Her daughter was gone. Again.

Chapter 1.5
AZAZEL

I looked down at my disheveled brother Raphael, who appeared to have suffered the same fallen fate that I had. From the look of the deep gashes on his back where his wings had once been, the Angel of Healing was in need of healing himself. Curled into a fetal position, the once-statuesque Raphael looked small and feeble, as he shivered on the cold, hard ground, his usually vibrant hickory skin tone ashen in color.

There was no love lost between us, the bitterness I felt from being used as a vessel to heal Archangel Michael still fresh in my mind; however, as a master tactician, I saw Raphael's misfortune as an opportunity to gain useful information for myself.

Nudging him with the toe of my expensive Italian loafer, I asked, "Oh, Raphael, can you hear me?"

Turning his head to gaze up at me, Raphael didn't, or couldn't, utter a word, as if he was shell-shocked. I crossed my arms in front of me and tsked in annoyance. How easy it would be to leave my fallen brethren where he was…but that would benefit no one, least of all me. Giving him a once-over, I looked at Raphael's naked body.

"I can't take you back to town looking like this. I wouldn't want anyone to see your…liabilities. That would just embarrass me."

With a wave of my hand, a simple green sweatsuit materialized on Raphael's body, along with black running shoes. Bending down, I lifted my wingless brother over my shoulder. I contemplated taking him through the shadows, but thought better of it, not for Raphael's safety and well-being, but because if he perished, I might not obtain the possibly valuable intel I was hoping for. Instead, I carried him a short distance to a local park. Placing Raphael on a bench, I sat next to him.

Although it was dark outside, the park was well-lit. A young woman who was jogging stopped in front of us. Taking note of Raphael's bedraggled appearance and languid demeanor, she asked me, "Is he okay?"

Studying her from head to toe, I worshipped every curve of her shapely figure before responding. "While your concern is much appreciated, good lady, this man is unhoused. I intend to take him to my home to care for him. We all must do our part."

She smiled at me approvingly. "That is so admirable of you, and in keeping with the new year." She reached into her fanny pack, pulling out a five-dollar bill and a business card, handing them both to me. "The money is for him. Also, I'm a social worker. When he's ready, he can come see me at the Department of Social Services."

I read the name on the card. "Joy Evans. The name suits you, Joy," I said, causing the woman of undetermined ethnicity to visibly blush.

"Thank you, sir. I need to go, but please have him call me. Happy New Year," she said cheerfully, jogging off.

"Same to you," I replied, my voice low. Reaching into my coat pocket, I took out my wallet, placing the money and business card inside, briefly looking at Raphael. "You don't need it," I chided.

I waited several minutes before tiring of Raphael's unresponsiveness. Standing in front of him, I looked around to make sure no one was watching, then slapped him so hard his head flung to one side.

"Snap out of it, man!"

Shaking his head as if clearing out cobwebs, Raphael finally showed signs of life. "Azazel?"

"Yes, it is I, once again rescuing an undeserving family member. You're welcome."

"Wh-where am I?"

I retook my seat before saying, "Salix Pointe. Now it's my turn to ask a question." I crossed one leg over the other, then folded my hands, resting them on my knee, taking a posture reminiscent of a television talk show host. "Now, Raphael, tell me what led to your downfall."

A befuddled look marred his face, as he tried to remember what happened. "As the Angel of Love, the Divine Matchmaker, I thought I was doing a good thing," he began, rambling. "I wanted to show that both sides, religious and spiritual, could exist in harmony, live in peace, and they did for a while, but there was always a price. So I gave them a do-over every time. But I did it all in secret, and then He found out."

Thoroughly intrigued, I prodded Raphael to continue. "There, there, dear brother. Tell me more, and don't leave anything out."

CHAPTER 2
TASMIN

"Get inside now," Octavian yelled to me and Elisa. "Dafari and I will try to find Attalah."

I watched helplessly as Octavian frantically crossed the veil, and Dafari the shadows, in hopes of locating Attalah.

I dropped to my knees, once again calling for my daughter, but she had vanished, just as quickly as she had arrived. But not before dropping bombs on us. Death. She said she was Death! And had been in Hell! How? Why? My child performed only good works in the short time she was on this Earth. Why in the world would her soul be banished to the likes of Hell? I had so many questions that needed answers, but I feared those answers would only lead to more questions.

"Tasmin," I heard Elisa say, as she knelt beside me, placing her hands on my shoulders. "Come on, Cousin, let's go inside. It's not safe for us to be out here, and we don't know how long Dafari and Octavian will be gone."

"I can't," I replied, tears rolling down my cheeks. "I need to wait for Attalah. She might come back, and I want to be here when she returns."

Elisa placed her hands on both sides of my face, turning my head so I had to look at her. I saw the sadness in her eyes, the same sadness I knew was in my own. "You heard her," she softly replied. "She said she won't be back until three days' time. I don't think she'd want you out here waiting for her. She'd want you to be safe, and the safest place for you right now is in the house."

Intellectually, I knew Elisa was right, but my head and my heart were in conflict with each other. My body felt rooted to Dafari and Elisa's porch, my heart trying to convince me that my only child would rejoin us sooner rather than later. But my head…it was telling me that was nothing but wishful thinking.

"I can still feel her, you know? Feel the tug of our maternal bond. It's strong, Elisa, so strong it's excruciating."

Elisa put her arms around me, hugging me tightly, resting my head on her shoulder. "You're an empath, Tasmin. I'm sure that's only heightening that bond between you and Attalah. I'm so sorry."

"Why?" I screamed, looking up at the sky. "Why are you doing this to us? Why does my family keep suffering over and over again? Haven't we endured enough?"

I knew we weren't supposed to question the Most High, but I didn't care. I wanted to know why our family had suffered perpetually for centuries. My and Attalah's hanging, Octavian losing his mind, and Dafari spending seventy-seven years in Hell in his place; Elisa living well-below her former status then losing her children. And let's not forget all the heartache and pain from this century. Elisa lost her parents and grandmother; I lost Aunt Noreen; Octavian's latent demon side was released; and Elisa and I almost died at the hands of two hateful Archangels, all because of some grand plan, *the greater good.*

"I'm sick of it! Do you hear me, sick of it and sick of you!"

Elisa quickly stood up, backing away from me. I didn't understand why until I looked down at my hands. They were glowing, and the brighter they glowed the hotter they became. The heat began to move up my arms then to my body, spreading equally from my chest up to my head and down to my feet.

"Elisa, what's happening?"

The moment the words left my mouth, I knew it was a dumb question. I was sure she was just as clueless as I was, the panicked look on her face confirming that.

"My word," I heard Octavian yell from a distance.

"Octavian," Elisa shouted back, "what is going on with her? She was really upset about Attalah, went off on…Him, and just started…glowing."

Quickly crossing the veil, Octavian appeared in front of me, while Dafari and his pet dogs appeared aside Elisa.

Kneeling down, Octavian placed his hands on my shoulders then asked, "My love, what ails you?"

"I-I don't know. I thought about everything that's happened to us and I got so angry…I'm just…so…angry, Octavian."

"Brother can't you calm her?" Dafari asked.

Turning his head to look at his brother, he replied, "I could, but I fear she's overloaded her empathic powers. Calming her will only temporarily quell her rage. But I think I have an alternative."

Octavian walked to stand behind me. Quickly standing me up, he grasped my arms, bending them at the elbows, my hands pointing outwards.

He leaned his head down, speaking softly into my ear. "Tasmin, I understand every bit of the emotions you are feeling, you know I do; but you *have* to release them."

"I can't," I replied. "It all hurts so much."

"I know, Poppet. It's as if once you've navigated getting pass the pain and trauma of one event, the next hits you like a bulldozer, and you never get a chance to truly exhale, yes?"

"Yes, yes to all of that. And with Attalah coming back...and finding out her soul ended up in Hell...and now, she's gone...again," I said between sobs.

"I fear that is what pushed you over the emotional brink. Tasmin, I promise you, as your one true love, the man who would lay down his life for you, and your once and future husband, we *will* bring our daughter back. But when she returns, Attalah will need her mother, so, my love, I need you to let...it...go...*Now!*"

Jutting my hands out in front of me, I released the rage, the pain, the hurt that I felt, off into the distance, screaming so loud I hurt my own ears. Then dimness overtook me.

Chapter 2.5
LILITH

"*Why? Why are you doing this to us? Why does my family keep suffering over and over again? Haven't we endured enough?*" Lilith heard, as she tended her flowers in the Garden of Eden. "*I'm sick of it! Do you hear me, sick of it and sick of you!*"

The cries were of a woman in pain, her tortured wails coming through loud and clear, as if they were being projected through a megaphone. Lilith felt every individual emotional wound she had ever experienced over her lifetimes. It felt like having a million paper cuts inflicted onto her psyche, each one more painful than the last. It was incapacitating. And then…there was nothing.

Regaining her senses, Lilith composed herself. She recognized the spiritual energy signature; it was that of Tasmin, the mate of her nephew Octavian. The fact that her heart-wrenching outburst reached her in the Garden of Eden told Lilith that Tasmin's wrath was directed at the Most High. She understood that outrage all too well. She had been there herself eons ago. But that was a story for another time.

Right now, she needed to further investigate the reason for Tasmin's fierce condemnation of the Almighty. She attempted to mentally reach out to the one archangel she trusted implicitly but got no response. She tried a second time, but the outcome was the same. A knot formed in the pit of her stomach. Lilith instantly knew that something was wrong.

CHAPTER 3
TASMIN

I woke up on Octavian's lap, his wings encircling me. Elisa was holding one of my hands in hers, the three of us seated on the sectional in her living room.

"How are you feeling, Cousin?" she asked.

"Drained…but at the same time, like a weight has been lifted. Octavian," I started, looking into his black eyes, "how did you know what to do to get me to release all that anger?"

He gently brushed several locs off my face, placing them behind my ear. "Sissy helped when she informed me of your emotional state upon Dafari's and my arrival, and I recognized that anger. It was the same type I felt when my parents attacked you and Elisa. Because my latent…curse was activated, my fury was heightened exponentially, and it was the reason why I had to distance myself from everyone until I regained my composure. But you, being an empath, absorb emotions like a sponge. You've been taking it all in without releasing it…that was, until Attalah appeared, and you couldn't contain it anymore."

"Thank you," I said, kissing him on the cheek.

"No need to thank me, Poppet."

Dafari walked up, a mug with steam wafting from it in his hand. "Drink this, Sister. Your signature lavender and chamomile tea with honey." He then sat next to Elisa.

"Thanks, Dafari." I took a long sip of the tea, savoring

it. My thoughts felt a bit scattered, but one memory stood out in sharp focus. "Elisa, when we made the pact of the coven, remember when we both saw Attalah with black wings?"

"Yes," she replied, "and a gray mist cloud surrounded Zafer and Safiya."

"It all makes sense now. Attalah is Death, hence the black wings, and—"

"Safiya and Zafer's souls are floating around somewhere in limbo, which explains the gray cloud. Their souls are together, protected by her magick, but I couldn't pinpoint their location," Elisa said, completing my thought.

"Why am I just now finding out about this?" Dafari questioned, gruffness in his tone.

"I would also like to know that," Octavian remarked.

Elisa's eyes peered from one brother to the other. "Because right after the ceremony, The Book Nook came under attack, so there wasn't time to discuss the matter. With everything that happened after that, I had put that memory in the back of my mind."

"Same here," I concurred. "Believe me; we weren't trying to hide anything from either of you."

"I believe you, Poppet. But in that same vein, Brother, how could *you* have forgotten that your own niece was with you in Hell, and that you brokered the agreement for her release?"

"As I told you all earlier, I believe I had something done to repress those memories. My gut is telling me that was a period of time I don't *want* to relive."

"Be that as it may," Octavian countered, raising his voice, "this is not about what you *want*, but what we *need*, and what we need is to know what transpired when Attalah was with you, and what arrangement you made for negotiating her release."

"And I said I don't remember!" Dafari stood up abruptly, eyes swiftly transitioning from their normal golden to red.

Within seconds I was on the sectional and Octavian was on his feet, face-to-face with his brother. "Then something must be done to facilitate the return of those memories, dear brother." Two sets of red eyes stared at each other, Octavian's voice taking a lethal quality that I had never heard him take before with Dafari.

Elisa and I, passing worried glances between us, hurriedly jumped to our feet, edging our way between our men.

"We all want to get to the bottom of this situation, but fighting amongst ourselves is *not* going to get us anywhere, wouldn't you agree?" She said this as she moved to stand in front of Dafari.

"Elisa's right," I said, looking up at Octavian. "Baby, listen to me. If Dafari is so reluctant to recall his time in Hell, and he did have his memory wiped, my bet is he was severely traumatized in some way. Instead of trying to force him to remember, which would probably breed resentment between you two, ***and*** may not work, I suggest that, like with Attalah, I attempt to 'see'," I said, making air quotes, "if any specific impressions appear to me. Dafari, that is with your permission, of course."

I immediately took note of the apprehensiveness on Dafari's face. I got it. I, too, would be hesitant to have someone probe my mind; my deepest, darkest, innermost thoughts and experiences, especially if it was something I was purposely trying to avoid.

"Dafari, I can't begin to imagine what you went through in Hell," Elisa said, "and I want to respect your feelings, truly I do, but finding our children's souls…we ***have*** to. Zafer and Safiya deserve to rest in peace, and I know in my heart that finding their souls will give us some peace as well. Please…" Her voice trailed off.

Dafari raised her chin with his finger. Looking into her eyes, he replied, "I want that too, Elisa. I just…I fear that once I open that door to those memories…it may change the way you feel about me."

Elisa placed her hands on her full hips before stating, "Dafari Battle, I have been with you through more than one lifetime, and we've stuck by one another through thick and thin. I know you; I know your heart. You are a good, fair, and honorable man. Taking the blame for Octavian and facilitating Attalah's release at your own expense attests to that. Whatever you did in Hell, I know you must have had good reasons. As you stated in your vows, we are bonded by a love that transcends time, and like your promise to me, nothing and no one will come between us, and that includes your actions in Hell."

Dafari took the back of his hand, rubbed it gently down the side of Elisa's face. "I will do what's necessary to give you and our children the solace you all deserve." He stepped from around Elisa to stand in front of me. "Sister, do what you must."

I nodded, holding my hands out for him to take. "I need you to open your mind to me, specifically the part that you've lock off even from yourself, if you can."

"I…will try."

After Dafari took my hands, he closed his eyes. I followed suit. He had indeed allowed me to enter his mind. I saw a door, apparently the entrance to those memories he kept locked away. I walked towards it, cautiousness in my stride. When I finally reached it, I touched the doorknob. It was warm. Not hot, but definitely warmer than I expected, putting me on alert. I opened the door just a crack. What appeared to be smoke wafted out; it had an acrid smell to it, with a strong odor of sulfur. I carefully peered around the door's edge.

Immediately, the image in front of me caught my attention. It was Dafari, standing in front of a table, some terrifying demons, who I assumed to be his judges, sitting behind it. I couldn't hear what was being said, but from the look of things, being that he was bound, it appeared to be his sentencing. Despite the fact that Dafari was not the one who committed the crime, his demeanor showed that he stood resolute in his convictions, no doubt to keep up his ruse to protect Octavian.

Once the sentencing was done, the scene changed. It was…Attalah! I still couldn't hear what was being said, but I saw her and Dafari. She was crying uncontrollably, Dafari, in his role as her loving uncle, comforting her. The next thing I saw was Dafari, Attalah, and Azazel engaged in conversation with some malevolent-looking characters.

The last scene was brief, and while it scared the living daylights out of me, I was, at the same time, intrigued. It was of a man, shackles clasped around his wrists and ankles, chains attached to four pillars. I recognized that man; Jebediah Thorton, one of the men who participated in my and Attalah's murders. The look on his face was one of defiance, until Dafari materialized out of nowhere, barbed whip in hand. Walking up to Thorton, he whispered something in his ear, something that had the man turning a ghastly shade of white, making him appear paler than his normal coloring.

Dafari then walked behind him, ripping his shirt. Eyes turning red, he lifted the whip above his head. As the scene began to blur, I saw the most perverse smile cross Dafari's lips, a look of sheer terror on Thorton's face. As he swung the whip to strike the first blow, the door slammed shut. I gasped, letting go of Dafari's hands.

"Tasmin, what happened, what did you see?" Elisa asked expectantly.

"I—"

I wanted to blurt out everything, and was about to, but we were interrupted. Dafari's dogs went into a frenzy, first growling then barking loudly, running in circles.

"Dorcas, Mimzi, to me," Dafari shouted. The dogs did as he commanded, sitting on either side of him.

"What is it, Dafari? Elisa asked.

"Are we under attack again?" I questioned.

Dafari held up his hand to silence us. A few seconds later, a look of annoyance crossed his face. "No, it's just Father. Normally, I would say ignore him, but he says he needs to speak with us and it's urgent. We all know he may be a lot of things, none of them good, but he would not lie about something like this. Ladies, if you will."

Elisa and I looked at each other. Dafari wanted us to briefly drop the wards on the house. Her gaze was a reflection of mine. Neither one of us wanted to see Azazel. I was sure Octavian and Dafari shared our misgivings. Despite that, we did as Dafari requested, raising the wards back up once we saw Demon Daddy walk from the kitchen. Why he didn't just materialize into the living room puzzled me, but I didn't care to address it.

"Ah, I see the bitches are here."

"Who are you calling a bitch?" Elisa asked defensively.

"I *know* he wasn't talking about us," I snapped.

"Calm down, my favorite daughter-in-law. I was neither referring to you nor the per—," he began then chuckled. "Virgin no more. The sweetest scent there is. Nephew, I see your celestial powers were enough to...," he paused, chuckled again, then continued, "penetrate that spiritual chastity belt of hers. Ah, sex before marriage; the best kind there is. You boys should ask your mother. She can attest to that."

"Uncle, mind your manners and show some respect, or leave," Octavian snapped, stepping in front of me.

"You are such a pervert," I retorted.

He took a healthy bite of an apple that appeared in his hand out of nowhere, chewing it and swallowing slowly for dramatic pause. "I've been called worse," he said then smiled. It was undeniable how much his smile was like Dafari's, except creepier, eviler, and more sinister.

"Father, I suggest you state your business then be on your way."

Demon Daddy huffed before saying, "Fine. I'll cut to the chase. When I said the bitches are here, I was referring to Dorcas and Mimzi. I, too, have brought along my own bitch. Oh, Raphael, come here."

CHAPTER 4
OCTAVIAN

Shock would not have been enough to describe what I felt after watching Uncle Raphael limp into the front room. The medicine man looked worse for wear. My eyes shot to Dafari. This couldn't be good, and how did Uncle Raphael come to be in the company of Uncle Azazel? Dafari glanced my way then shot an accusatory look in his father's direction. I assumed he had similar thoughts.

"What happened to him?" Tasmin asked.

"Besides having his wings ripped from his back and then being tossed from the heavens? Nothing a good bath and hot meal wouldn't fix…eventually anyway," was Uncle Azazel's response. The look on his face said he was either offended by Uncle Raphael's presence or disgusted. Maybe a little bit of both.

"Just great," Dafari growled, turning his ire toward our uncle. "What did you do, old head? Piss off your father?" he then asked, his question dripping with sarcasm.

Uncle Raphael's hickory-hued skin looked ashen while he moved like he was too weak to even stand. When Tasmin and Elisa rushed to his side to give him a hand, I, Dafari, and Uncle Azazel didn't make a move. Demon Daddy was too busy enjoying the position his brother was now in. I, for one, didn't trust any of them as I once had, and judging by the hard set of Dafari's jaw, he found Uncle's arrival just as suspicious as I did. Still, when Uncle Raphael's seven-foot frame dropped to one knee and the women crumbled under his weight, both my brother and I moved in to assist him.

Once we placed him on the sofa, he sat silently while his shoulders moved up and down in the same slow rhythm. We then had to endure his heavy, labored breathing as we listened intently while he told us of his plans and how he had been trying for millennia to see it through. Repeatedly restarting the process of trying to have the holy and the magick wielders live in harmony.

He turned his sallow green eyes to us. "My brothers and sisters attacked me on His orders. I barely made it out alive," he croaked out then coughed violently. "If Michael and Gabriel hadn't literally kicked me out of the veil, they would have killed me…" Whatever else he had been about to say got lost in the incessant hacking. It sounded as if he was coughing up a lung.

While I, Uncle, and my brother didn't make another move in his direction, Tasmin and Elisa jumped into action. Tasmin rushed to Dafari's guest bathroom while Elisa ran for the kitchen. A few seconds later, both women returned. Sissy had pure Sidr honey, a lemon, tea leaves, a small black teapot, and organic cayenne pepper while my love had over-the-counter pain meds, which was an odd find, considering Dafari would never need it.

"I'm human, Octavian. I need it," Elisa said as she quickly opened the jar of honey, it's sweet, sugary, and earthy smell covering the small space between us.

My mind was wide open, so I didn't fault her for picking up on my thoughts. Seconds later, she set the small teapot on the floor and mumbled something to Tasmin. After a small pricket relieved itself of its candle, it sailed across the room to settle beside Elisa. She then snapped her fingers and a single, blazing flame floated underneath the holder before the small teapot righted itself, hovering directly over the flame.

"If what I'm thinking is correct, because he was literally thrown from another plane, and with such violence, his body wasn't given enough time or space to adjust to Earth," Tasmin said to Elisa as they worked separately, yet together.

"I'm thinking the same. And he's in a lot of pain. His mind is wide open, and he keeps fighting to close it, expending far too much energy," Elisa added, she and Tasmin now touching fingertips, creating a bright dome that hovered just above his head. "It's giving me a headache and making my third eye burn."

"We should convene alone later so I can help with that," Tasmin added, laying a comforting hand on her cousin's back.

I rolled my shoulders to stave off the instant lust I felt seeing my wife in her element, using her powers as she had done in times past. When I glanced at Dafari, his eyes were squarely on his wife, and I could tell by the way he took deep, controlled breaths that he, too, was suffering. Fighting between staying focused on the moment and grabbing his woman like he was a caveman and running off with her.

There was something primal about a man seeing the woman he loved practicing her craft, with no need for his physical help, but just his presence alone gives her the extra push she needs to get the work done. Brother and I were used to this. Seeing them use their magick to heal those who couldn't heal themselves. We'd seen them do it countless times on plantations.

"She's not your wife yet," Sissy said, cutting a quick, amused glance in my direction.

I caught the smirk she tried to hide when Tasmin looked

over her shoulder at me. "Not yet, but soon," Tasmin assured me, voice soft, firm and sweet, with a silent promise she had no intention of breaking.

I didn't know if she intended to, but she opened herself up to me in that moment, and I felt the longing...the need to be my wife again. Dafari was smart enough to back away, hand covering his nose to lessen the sweet aroma Tasmin had just sent my direction. Brother backed so far away, he disappeared into a shadow as it would lessen the smell and its effects. Uncle Demon Daddy only bristled, rolled his shoulders then made a show of sniffing the air. Turning, I stood face-to-face with him, practically daring him to say or do anything else while her scent was in my nose.

"A sword measuring contest in the middle of us trying to heal is such disrespect to us, our craft, and our powers," Elisa said, the curtness in her tone noted. "Please stop. She will not be able to work if you keep it up, Octavian. Ignore him."

A wide, jagged tooth smile adorned Uncle's features as he stared me down. "Best listen to your...Sissy, lest we come to blows, Nephew, and I would hate for that to happen especially since we've all been getting along so famously..."

I heard Sissy's warning, but Uncle had tap danced on my last good nerve and I got ready to say as much until I took notice of Uncle Raphael trying his damnedest to get away from the witches, Tasmin specifically.

"*Please*," he begged on bated breaths, "please get her away from me..."

Hurriedly, Tasmin put the pestle down and moved to sit next to him on the sofa much to his chagrin. I didn't know if Uncle had ever taken to lying with what the heavens offered for his pleasure, but I did know he had never been one to dilly or dally haphazardly. Unlike Uncle Azazel, he was probably truly offended by her scent in his nose. It went against his chastity.

The women ignored him though, working in tandem to get medicine in him. Elisa worked at a frantic pace, squeezing the lemon into the teapot, adding a generous helping of the honey, a sprinkle of the cayenne, and then the tea leaves as she muttered a spell. Tasmin snapped her fingers three times and from the kitchen we heard water running. Next, Elisa waved a hand, and no more than a second later, a stream of water floated from the area, dropping directly into the teapot.

Next thing we knew, Tasmin and Elisa were forcefully urging Uncle to lie back on the couch after he tried unsuccessfully to get up. The seven-foot angel was in a weakened state, but still put up a good fight, pushing and shoving at the witches, who wouldn't let up. If I didn't know any better, it would look as if they were kicking his arse.

"You have to get something in your system," Elisa firmly stated, grabbing Uncle's left arm when he shoved at her again. "You've fallen and more than likely need an earthly healing before any of your powers can regulate to this plane."

Tasmin had a hold of his other arm, pinning it between her thighs as she straddled his lap, careful not to sit directly on him. "You're burning up with fever and are in so much pain that it's hurting me because *I can feel it*. You're also dropping Elisa in and out of your memories, harming her as well. Now, *relax*!"

Elisa brought Uncle's muscled arm down to pin it under Tasmin's other leg. Quickly grabbing a fist full of the pills she had expertly crushed into powder, Tasmin slapped her palm across Uncle's face. Then in a move that shocked even me, she punched him in the gut, forcing him to inhale the white substance.

"As soon as the effects of the pills hit, Cousin, pour the tea down his throat," she yelled at Elisa.

Elisa picked up the teapot, twirling a finger over it before snaking an arm around his neck. Forcing his mouth open, she waited for Tasmin's signal. Uncle Raphael roared with anger, trying to fight them to no avail.

When he took a deep breath, his green eyes shot open. "Now," Tasmin ordered, and before Uncle could thrash about anymore, Elisa had the tea pouring in a messy stream down his throat.

"Being of light, soul so pure, how much more torture must you endure? Thine touch is healing, but you are weak, let us administer the healing that you seek," they chanted in unison as they released their hold on him.

"Doctors really do make the worst patients," Tasmin mumbled.

"Poppet, not to question your skill, but why not just heal him outright? You're more than capable," I said, watching her closer now.

"He is very…and I do mean very unstable. He's hurting both Elisa and me trying to stabilize himself. He's so vulnerable, open and raw… and any empath in his immediate vicinity will feel his pain directly. Elisa is telepathic, and his mind is like an open space full of land mines, which he keeps dragging her into, because he cannot control it or close his mind off to her. If I were to go in and try to heal him with my powers, I could injure myself. Think of touching a live electric wire. I don't want to risk myself or Elisa getting hurt."

No more than a few seconds later, Uncle Raphael's body visibly relaxed. His breathing stabilized and his manic, urgent need to get away from Tasmin's aroma took a backseat to the euphoria he felt.

"Normally I wouldn't administer any type of medicine that way. I took the risk that him being thrown from Heaven would make his central nervous system just unstable enough for his angelic blood to override his body trying to adjust to becoming human, per se."

"Why not just administer it the normal way, oral in this case?" Uncle Azazel asked.

"Having him inhale the pain medicine as opposed to swallowing it will get it into his blood stream quicker. Drugs delivered orally encounter acidic or enzymatic degradation in the stomach and may break down during the first-pass effect. That would lead to a huge possibility that it wouldn't work, considering he's angelic and all. I mean it's the same for humans, but because he is who he is, I'm flying by the seat of my pants here.

However, drugs can be delivered via alternative methods like through the nasal cavity. The makeup of that region is such that it can provide a direct path to the central nervous system immediately and relieve him of his pain." Tasmin explained all of this while she and Elisa stood watch over Uncle Raphael who was now sitting up straighter.

Elisa picked up where Tasmin left off. "And believe it or not, your scent will also help. It's euphoric to his kind...so much so that when they walk the walk—when they're true believers— it offends them to be in the presence of a woman in heat, no matter the reason."

Like it wasn't even a second thought, she pointed a finger and made the teapot pour a fresh mug of tea then floated it to Uncle Raphael while she kept conversing with Elisa. "It's something he will have to get over for the moment, considering its effect will give him a shot of straight dopamine," Tasmin concluded.

"I was wondering why you crushed the pills, then I remembered... I haven't seen you do it since back on the plantation, Cousin. Remember the opium powders we stole from a German doctor? You would let the enslaved men inhale it from time to time to relieve their pain from being in the fields, but especially after one was whipped," Elisa said, her voice low but expressive. "And for the enslaved women, we stole cannabis extracts…"

"Yes, and even then, you were always right there with me, magick in hand, amplifying any human medicines I gave to them."

"Balance. We always had balance. One thing was never better than the other, but they worked together to amplify the other's abilities."

The ladies shared a moment and I felt ashamed of myself, but only briefly. Tasmin's casual way of dropping knowledge behind the method to her madness reminded me that while I was indeed a walking encyclopedia, she was just as intelligent. My sexual attraction to her intensified as she explained herself.

I moved closer to Tasmin, just to ensure she was okay, and immediately regretted it. Like a hit of the purest Angel Dust, her arousal slammed into me head on.

Wiping my nose with the back of my fist, I asked, "Are you okay? Uncle is pretty strong, even in his weakened state." My voice came in rough, and I felt my body bulk against my will, but I knew now was not the time to be thinking of bedding my woman. And yet, I couldn't help it.

Our daughter had just shown up, dropping more bombs on an already fractured family unit, and now another uncle had been tossed out of Heaven. I needed to stay focused.

"So you both understand then, why my plan can work?" Uncle Raphael asked, voice a lot calmer and stronger now. "Understanding that two different things can coincide with one another, in harmony with neither side having to give up anything to do so?"

"Of course we understand," Elisa agreed, "especially after learning we're descendants of the Sybils, but what we don't understand is why He would be mad enough about it to kick one of his top-ranking archangels out of Heaven."

"Things have to always be the way He demands it, haven't you all learned that by now?" Uncle Azazel chimed in, impatience now lacing his tone. "It's His way or the highway."

"Would that explain why Uncle Izrail was here?" came from the shadows, causing both Uncles Azazel and Raphael to whip their heads in my brother's direction.

"You two didn't know?" Elisa asked both uncles.

"The Fallen wouldn't know. Izrail would have made sure of it. As to why I didn't feel his presence, well…look at me," the medicine man spat.

"Is that why your front yard looks as if a tornado hit it?" Uncle Azazel asked, looking toward a shadow in the room.

Dafari responded with a solemn, "Yes."

The two uncles passed knowing glances between one another, annoying me further.

"Since you two seem to know something about this, maybe one of you can explain how and why my daughter is Death and how her soul ended up in Hell," I snapped, not even realizing the deadly tone my voice had taken.

Uncle Azazel chuckled, sliding his hands into the pockets of his slacks. "Ah, yes, I was wondering when that tidbit of information would be revealed."

"So, you knew this whole time?" Tasmin asked.

"More or less. It wasn't my place to reveal that bit of information as none of you were in the head space to receive it well."

"Do you know where Zafer and Safiya are?" Elisa asked.

Turning red, appraising eyes in her direction, he looked her up and down, then down and up again before responding. "Do I know where they are currently? I do not."

Elisa didn't flinch, but her eyes gave away the slight she felt at being ogled by her father-in-law.

"You said currently, which indicates you may have known where they were before?" Dafari came out of the shadows to ask, standing directly in front of his wife now.

Instead of answering outright, Uncle crooned, "Perhaps…"

"Father, please."

"I'm sorry, Son, no matter how much you plead, I have no idea where they are, and was sworn to secrecy before now. What can I say, being a demon of my word means something to me when it comes to my grandchildren." And with that, he smiled lecherously and was gone before we could even ask him to explain more.

"Father," Dafari yelled to which he got no response. Roaring with contempt and anger, my brother's lack of control over his rage at the moment told me that he, too, had his woman's scent in his nose.

I needed to get out of that house. Uncle Raphael was now gazing at the both of us with something akin to antipathy on his features. "Have you two no control over your senses where these women are concerned? Wearing your lust and need to copulate on your sleeves as if you're mere man with no decorum! Have either of you no more pride in who you are?" His voice, while still frail in some ways, was laced with disapproval.

The more he spoke, the more my own anger bubbled to the surface. "I cannot speak for my brother but pardon me if decorum is the last thing on my mind." Wiping my nose again, I kept going. "My *dead* daughter just dropped down on my brother's doorstep, my parents tried to kill my wife, then my aunt tried to finish the job, and you, in all your angelic glory just dropped into our lives only to tell us that you are indeed your father's son because you took the trajectory of our lives into your own hands." I stared at the being head on, not giving an nth of a damn about respect at the moment. *"I ain't got no bloody-fucking-pride left!"*

And before I could say more and break the little bond one of my favorite uncles and I had, I yanked the front door open and stormed out.

CHAPTER 5
DAFARI

"Octavian," Tasmin yelled, getting up from her seat, intent on running after my brother.

Quickly placing a hand on her shoulder, I replied, "No, Sister, allow me. My little brother is not in the right frame of mind to…talk to you at the moment.

I could tell Tasmin was about to object until I saw the wheels in her mind turning, figuratively speaking. "Oh," was her simple reply.

I nodded, then stepped into a shadow, materializing on what was left of the front porch to stand at Octavian's side.

"Feel better now?" I asked.

"No, thank you very much."

Octavian was in a bad way. Despite providing needed distance between himself and Tasmin, he showed the tell-tale signs of a being caught in the thrall of his woman's scent; that is, a being with partial demon blood. Had Octavian still been a full-blooded angel, while he would have been enamored with Tasmin watching her work her craft, as he had been in the past, he would not have had the reaction to her that he was currently experiencing. And he most assuredly would not have admonished Uncle Raphael the way he did, although he deserved no less. Sitting on the porch's damaged front steps, Octavian rubbed his palms down his face, as he took in rapid, jagged breaths. I sat down next to him.

"Welcome to my world, baby brother," I said, placing a hand on his shoulder. "Now you know what it feels like to have the aromatic scent of your woman invade your olfactory sense, driving you to utter madness."

While I had deep affection for my brother, I felt a perverse satisfaction watching him suffer the way I had not too long ago at Elisa's shop shortly after her full powers had awakened. I was drawn to her like an addict to the most potent drug. I was having trouble coming down from Elisa's honeysuckle-scented high and had gone to The Book Nook to seek Tasmin's help. Realizing she was there with Octavian, I hid in the shadows. Unfortunately for me, I had accidentally left my mind wide open. Octavian caught me watching him and Tasmin when they were engaged in an...intimate embrace, and he handed me my head for it.

"Is this...how it is...for you, Dafari?" he asked, attempting to slow his respirations.

I nodded before responding. "Elisa's fragrance, while heavenly, makes me want to commit the most un-heavenly acts. Then again, you already crossed that line in Heaven itself," I said with a slight smirk.

"Dear brother, let me remind you that Aunt Lilith sanctioned and blessed our...visit to the Garden of Eden," he snapped.

I could tell Octavian was becoming more exasperated, his nerves raw, despite my poor attempt at bringing levity to the situation. My, how the tables had turned. Now, I truly understood how he felt whenever he tried to lighten the mood during one of my episodes. I had been where he is now on many an occasion and sympathized with his plight. As my brother's keeper, the burden fell on me to see him through this crisis.

"Octavian, we have much to do and very little time to do

it. Which is why I need you to get a handle of your emotions. I can help you with that, if you allow me."

He let out a hard, resigned sigh. "I will do what I must. I need to keep my wits about me, and…the last thing I would ever want to do is hurt Tasmin."

When he looked at me, I actually saw fear in his tearful black eyes. While Octavian was not an incubus, and possessed far less demon blood than I, Father's activation of that blood created significant changes to his DNA, and he could unintentionally hurt Tasmin while in the throes of passion.

"All the more reason for us to get you under control as soon as possible. Agreed?"

"Agreed," he replied. "And thank you, Brother."

"Don't thank me yet. We'll start first thing tomorrow morning at five sharp. In the meantime," I continued, taking off the amethyst, black tourmaline, and clear quartz bracelet Tasmin has created for me to calm my urges, "while Tasmin created this for me, being that you're my brother it should work the same for you. Wear this until she can make you one of your own."

Octavian stared at me, a confused look on his face. "But you were also affected by Tasmin's pheromones. Won't you giving that to me make it worse?"

"Dear brother, while it won't make it better, Tasmin is not my woman; therefore, neither you nor she need be fearful of me."

After a minute or so, Octavian accepted the bracelet, placing it around one of his wrists. "Again, thank you, Dafari. I feel somewhat better."

"Good. Now let's get back in there. I dare not think what's transpiring between Uncle Raphael and the ladies. After the way you stormed out, I fear he may take it out on them."

When Octavian and I walked through the front door I realized I wasn't far off the mark.

"My nephews have lost their God-given minds, acting like witless, lovelorn buffoons when it comes to you two. Perhaps I made a grave mistake with your pairings," we heard Uncle Raphael say.

"Oh, you have got a *lot* of nerve," Tasmin exclaimed, her sheer defiance overpowering her diminutive frame. "Your nephews are the best of *all* of you, hands down. They have sacrificed time and time again for others, gone above and beyond to help those in need. I didn't see any of you down here going to bat for the likes of us humans. Instead, you sit on your lofty perches judging us. Speaking for myself, even if you hadn't orchestrated Octavian and me being together, I still would have been drawn to his kindness, compassion, and strength."

"I feel the exact same way about Dafari," Elisa added, her hands once again placed on her full hips, a stance she often took when she was annoyed. "Despite his parentage, he is giving, selfless, and damn near fearless. Let me say that both of your nephews go hard not just for me and Tasmin, but for *everyone* they love or care about. Oh, and if my *husband* wants to act like a witless, lovelorn buffoon because of me, I'm right there with him, because I love him just the same."

Elisa's last line stirred something within me, not that the rest of her words didn't, but hearing her acknowledgement of how much I loved her meant everything to me. No matter how we were brought together, we were each other's destiny.

"By the way," Elisa continued, "you're welcome."

"For what?" Uncle Raphael asked, disdain in his tone. "Eh, I guess some small thanks are in order."

"You guess?" Tasmin parroted. "Why you—"

Octavian was through with Uncle and his impudent behavior towards the women, stating, "Ingrate! You should be kissing the ground Tasmin and Elisa walk on. Considering all that our family has done to them, they could have easily declined to provide aid, but it's not in their nature."

"I am not the rest of the family," Uncle declared emphatically. "I only—"

"Changed the course of our lives forever without our knowledge or consent? Did you ever stop for one moment to consider the ramifications? I dare say no, you did not. Dafari and I have to go through entire lifetimes watching Tasmin, Elisa, and our families live, grow older, and eventually die, leaving us to mourn them over and over again. There were times the grief was unbearable. Then there was the anxiety from waiting decades for them to be reincarnated, grow into adulthood, and hopefully reawaken and remember us."

I seconded every emotion Octavian described. Watching my love live out her mortal existence on this plane then transition to the next was definitely a low point for me. Being here in Salix Pointe waiting seven years for Elisa to remember me was beyond maddening.

"Not to mention when Elisa and I reawaken, we retain the memories from our previous lives. I don't mind the good memories in the least bit, but the bad ones; I would do a*nything* to forget those." Tasmin's voice trailed off as she visibly shuttered.

Octavian pulled Tasmin into a supportive hug, before saying, "This may not be my home, Uncle, but I have half a mind to throw your wingless arse out on the streets to fend for yourself."

Despite not being fully recovered, Uncle Raphael stood slowly on unsteady legs, walking to stand in front of Octavian. "Nephew, you would discard me as if I were a piece of trash?" There was a challenge in his tone.

A lesser being would have been intimidated by the

hulking figure looking down at him, but not my brother, who stated pointedly, "In...a...heartbeat."

Although Octavian was managing the situation quite handily, I felt the need to step in. "Uncle Raphael, this *is* my and Elisa's home. As such, you should be mindful to watch your tongue and your tone when addressing my wife and Tasmin, the two women who brought you back from the land of the dazed and confused to being a...somewhat lucid individual. Remember, you are a guest, but that can easily be remedied. We've had more than our fair share of party crashers as of late, but at least they showed gratitude for our hospitality. I suggest you follow suit."

I looked at Elisa and Tasmin. The shadow of battle-weariness surrounded them. After all that had occurred this day, I was not surprised. Attalah's return; our fight with Level three Messengers; Father rudely pawning off Uncle Raphael for us to tend to; and finding out our relationships were a part of some grandiose social experiment. While Octavian and I didn't require sleep, as humans, Tasmin and Elisa did.

Taking Elisa by the hand, I affirmed, "Now that I've made myself abundantly clear, I suggest we all retire for the evening, as we've all had a long, extremely trying day. Uncle, Elisa and I will show you to a guest room. I'm hoping you will have a more...agreeable disposition by tomorrow morning."

That was more of a demand than a request.

As Elisa and I lay in bed, I felt her silent tears fall onto my bare chest. Not wanting to intrude on her innermost thoughts, I gently stroked her thick mane, hoping to somehow soothe the immense pain I knew she was feeling. I felt it too, but I needed to remain strong for her. The thought of our beloved children's souls being out there somewhere, with Heaven and Hell both vying for them made my blood boil. It angered me knowing that Zafer and Safiya's souls were being used as pawns in an otherworldly pissing contest.

"Dafari, we have to find them," I heard Elisa utter, her voice low.

"I know, my love, and we will," I replied in a reassuring tone.

"But how? We don't know where their souls are; not even a general vicinity."

Elisa sat up a bit, leaning on one elbow. I followed suit. While it was dark by human standards my supernatural vision allowed me to see my love, her beauty clear as day. Her cheeks still wet with tears, I used the pad of my thumb to wipe them away.

"Your father definitely knows something, but he's being cagey and cryptic, as usual. It's like this is all a game to him, and playing with people's lives, and souls, is run-of-the-mill."

"Unfortunately, you are correct on all counts. Father rather enjoys keeping us off balance. As to why he does it, I cannot begin to speak for him. What I can say is I will do whatever's necessary to get the information from him; keeping his word as a demon be damned! And..." I paused not sure I wanted to finish my thought for fear of giving Elisa false hope. She moved a stray lock of hair off my shoulder.

"What is it, Dafari?"

"If it means locating the souls of Safiya and Zafer, I will find a way to unlock my memories."

Elisa's dark brown eyes lit up. "Honey, are you sure? I don't want—"

I placed a finger over her lips. "I will do whatever I have to for you and for our children, no matter where it leads."

"I love you," she said, then leaned in to kiss me.

Her full lips were soft, and the scent of honeysuckle began to suffuse the air in our bedroom. Her tongue sought out mine with urgency.

Breaking our kiss only momentarily, she said on a breathy whisper, "Make me feel better like only you know how."

Judging by the strength of her scent, her need for healing was great, but I needed confirmation that was indeed what she wanted, as her consent was of the utmost importance to me.

"Elisa, are you sure?"

Instead of answering me, she sat up, pulling her thigh-length nightshirt over her head, dropping it on the floor. As she lay on her back, I looked at her large breasts, dark berry nipples already hard in anticipation. Her thick thighs spread slightly, stirring up everything incubus in me. I moved closer, kissing her, while fingers of one hand traced down between her breasts to her abdomen, finally settling inside her silk panties. She moaned as I slid two fingers inside her, milking that spot that had her raising her hips. I lowered my mouth onto one nipple, tongue encircling it, lips sucking on it. I then moved on to the other one.

The way Elisa's body writhed as I stroked her womanhood told me she wanted more, and I wanted to give it to her. With just a thought, I removed her panties and my boxer briefs, the barriers between us gone. I removed my fingers, placed them in my mouth, sucking her sweet juices off. Positioning myself, I placed Elisa's legs in the crooks of my elbows. I slid my rock-hard manhood inside her then grabbed her waist. Gave her slow, hard thrusts, just the way she liked it. I watched as she bit her bottom lip, grabbing the sheets, her back arching as I gave her exactly what she wanted; a little pain with a lot of pleasure. My job, my joy, was to please her, taking away her pain in any way she desired.

Placing her legs back on the bed, I covered my body with hers, continuing to stroke her insides. Tilting her head to the side, I kissed then licked the side of her neck. Bracing herself for what was to come I felt Elisa's fingers press into my back.

"Elisa," I whispered in her ear. "Do I have your permission?"

"Ye-yes," she replied, shifting her position, exposing her neck even more.

My fangs dropped, allowing me to penetrate her supple flesh. Elisa screamed as an earth-shattering orgasmic wave overtook her body; I roared as one overtook mine.

CHAPTER 6
DAFARI

The next morning, Octavian met me in my sanctuary as I was already in meditation. One thing about my younger brother; promptness was always one of his strong suits.

"Good morrow, Brother."

"Good morning," I replied. "Close the door behind you."

Once he did as I asked, I motioned for him to cross the small bridge separating one side of the room from the other.

"Have a seat," I instructed.

Octavian joined me on the circular moss island, mimicking me, sitting in a cross-legged position. His eyes then panned around the entire room, a look of wonderment on his face. Unlike Elisa and Tasmin, Octavian had yet to experience the tranquility and healing atmosphere of my sanctuary.

"How was your night?" I questioned.

"I'm sure it was nowhere near as satisfying as yours," he replied, crankiness in his tone. "All night, I tried to diminish the anger I felt, and still feel, towards Uncle Raphael. I didn't want to subject Tasmin to my angst, and...I still wanted her in the worst way. That is why I slept in another bedroom. The bracelet helped some, but not enough to keep me from the need I felt for her."

"That is understandable. Our bond as biological brothers

notwithstanding, the bracelet was made specifically for me. That said, since you are still quite distressed, I suggest we get started. I need you to open your mind to me."

He raised an eyebrow skeptically. "Why, may I ask?"

"There is something I want to share with you, a memory that may help with your current situation. No worries, little brother, I promise not to invade your privacy."

He sighed resignedly. "Let's get on with it then."

"Relax, close your eyes, and open your mind…"

"Dafari, why don't Father and Uncle Azazel like each other? They are brothers after all," a five-year-old Octavian asked my twelve-year-old self, as we sat at the edge of the lake behind our Windermere, England home.

"It's…complicated," I replied.

Complicated, perhaps, for a five-year-old full-blooded angel to comprehend, but not me. My parents divorced when I was younger than Octavian was now, mainly because Father wouldn't give up his demon ways for Mother and she couldn't accept him for who he was. After they split, Uncle Michael was there to swoop in and pick up the pieces of her broken heart. They eventually married and had Octavian. That was enough to cause tension in any familial relationship.

"What's complicated mean?"

I sighed before answering. "It means something is difficult to explain."

"And why didn't Mother believe me when I said I broke the egg?"

"Because you are her favorite."

My precocious little brother was always full of energy and full of questions, which, at times, irritated me to no end. Right now was one of those times, as I was seeking peace and quiet. Earlier in the day, Octavian and I were playing in the house when he accidentally knocked over one of our mother's favorite Fabergé eggs, damaging it. Not wanting him to get in trouble, I stupidly took the blame. Mother accused me of doing it on purpose, saying that I did it because Michael gave it to her, and that I was very much my father's child. Octavian then tried to own up, but it was too late. She would have none of it, instead choosing to believe that the favorite son tried to protect me. *Oh, the irony.*

The lake was where I would come to when I needed to calm down and center myself, something Uncle Michael had taught me some time ago due to my anger issues, but it was rather difficult to do with Octavian underfoot.

"Didn't we agree that you could come along only if you were quiet?"

"Yes, but…"

"Octavian, I'll make a deal with you. If you can be quiet for five minutes, then you can talk and ask all the questions you want."

"You promise?"

"Yes, I promise."

As we sat at the lake's edge, we watched as the sun began to set. I looked over at Octavian, noticing how fixated he was as the burning orb seemed to dip lower and lower until it hid behind the mountains on the other side of the lake. It was at least thirty minutes before he spoke again. From that point on, whenever he needed to refocus and center himself, I would always take him to our spot at Lake Windermere.

When I opened my eyes, Octavian appeared to be in a meditative state. It seemed as if my plan had worked. Not wanting to disturb his few moments of peace, I silently stood, crossing a shadow into my kitchen. As I did, I heard a knock at the front door. It wasn't even six yet. Who could be darkening my doorstep at this time of morning? When I opened the door, my curiosity turned to displeasure as I saw my father on the other side.

"What are you doing here so early, Father, and why did you knock on the door? You never knock, you just make your presence known." I stated, stepping onto the front porch, closing the door behind me.

"Now, Dafari, is that any way to treat someone bringing big news? And I knocked because of the hour. I do have *some* decorum. Where are Octavian and your women?"

"I assume Elisa and Tasmin are still resting. They had a time dealing with the likes of Uncle Raphael. Thanks for that, by the way."

"Anytime," he rejoined.

I cut my eyes at him. "As I was saying, Octavian is in my sanctuary. He's had a rough time dealing with his emotions after your...gift, and everything that happened yesterday didn't help."

"And I thought he was improving."

I stared at him. Father knew damn well that Octavian was struggling. The least he could do was not make light of it.

"Son, I have to ask; is it wise to have your brother wax on and wax off in your personal space?"

I scoffed. "Better him than you. Him I trust."

Placing his hand over where his heart should be, he replied, "Dafari, Son, fruit of my loins, I am wounded."

"No, you're not."

He chuckled, then said, "You're right."

I leaned against the door, crossing my arms in front of me. "It is too damn early for your antics, Father. Please tell me your news so I can get back to Octavian."

He sighed, looking at his well-manicured nails before continuing. "Word has it there's a big shake up going on," he stopped, lowering his voice, pointing overhead, "up there."

"What kind of shake up?" I asked, my interest piqued.

"No idea," he replied, voice returning to normal. "All I

know is it's big. They're scrambling down below, preparing for the worst. I assume it's the same above. I believe the reorganization began with Raphael's dismissal. I would bet anything more are to follow."

Just as Father was prattling on, I saw two crashes as if meteors had fallen to Earth. I immediately knew who was showing up at my home at this ungodly hour. The day had just begun, and it was already off to a bad start. Could it get any worse?

Chapter 7
ELISA

*I*n my dreams, I was floating in and out of time. Memories of my children filled me with so many emotions that my nerves felt raw. Tasmin was in my dreams with me. I didn't see her, but her energy was ever present. Things were chaotic. Voices tuned in and out. Some blended making things seem more demonic than they actually were, and then with clarity, I heard them...my adult children...

"Mama saw us this time..." warped into "I know, but she still doesn't know where we are..."

"Zafer... Safiya..." I tried to scream. I said tried because it felt as if my lips were sealed shut.

I futilely struggled to speak until another voice captured my attention. "So many times, in so many lives, our daughter was wronged, and the one time..."

As her voice faded, tears clouded my vision. It was richly southern, but smooth and comforting. She had the kind of voice that soothed a child's fear just by hearing it. I missed her so much...

"Mama..." I cried softly.

"We didn't choose wrong, Akasha. We picked the best option from what was presented to us..." The deep male baritone with the southern drawl made my heart race.

Trying to catch my breath was difficult. "Daddy..."

THE RECKONING & THE REAPER

As their voices faded, the dreams spun wildly, scenes forming and disappearing just as quickly...then I smelled the burned cinnamon. I was standing in front of Tarot Readings, Charms & Runes, a small shop in town that did just what the name alluded to, but before I could question why, the scene closed in on itself.

My eyes shot open, and in an instant, I was out of bed and rushing downstairs. My anger making the earth beneath the house quake. Random items crashed to the floor. Doors flew open and then slammed shut, as did a few windows. Barefoot, I didn't care that I was still in nightwear, nor did I give a damn that I felt Azazel's presence. Decorum an afterthought, I leapt off the last stair.

Yanking the front door open, and then storming onto the porch, I came face-to-face with my husband's mother. Taller than the average woman and built like an Amazon, her ropey braids were pulled back from her face, putting her striking ebony features on display. Her dark skin was the same as Dafari's, and her eyes just as haunting, adding to the things that identified her as his mother. While Michael—who immediately turned away from me probably because of my nightgown— was dressed in all black and looked as if he was about to go into battle, she was in only white garb that had been strategically wrapped around her battered and bruised body to look like a long sarong.

I didn't care that she and Michael looked like they had just dropped in from a fight. Nor did I give a damn that she gazed down at me as if I was but a fly sent to antagonize her.

"What do you want?" I asked plainly.

Breathing seemed to be laborious for her, but she gazed from me to Dafari like she was trying to figure something out. "You married her," she then said, casting a disappointed look in her son's direction.

Dafari sighed heavily then stood to my right, his hand

easing down to hold my wrist with the bracelet. Then he let the pad of his thumb gently graze my palm. "Answer her question, Mother. What do you want?" he responded.

Silence settled between the three of us, before Azazel's cocky chuckle drew my attention his way. Unlike Michael, he didn't turn away, but took in the sight of his ex-wife and me equally, pausing to study me with a slick grin before turning to his ex-wife. "Well... isn't this a sight," he crooned. "To what do we owe the honor?"

"Go to Hell, Azazel," was her frosty reply.

"Will you be joining me? Heard the place needs a new mistress now that Eve has escaped, and I would love nothing more than to have you as a *hetaera* in my chambers..." Even though his voice was smooth and honeyed, the underlying threat made my flesh crawl.

While the woman bristled, she didn't respond verbally. Her gaze still bouncing between me and Dafari.

"Please do not forget that there is still a target on your back, Brother," Michael warned, angling his head just enough to send a glare of madness toward Azazel.

Dropping his hands, Azazel stepped forward. "Was that a threat?"

Turning fully now, Michael moved closer to his brother, lessening the gap between them a bit more. "Does it need to be?" he growled.

"Father...Uncle, please refrain from using my home as your arena. Uncle, state your business, and Father—"

"Say. Less," Azazel growled and then backed away, but not before shooting a menacing scowl at both his ex-wife and his brother.

"Nephew, please ask your wife to properly clothe herself so that we may speak face-to-face," Michael asked, his voice taking on a terrifying chill as he worked to calm his breathing. He rolled his shoulders then put his attention on Dafari.

"No. You showed up to our home, unannounced first thing in the morning, and make demands? I think not. If her state of dress offends you, gouge out your own eyes as the Book advises. Otherwise, say what you need to say."

My gown was loose and stopped knee-length. However, anytime I moved it clung to any and every curve my body owned. Michael acted as if I'd stepped outside in lingerie.

You have on no undergarments, and you have my scent all over you. Not to mention your own, Dafari shot my way telepathically. *Same as with Uncle Raphael, it offends his chastity.*

Chastity? What chastity? He's got a whole wife!

"My son, thy do make me…proud," Azazel crooned cockily, while folding his arms across his muscled chest.

With his long, shoulder-length hair curtaining his exotic face, it was easy to see why he was the king of incubi. Standing as if he ruled all the land, he scoffed at his brother who had turned around to face the pair just as Octavian and a very angry Tasmin stepped out onto the disheveled porch.

"There are other fallen who are gathering, amassing forces from all sides," Michael snapped then turned to his wife who hadn't taken her eyes off Tasmin. "Our sons have made their decisions, Eset."

"Mother…Father, what are you doing here?" Octavian asked, his cadence a lot calmer than it had been the day before, but there was still some indifference. Placing himself whereas he was flanking Tasmin, he waited for an answer.

"It's been like a revolving door around here," Tasmin mumbled then sent a look of concern my way.

Are you okay? she thought.

Outside of a few bad dreams, I was coping very well until she showed up, I sent back.

Are we going to talk about exactly who she is when we're alone later? she asked.

Oh, we are most definitely going to talk about it…

I could tell Octavian and Dafari were privy to our conversation as they each cast pensive gazes in our direction. To have their wives and mother at odds had to be disconcerting. Although…their mother did try to kill us…

Will you put up a black box for a second? she asked.

Without question I closed our conversation. *What's wrong?* I shot to her.

You are aware you look as if you've been ridden hard and put up wet, right? And not in the traditional sense of the saying. Like…it's pretty obvious you've had a pleasure bite as well. You're dark skinned and I can see the bruise…

Holy shit. That better explained Michael's reaction to my presence.

Chuckling inwardly, she thought, *Dang, Cousin… making up for old times?*

A ghost of a smirk appeared on her face, making me groan internally. *Is it really that obvious?*

Raising her brows, she discreetly nodded once. *Rode very, very hard. Put up very, very wet…*

"Lucifer Morningstar is on the move and for some reason, the battle to collect as many souls as possible is just as important as the final battle. Gray-Walkers have been disappearing all over the world," Michael said, breaking our mental conversation.

"What does that mean?" Tasmin asked as if she had been paying attention all along. "And what does it have to do with us?"

"Because of you two," Eset said, looking from me to Tasmin, "both sides are scrambling to reinforce their numbers."

"How much time do we have? Days? Months? Years?" Octavian asked.

"We don't know. With Eve still being topside, Hell is off balance," said Michael.

I'm surprised they haven't mentioned Raphael, I sent to Tasmin.

I do find that odd, but that could be a good thing. With him being tossed out, perhaps two of Heaven's best warrior archangels not knowing he's here is for the best...

Eset continued, "Souls and Gray-Walkers are key ingredients to any battle, as it's hard to kill a soul, but in the right hands, the power a soul possesses can be harnessed to be used as their captors see fit. Tainted souls, those willing to commit the vilest of acts, can be manipulated to possess bodies of those like angels serving periods of atonement here on Earth, right in battle. Essentially causing them to turn on their own side.

On the other hand, Gray-Walkers can only be killed by heavenly forces, giving whoever controls them an almost unstoppable advantage in battle." She paused, coughed once then took deep, hard breaths. Michael was at her side in an instant, assuring she was okay. Once she recovered, she said, "Coming into your powers has tipped the scales. Just now, before we dropped in, there was a battle outside Salix Pointe."

Tasmin looked at me then back to Eset. That wasn't something we wanted to hear. After reawakening, we knew there was more to this place than met the eye. We still had so much to learn about our coven and the town itself that having to battle for it seemed unfair. To now have to go to war to keep the whole town— and probably the whole world— safe seemed like another slap in the face on top of every-damn-thing else!

Where are my damn children? my mind screamed, causing Tasmin to slightly startle before catching herself and shooting a worried glance in my direction. I would have to apologize for scaring her later. She probably now thought I was going crazy as I slammed that part of my mind shut.

"Demons and Messengers," Michael said. "Levels three and four Messengers were headed here at the behest of Izrail. The demons were courtesy of Lucifer himself. When the two sides collided, a fight ensued in the shadows that spilled over into the veil, and then back into the human world. We've just come from its aftermath."

"Wait, back up," I said, confused about something. "If Gray-Walkers can only be killed by heavenly forces, and if the other side has them, isn't that a loss for their side considering you're literally angels from Heaven?"

"Just because *we're* fallen doesn't mean we aren't still beings created in Heaven," Azazel answered. "Gray-Walkers are neither good nor bad, light nor dark. We walk the middle."

Octavian added, "Until controlled by a more powerful entity, and then they can be used at will."

Azazel nodded proudly at his nephew. "Correct, Octavian. Lucifer or any other powerful fallen can control them as well. A horde of Gray-Walkers is just as dangerous as a coven of vampires or a pack of werewolves."

"And what does that mean for you?" Tasmin then pointedly asked Azazel. "Who controls you if they get—"

Cutting her off, Azazel chuckled arrogantly. "My sweet doctor, please be serious. Me? Controlled? Not even the one who created me could do that. Hence, my coveted fallen status." He made a show of spreading his arms with a showman's grin.

"While he has a point," Michael cut in now, ignoring Azazel's antics, "what's more important is that you four do whatever it is you can here to secure this place. We don't need you or Tasmin falling into the wrong hands."

"As opposed to what?" I asked.

"Us falling into your hands?" Tasmin wanted to know. "Seems as if your warning is a bit biased considering you and your wife have already tried to kill us. The Angel of Death sent Messengers after us. How are we to know which side is **'*the wrong hands*?'**" she said, putting the last three words in finger quotes.

"I mean as far as we know, you and she could be here now to do His bidding for *the greater good*," I snapped sarcastically.

"They do have a point," Dafari added. "The fact that they are safer with my father isn't saying much at all."

That got a hearty guffaw out of Azazel. "Touché, my son."

"And I for one, don't trust either of you, still. Yes, you helped us fight off Eve and her minions, Michael, but even with that fact, don't expect me to lay out the welcome mat willingly. As far as you," Tasmin said, facing Eset now, "I wouldn't trust you even if I *could* trust you."

"Make that two of us. Looks like my cousin and I are on our own, outside of Dafari, Octavian, and our coven. We don't need your help, especially since it seems to come with the condition that you'll only help us if you can control us afterwards," I said coolly.

Eset sucked her teeth. "You two think you have all the answers? Two witches with miniscule powers here on Earth are going to tell me—"

I had visions of using the power of the wind breezing overhead to throw her clear into the yard. "Don't disrespect our powers because it looks different than yours. I'm a proud Black witch, and no matter the lifetime, I always will be. I also love your son…that doesn't change either. It never changes, Eset."

"You have a lot of nerve compared to the last one of mine you're tapdancing on," Tasmin said on an exasperated sigh.

"However, because I love your son, I'm going to extend you the grace you have never extended to me. We don't have to be enemies."

The light breeze on the wind picked up now, making the trees rock and sway violently while random pieces of broken wood started hovering just above the ground. I felt Dafari's hand grip mine. Saw when Octavian moved closer to Tasmin, probably to try to calm her down.

"Now, Eset, how rude of a guest you are, insulting the witches on their own turf? Tsk...tsk...tsk... Might I suggest you don't underestimate them? They're very comfortable in their powers," Azazel quipped, and I couldn't tell if he was being sarcastic or antagonistic...or both.

"I think it's time we took our leave," Michael said. "We'll be back when we find out more. Hopefully next time, we'll all be in a better place emotionally."

He took a hold of his wife's hand then escorted her off the porch. A few seconds later, a white tornado-like tunnel swooped them up toward the heavens.

Chapter 8
TASMIN

Despite protestations from Octavian and Dafari, Elisa and I decided to venture into town for a bit. Rufus was managing both The Book Nook and Elisa's Coffee Press and was doing an amazing job. However, as much as we trusted Rufus implicitly, we felt the need to check on our respective businesses. That and we wanted to talk without listening ears and minds, around.

"...and did you hear the way she said, 'You married her.'?" she asked, imitating Eset's vocal pattern to a tee. "And the scowl on her face when she said it. I cannot with her!"

Elisa was fit to be tied; we both were. Having Eset and Michael pay a visit on top of all the other drama and this year was definitely starting off on a low point.

"Yeah, your mother-in-law is a piece of work," I said, laughing to myself as I kept my eyes on the road, knowing Elisa would immediately have a response to my comment.

"Oh, so that's how it is, Cousin?" she asked with a giggle. "Okay, I'll give you that, but *only* because you and Octavian aren't legally married...yet. But you just wait."

"Oh joy, oh bliss," I remarked sarcastically. "If I didn't love him so much...but I do, and regardless of whom his parents are, nothing's going to stop me from marrying him...again."

"Or maybe in spite of them, perhaps?" My cousin knew me well.

"Maybe a bit of both," I said smirking. An idea forming, I turned to Elisa. "I know we had planned to go into town, but I have a better idea."

Elisa raised an inquisitive eyebrow. "Do tell."

Within fifteen minutes, I had pulled up in front of the mayor's mansion.

"So we're doing this?" Elisa asked, getting out of the car.

"Oh, we're definitely doing this," I stated resolutely.

"Then let's go."

I paused momentarily, looking around, scoping out the area. There wasn't a living soul in sight, although it wasn't unexpected. The holidays had fallen on a weekend, so it didn't surprise me at all that the mayor's mansion was closed to the public. That just made things easier for us.

"Let's keep our minds open to each other," I said.

Elisa nodded, sending me a telepathic signal. Standing in front of the thick, carved wooden double doors, the bracelet on my left wrist began to glow, as did the one on Elisa's right. Elisa and I raised our arms with the bracelets, hands pointed towards the door. The energy blasts we released blew the doors open with ease, allowing us entry into the building, not caring one way or the other if they heard us. Once inside, I noticed how dark the foyer was, save for a few auxiliary lights. To my left sat a small, oak entryway table with mail piled on top of it.

"I wonder if Ephraim and Ilene are even here." she thought, as she riffled through the mail. *"Neither of them has*

been seen since we body jacked them before the big battle, which is unusual for them, especially around the holidays. We were so caught up dealing with Eve, then my wedding and Christmas that I didn't even think about what a show they put on every year. This place should have been decorated to the nines, with a huge Christmas tree out front and one in this very foyer. They usually keep everything up until right after New Year's Day."

"Maybe they skipped town. After the way the coven took them down, it wouldn't surprise me."

Elisa huffed then conveyed, *"The town would be better for it if they were gone."*

"You'll get no argument from me. I still say we look around. If we don't find them, whatever, but maybe we can find a clue to where they went. Let's start with the mayor's office."

Using the memories from the night of the jubilee, I walked in the direction of Mayor Lovett's office. Upon reaching it, Elisa put her hand on my arm.

"Wait. Ephraim's in there, and so is Ilene. I can hear their thoughts loud and clear, which is odd because they were always so good at cloaking them."

I shrugged. *"Maybe they're not masking them because they don't think they have to. They probably think they're the only ones here."*

"True, but I just thought about something. Ephraim is a powerful warlock. Even though he and Ilene are here, none of the staff is. With all that they're hiding, don't you think they'd have some sort of...supernatural alarm system? They probably couldn't hear us blow the front doors open from way back here, but if there were magick wards up, they would have been tipped off for sure."

"And I'm guessing neither of them were in the security room to see us," I said, nodding my head in the direction of

the door to the left of the mayor's office, a name plate with the word **SECURITY** on it. *"Well, there's only one way to find out what's really going on."*

As we did to the mansion's front doors, Elisa and I used our energy blasts, opening the office door in no time flat.

"H-how did you get in here?" a shocked Ilene asked.

"Through the front door, like anyone else," I snarkily replied.

"What is the meaning of this intrusion, Tasmin and Elisa?" the mayor asked, acting just as dramatic as Ilene. He moved to stand next to her.

"We'll be the ones asking the questions, Ephraim," Elisa stated with authority.

Two wood and leather armchairs sat in front of the mayor's desk. Using my telekinesis, I turned them around to face me and Elisa. I waved a hand, signaling Mayor Lovett and his wife to each take a seat. Once they did, I communicated with Elisa telepathically.

"The Virginia creeper vines on the side of the house; after I open the window, I need you pull some in here. We need a captive audience."

Elisa smiled and nodded. Not wanting to damage the pristine stained-glass windows, I used my powers to turn the latch then carefully opened the panes. Elisa thrusted her arms forward. As she retracted them, long strands of the vines followed. The path they took mimicked her hand motions, the vines firmly securing Ephraim and Ilene to the chair's parts. Once they were confined, I took a moment to allow my eyes to scan the room. They were packing, and hurriedly from the looks of it.

"Going somewhere, Mayor?" I asked, sitting on the leather couch directly across from them, Elisa joining me.

"Ye-yes, well, Mrs. Lovett and I were planning a little

getaway, an extended holiday of sorts," he replied, chuckling nervously.

"Really, Ephraim?" Elisa asked skeptically, raising an eyebrow.

"Husband of mine, I think that witch is reading our minds," Ilene exclaimed in her true Southern belle fashion. "Make her stop," she whined.

"Alas, *mon amour*, if only I could."

"Ilene, you might want to watch how you address my cousin and me, especially since she can tighten those bindings with just a mere thought, right, Elisa?"

I watched as Elisa constricted the vines surrounding Ilene's forearms, moving her hands in circular motions, Ilene's skin blanching, becoming even paler than her normal pasty complexion.

"Ouch, you're hurting me, and I can't feel my fingers," she complained.

"I'll stop, but only if you watch your mouth. Deal?"

Ilene poked her non-existent lips out before saying, "Fine."

"Now that that's settled, let's get down to business. We all know Elisa can read your minds, so don't even try to lie," I instructed. "And on that note, why *can* Elisa read your minds now? Both of you were so good at blocking her."

Mayor Lovett let out a long, hard sigh before responding. "*Ma chère et douce épouse* and I can…no longer do that, much to our displeasure."

"And why is that, Ephraim?" Elisa queried.

"Don't tell them anything, Ephraim. We still may be able to rise above this and attain our once and former glory."

With a twirl of her index fingers, Elisa once again tightened Ilene's bindings, this time the ones around her legs.

"Okay, okay, I'll be quiet," she shouted.

"Promise?" I asked.

"Yes, yes, I promise."

"You're lucky it wasn't the ones around your chest," Elisa noted, slightly loosening Ilene's leg vines. "Ephraim, as you were saying."

"If I tell you what you want to know, will you let us go?" He looked from Elisa to me, genuine fear in his eyes.

"Sure we will...as long as we know you're no threat to us," I replied. "So, Mayor Lovett, enlighten us." I leaned my elbows on my thighs, chin resting on my folded hands.

"I'm not sure if you were aware, but I am a direct descendent of Madame Marie Delphine LaLaurie."

"Believe me, we are very much aware," I retorted. "We also knew about her Faustian bargain with Mephistopheles. She sold her soul in order to gain immortality, promising, in return, to serve Mephistopheles's master, who turned out to be the demon, Eve. But what does that have to do with you not being able to prevent Elisa from reading your minds?"

"It has everything to do with it," the mayor said, raising his voice. "I apologize. It's just that...anyway, Marie didn't just sell her soul, she also sold the souls of my entire male line, as well as those of her handmaiden and her descendants, of which my beloved is one. Because of that, as long as the deal was in place, we were all locked in servitude to Eve."

"So, you're telling us that for over a century and a half, because Marie roped your ancestors into her contract, both of your bloodlines were forced to carry out Eve's will? Do you really expect us to believe that?" Elisa looked incredulously at the mayor then his wife.

"It's the truth," Ilene chimed in, her shrill voice showing her desperation. "We, nor our ancestors, had a choice. Whatever Eve wanted us to do, we had to comply, no questions asked. If anyone opposed her, it didn't turn out well, if you know what I mean."

"Although...," Lovett began.

THE RECKONING & THE REAPER

"Go on," Elisa prodded.

"It wasn't all bad. As long as we continued to do her bidding, Eve bestowed on us certain...gifts."

"You mean that fact that you're a wizard and have used your powers to benefit you and Ilene, manipulating the people of Salix Pointe for years?" I asked.

"How did y'all find out? That paramour of yours made it known to me that he was aware of my status as he was accosting me in front of the townsfolk."

"The how is not important, the fact that we do know is. And the way we heard it, and not just from Octavian, you came at him first, so you had it coming. And speaking of Octavian, let's go back to the night you were our...guest at Dafari and Elisa's home."

"You mean the night you almost killed me?" Mayor Lovett barked, fear and fire in his eyes.

"Yeah, that night," I said, unbothered by his accusation. I had since come to terms with my actions that night, and his righteous indignation meant nothing to me, considering all he had done.

"How is it that your and Ilene's energy signatures were the same as the ones from the night...two of my ancestors were hanged in 1855?" I felt he didn't need to know the truth behind the hangings, but my attempt at subterfuge turned out to be futile.

"Come now, Tasmin," the mayor began, "cards on the table, Eve filled us in on your very...*colored* histories." I didn't appreciate the way he said colored, his dual meaning clear. "You mean the night you and your daughter, was it, were hanged?" A slight smirk crossed his twisted features.

"I suggest you watch how you talk to my cousin, Ephraim, and just answer her questions. No snark allowed, understood?" Elisa twirled a finger, the vines around the mayor's chest constricting, his face becoming flush.

He regarded Elisa then me, saying on labored breaths, "Under…stood. My apologies, Tasmin. I'll tell you what you want to know." Elisa loosened her hold on Lovett, his complexion returning to normal. "That energy you felt had to be from my ancestor, Philippe Lovett, and Ilene's, Zoë Beauchamp, Marie's handmaiden. Philippe was part of a local group that was bound and determined to quell any slave rebellions. Your deaths were meant to send a strong message to any slaves who tried to escape or help others do the same. I swear on my life, it was him who was there that night, not me."

While my gut was telling me his emotional response was sincere, I was a bit emotional myself, the horror of that night once again flooding my mind. I dug my nails into my hands, attempting to keep my anger from bubbling to the surface. Composing myself, I telepathically spoke to Elisa.

"I sense he's being truthful, but can you read his mind just to make sure?"

"Of course I can," she replied, *"but are you okay?"*

"I will be, once we get home."

Elisa nodded in acknowledgement. *There's no deceptiveness from him. He's on the level, and since this* is *the mayor, that's not a phrase I use lightly. I'm glad we at least got this cleared up, for your sake."* She placed a supportive hand on my shoulder.

"Yeah, so am I."

My burning question answered, Elisa continued with the interrogation.

"Tell me, Ephraim," Elisa began, "was it mainly your powers that allowed you to steal the mayoral election time and time again, because there are only so many people in this town you can blackmail for their vote. Most are morally above reproach."

"Elisa, the term stole is so harsh; I'd more say appropriated the office."

"However you try to spin it, it wasn't a free and fair election, and the position was never rightfully yours," I admonished. "I'm guessing Aunt Noreen could only do so much to stop you."

"Ah, the fair Noreen Chadwick. Despite her and Amabelle Nall being formidable foes, they were no match for the powers bestowed upon me by the all-powerful Eve."

"Exactly how long had Eve been eyeing Salix Pointe?" Elisa questioned.

"Eve hungered for the epicenter of magick for decades. That *gemme* could tip the balance for good or evil, depending on who had possession of it. As such, my Ilene and I were tasked with…procuring it. I tried to buy that infernal bookstore from your aunt Noreen many times, but she always refused. Once she was…no longer with us on this plane and you came to town, *chère*," I shot him a scathing glance, "I mean Tasmin, I thought it would be easy to buy the property from you, but, not unlike your aunt, you turned out to be a challenging opponent, especially with the help of Doctor Battle and his brother. And the two of you together…you've thwarted me at every turn. I couldn't understand how that was possible until Marie revealed to us who, and what, you two are, powerful witches. But now…we haven't heard from Marie in weeks, and my powers have all but disappeared."

"Oh, you don't know?" Elisa inquired.

"Know what?" Ilene countered.

She and I shared knowing glances before Elisa gave them the news. "Marie is dead."

"Dead?" the Lovett's shouted in unison.

"Yes, dead," I replied, a sense of satisfaction in my words. "After Eve got what she needed from Marie, she found her…

expendable, so she had her taken out, by Azazel no less." I thought back to how Demon Daddy ripped Marie's beating heart from her chest, only to drop it on the ground and stomp on it like one would do to a scurrying roach.

The mayor dropped his head, defeat written all over his face. "That explains it. I was wondering why I no longer felt that familial bond with her. With Marie dead, the deal that she made ended. We're no longer in servitude to Eve, but that also means that all the powers she bestowed on us are gone."

"My loving husband, what ever shall we do now?" Ilene asked, reminiscent of a damsel in distress.

"Leaving Salix Pointe and never coming back is an option," Elisa said, a smile crossing her face.

"I wholeheartedly agree with my cousin. And if you don't leave, I see a recall election in your immediate future. The choice is yours."

With that, knowing that the Lovetts were essentially harmless, Elisa released them from their restraints. We both stood up, briefly looking at the downtrodden couple, then left, leaving them to ponder their own fates.

Chapter 9
OCTAVIAN

"What's on your mind, Brother?" Dafari asked as we sat in his home office.

Things had calmed down after my parents' abrupt visit earlier that morning. The ladies were gone, and my mind was all over the place. Mostly, it was on my daughter, Attalah.

"Attalah said three days, but it's already starting to feel like forever," I replied, more shaken than I cared to disclose. "What is she doing? Where is she? Where are Zafer and Safiya? Why don't you remember anything from your time in Hell? Uncle Morningstar is sending demons to Salix Pointe. On top of all that, we've got Uncle Raphael who was kicked out of Heaven. I've got many questions and very little answers. I feel as if my mind is no longer my own, Brother."

"Same here, and just so you know… I've told Elisa that I intend to find a way to have my memories restored."

"How in bloody hell do you plan on doing that? I mean you don't even remember what you had done or who you asked to help you do it."

"Yes, but I know my way around underground New Orleans fairly well, and if I'm my father's son, I can bet that is where I went."

"So when do you plan on leaving?"

"As soon as I speak to Elisa more about it and then to all of you, including the coven...and... I can't believe I'm saying this but...Rufus. I think I'll feel better knowing he's around more in my absence. I know Uncle Raphael is here, but he's not in good shape, and we don't know what he's capable of yet or if he even still has powers."

I nodded, understanding his logic, especially since Rufus was a fairy, one of the most powerful magickal beings there were.

"While you do that, I'll do all I can to help find out where Zafer and Safiya are. Perhaps, once you have your memories back, it'll also help in that regard as well."

Comfortable silence settled between us as we sat at his desk, him behind it with me sitting on the other side. After my parents had left, so did Uncle Azazel. Under the guise of needing to get information on where his grandchildren were, he disappeared before we could ask him any pertinent questions.

Dafari finally said, "I'm going to get dressed and head into the office. I think it's important we keep up appearances during this whole thing. As a cover for my absence, I'll start letting my clients know that I'll be out of town for a few days, possibly weeks, if this excursion takes longer than expected. Speaking of appearances, what do you plan to do as far as your work?" After asking this, he stood and started making his way to the door, but not before polishing off the last bit of his aged rum.

"I need to make a call to the university, and possibly make a trip of my own to square things away back there. With Tasmin being here, I feel Salix Pointe is where I belong."

Nodding, my brother deftly pulled all his hair back into a ponytail, tying it with a leather band he had around his wrist. "Then you should probably start looking for your own place.

Not that I mind you being here, but I'd like for Elisa and me to have some sort of privacy for a while, without random family members dropping in on us unannounced. And again, you're always welcomed, as is Tasmin, but I know you understand what it is I'm asking."

Standing, I, too, finished off the last of my drink. "I understand. I'll start looking forthwith. Staying with her parents has been an experience, that's for sure," I said, sensing Dafari noted the sarcasm in my voice.

"You need to talk?" he asked, stopping just outside his office door.

"No…it's just…Jewel has been a bit standoffish. She's stayed locked away in their room most of the time, and when she does come out, she acts as if she can't stand the sight of me or Tasmin, which is odd considering she's her daughter."

"Have you spoken to Tasmin about this?"

"Not in any detail, no; however, both of us have made note of it. Whatever the case, it could be that she is just shaken up because of the battle. They have a lot to process with finding out their daughter is actually a reincarnated soul."

"This is true. I'll see you this evening unless something dictates otherwise."

With that, he headed upstairs, and I made my way to the kitchen. I didn't expect to find Uncle Raphael standing very still, as if in meditation, by the sink. He was shirtless and the large gaping wounds where his wings had once been made for a ghastly sight. He kept his eyes on the horizon while each breath he took caused his massive back to expand in such a way that it looked as if it caused pain.

"It does," he growled. "Even though I can feel the wounds healing, the pain is still more than I can bear on this plane."

"That answers at least one of the questions Dafari and I

had about if you had any powers still," I murmured, moving across the kitchen to start a pot of coffee. "Have a seat. Until we know exactly what condition your body is in, it's best we treat it as if you're human. I'll fix you something to eat. Get some kind of sustenance in you and go from there."

"Perhaps a bit more of that tea the women gave me yesterday as well?"

I started the water for tea and grabbed items for a quick vegetable omelet. Uncle Raphael's silence during this unnerved me. For that reason alone, I closed my mind to him. I wasn't sure what to make of him just yet. Didn't know exactly where his loyalties were placed at the moment. Sure, he had been thrown out of Heaven; however, some of my uncles were known to do anything to get back in His good graces.

"No one could have ever convinced me that my father would kick *me*, of all his sons, out of Heaven," he finally said after I'd set out the tea and its fixings.

Sitting a saucer with the omelet in front of him, I scoffed. "Surely you're joking?" I asked, a bit perplexed. "I mean considering…"

When Uncle's gaze met mine, I saw the seriousness there. "I've done everything He asked of me. Everything. And the one time he finds out I'm trying to bring peace, not war and calamity, but peace between religion and magick, He deems me unfit? I have never strayed, Nephew. Not ever. So why would I think *He* would cast *me* out? Surely he'd let me plead my case, no?"

After hearing the obvious pain in his voice, I brought my sarcasm and highhandedness down a notch.

"To have my brothers and sisters attack me, violently rip my precious…precious wings from my back and then kick me out as if I was no more than a wayward Fallen? What could I have done? Peacefully coexisting amongst all his people is what He wants, no?"

Uncle sounded broken, fractured in a way I'd never heard. And I found myself praying he didn't shed tears. An angel's pain could be felt through all its bloodline, and when an angel shed tears…it was excruciating for all those around.

"I…I don't have the answers, Uncle. I don't think any of us do, but by now, we all know that when things aren't going His way—"

"I'm at a point where I'm questioning exactly what *His way* is," he said, cutting me off. He turned back to his breakfast, picked up his mug, and then sipped his tea quietly.

I didn't know what else I could do for him or say to him, so I exited the kitchen to give him space. On the way up the stairs, I passed Dafari. Jet black hair now hanging in thick waves around his shoulders, he was dressed in a black turtleneck with tan trousers. He looked more like he was going on a date as opposed to his office. Sometimes he reminded me that he was his father's son in the smallest of ways.

It was clear that he'd heard our conversation in the kitchen based on the conflict I saw on his face. "We'll discuss it more later," he said. "When the ladies get here, I'm sure they'll also have some things to share. Might as well get everything out there all at once."

"I agree. I'm going to check on Tasmin's parents and then head into town," I told him.

"Be careful and stay vigilant."

"You do the same."

Thirty minutes later, I was dressed and headed to Aunt Noreen's house to do a wellness check. Attalah had asked for three days, and this was only day one. I didn't know if I could just sit and wait for her to show up again and not go completely mad.

Tasmin's painful cries and pleas to the heavens replayed in my mind. I hated I couldn't do anything to take her grief away. Attalah had to come back with answers to all our questions. There was no other way around it.

I stepped through the veil into Aunt Noreen's front room, expecting to find Silas and Jewel, but the house was completely silent. Even weirder, the place was eerily dark. Too dark as the sun was shining brightly outside, even with the threat of rain on the horizon.

"Silas? Jewel?" I yelled, walking through the front room toward the kitchen. I then went to the foot of the stairs and called up. "Mr. Pettiford?" Again, silence. "Mrs. Pettiford?"

Suddenly, I heard movement to my left. Turning to head back toward the front room, I stopped upon seeing Silas come from the spare bedroom.

Tying his robe, he squinted as he took me in. "Octavian? What are you doing here? Everything okay with my daughter and niece?"

"Top of the morning to you, and yes, everything is well," I said, not completely comfortable telling him the whole truth at the moment. "How is Jewel? And may I ask why it's so dark in here?" Before waiting for him to answer, I walked over the bay window and snatched the curtains open. A burst of pure sunlight lit up the cozy area.

Silas threw an arm up, squinting from the brightness. "Jewel has been feeling rather sickly. Frequent headaches and upset stomach. She can barely hold anything down. The slightest sound or pinch of light makes it worse. She's not been feeling well since having that pie Rufus made."

THE RECKONING & THE REAPER

"Why hasn't she reached out to Tasmin about this?" I inquired, something about the whole thing making the hairs on the back of my neck stand up.

"She doesn't want to worry her, and she said once the headaches wear off, she'll be okay. Until then, I've been trying to make things as comfortable as possible for her."

"Is there anything I can do to help?"

He shook his head. "I want to say no, but I suppose you should tell Tasmin to stop by and have a look at her. I'll just feel better about her recovery, you know?"

"I'll do just that, but you're not looking the best yourself. Perhaps she should take a look at you, too..."

Silas looked at me as if he was about to respond then stopped, tilting his head slightly to the right as if listening to something only he could hear. "You know, sometimes I swear I can hear Jewel calling me...even when she isn't," he said, a frown on his face.

I didn't hear anything. Not even the buzz of appliances. "That...is indeed odd. Are you sure everything's okay here, Silas?"

"Yeah, just need some rest. Haven't been sleeping well. I wake up feeling like I've been hagridden."

"I beg your pardon? Hagridden?"

"Yes, some of us deeper down south may say a witch was riding our backs. It's quite different than a boo hag, which is similar to a vampire and a sleep paralysis demon, but instead of blood, they drain your energy and steal your skin. With a witch riding you, it feels like you're conscious but unable to move. Something has control of you, and you can't even scream."

"Not the type of witch I'd want to run into, that's for sure. Perhaps you and Jewel should get out the house. Take a trip down to the café. Get some fresh air?"

"Maybe I will talk Jewel into stepping out. Some time away from home may help her heal faster."

Just then, a very strained, "Silas..." came from the direction of the bedroom.

"Yes, I'm coming," he yelled then turned to me. "I need to check on her. Don't forget to tell Tasmin to stop by."

Soon after, he was making his way toward the bedroom. Jewel sounded horrible. Her voice was dry and brittle, like if she were to cough, out would come dust. What exactly had Rufus put in that pie— if it was the pie that had caused this lapse in her healing? My gut was pulling at me hard, and while I couldn't put my finger on it, something here was off.

No more than a few minutes later, I was inside of The Book Nook. Tasmin hadn't arrived which made me wonder exactly where she was. Just as the thought crossed my mind, I saw the lights flicker on in Elisa's café. Not knowing whether it was she or Rufus who was about to open, I waited by the window, peeking out at other parts of the street every so often.

Not too many people were out and about yet, but there were several business owners taking down their holiday decorations. Now that the new year was here, it was time to move on from the festive nature of things. Dense fog hung low as far as I could see. An occasional taillight could be seen here and there. Two joggers kept pace next to one another across the street while an old man moved at a snail's pace heading toward the park.

I turned my attention back to Elisa's café just in time to see Tasmin making her way to the bookstore. Not wanting to startle her, I flipped on the lights in The Book Nook then casually waved at her from the window. Upon seeing me, she smiled wide, and then hastened her steps.

"It's safe to say, I expected you to be here," she said as she entered the store.

"Did you now? Well glad to have met your expectations, Poppet."

After locking the door behind her, I quickly lifted Tasmin into my arms. Now that she was reawakened, showing her this kind of affection did my heart some good. She wrapped her legs around my waist easily, bringing her lips to mine in an intense kiss. With all that we had going on, I was glad she was even in the mood to receive this sentiment. I needed it and her. Trying to sleep last night had been torturous.

Keeping my hands on her waist, I placed her back on her feet. "Pray tell, short one, where have you and Sissy been?"

"Paid a little visit to the mayor's manor."

"Did you now? Any new information to share?"

As she was getting ready to respond, "Thank goodness one of you are here," caught us off guard. I whipped around to see Afolabi, the disembodied spirit that had been trapped inside of Ilene's cat, Disemspi. Still dressed in the shabby clothing enslaved people used to wear, he looked dirtier than he had before. His transparent form didn't quite hover nor was he standing…per se.

"Afolabi? Where have you been and where is your wife, Aziza?" Tasmin asked.

"She's back on the other side. I would have made myself known at your brother's home, but I am afraid of leaving this bookstore. It protects me and Aziza; however, she is too terrified to cross back over to this side."

Tasmin moved closer to the spirit. "Why?"

"Our bloodline is being attacked on the other side," he spat urgently.

"What do you mean attacked?" I asked, almost incredulously.

"Messengers, demons, and everything in between are coming after our souls on the other side. If Tasmin and Elisa aren't able to commune with the Ancestors, it limits how much magick they can use. Sure, they can still use all their magick, but the power behind it may not be as strong." Turning back to Tasmin now, he said, "Our resting places are being disturbed, but for now, our familial line is holding strong. I don't know how much longer we can.

I want you four to understand how serious and dire this is; there are those from our line who did not walk the side of good. They, too, can be summoned to do dark deeds. And those deeds can be turned against us and the coven, especially you and Elisa. Which is why even though she and Silas are necromancers, I must warn them against trying to contact any of us for now. It would be too easy to be intercepted and then, who knows what would happen."

"Sounds like they are coming after all of you very aggressively, and from all sides," I said to Tasmin. "And it makes sense they would go after the whole bloodline, especially when we consider what Afolabi just disclosed."

"I can honestly say that is something Elisa and I haven't even considered…"

When Tasmin's face fell into a deep scowl, I knew she was calculating something in her mind. She gave her attention back to Afolabi. "With those who have crossed over, do all of you communicate with one another?"

"For the most part, yes."

"Do the names Zafer and Safiya ring a bell?"

Looking taken aback, Afolabi nodded. "Of course they do."

"Would you happen to know where they are? They're a huge piece of this puzzle—"

"Because their father is half angel and half demon, they move a bit more freely than we do. Zafer…is very powerful, almost to the point he's uncontrollable. Safiya, too, is powerful, but her brother is frightening, especially when upset."

"Well of course he's powerful. Look at who his parents are," I quipped, a bit of pride in my voice for my nephew.

"No, you don't get it," Afolabi said, checking over his shoulder as if he expected someone or something to jump out at him. "Zafer can possess other souls, entities, and beings the same way he would a human, and that's on top of everything else."

"Bloody hell," I groaned, the explosiveness of the revelation causing me alarm.

Tasmin's hand gripped my arm. "No wonder all sides are after them."

Suddenly, the lights in the bookstore flickered off and on. Several books fell as the ground shook. Keeping Tasmin secured safely behind me, I moved us away from falling books and other items. It was over just as quickly as it started, but when the lights finally stopped flickering, Afolabi was gone.

CHAPTER 10
DAFARI

I finished all the calls to my clients, letting them know that I would be away from the office for a few days. Gratified to be done with the chore of contacting all of Salix Pointe's pet owners, I felt Elisa's presence at the café and was anxious to pop in on her since she wasn't there when I arrived in town.

As I was about to lock up and walk over to the shop, Octavian reached out to me telepathically.

Dafari, you need to get to the café immediately, he said, urgency in his tone.

What's going on?

Tasmin and I will explain when you get here.

Not wanting to waste any time, I locked my office up tight, including putting up my own protection spell, then headed through the shadows. Not sure if there were any customers at the coffee shop, I made sure to cross into a shadow in the café's kitchen. As soon as I walked through the door to the dining area, I realized my caution was for naught. The shop was empty save for Elisa, Tasmin, Octavian, and Rufus.

"Thank goodness," Elisa said running to me, pulling me over to the table where the others were seated. "The coven members are on their way, but Tasmin and Octavian wanted to talk to us first."

Without looking at Elisa, so as not to make it obvious, I shot her a telepathic message. *"We're talking freely in front of Rufus now?"* Not that I minded, I just wanted to make sure that was what we were doing.

"Yes. Since he was already here when I arrived, we decided it was time we loop him in. We need all the help we can get."

"I wholeheartedly agree," I concurred. Elisa and I joined the three, taking seats at the table.

I arrived in the middle of Octavian explaining to Rufus that we had figured out he was a fairy, to which Rufus let out a hearty, "Whew. Glad that cat's outta the bag, so ta speak." His comment made me think of Ilene's mangy cat Disemspi, and how Afolabi's spirit was trapped inside him. "I wanted ta tell y'all for a while now."

"Are there other fairies in town?" Elisa asked.

"Nope, Elsie, I'm the lone yumboe in all of Salix Pointe."

"Yumboe?" Tasmin questioned.

"That's right, Tasmania," he replied, then continued on. "Yumboes are fairies from Senegal, West Africa. While a lot are still there, some migratated decades ago, settling in the Americas." We knew Rufus well enough to know he meant migrated.

"That makes sense," Octavian cut in. "I've read about the yumboes in my studies. From what little is written about them though, they only grow to be around two feet tall and are silvery white in color, of which you are neither. They are also said to be the spirits of the dead, attaching themselves closely to human families. Quite benevolent creatures from what I've gathered."

Rufus nodded his head a few times before continuing. "Correct on all counts, Octovian. But that was my Ancestors. We somewhat different now because of my Yom-Ziza."

Octavian, Tasmin, and I exchanged confused glances. "His grandmother," Elisa said, clarifying.

"My Yom-Ziza took up with a human man, which means we got human blood in us, so there's no need to latch on ta humans no mo'. And being that my grandpaw was a tall man, those of us that came after were taller and looked more human. We also learned how to hide our glow…that is, unless we wanted someone to see it." All of a sudden, Rufus's appearance quickly turned to that of a creature whose silvery form was quite a sight, causing both Elisa and Tasmin's mouths to drop open. Just as quickly, he turned back to the man we were all familiar with. "Because Yommy fell for someone who wasn't her kind, she was ostrapasized for it."

"Ostracizing a being for falling in love with a human. Sounds familiar." Tasmin quipped, looking from Octavian to me.

"Dey treated us so bad that when I was old enough ta leave, I ended up here, in Salix Pointe; didn't know why, but it was like I was led here. I made the same mistake Yommy did; fell in love with a human, my soul mate Roberta. That woman stole my heart, I tell ya. She's long since passed, but I loved this town so much I stayed. The yumboes been chasin' ole Rufus ever since, but the magick of Salix Pointe keeps me safe and allows me to do this."

We watched in awe as Rufus completely disappeared from sight, only to reappear within seconds.

"Rufus, my good man, we were all quite curious as to how you knew little Nazila was at Dafari's home, and her mother was in distress."

"Well, Octovian, that there is easy ta explain. I can sense when a child is in trouble. I sensed it when she was first attacked, but by the time I tracked her, 'cause we some good trackers, she was already at Dayfari's, so I knew she would be safe. But when y'all was out there at Doc Benu's place fightin'

THE RECKONING & THE REAPER

the big bad and all, Nazali was all alone and scared with her sick mama, Tanisha. I had ta do sumin'," he said, butchering both of their names.

"And because you're good, you were able to get past the wards and into the house," Elisa said in a low voice, almost as if she was thinking out loud.

"Rufus, if it wasn't for you, Tinashe might not have made it. I think I can speak for all of us, including Tinashe and Nazila, when I say thank you," Tasmin chimed in.

"You are quite a surprising individual, Rufus," I noted. "I'm glad you're on our side."

"Yes, we're all glad," Elisa said in agreement. "You've done so much for us, and, truth be told, you're like family."

"Awwww, I really 'preciate that Elsie, 'specially since I ain't got no family here. And speakin' of family," he said, changing the subject, "before yours gets here, Tasmania, I been meanin' ta talk ta you. Somethin' ain't right wi'cha mama."

"Yes, I know. She doesn't seem to be recovering from Eve's attack the way we all thought she would. Plus, Octavian and I have noticed her...let's just say, change in personality. It's as if she doesn't want either of us around."

Rufus shook his head from side-to-side, his sparse comb-over hair moving with him. "See, dat's what I'm talkin' 'bout. Sumin' ain't right wi' her. When we had Christmas dinner, the way she reacted ta the sweet tater pie—"

"If I recall correctly, when Jewel inquired as to what was in the pie, you said you added your two special ingredients, Madagascar vanilla and West Indian cinnamon," came from Octavian.

"Well, yeah, but there's one more that I didn't mention... fairy dust." We all looked at Rufus quizzically. "It's like this; together Gascar 'Nilla and West Indian cinnamon hep ta get rid of negative energy in the body and make ya happy. But add fairy dust, and bam!" he said, banging his stubby hand on the table in dramatic fashion. "Them effects is magnifified."

"You mean magnified?" Elisa asked.

"Yeah, that's what I said, Elsie, magnifified."

"So it sounds as if the mixture is like endorphins on speed, which explained the extremely pleasant high we felt afterwards. But, Rufus, what does that have to do with my mom?"

"Well, Tasmania, fairy dust don't sit well in the craw of someone that's got," he stopped briefly, looking around as to make sure no one was eavesdropping, then he whispered, "evil in 'em. The only time I seen that type of reaction was when I was a Yomboe young'un, back when my folk was goin' up against these creatures called Abiku elves. Ya see, while we protect churrin, Abiku elves steal dey souls. They would cozy up to a child, share food and drink with it, and the child would eventually die."

"Oh, my gosh, that's horrible," Elisa exclaimed.

"Well we wasn't haven't, no we wasn't," Rufus stated emphatically. "We started trackin' 'em, and when we found one going after a child, we started adding Yommy's special spice, as I like to call it, to all the food and drink in the home. It would make dem Abiku elves so sick that dey would leave dem churrin alone, for good."

"Wait a minute, Rufus," Tasmin began, talking with her hands emphatically, "are you telling me that my mom is evil?"

"I'm not sayin' dat, but I am sayin' sumin' gotta hold on her."

Gently placing a hand on Tasmin's forearm, Octavian said, "Poppet, what Rufus is saying actually makes sense. With everything that went on at the bookstore, I forgot to tell you what happened when I went to check in on your parents."

We all looked at my brother expectantly, waiting for him to continue. He quickly recounted all that occurred when he was at Noreen's home.

"Octavian, why didn't you contact me right away?" Tasmin was almost yelling. "I would have shot over there immediately."

"Because, my love, something wasn't right, and while I didn't get to lay eyes on Jewel, Silas looked like death warmed over. I wanted to discuss the situation with you first before going back over there, and I would have had it not been for Afolabi showing up when he did."

My ears perked up immediately. We hadn't seen Afolabi the spirit, or his wife, the ghost Aziza, since The Book Nook was attacked. "Afolabi? He appeared to you?" I asked.

"He did," Octavian replied. "And since this part relates to the family, I wanted to share it with you and Elisa first before the coven arrived." After they disclosed the information given to them by Afolabi, we sat for a moment or two in stunned shock before speaking.

"So…I can't contact Mama Nall or my parents? This is insane! Our bloodline is under attack, and they're purposely trying to diminish our magick? To what end? What the hell is really going on? Dafari, they want to use our babies as pawns in this…twisted war of theirs."

I sensed that Elisa was doing everything in her power to hold it together. I slid my hand over hers, squeezing it supportively.

"Elisa, even in death our children are strong; Afolabi said as much."

"Yes, but he also said Zafer was almost uncontrollable. If the other side gets a hold of him —"

"They won't," I said, cutting her off, attempting to ease

her mind. "We will find them, my dear, I promise you." That was a promise I intended to live up to.

"Yes, Cousin, we're going to do all we can to locate their souls." Tasmin gave Elisa a reassuring glance. "I just wish Afolabi had been able to tell us who the two beings that can contain all that power were before he was whisked away."

"As do I," Octavian stated.

Tasmin turned to Rufus, steering us back to the most immediate crisis. "It's been a little over a week. How long would it take for the effects of your…special spice to wear off?"

"No tellin', but what I can tell ya is if ya mama is still sick, then that ain't good."

Despite her obvious worry for our children, being the team player she was, Elisa pulled herself together quickly. "We also need to address what Silas told Octavian about feeling hagridden. Cousin, you and I both know that if a witch or some other entity has its clutches in him your attempt to heal him may end up being at best temporary, at worst useless without him being free of whatever it is."

"Then there's the risk of it latching on to you, Sister," I interjected.

Tasmin sighed dejectedly. "Then we need to find out for sure if some evil being has control of my parents, and, if that is the case, we need to figure out which one it is."

Elisa stood up. "Silas, Jewel, and the Widows should be here soon. I say we try something with Rufus's special spice."

"Good idea," Tasmin replied. "But not dessert, because clearly my parents think Mom's still sick because of Rufus's pie. She does love hot chocolate, so that could work."

"And I know just the recipe to make," Elisa said.

"In the meantime, if Jewel has been taken over by a maleficent force, I think it best not to discuss anything in her or Silas's presence. Are we all in agreement?" I queried.

Everyone nodded.

"Dafari, can you help me in the kitchen?"

I followed Elisa, knowing I needed to speak with her regarding my quest to restore my memories. She opened the large pantry, walking inside to fetch what she needed to make the hot chocolate.

"Honey, do me a favor and grab ten mugs," she yelled.

Doing as she asked, I fetched the mugs from the cupboard, then set them out on the marble counter, lining them up one next to the other. Elisa walked back over, placing all the required items down.

Before she could start her task, I turned her to face me, taking her hands in mine. "We will find them, Elisa."

Tears had begun to well up in her big brown eyes. "How can you be so sure?"

"Because, wife of mine, our family is strong, persistent, and tenacious. Tasmin and Octavian will work ceaselessly to discover the whereabouts of our children's souls, as will I." I knew we would all do our best to locate Safiya and Zafer…or die trying. "That being said, I wanted to tell you that I was planning to travel to New Orleans in order to see about retrieving my lost memories. Afolabi's brief appearance to Octavian and Tasmin speaks to the urgency of my doing that."

Elisa looked up at me, a myriad of emotions reflected in her eyes. "As much as I want you to stay here, I also ***need*** you to do what's necessary to find our kids. But please, Dafari, promise me you'll be careful. I can't lose you too."

She touched her hand to my cheek. I turned my head, kissing her palm. I then leaned down, kissing her forehead. "I will do my best."

"I'll accept that," she replied on a whisper. Sighing heavily, she said, "Let's get to work. The others will be arriving shortly."

After we added heaping teaspoons of African cocoa powder, she added the West Indian cinnamon and Madagascar vanilla. We then added hot milk to the mugs. As if on cue, Rufus came running to the back.

"Elsie, they heah," he said.

"Right on time. Rufus, if you will."

Understanding what Elisa was asking, he pulled a small bottle containing a golden substance that resembled glitter out of his apron pocket. I assumed it was his fairy dust. As he sprinkled a bit into each mug, Elisa followed behind, stirring each one thoroughly. She topped the cocoa off with whipped cream and rainbow sprinkles. Placing the drinks on two trays, she allowed Rufus and me to carry them to the dining area.

By then, several tables had been pushed together to make one long table. The Merry Widows sat at one end, with Martha at the head of the table, her sisters, Cara Lee and Mary Ann, seated next to her. Tasmin sat beside Cara Lee, with Octavian sitting aside his lady. Tasmin and Octavian sat across from Jewel and Silas.

What immediately caught my attention were Tasmin's parents. Jewel looked robust and healthy, her eyes vibrant and smile radiant. Silas on the other hand, to coin Octavian's phrase, looked like death warmed over. His eyes were sunken and had dark circles around them and, although his complexion was normally cinnamon-hued, at the moment his skin looked ashen in appearance; a veritable walking dead. Knowing Tasmin, it took every bit of strength she could muster to not attempt a healing.

"Tasmin, I appreciate you worrying about me, but as you can see, I feel much better," Jewel spoke jovially. "I just didn't want to bother you, sweetie. Your father on the other hand; I think he may have caught what I had."

"Mommy, you would not have been bothering me. What

good are my powers if I can't use them?" Tasmin's poker face was strong. "And Daddy, we'll see about getting you all squared away in a bit, okay?" He simply nodded. I noted that he hadn't spoken at all.

Tasmin touched Silas's hand. It was subtle, but she flinched, pulling back slowly. My little brother could read and see energy, including auras, while I, in contrast, could feel when something was off, my own form of intuition. My gut was firing away, alerting me that something was amiss.

"Hey, everybody," Elisa said once we reached the tables. "Glad you all made it safely."

Rufus and I began placing mugs of the steaming cocoa in front of everyone. I made sure to give Jewel and Silas theirs, so as to not cause Jewel to suspect Rufus of any wrongdoing. I also gave Tasmin and Octavian mugs, keeping the last one for myself. Once everyone was served, Elisa, Rufus, and I took our seats. We kept to small talk, holding strong to our pact to not discuss anything vital in front of Jewel and Silas until we knew whether or not one or both of them were touched by evil.

"Who made the cocoa because it is absolutely divine," Martha said, thoroughly enjoying the blend.

"I did, Martha, and thank you."

"Yes, Elisa, it's so delicious," Cara Lee added.

Mary Ann chimed in, "What kind of cocoa is this? I must have some for the house."

"It's African cocoa powder. Remind me later to tell you where I order it from."

Mary Ann thanked her. As covertly as we could, Tasmin, Elisa, Octavian, Rufus, and I watched Jewel. She drank the cocoa slowly, making conversation with everyone, laughing and having a good time, as if her husband didn't look like he would keel over at any moment. Suddenly, just as she did at

Christmas dinner, she began to cough, mildly at first, but then it became more vigorous.

"Mommy, are you okay?" Tasmin asked, simply for appearances, as Jewel's reaction to the drink confirmed our suspicions.

"Yes...I'm fine," she said between coughs. "Some of the cocoa went down the wrong way."

We knew that was a lie.

"Let me get you some water," Tasmin said.

"N-no, sweetie, it's okay. All that coughing did make my head start hurting again though."

"Here, let me heal you." Tasmin started to get out of her seat.

Those of us who knew what was going on looked at her curiously. What was she doing? She knew she wasn't supposed to attempt to heal either of her parents. I was hoping that Tasmin wasn't thinking that because she could heal herself, she would be fine, because none of us could make that assumption.

"No," her mother exclaimed, causing all chatter at the table to come to an abrupt end. "I-I'm sorry, Tasmin, but I don't want you to expend your valuable energy. I think I may have pushed myself too far. I just need to go home to rest, and so does your father. If you want, you can come by the house later to heal us, okay?"

Tasmin studied Jewel tentatively. We shared the similar gift of intuition, so I was keenly aware that she was feeling the same as me; she knew something was unquestionably wrong with her parents.

"Okay, Mommy. Octavian and I will come by later."

It wasn't lost on me the look that Jewel gave when Tasmin said Octavian would be accompanying her.

"Umm, okay. We'll see you two later. Silas, honey, let's go. We're sorry, everyone."

We all said our respective 'feel better' then Tasmin, with Octavian in tow, walked them to their car.

After they returned, Tasmin locked the door behind them. Once she took her seat, she inhaled deeply. I could tell she was doing her best to remain calm. The words she spoke at the time almost seemed like an understatement. "We've got a really huge problem on our hands."

CHAPTER 11
SAFIYA

She felt it as soon as she opened her eyes. She knew her brother was no longer under her protective spell. The grounds beneath her shook violently, and it felt like rumbling thunder was walking the earth. Vicious lightning strikes touched the ground in hard, rapid beats of fire bolts.

"Zafer," she yelled, trying to find her balance.

Oh God, where is he? her mind screamed!

Absolutely terrified of what all this meant, she called for her brother again. "Zaferrrr!"

She didn't want to, but she had no choice. Safiya had to leave the safety of her magick to find her brother. Waving a shaky hand, she watched the once serene hiding place she had carved out for them disappear. She tumbled forward awkwardly, not having time to brace for impact.

In an open, lush green field stood her shirtless brother. In only black trousers that fit his tall, athletic frame perfectly, from behind he resembled their father. So much so, she had to do a doubletake to be sure of who and what she was seeing. Long, thick black ropes of hair hung midways down his broad back. His breathing was so intense that Safiya could see his muscles ripple and roll like steel cables underneath his dark brown skin. Fists balled at his side, he stood as a warrior would, ready to go into battle.

"Zafer! What are you doing?" she tried to scream over the

roar of the wind, but she was sure her voice was drowned out.

The grounds quaked again, knocking Safiya backwards, but she righted herself quickly. Something wasn't right, the sun was turning orange and the more her brother stared at it, the deeper the orange became until it was…blood red…

Horrified at even the thought of what her brother was doing, she felt frozen in place. *"Zafer! You fool!"*

Quickly scrambling to her feet now, she watched her brother then turn his ire toward the moon. It darkened second by second, drawing the now blood red sun toward it in the process. Barefoot, she raced toward the ***arrogant bastard*** her mother had birthed! She should have known he was up to something when he acquiesced to all her demands in order for them to make this trip. Zafer didn't like taking orders. From anyone. Sometimes it was hard to get through to him when he was in a mood. Again, so much like their father. However, his determination was every bit of their mother.

Just as she was within touching distance of her brother, a white-hot lightning bolt coming at the speed of light crashed dead center into her brother's head. The force of it so powerful, both of them went flying across the field. They landed with a hard thud against the ground, but her brother got the brunt of it. Bolt…after bolt…after bolt chased him as he hopped to his feet.

Grabbing for her arm, he yanked Safiya up and they ran for their lives. Safiya was hurting and she shouldn't have been. She wasn't human. She wasn't dead either, but for the first time in a long time, she felt physical pain. That was how she knew her brother had crossed the line. As soon as the thought formed a gale force of wind tossed them in the opposite directions.

And suddenly… the ground opened and coughed up an

angry orangish-red blaze. A maleficent, terrifying form took shape amongst the flames. Terror gripped her heart, and instantly she knew they'd made a mistake.

ZAFER

He knew their Granduncle Morningstar had found them. Just like he was aware Heaven had opened its gates and sent the calvary after him.

"Fuck," he murmured aggressively, sensing his sister's fear.

It stabbed him in the heart and created an ache he hadn't felt since he watched his mother slowly lose her grip on reality after Safiya had disappeared. From where he was, he couldn't do anything to ease his mother's pain…and in the end, he hated himself even more for adding to it. He knew Safiya now felt the same.

His vision had gone from blurry and white to now being able to see everything so clearly that he wondered if he was experiencing the effects of the mushrooms he and Safiya had partaken the night before. Instinctively though, he was sure that wasn't the case. All of his powers felt amplified in such a way that he knew he had gone too far this time.

The angry thunderbolt had slapped him in the center of his head and caused blinding pain…but only for a few seconds. And then, just as quickly, the pain morphed into something else. Something more…defiant in nature. The surge of white-hot power he felt fed something sinister in him. His body had literally rejected the pain. Zafer…was amazed.

But he didn't have time to relish in the moment. His sister needed him. Finding his balance on the shaky ground, he yanked his sister back from the edge of the burning pit just as he was grabbed from behind. Fear gripped his heart as he watched his hold on his sister's hand slip, and she went flying into the clutches of Lucifer himself.

More than likely too frightened to think quickly enough to use her magick, Safiya was flailing wildly as she struggled to get out of his grasp. Their granduncle had managed to trigger the only flaw in his sister. If ever she got so scared that she felt it in her soul, her magick froze, and that only happened if she was afraid for a person she loved. It was another surprise the afterlife had for them. The second surprise happened when they realized that Safiya could tap into her brother's powers. At will. It was how she was able to always secure them a safe place to rest.

He had to get to his sister. Fighting the hold the heavenly beings had on him, he swung his elbows backward, knowing the move would cause some of the feathers from his black, leathery wings to break the skin on his back. Zafer's wings weren't like anything the 7th Battalion had ever seen. And the ones holding him soon realized why.

His wings were sharp, and poison filled his feathers when in fight mode. They also injured heavenly beings like angels —sometimes fatally. It was something he only learned of after his sister had joined him on the other side. Angels had been sent after them for the first time, and because neither of them knew exactly why, they had to learn to defend themselves while on the move. They had been cornered in an alley on a side street, in a world humans would never know existed, when Zafer's anger at the fate that had befallen his family manifested. It was one of many times to come.

Just like then, the feathers ripping through the angelic beings caused him instant gratification. "Get off me," he growled low as one of the angels' grip tightened then loosened as its pain intensified.

Pleasurable pain raced up and down his triceps. To the naked human eye, black, thick feathers protruding from the back of human arms and shoulders made for a scary, mind-boggling sight. Racing forward, as he felt his wings get longer and the poison pulsate through his veins, he charged at his granduncle.

He had only a few seconds, but if he could get Safiya out of their granduncle's clutches, he could get them to safety. He was that smart, and he was that good. Morningstar was in his true form and the thought of his sister being dragged to Hell angered him.

As Morningstar's madness intensified, Zafer's wings finally ripped through his back and he took flight. His massive wingspan almost blacking out the little light shining over the land. Using his wings, he sliced at his granduncle at a frighteningly fast clip, catching the being off guard. His sister's screams increased his fury. Behind him, he felt the 7th Battalion regrouping with new ones heading through the veil.

He heard hellhounds in the distance and knew the exact moment they came charging in from the shadows. It all happened so quickly.

In order to keep Zafer's wings from his face, Morningstar roared back, throwing up a shield that forced him to drop his grip on Safiya. The hellhounds were almost on her in seconds.

Zafer knew she was still shell-shocked, so to speak. Flying straight down, he rushed to stand in front of his sister, guarding one of the most precious things in his afterlife. Just as the hounds took a running leap at them, Zafer waved his hand and threw up a dome-like shield. Several of the hellhounds disintegrated on

THE RECKONING & THE REAPER

impact. The others slowed just in time to save themselves.

So pleased with himself, Zafer almost forgot about the heavenly forces that were behind them. If he had been human, or even a lesser being, the sight of archangels in their true, soul-churning form would have scared him to death. And while they tried their best to tear through the dome, they couldn't. Neither could Morningstar or his minions. While both factions clashed outside the dome, there were still those who were trying to penetrate it.

Zafer knew he had to get his sister to calm down enough so she could get them out of there. However, turning to look at her finally, he saw she wasn't in good shape. His sister looked sick, something that should have been impossible.

He dropped to his knees then cradled her shivering body in his arms. With her eyes closed, she said, "It...hurts, Zafer...I feel...pain...Why?" Her 'why' had come out on a strangled whisper. "What.have.you.done?" Those last four words stabbed at his heart.

But, "You have to get us out of here," were the only words he said to her.

Tears leaked from her beautiful eyes. She looked so much like their mother at times, it hurt to gaze at her. They clashed often because it was easier for him to piss her off and have her storm away than to deal with the guilt he felt anytime he laid eyes on her. He had to get her to safety. He couldn't lose her, too. They had already lost so much.

"Why are...you shutting me out?" she asked, finally opening her eyes. Then, she gasped. "Zafer, your face."

He frowned, unsure of what she was speaking of until he caught his reflection against the dome. Down the middle of his forehead and covering his right eye was a white streak that went all the way up into a few locs of his hair. His once golden eyes were now mismatched, with one being so gray it was almost white. Something he would have to worry about later.

Giving his attention back to her, Zafer said, "Safiya, please. We can talk about whatever whenever you want, once we get out of here."

As soon as the words left his mouth, a jagged crack appeared on the left side of the sphere. Without a word, and more than likely sensing imminent danger, Safiya laid her hand against her brother's heart while closing her eyes. She could create any world she and her brother needed to hide. She only needed Zafer to think of a location not many would seek them out. When he thought of Mount Hermon, she knew she had to call in for backup once they got there. Zafer was too strong, and he was starting to use his powers in ways that put the literal fear of God in her. She only knew of one being who would recognize her trail, only one who would even know what to look for. Their grandfather, Azazel.

CHAPTER 12
ELISA

"Silas is being hagridden in theory, but in reality...It's not a witch riding him, per se. If it were as simple as a that or a boo hag, it would be easier to get rid of." I glanced at Tasmin, knowing what I was about to say could make her uncomfortable, but it had to be said. "If they are still actively having sex, she could be quite literally...sucking the life out of him."

Tasmin sighed loudly. "While I don't want to imagine my parents having sex, this is good to know. I'm worried..."

"Sissy, are you saying that whatever has taken over Jewel is using her sex to weaken the man?" Octavian asked, and then he did something that, if I hadn't been paying attention, I would have missed. He ran his tongue across his front teeth from one incisor to the other.

I cast a quick glance at Dafari and saw he, too, was watching his brother curiously.

I said, "In a nutshell, yeah, and that's what worries me. For a boo hag, all you have to do is wait until they shed their skin at night, find where they hide it, and then sprinkle salt and pepper all over it. Once the boo hag returns from her nightly hunts and tries to redress in the skin, she won't be able to. The salt and pepper would make it impossible because it would burn the witch damn near to death."

"Which is how I know it's something more sinister," Tasmin added.

"Yes, but I feel like we're missing something," I said, standing so I could help Rufus with the cleanup.

I wanted to speak to my cousin alone. There were things we could discuss in private that we wouldn't in mixed company. She and I had been hit with a hell of a lot in a short time, one thing after the other. And it hadn't stopped or slowed down.

Martha reached for her staff, the gold kaftan she had on flowed down and covered her feet. Laying the hand-carved piece of wood on her lap, her brows furrowed. "Remember when we came to Christmas dinner at Elisa and Dafari's place, and I was feeling okay after the battle? Then when Jewel and Silas showed up, I started getting sickly again? Something in her has put roots on him. Whatever has taken over her body is using Jewel's natural witchy practices to also suck the essence right out of him, and if it goes on too long, there will be no saving him."

Cara Lee nodded, a worried frown marring her features. "And the same will happen to Jewel…"

"What do you mean?" Tasmin asked.

"This…is something my sisters and I have been discussing since we left the dinner. Whatever has a hold on Jewel is so strong that if we don't free her soon, your mother will never be the same."

"We been meaning to come see you four and discuss it, but with Elisa and Doctor Battle's nuptials, we really didn't want to intrude," Mary Ann said.

"Wouldn't have made a difference," Dafari growled low. "Everyone, their parents, and their uncles have been dropping by anyway. You would have fit right in."

Completely missing the sarcasm and annoyance in his words, Mary Ann continued, "If we do manage to somehow

THE RECKONING & THE REAPER

save her, if not done before the entity takes full control of her faculties, Jewel will just be a shell of herself."

"And she will keep draining every bit of Silas' magick and energy until he succumbs and dies," said Martha.

Octavian wrapped a protective arm around Tasmin when she visibly stiffened at Martha's words. "It's okay, Poppet. We'll figure it out. Trust me."

Before making another comment, I discretely watched my brother-in-law. Cringing as if it pained him, he ran his tongue over each of his incisors again. And just like a few moments before, Dafari, too, watched his brother. Octavian's behavior was peculiar...because the only time I'd seen that action was when Dafari was fighting with himself to drop fang. Octavian had never, in any life, had fangs. When Dafari's eyes found mine, I knew he was thinking the same thing.

Standing, he moved toward the kitchen, "Brother, may I speak to you for a moment?"

Once they had disappeared into the kitchen, I turned my attention back to the subject at hand. "Does anyone have any haint-blue paint or know where to find some quickly?" I asked.

"I shole do," said Rufus. "I can get out to Herschel's and get him to let me get a coupla' pints. Sho' can."

"And some dirt from Mama Nall and Aunt Noreen's graves," I added.

Tasmin turned her attention to me. "Are you thinking a goopher bag, Cousin?"

"I am..."

"I can get the dirt for you two," Mary Ann volunteered.

"Make sure you get it from directly over their hearts. Normally, it has to be collected just before midnight, but in this case, we have to make an exception. Also, leave a dime on their graves so nothing evil can follow you home," Martha told her.

"I'll go with Mary Ann," Cara Lee said.

"Rufus, before you leave, will you set the ovens and put in the prepped bakery?"

"No problem at all, Elsie!" And with that, the man headed toward the kitchen.

Tasmin sighed loudly, dropping her head in her hands. "My parents are very much in love and happily married. It's why whatever has its hook in my father is so detrimental to his health. His and my mother's heartstrings are intertwined. Getting graveyard dirt from…his mother—" Tasmin stopped abruptly then said, "I'm sorry, but it really just hit me that I didn't get to know my paternal grandmother, who was Mama Nall, and I know that was random…"

I walked over to hold her hand. My cousin was shivering she was so emotional. "No, you don't have to explain. I get it. Silas is my father's brother, and I had no idea. Once we get your parents free, and after I've communed with my parents and Mama Nall, maybe we can try to have a family meeting, ghosts and all." I chuckled which made Tasmin do the same.

Soon after, the Widows and Rufus left. It was time Tasmin and I dug deep into our southern hoodoo roots.

Afterwards, I said to Tasmin, "When you and Octavian go to see your parents tonight, try to get Jewel out of the house. I'm going to ask Rufus to use his magick to paint the top front porch's roof haint-blue. He can probably do it in record time."

Tasmin nodded while helping move the tables back to their places, as it would be time for me to open soon. "I'm going to look in the basement of the bookstore and grab those cobalt blue bottles I saw down there. There is a tree near the creek that has empty branches. When I used to visit as a kid, I would see those bottles on that tree."

"Bottle trees are another Gullah tradition with African roots that goes back centuries," I added. "Meant to capture evil spirits and prevent them from entering homes."

Tasmin spread the last cloth over a table before turning to me. "Right, and I'm going to put them on that tree."

"I still say sprinkle that salt and pepper in whatever bed they're sleeping in. Perhaps also use some of the black salt we made that has Octavian's blood mixed in? Might not be a boo hag, but it's kind of behaving as one…"

I was about to get ready to say something else until a tall, mocha-colored man with curly hair and green eyes walked to the door of the café. I glanced at my watch to see it was past time for me to open. Dressed in a gold-colored dress shirt that hugged the muscles in his upper body and black dress slacks that made each powerful stride he made even more noticeable, I took in attorney Adour-Nuru Citali Daystar. A black Audemars Piguet watch on his left wrist matched the black bracelet on his right. Dangling from his left earlobe was a golden earring. His green eyes never left mine, and when he smiled—so easy and calming— my knees almost buckled.

Holy hell! What was that? my mind screamed.

I'd never felt a wave of sensuality hit me dead on like that. Not even from my husband. It landed right in my womb and settled like a warm embrace…and then traveled further down south. The feeling was so strong, I had to grab ahold of the nearest table to steady myself.

"Elisa," Tasmin said on a gasp. "What…in…the heck… was that?" she asked, breathlessly, but still trying to help keep me balance.

"You felt it, too?" I asked, almost terrified, but also…My breasts swelled, nipples pebbled into hardened berries, and my vagina thumped between my thighs, and I still couldn't break the man's gaze.

"Oh yeah...how could I not feel...*that*. But apparently, it hit you harder."

"*Hello, Beautiful,*" I heard in my head, clear as day.

He...was in my head, and that terrified me. Moreso because I hadn't given him permission.

As if he was reading my mind now, he opened the front door, and walked right into my café. And just as quickly, Dafari came stalking from my kitchen followed by a very annoyed Octavian. My husband's eyes were red as fire which told me he didn't give a damn about Adour-Nuru seeing his power.

Walking to stand directly in front of the attorney, with Octavian flanking his left side, Dafari asked coolly, "May I help you?"

A lopsided smirked took over the attorney's features. "I came to get coffee—"

Taking a deep breath, my husband rolled his shoulders. "She's not open."

Adour-Nuru shot a quick, devilish glance my way, and I felt completely naked. Exposed. That was until Octavian moved directly in front of me and Tasmin.

"Her front door was open. I assumed—"

"You assumed wrong. Please leave my wife's establishment."

When Adour-Nuru chuckled, it settled all over my body, and I groaned as I crumbled into the chair behind me.

Tasmin rushed to my side. "Cousin? What is it?"

I was so out of sorts, I couldn't even telepathically connect to her. My hands started to shake so badly, I had to wonder if I was about to pass out. However, I didn't have time to think about that before both my husband and my brother-in-law moved in like they were about to get into an outright brawl in my coffee shop!

"No, no! Please, Dafari and Octavian. You'll tear up my shop," I cried, trying to get my senses about me.

"I'm leaving, I'm leaving. Oh…and congratulations on the wedding, yeah," said Adour-Nuru as he calmly backed out the front door, but that arrogant smirk never left his face.

CHAPTER 13
TASMIN

"You need to ward this place against Daystar *immediately*," Dafari bellowed in Elisa's direction the moment Adour-Nuru left the café. "I warned you about him, Elisa." Eyes still red, his words were stern and scolding.

Elisa, who still appeared dazed from whatever it was Adour-Nuru had inflicted upon her, tried to answer, but seemed to be having difficulty getting her thoughts together.

"Hold on, Dafari," I said, speaking up for her, walking to stand in front of him. "While I totally agree with you, you need to calm down, brother of mine."

"How can I when an incubus, a *full-blooded* incubus at that, is trying to at the very least mind fuck my wife?" he demanded, looking from me to Elisa, eyes as thin as slits.

Octavian took several steps towards us, but I held up my hand, halting his approach. Unfazed, I crossed my arms in front of me. "Because, Dafari, you flying off the handle is not going to solve anything, now is it?" I stared up at him waiting for a response. All I got for my trouble was a hard grunt. "Good, now that cooler heads have prevailed…for the moment, how about you go tend to your wife? In the meantime, I need to run to the bookstore. I think I know what we can use to ward this place off from attorney Daystar. Octavian," I said, nodding my head towards the door.

Octavian began to follow me but stopped. Pivoting to face Elisa and Dafari, he queried, "Sissy, considering most of the coven has tasks to fulfill today, and you've been through quite an ordeal, would it be an imposition if I recommend you close the café for the day?"

"I think that is a reasonable suggestion," Dafari chimed in, kneeling in front of Elisa, who appeared to be more lucid. He placed a hand on her cheek. "How are you feeling?"

"I-I'm okay…I think. Adour-Nuru's an incubus? No wonder what he did hit me like that. It felt similar to whatever it is Demon Daddy does when he's feeling—"

"Roguish?" came from Octavian.

"Wicked? added Dafari.

Not wanting to feel left out, I threw out a word. "Vexatious?" Everyone gave me curious glances. "What? I learned that one from Octavian," I stated, garnering a light chuckle from Elisa, a look of pride from Octavian, and a head shake and slight smirk from Dafari.

"All of those," Elisa acknowledged, "but Dafari, how did you know to come out here?"

"Our minds are open to one another, remember?" He stroked her hand tenderly.

"Yes, and I'm glad for that," she replied, relief in her tone. As she began to stand, Dafari rose from his knee, helping her up. "Octavian, you do have a point. I'll close for today. I have to finish what Rufus started, but other than that, the shop will be closed to customers. We can take today's goods to the shelter and food pantry, because I'd hate to see all that food go to waste."

"Splendid," Octavian replied. "Tasmin and I will fetch what she needs from the bookstore and shall return straight away."

Octavian and I left Elisa in Dafari's capable hands. I wasn't too worried because I knew exactly where the supplies

I needed were and we'd only be gone for a short time. Also, I figured Adour-Nuru wouldn't be stupid enough to return so soon after running up against Dafari *and* Octavian...at least I hoped he wasn't.

Octavian waited for me while I quickly ran to the basement to gather my supplies, including the cobalt blue bottles and the black salt containing Octavian's blood. Tossing everything in a knapsack, I headed back up to find Octavian looking in a mirror. He had lifted his upper lip and appeared to be examining his perfect teeth and gums, pressing on and around the upper front and lateral teeth, flinching as he did. I had never seen him do that before. As far as I knew, angels didn't have dental issues, at least mine never did.

I reached up, placed a hand on Octavian's shoulder. "Are you okay?"

"Poppet." He almost jumped, turning to face me. "I didn't hear you come up the stairs."

"That's because you were so busy looking at your teeth. Something wrong?"

"No, it's nothing."

I looked down, noting how Octavian's hands were balled into tight fists. My eyes panned back up to his. His brows creased and his eyes were squinted.

Tilting my head to the side, I retorted, "Are your palms burning? How's that ringing in your ears working for you? No need to answer that, I already know. Stop lying, Octavian, and spill it already."

He let out a long groan. "I don't really know what's wrong." He shrugged. "My gums have been itching recently, but I have no idea why. In the café, Dafari told me that he noticed that I was doing something odd. Then he mentioned something about fangs, but—"

His last statement made the hairs on the back of my neck

stand up. "Fangs?" I asked louder than expected. "Octavian, are you developing fangs?"

"Honestly, Tasmin, I don't know. I wish I did, but I'm as much in the dark as you are." He placed his hands around my waist, pulling my body flush with his. "And, at present, my love, we don't have time to ponder my latest demon blood conundrum. We need to get back to Elisa and Dafari, then on to our other tasks, yes?"

While I was aware his point was valid, I knew Octavian well enough to know he was attempting to deflect from his problem. My intent was to call him on it, but as I studied his black eyes, I suddenly felt as if I was being mesmerized. I tried to pull my gaze away from his but couldn't, the same way I tried the first time Octavian and I trained together and I bested him during martial arts sparring. He ended up on his back, and, somehow, I ended up on top of him. This moment was reminiscent of that one, and yet, it was heightened to the *nth* degree. I had gotten lost in his eyes many times before, but not like this.

With his arms around me, I not only felt his physical hold, but an even stronger emotional one, one mixed with powerful sexual undertones. My breath hitched as my body reacted to whatever it was that I was feeling. And then…and then, he leaned down and kissed me. At first, it was slow and gentle, like so many of his kisses, but then it became more aggressive, not just on his part, but mine as well, my tongue eagerly seeking out his. He picked me up, my legs viscerally wrapping around his waist. He turned around, backing me up into a wall. As his need pressed against my lady parts, rational thought began to elude me.

I knew we were in the middle of an extremely important task, but right now, it was the furthest thing from my mind. I never wanted Octavian more than I did at this moment, and that was saying a lot. If this was even a small glimmer of what he was going through, I felt for him. He intensified our kiss, had me feeling like I was drunk on love and lust. What was I doing? I was the responsible one, the person everyone always counted on to come through, but now… Elisa and Dafari were waiting for us back at the café…my parents were waiting back at Aunt Noreen's…none of that mattered. All I wanted was for Octavian to be inside me. I needed that like I needed to breathe. I thought he wanted the same until…he abruptly stopped.

"Tasmin, my love, we can't."

"Why…not?" I questioned as I kissed his neck.

Lifting me from around his waist, he gently placed me on the floor, putting space between us. He once again faced the mirror, staring at his reflection for some time, as if he was gazing at a stranger. He slowly breathed in and out several times before responding. "I apologize; I don't know what got into me. We have to get back to Elisa's shop."

It was a buzz kill, but I couldn't disagree, my common sense finally kicking in. "Yeah, you're right. But before we do, are you okay?"

He rubbed his palms down his face. "No, I'm not. I feel…out of sorts, as if I have no control over my faculties. Dafari is trying to help, but I fear it's not working."

I closed the gap between us just enough to reach out and hold his hands. "You've only just started working with him, Octavian. Be patient and give it time."

"Time is not a luxury afforded to us, Poppet…however, I will exercise some patience…for now, for you."

I smiled up at him, silent understanding passing between us. We did need to head back, but I wanted to check something before we left The Book Nook. "Octavian, can I take a look at your wings?"

He raised an inquisitive eyebrow. "Of course you can, but may I ask why?"

"Just a hunch. It could be nothing, but I want to be sure."

He shrugged but acquiesced, unbuttoning then removing his black shirt. I never tired of looking at his perfect pecs and well-defined abs...but now was not the time for self-gratification. Octavian unfurled his wings and, while they still resembled an angel's, some of the feathers were pure black. There weren't many, but it was enough to be disconcerting. The expression on Octavian's face told me he felt the same.

"My word," he uttered in barely a whisper. "What is happening to me?" He quickly retracted his wings, putting his shirt back on.

"If I had to make an educated guess, your body is reacting as if it's had a bone marrow transplant. You now have two sets of DNA, yours and Azazel's, effectively making you a chimaera, an organism containing a mixture of genetically different tissues. Thing is your physiology is different from that of humans, so these...changes you're undergoing are completely foreign to me. All I have to go on is what I'm seeing. You've been experiencing emotional and physical affects; your days' long initial transformation after the battle with your parents, change in temperament, intermittent red eyes, and now your wings." I purposely left out the part where I felt as if he had me in his thrall. Octavian was already going through enough.

"Damn Uncle and his demon blood," Octavian exclaimed, understandably upset. While Azazel claimed that he activated Octavian's latent demon blood in order to allow him to save us, knowing him, his actions were nowhere near being completely altruistic.

I rushed over to him, standing on my toes, placing my hands on his face. "Baby, we'll figure this out, I promise you. You believe me, right?"

"Of course I do, my love. I-I just don't want to run the

risk of hurting you or anyone else I care about. I would never forgive myself if I harmed any of you." I saw the consternation in his eyes, and it was tearing at my soul.

"Octavian Jerrod," I began, "you would never hurt us, regardless of the changes you're going through. I believe that with all my heart."

Taking both of my hands in his, Octavian kissed one palm then the other. "You have more faith in me than I do myself right now, Tasmin."

"I have enough faith for the both of us." I pulled him down by the collar of his shirt, placing a light kiss on his lips. "Now let's get back to the café, shall we?"

We made sure everything was locked up tight then headed over to Elisa's. Once we entered the shop, the scent of freshly baked goods bombarded us. We walked back to the kitchen where Elisa and Dafari were; she was checking pastries in the oven while he was cutting a caramel crunch cake and placing the individual slices in plastic containers.

I couldn't help but laugh inwardly watching him. In our past lives, although he could cook, Dafari had never been one to venture into the kitchen often unless it was to sample what Elisa was cooking. But now, in this lifetime, not only had he been a great help to her at the café, he did much of the cooking at their home, in large part thanks to his friendship with Aunt Noreen.

"You're really working that apron, brother of mine," I teased.

Dafari looked at me, a combination of a scowl and a smirk on his face. "You're lucky it's you who made that comment, Sister."

"As opposed to Adour-Nuru?" Elisa asked, taking a pan of apple tarts out of the oven.

"Speaking of the incubus," I started, pulling items out of my knapsack, "I have everything we need to keep him at bay;

coral to ward off visitation from said incubus, and clear quartz to amplify the effects of the coral. We can put the chunks of coral and quartz in the corners of the shop and around the building. Elisa, I'll also create a bracelet with coral and quartz beads for you to wear. Dafari, although you're half-incubus, this shouldn't affect you because you and Elisa are soul linked."

"Even if it does affect me, I will deal with whatever discomfort comes from it. Besides," he said, walking over to Elisa, kissing her cheek, "our love, our bond is stronger than any amulet."

"Well said, Brother. If all goes as expected, that will be all we need to keep that ne'er-do-well away from Elisa," Octavian chimed in.

"And if not, I'll deal with him, personally." Dafari's tone held lethality.

"Let's hope it doesn't come to that," I remarked. "Guys, why don't you two cover the outside while Elisa and I handle in here?"

Dafari, raising a suspicious eyebrow, removed his apron, placing it on the counter. "Octavian, is it just me or is Tasmin trying to get rid of us?"

"It most assuredly is *not* just you, dear brother." Octavian reached down, hugging me from behind. "Feel free to talk about me when I'm gone."

I handed them each a bag full of crystals, watching as they headed out the backdoor.

"Okay, what's going on?" I turned around to see Elisa, arms folded across her chest, eyeing me intently.

As I walked to the corners of the room, strategically placing crystals, I reiterated all that happened with Octavian at The Book Nook. I had to admit that I was glad we had our full memories back, because she was the one person I could tell absolutely anything. I continued my tale as we moved to the dining area to arrange the crystals around the room. Once that was done, I set myself up at a table, ready to create Elisa's bracelet. While I was laying out my materials, Elisa walked behind the counter. When she returned, she had two steaming mugs in her hands.

"A caramel apple spice with extra caramel and whipped cream for you, and a white chocolate mocha with a shot of espresso for me."

Thanking her, I gladly accepted the cup, resting it on the table.

Elisa sat across from me, taking a long sip before saying, "It sounds like Octavian didn't even realize what he was doing."

"I know, and that's what worries me. He even said he felt like he didn't have control of himself. When he went into his self-imposed lockdown after the fight with his parents, it seemed as if he had gotten a handle on things, but ever since our battle with Eve, he's become increasingly unstable. He's afraid, Elisa, and I'm afraid for him. Problem is I'm completely out of my depth in this situation, and I have no idea how to help him." My voice trailed off as I strung crystals on the elastic string.

Elisa stopped me, placing her hands over mine. "You *are* helping him just by being there." She paused for a few seconds. I could tell she was deep in thought. "I know he's not completely healed, but maybe Raphael could do something. It's the very least he can do since he's been the houseguest from Hell."

I couldn't help but laugh at what she just said. "I guess, but I don't think he's capable of healing anyone right now, and with his bad attitude, he may not want to help. Plus, I don't think what's happening with Octavian is something that can be healed, or reversed for that matter. I believe he can only learn how to live with it."

I stopped speaking, apparently too long for Elisa's liking. She blinked slowly several times. "Tasmin, I know that look. What's going on in that head of yours?"

I finished her bracelet, tying off the ends of the elastic cord. Handing it to Elisa, I stood up then began pacing back and forth, knowing full well that what I was about to say wouldn't go over well, understandably so.

"You're not going to like it. Heck, I hate it, but we need to get to the bottom of what's happening to Octavian and we need to do it with a quickness. On top of that, Octavian needs to learn how to control parts of this…metamorphosis he's experiencing. As much as Dafari wants to help his brother, he can't really teach him because he was born half-demon and grew into his powers as a fledgling. The only person who can truly see him through this is the one person…demon who caused this hot mess to begin with, and that's —"

"Don't say it," Elisa demanded, covering her ears.

"Azazel."

"I told you not to say it," she replied then exhaled loudly. "Just when I thought we could steer clear of him for bit…but I get it. If this is what it takes to help my brother then," she swallowed hard, gritting her teeth, "so be it."

I was glad to have Elisa on board. While her trepidation was justified, and as much as we both preferred to have nothing to do with Azazel, he was a necessary evil, in more ways than one. That said, I was going to do whatever I had to in order to help the man I loved…even if it meant dealing with the devil.

Chapter 13.5
GABRIEL & URIEL

Gabriel, the Messenger Angel, and Uriel, Angel of Wisdom and Enlightenment walked in the midst of the early-morning crowd in Midtown Manhattan, the high archangels seeking to evade detection from Above. Being the angel involved in science and education, Uriel was able to come up with a way to cloak their energy signatures. The large crowd helped to keep them hidden even more.

"Must we stroll amongst this throng of humans?" Gabriel questioned, his Barbadian-accented voice fitting in perfectly with the melting pot that was New York City.

"If you want to speak freely without fear, then yes," Uriel retorted, sounding as if he resided in Spanish Harlem.

Like their other angel brothers, neither the Messenger Angel nor the Angel of Wisdom shared a resemblance. Archangel Gabriel, with his caramel complexion; almond-shaped, hazel eyes with flecks of green; full lips, and locs made him a standout in any crowd. Dressed in a winter white linen-wool blend suit, cocoa-colored dress shirt, cognac leather dress loafers, and a full-length, acajou-colored wool coat, he garnered the attention befitting his station.

Like his brother, the amber-complected Uriel, who stood an inch shorter at six feet three, was a head-turner, as well. With a well-lined tapered fade, piercing gray eyes, round lips, and five o'clock shadow, he garnered more than a few admiring looks from passersby. As his signature color was red, he donned a ruby-colored, double-breasted wool suit jacket with matching pleated wool trousers. His look was completed with a button-down dress shirt, polished calfskin Oxfords, and a cashmere overcoat, all in black. Both high archangels looked as if they were ready for a Wall Street board meeting.

"Michael was tortured for failing in his mission," Gabriel stated as they walked briskly along 34th Street. "Raphael, on the other hand, blatantly violated His edicts. By coupling those witches with our nephews, he bucked all convention."

"I understand that, but did we have to be so harsh with him?" queried Uriel.

Gabriel looked to his left and his right, as if checking for listening ears. "You know better than to question His rules. Raphael went against the natural order of things. Had we not carried out His instructions to the letter, *we* would have been involuntarily joining our dear brother here on Earth, wingless and powerless."

"I am well aware that Raphael violated His rules, but was that such a bad thing? Our nephews are persona non grata for falling in love with human women, but those women also fell in love with them. The way Raphael's powers work, if their attraction wasn't mutual, the pairings would have never occurred."

"That's all well and good, but those humans are **witches**, Brother; and let us not forget, those same witches have Nephilim blood running through their veins."

"Yes, but they are witches who **help** those in need. They protect people, have defended the people of Salix Pointe with their very lives. Doesn't that, by all definition, make them good? Clearly, their DNA does not define who they are," Uriel retorted.

"Be that as it may, I don't make the rules and neither do you. Our job is to enforce them," countered Gabriel. "You know we have to be careful with our every move from here on out. Bad enough we were complicit in aiding our reprobate brother Azazel, with a plan *you* concocted, no less. Mind you, it was to help Brother Michael, but I don't dare think of what would happen to us if our deception was ever discovered. Uriel, I wouldn't fret over Raphael. He's with our nephews and their witches. I'm sure he's recovering quite nicely."

Chapter 14
OCTAVIAN

Tasmin and I made it back to her aunt's home just after dusk. The sun fading over the horizon was normally a beautiful sight, but this evening, it annoyed me. As a matter of fact, everything grated my nerves more than usual, and instinctively I knew it was because of whatever was going on with me.

Back in the bookstore, it felt as if I was having an out-of-body experience as I watched myself—somewhere from the recesses of mind—aggressively tongue my woman down… but with a passion and hunger I hadn't quite experienced before. I wanted her in the most primal of ways…In ways that would surely be frowned upon in most places. And even stranger, the urge to bite her, so to intensify her pleasure and mine, was so strong I had to pull away. Something in me, another side of me, yanked me back down to reality before I could completely lose myself.

Now, as we stood just outside the front door of her aunt's home, I couldn't help but gaze down at her. While we were here to try to save her parents from whatever had a hold on them, I wanted to rip her jeans down…and—

"Heyyy, Octovian and Tasmania," broke me away from my lascivious thoughts.

We looked down near the wooded area where a brook separated Noreen's home from Elisa's old home. Rufus was coming through the dense brush with a can of paint. The short, squat man managed to smile brightly while holding a serious intensity in his gaze.

"Good evening, Rufus," I greeted.

"Rufus! Thank you so much for coming," Tasmin whispered. "I don't want to waste too much time. Can you go around back and start painting the window seals and back door?"

"Shole can, and I don't blame ya a lick for not wanting to waste time. I'ma get right on it. This place got some freaky energy 'round it, and Noreen wouldn't stand for it," he told her as he practically jogged and skipped to the back of the house.

Tasmin looked over at me. "We got the bottles on the tree in good time. Let's get the rest of this done, and remember, no matter what they say, we get both of them out the house."

"As you wish, Poppet," I responded, more than willing to follow her lead this time around.

No more than a minute after Tasmin knocked at least three times, Silas opened the door. He looked better than he had earlier, but not by much. The faint hint of sulfur wafting from the house was offensive to my senses. Black rings around his eyes made him look racoon-ish in appearance. His shoulders sagged and he presented as if standing caused him great exhaustion. The man was dressed in thick pajama bottoms with a matching shirt. On his feet were slippers and his robe was tied at the waist.

"Hey, Daddy," Tasmin said sweetly, while trying to mask the fact the odor coming from inside was off-putting.

Silas' weak gaze landed on his daughter, then me before going back to Tasmin again. "Tasmin...Octavian...what are you doing here?"

"Remember earlier, I told Mommy we'd be by later to try to see what we could do to help you guys get better?"

Confusion clouded the man's features before he took a deep breath while nodding. "Well...come on—"

"No...no, Daddy. I was thinking some fresh air would help both of you. You come outside and wait with Octavian while I go get Mommy."

"Silas, why don't you step down here with me," I suggested, pointing toward the yard, near the bottle tree. "I hope I'm not overstepping my bounds here, but the house could really use airing out. Whatever sickness you and Jewel have contracted has a putrid odor emanating from inside."

"He's right, Daddy. I'll let some windows up so the house can air out." Before Silas could respond, Tasmin had stepped inside then ushered him out.

As soon as she closed the door, I felt when Tasmin opened her mind to me completely. It was how I knew she no longer trusted her mother. With her mind open, she would be able to show me things that I wouldn't be privy to while outside with Silas.

I studied the man, watched his breathing go from erratic to calm in a matter of seconds. "When I'm not around Jewel, I tend to start feeling better," he said without being prompted to do so. "It's something I've been noticing..."

"She's not Jewel as you know her. I think it's okay if we all admit that now," I said matter-of-factly.

I knew my powers were a bit shifty at the moment, but I was also aware I hadn't lost my ability to bring people peace with just a touch. Maybe that had been intensified as well? Reaching out to lay a supportive hand on my soon-to-be father-in-law's shoulder, I watched the man relax further. Some of the burdens that were weighing him down lifted instantly. He stood up straighter, shaking his head as if to clear it.

"When we…were intimate…things felt differently, and I couldn't bring myself to say that aloud, but my gut wouldn't let it go…"

I nodded once, finding it curious that the man wanted to speak so freely and openly. "Tasmin is inside now. We're putting a few plans into action."

Rufus jogged around to the front of the porch. As the little man hummed, he stuck the paint brush in the bucket and then started waving it back and forth as he splashed paint above his head. And in the next second, he stopped.

"Wait…is that…Rufus?" Silas asked, his eyes squinted as he tried to get a better look on the porch.

"It is, and it's something we'll have to explain later."

As tiny flashes and faint explosions of haint-blue light covered the porch's ceiling, Silas' eyes widened. Rufus turned in our direction, raising his hand to wave before he suddenly turned his attention to the house then snapped his fingers to vanish.

Tasmin's thoughts slammed into mine, showing me things that had happened just moments before.

"Mommy, are you almost done in the bathroom?" I heard her ask Jewel.

"Ju-just…a se-second, love…" Jewel's voice sounded like a broken record.

As Tasmin shot quick glances at the bathroom door, she sprinkled the bed with the black salt and pepper she had grabbed earlier. Careful not to make it obvious the covers had been tampered with, she lifted them enough to place the mixture and then put the covers back as they were.

Seconds later, she moved quickly around the room, chanting spells as she placed several protection crystals. My woman was confident in her abilities as she went about her tasks. Those jeans cupping her derriere just right when she got on all fours to strategically hide crystals throughout the cozy home.

Focus, man, I berated myself internally.

Now, Jewel inched down the front steps timidly. "Oh… Tasmin, baby, won't you let Silas help me. I don't want to burden—"

"Don't be silly, Mommy. You're no burden to me. Come on, let's walk near the brook. That way, you can be close to the house just in case you need to hurriedly get back inside. Octavian, Daddy, you guys can follow us. I figure a nice, long walk will do her some good."

While Tasmin's voice was light and wispy, her actions showed she was in no mood to negotiate. She looped her arm through Jewel's and then led them in the direction of the babbling brook. Silas jogged ahead of me to be nearer his wife and daughter, but I noticed he walked behind them as opposed to being on the other side of Jewel.

Tasmin made random small talk, asking questions about her childhood and other frivolous things. Jewel grew weaker by the moment. I could tell by the way her shoulders drooped and legs sagged.

Miss Noreen's home and the surrounding area were charming in their simplicity. The exposed beams, stone accents, cobblestone drive and pathways, along with its prominent columns all made for a cozy, picturesque sight.

The trimmed back tree limbs and neatly manicured shrubbery framed the backyard walkway. The serpentine brick path was flanked by all types of flowers and plants and would normally be filled with the noise of insects and wild animals scurrying about. Tonight, however, I noticed that it was completely silent. Nothing moved, croaked, fluttered, or flew overheard.

My instincts kicked into overdrive, and something in the

back of my mind would not stop screaming that danger was near. Tasmin and her parents had stopped walking, and I made note that Jewel's stance was odd. I had to wonder if the woman's transformation during the battle with Eve had left her bones deformed in some way that we hadn't noticed before.

I quickly put that thought to bed when I remembered how well the woman seemed to be getting along at Elisa's café earlier. They were near the brook now, and something about the water unsettled Jewel.

So many things bombarded me at once. Rufus had said his Yom-Ziza's special flavoring would bring up any evil inside a person, or something along those lines. So that told me that Jewel was already compromised before then, but what if…it was during battle that she was infected…or perhaps the moments soon after battle? It was right around the time…Eve…went missing—

And then it all hit me like a ton of bloody bricks.

"Tasmin and Silas, move away from her now," I yelled, sprinting toward the three.

Jewel's head ripped around at the speed of light. Blood red eyes bore into me, and before Tasmin or Silas could react, she shoved both out of her way and raced back toward the house. Tasmin almost fell but righted herself quickly. Jutting her hand forward, she sent a lawn chair flying in the direction of her mother. Jewel shrieked, ducked the chair, and then tried to run for the back porch only to pull up short as she spotted the now haint-blue door.

Tearing back down the steps, she raced toward the front yard, but she would have no luck there either, especially when Tasmin threw a handful of the black salt in her direction. An ear-splitting scream like I had never heard rent the air.

"She's trapped," yelled Silas.

"We can't allow her to leave. Not now that we know who

THE RECKONING & THE REAPER

she is. I'm sorry, Poppet, but... Eve has taken over your mother's mind and body," I informed Tasmin once she had run over to me.

So many emotions passed through her eyes at once, it was hard to tell what she was thinking. "What? Eve? How do you know?"

Before I could answer, a painful sob made all three of us turn in time to see Jewel's body writhing on the hard ground. Tasmin tried to run for her mother, same as Silas, but I stopped them.

"She's in pain," he yelled angrily. "We need to help her!"

"No! She will try to latch on to you if you get too close. She is an unstable creature without a viable body to inhabit. Literally, any *body* will due," I shouted. "I know you hear your wife's voice but remember what kind of evil we're dealing with!"

"We have to do something! We can't let her have free reign over Salix Pointe," Tasmin cut in.

"Oh...shit..." Silas' frightened declaration made Tasmin and I look toward her mother again.

Her body now lay prone. She was so still we didn't know if she was alive; however, Eve's demonic form could be seen hovering just above her body. It was a hideous, but pitiful sight. So misshaped and discolored, no words would be able to rightly describe what I was looking at.

Even more mind boggling were the flames rising from beneath her. Sulfuric ash mixed with plumes of dark gray smoke hissed up from ever widening cracks in the ground. Fast-moving, erratic gnarled fingers grabbed and slashed at Eve, yanking her this way and that.

"What on earth is that?" Tasmin yelled.

I grabbed her, shielding her behind me just in case whatever was ripping at Eve decided to come in our direction.

Silas flanked us now, eyes wide with fright and disbelief as he stared on.

Eve's disembodied cries of "No…please! No! Helllppp me," chilled me to the bone.

She thrashed about, clawing at dirt, grass, anything she could get her hands on to keep her descent to Hell from happening. It was of no use. The oversized tail of the largest reptile I'd seen in all my years—and I'd seen some things—coiled around the fallen demon's waist and yanked her down to the bottomless black pit.

Chapter 14.5
LILITH

Lilith felt Eve's terror register as soon as he dragged her to hell. She was terrified and in so much pain that even Lilith was shivering. No one would ever understand why, even after all Eve had done, she still loved her. Eve was her sister and always would be. She would have given anything to be able to go back and try to talk her younger sister out of becoming one with Adam. She was doomed before she started.

"Leave her alone," Lilith screamed, her anger quaking the grounds on the Seventh Level of Heaven.

She felt the fire lick her skin. Smelled the rancid stench of rotting flesh. It was as if she was right next to her sister, feeling every modicum of pain and torture. He was enjoying torturing Eve. Lilith knew it. It was his way to take pleasure in the chaos he created. Eve had not only escaped but tried to take control of the ultimate power on her own.

Tears of frustration stung Lilith's eyes. At one point in time, Eve had been an innocent, caught in a war between father and son. She was used as a pawn to further one's agenda. Rage flowed through Lilith's veins like molten lava.

Oh, Morningstar would pay, and he would pay severely!

CHAPTER 15
OCTAVIAN

It was two hours later, and I sat in a shower at my brother's home. The hot water felt good as it washed away the day's troubles. My mind was on everything and nothing all at once. While Tasmin was laying out our night things in the bedroom, I could no longer stand in the presence of my own funk. And that was more figurative than literal.

Human magazines said cold showers helped with things such as this, but maybe because I was more angelic, I found that hot water actually worked better.

My mind traveled back to the moments after we got Jewel to the basement of the bookstore... where Tasmin, along with my brother, had set up a makeshift triage for her parents. With Rufus's help, Elisa and I were able to clean and sterilize the area as much as possible. I had a feeling his fairy magick helped more with that than anything else.

Uncle Raphael also volunteered to come along to help, telling us being in the house all day with only his thoughts to keep him company was maddening. He wanted to test his medical prowess on this plane to see just how much power he did or did not still have.

Now, Jewel lay silently, an IV bag that my brother had procured from Doc Benu's office set on an IV pole next to a cot we'd also taken from the doc's clinic. Silas was laid out on one of the small sofas from the bookstore that we'd also moved to the basement. Elisa and Rufus had whipped him up a mug of tea that had been infused with magick. After checking Jewel's vitals and making sure she was stable, there was really nothing else Tasmin could do for her, even though she had wondered aloud if she should try anyway.

"There is no way that thought should have even crossed your mind, Doctor," Uncle Raphael fussed, but he was gentle in his delivery. "I understand this is your mother but think about how it felt when you first tried to heal me. Now imagine trying to go in to heal your mother after an original evil has taken up residence..."

Sighing, Tasmin gazed at her mother. "I know, trust me... I know... She's just going to have to rest. We don't know and can't tell what kind of, if any, damage has been done to her body yet," she said to the room at large. "I don't feel safe with them anywhere else. We know the bookstore is the epicenter of magick, and I'm hoping that it shields and protects them if whatever came for Eve decides to double back."

"Everything in me thinks it was Uncle Morningstar who snatched her down," I said. "It's safe to say she won't be coming back."

"The Devil always gets his due," Uncle Raphael replied. "Even though we have no idea if he came directly or sent henchmen, we know she's been dragged back to Hell, and for now, that's a plus for us. One less thing to worry about."

"This has been the longest day of my life it seems. I swear last night and today just blurred together," Elisa tiredly said then tried— unsuccessfully— to stifle a yawn. "I am truly drained, and that's on top of me dreading Dafari heading back to New Orleans."

"I'll be as careful as possible," my brother assured her, taking her hand in his then kissing her palm.

"Why don't y'all go on and get outta here. I can keep an eye on ya folks for the night. I ain't got a heap I need ta be doing," Rufus cut in, reminding us he was still in the room. The little man moved so silently sometimes; it was easy to forget.

Uncle Raphael moved around the cot, studying Jewel as he took notes. He shadowed Tasmin earlier, taking in all she was doing as if it didn't come second nature to him. "I think I'll stick around as well. I'd like to test my skill and knowledge while trying to figure out what my next move will be. My spirit is unsettled, and I feel as if…things have shifted."

After a few more exchanges between us, all things considered, we took them up on their offer.

Dafari had asked that he have his own space back, but for now, Tasmin and I went back to the guest room at his place. There was no way we could go back to Noreen's. Not until the place had been physically and spiritually cleansed.

My mind was a jumble of things and emotions… For as serious as our situation was, my body's needs were drowning out anything that didn't lead to its satisfaction. I needed to be inside my woman's body. *Immediately.* I didn't know what was happening to me and why it felt like I was no longer in control of my own person. I couldn't stop the longing for Tasmin no matter how hard I tried.

That was why as soon as we made it home, after she and Elisa had been conversing in the kitchen for about ten minutes, I took Tasmin's hand and guided her right to our room. It was much to Elisa's chagrin, as she clearly wanted to discuss what had happened with Tasmin's parents more. I'd apologize to Sissy later. Right now, I needed to be selfish with my woman's time.

I didn't stop walking until we were in the bedroom, and to make sure nothing would be heard once Tasmin and I were locked in, I threw up a sound barrier, cocooning us in our own mood while keeping everyone else out. Any other time, the natural stone of the shower would appeal to me. Right now, though, I couldn't even be bothered to care.

Tasmin entered the bathroom. "Everything is all laid out," she said.

"Sound goods. Mind if we chat for a bit?" I asked.

Shirt already removed, I watched on as she rid herself of her socks and shoes then peeled off her jeans. Next came her bra and panties. Tasmin's nude body put me in a trance. I didn't pretend to hide my lust either. I stared on greedily as she released her locs and allowed them to curtain her shoulders and face.

"You're so damn beautiful," came out huskily as I fought with my body not to bulk.

I didn't recognize my voice and judging by the way Tasmin stilled, she was having a hard time with it as well… but in the same breath, I could smell how it affected her body.

Smiling tiredly, she finally looked at me, taking in my nudity the same as I'd done hers. "What's on your mind?"

"I need to make a return trip to London. Put an end to my life there. With you being back into your full powers and us on the way to remarrying, my life is here with you now…"

Easing the glass shower door open a bit more, she stepped inside, allowing the steam to envelop her. She moved closer in my direction, stopping short of closing the distance. "How long do you plan to be away? I mean with Dafari leaving I don't know how I feel about you being gone as well."

I reached for her hand, needing something of hers to touch. "I don't plan to be away that long. Maybe a day at most."

"Okay… and maybe once you get back, we can discuss

your…condition. I was thinking…your uncle could help you more than anyone right now."

Feeling her pulse quicken as my eyes traveled the expanse of her body, my gums tingled and burned. I ran my tongue across the top row of my teeth to try to ease the pain. "To be honest, you could suggest I share libations with Lucifer himself, and I'd agree."

She chuckled so light and sweet that I felt my muscles expand…every last one. When she picked up the loofa and lathered it with peppermint soap, I watched from somewhere beside myself as she took her time washing me from head to feet. It was quite an erotic experience for a man's woman to be gentle with his body. Sure, I was this supernatural angelic being, but now…Tasmin made me feel like…a man. Human.

Not wanting this moment to belong to only her, I grabbed the other loofa, remembering the healing properties of peppermint. I was very thankful in the moment that I remembered some of the things she taught me all those lives ago. She even tilted my head back and grabbed the smaller, extendable showerhead so she could wash my hair. Lathering my loofa well, I began to wash her body. I used my gift of touch to loosen and take away some of the stress and worry riding her. Watching her shoulders relax and tension leave her immediately soothed me.

It was nice, but I needed to touch her in a more intimate way. So, I dropped the loofa and then used my hands. Rubbing, massaging, and kneading places where I knew she felt the angst of the day most. Cupping a gentle but firm hold on the front of her neck, I let my thumb make small feathery circles against her pulse.

I was putty in her hands when she gently massaged and washed my rigidness. There was no need to bother to hide how turned on she had me. It would have been impossible to anyway.

I had to sit down as my heart rate kicked up. I'd known hunger before, but tonight, I was ravenous for her. My heart beat a different rhythm, and I was so rigid, it ached deep within my soul. I had to calm down, lest I take her hard and fast. While Tasmin was more than enough woman to take all of me fully, I did not want to risk hurting her. The power coursing through my veins was new to me. I had to be careful.

"I'm not afraid, Octavian, even though something tells me I should be," she said softly.

Oh, she should be afraid…she should be very, very afraid, echoed in my mind.

Now I needed to stand again. Rolling my shoulders, I tried to ground myself as I watched her. Her perky breasts swelled with the need to be kissed. Her small brown nipples were ever hardening, drawing my attention and making my mouth water.

"I want you just as badly as you want me," she confessed.

My eyes were drawn to the minimal hair covering her vagina, and I licked my lips. Something was happening to me. I felt it in the way desire crawled just underneath my skin.

"Tasmin—"

"Shhh," she told me, laying a delicate finger against my lips. "Just…take me. However you want me…whatever that looks like…have me…"

Her words dripped with a sensuality that gripped and stroked my manhood like a famished lover. The pleading in her voice fractured what little resolve I had left. Staring up at me with big, wide expressive eyes, the yearning I saw there egged me on. I pulled her to me, mouth crashing against hers. The sweetness of her lips had my tongue eagerly searching out hers. Tasmin's need for me pulled a rough moan out of me, and when her hand slid down between us, found my hardness, and then proceeded to stroke me again, it took everything in me not to take her down right there.

I reveled in the feel of her hands driving me a little bit closer to madness. My body vibrated when my pre-excitement coated her fingers. Hands slid down her back now, gripping her backside, spreading her wide. Her shutter of desire entered my psyche and shook me to the core.

I had to stop.

Had to let her go.

My gums ached worse now. I needed to bite something.

Specifically, her…

Trying to push her away, I groaned low. "Baby… Tasmin…sweet…heart…"

My words escaped me, and I didn't know where to place my eyes. The water seemed to intensify my want for her. Tasmin's rich brown skin looked even more enticing under the spray from the square showerhead. Her long locs now cascaded over her palm-sized breasts. Rivulets of water flowed down the flat planes of her stomach and drew my attention back to where a meal awaited me. Her nudity was adding to my ecstasy. I closed my eyes, taking in deep, controlled breaths.

When I opened them, red reflected back at me from the glass door. She gasped and for a second looked as if she was too scared to say anything. Then…she came at me harder. Pushing me underneath the spray of the water until my back slammed against the wall. Her frenzied kiss made me aggressively grab her waist once more. I was set to put my foot down about needing some space to think, but as soon as my hands touched her again, I lost it.

She felt too damn good and pliable in my hold, and suddenly, I couldn't get enough of her. I fisted a handful of her locs, needing the control it allowed me. She smelled divine, her body readying itself for my invasion. Her petals blooming in anticipation of...me.

My gaze never left hers as I lifted her around my waist. I felt my gums burning, but this time I didn't care to try to stop whatever was happening. My gut told me to just give in to it. I felt when my canines lengthened. A painful growl erupted from me when one nicked my tongue. I knew she felt something shift when she pushed back to get a better look at me.

I didn't give her time to speak or resist. I didn't want to ruin the moment with words. Just the feel of her skin was doing something to me. The smell of her arousal and her touch both aphrodisiacs. I tore away from her mouth, nuzzling her hair away from her neck. I rubbed my face against her shoulder, kissing her collarbone as I eased her down on my hardness. We were so close one would have thought I was breathing for her.

Her faint gasps and whimpers, as the little resistance from her body adjusted to take me all in, drove me a little more over the edge. "So...wet..." I growled low.

She felt too good for me to take her standing up. I needed a bed. I needed her body under my complete control. With just a thought, we were back in the room on the bed. Once she was on her back, I eased out of her, pushing her knees back to her ears. Without hesitation, I planted my face between her thighs, sucking her core bud into my mouth with fervor.

I let my tongue have its way with her then plunged deep into her psyche. Invading the most private parts of her mind and body. As I sucked on her clit, I homed in on the throbbing within her vaginal walls. That pulsating ache where desire was buried deep... I took it and made it ricochet all through her body.

Her scent flooded my senses as I lapped and drank at her love. I buried my nose in the dewy folds of her vagina, trying to taste my way to the end of her rainbow. A stream of slick sticky wetness seeped from her plump slit. So wet, she was dissolving any common sense I had. So attuned I was to her body, I could hear her desire pulsing between her thighs. This was new territory for me. I'd known my woman's body many times, but this? Never like this.

I spread her wider. Opened her up with deep kisses, allowing her to feel every stroke and lick of my tongue. While her fingers massaged my scalp, holding my face close to her, I grabbed her hips tighter as I sucked on her clit then trailed my tongue down to circle her throbbing entrance. I set all those nerve endings ablaze, probing with my mouth, seeking to rewire the entire way she responded to me sexually.

And there it was…the sound I had been waiting for. The breathless gasp followed by her sweet guttural moan. When I lifted my head to witness the aftermath of my handiwork, I was rewarded with her head lolling from side to side as her skin glistened with the sheen of her first orgasm.

Her kittenish moans turned into sharp inhales that shot right to my groin. My shaft filled with all the blood that was left in my body. I felt it oozing from the tip and I had to chuckle inwardly being that she, too, had me leaking.

"Please, Octavian," she cried passionately, but I didn't know what she was begging for.

Tell me what you need, Poppet, I shot to her mentally.

"Octavian…my…God…"

I can be…

"I need you…"

To do what?

"Come…inside me…now…"

I chuckled again. This time so she could hear. Some part

of me got a kick out of the moment. I had the always-in-control Doctor Tasmin Pettiford so out of sorts she couldn't form a complete thought? That fed the arrogance in this new part of me.

Releasing her thighs, I slid up her body with ease, forcing myself to ignore the beat of her pressure points. I wanted to kiss her again, but the need to watch her as I thrust inside her was greater. The need to nick the inside of her thighs strong. I didn't use hands to find my way inside her, filling her up until my pelvis touched hers.

Our mouths so close together, I caught her heated gasp then swallowed it down.

"Oh…Octavian…what…is…happening?" she crooned softly.

I moved against her in small, gradual strokes…

Felt my muscles expand underneath my skin as I dragged my nose against the throbbing vein in her neck.

Her contracting around me made it feel like electric shots of adrenaline were running through my veins. My arms wrapped around her tighter. Grip on her backside way more aggressive than she was used to while I moved in and out… then out… then inside of her. *Again…*

…and again…

Tasmin didn't back down though. As I sank deeper, she wrapped her legs tighter around my waist, urging me to keep going. I didn't recognize my own sounds. Animalistic in the way I moved against her. I threw my head back, needing to be more verbal as my canines and gums throbbed incessantly.

Bite her, my mind screamed.

I couldn't. Was too afraid. I didn't know what I was doing, but dear…God…why did she tilt her head that way? Inviting me in for the kill…

No… I can't…

"Please, don't stop," came out on a pant from her.

Your pleasure...her pleasure... bite.her.now!

My nails got longer, dug into her cheeks and thighs... Unbridled lust took a hold of me. My movements against her now wild and the rabid need to sink my teeth into her neck overrode any logic I had left. Before I could stop myself, as the muscles in the back of my thighs burned...abdomen constricted and body hummed with the need to release, I sank fangs I didn't know I possessed until this very moment, deep into the erogenous zone of her neck.

And it was...glorious.

Delirium hit me immediately, especially when she in return bit down hard, right on that sensitive area between my shoulder and neck. There were no fangs, but the intent behind it was just as potent. Ohhh...my woman bit me as if she was proficient in the art of odaxelagnia. Explosions of lights erupted behind my eyelids. The last bit of decorum I had faded. The breath I'd been holding wooshed out with her name in guttural release.

Throwing my head back, I saw the injury to her neck, but she wouldn't let me go as I released inside her. She kept begging me not to stop. What was I to do?

Kiss the wound, my mind screamed.

Never in my life had I ever done something so damaging to her. I couldn't make out what I was seeing. Yes, there were trails of blood, but something else...What was that golden, silvery like substance oozing with the red liquid? I dipped my head to taste it and felt every piece of the orgasm riddling her body on the cellular level. A transference of energy unlike anything words could explain. I'd emptied myself inside her but couldn't bring myself to leave the snug and rhythmic walls of her body. The consequences of my actions from our night of passion would be something I'd have to think about tomorrow...

CHAPTER 16
DAFARI

When we returned home, everyone was still wound up from all that had occurred on this exceedingly long day. It wore on each one of us. As such, Octavian and Tasmin had retreated to one of the guest rooms to work out their angst as they saw fit, while Elisa and I withdrew to our suite. After a little more discussion on Eve's possible demise, my wife and I turned in.

Long ago, I discovered that reading poetry to my beloved helped Elisa to calm her mind and relax. After we had changed for bed and were settled, I fetched a book from my nightstand drawer, *Love Poems* by Nikki Giovanni. Her head resting on my lap, I read to Elisa for over an hour, stroking her thick, curly mane as I did so. Eventually, her slow, even breathing told me that she had fallen asleep. However, I read one final poem, entitled *Love Is,* for good measure.

"Some people forget that love is tucking you in and kissing you "Good night" no matter how young or old you are. Some people don't remember that love is listening and laughing and asking questions no matter what your age. Few recognize that love is commitment, responsibility, no fun at all unless…Love is you and me."

The words on the page rang true; love was a commitment, as well as a responsibility, and…it was me and Elisa.

Our love had withstood the test of time, despite all obstacles. My mind wandered to my upcoming travels to New Orleans. One way or another I had to get my lost memories back... despite my reluctance. For me to have my mind wiped clean, I knew I must have committed some heinous acts.

While I knew retrieving those recollections could be the key to finding our children's souls, I hoped that our love could survive whatever it was I had done. Elisa said she knew whatever actions I had committed in Hell must have been for a good reason and that nothing, including Hell itself, would come between us. I prayed she was right. Shifting my position to lie down, I placed Elisa's head on my chest, my arm encircling her waist. I allowed myself to drift off, a pleasant dream beginning to play out in my mind.

"Umm umm umm!" said the brown skin woman with glistening hazel eyes, taking another bite of the Gullah red rice. "You've truly outdone yourself this time, Dafari."

I poured her a glass of Pinot Grigio before saying, "Thank you, Noreen. I can honestly say I've learned from the best."

"I bet you say that to all the girls." Noreen's gentle ribbing actually brought a smile to my usually dour visage.

I sat next to her at my kitchen island, sipped on my own glass of wine. I typically wasn't a wine drinker, hard liquor being more my libation of choice, but when I was with Noreen, I always acquiesced and drank what she was having. There were those who never understood my friendship with Noreen Chadwick; then again, it wasn't for them to understand.

According to my father during one very heated...discussion, Noreen regarded me as the son she never had. She treated me as such, giving me the motherly warmth and tenderness I never received from the angel who birthed me. I cherished our Saturday afternoons together, as they always brought me joy.

"Congratulations on your nuptials, by the way." Her eyes held a glint of mischief.

I looked around, a bit confused. "Wait, this is a dream. A memory from several years ago. How—"

"What, you think we don't get all the latest news in the spirit world?"

A sense of panic overtook me." Spirit world? Did I somehow die in my sleep?"

Noreen let out a soulful laugh. "No, Dafari," she started, touching my hand. "You're not dead…but I am, remember?"

I shook my head several times, a feeling of sadness overcoming me. "Yes, and for that, I am truly sorry."

"Chile, why are you apologizing? You didn't do it; Michael did, with some help from Martha. That still boils my water. Sacrifice my left eye," she said in a perturbed tone.

I chuckled inwardly. I had truly missed Noreen's quirky nature.

"I know, but he is my stepfather."

Noreen placed a supportive hand on my shoulder. "Dafari, you are not responsible for the actions of that mangy angel. But enough of that; tell me what's on your mind. Those lines in your forehead tell me it's something big."

I tried to comprehend what was happening before answering her. This was more than a run-of-the-mill dream. The food and wine…the smells and tastes were so real. Then there was Noreen herself. Her salt-and-pepper hair was set in a neat bun, her attire a two-piece plum-colored pantsuit with sensible black flats on her feet. She smelled of fresh carnations. Her favorite carnation was of the purple variety, which was fitting, as it symbolized leadership, royalty, and nobility, all qualities that represented Noreen in spades.

"I thought this was just a pleasant dream, a memory from happier times. But it's clearly more than that. How is it that you are here, speaking with me in the present?"

"This is your dream, my dear friend, you tell me."

With the fate of the world at stake, and considering Noreen's spiritual nature, I rightly assumed she was fully aware of what was occurring on the heavenly plane. She advised me that Silas had initially kept her up to date on all earthly goings on, but recently, communication had ceased. I knew it was because of Eve. I took my time catching Noreen up on events since the last battle.

"Our family can't catch a break. There's so much happening, and I can't do a damn thing to help," she replied, annoyed. She swigged down the last of her wine then quickly refilled her glass. "I can't believe my poor niece Jewel was possessed by Eve, and that demon wench practically drained the life out Silas. Now that's a bitch, in more ways than one. Now, word has it that torture is her punishment." Noreen rarely used profanity, but when she did, it was quite amusing.

"Yes, but at least we have a better handle on that situation, in large part thanks to Rufus. We have been quite fortunate to have him on the team. He was integral in releasing Eve's hold over Jewel, as well as helping my Uncle Raphael nurse Jewel and Silas back to health."

"That's Rufus for you. He's always been one of the good ones."

I looked at Noreen curiously. "You knew Rufus was a fairy?"

"Of course I did. I knew all of Salix Pointe's magickal residents," Noreen said, then laughed heartily. "The same way I knew what you were the moment you showed up in town."

"And yet, you two never said a word."

"Why would I?" she questioned, crossing her arms over her chest. "That was for you to share, if you chose to. As long as you weren't harming anyone, it wasn't my business."

"But my lineage—"

She hastily interrupted me. "What about it? What you

are doesn't define who *you are, Dafari Battle. If that was the case, I wouldn't have been with my Adofo. He was the best of the best. I still miss him dearly."*

I listened as Noreen regaled me with stories of her still-missing paramour, Adofo Ange-Diable, the veterinarian I replaced, as well as the circumstances surrounding his disappearance.

"We, meaning the coven, never figured out what happened to Adofo. We tried all manner of conventional and non-conventional means to locate him, but nothing. There was no trace of him on Earth, not even a residual energy signature, which is why I know something untoward happened to him," she finished, her expressive eyes revealing the immense sadness I imagined she felt.

I lightly touched her hand. "I'm so sorry, Noreen. I'm assuming you attempted to find him here, in the afterlife."

She sighed heavily. "Yes, I, along with Amabelle, Duma-Nolan, and Hondo, have tried, but just like on Earth, there's nothing."

I felt her pain and told her as much. "We haven't been able to locate the souls of our children, Zafer and Safiya, either."

"Word has it through the spiritual grapevine that your son created quite a holy hubbub recently. He got the attention of hellhounds, the 7th battalion, and *Morningstar. Way I heard it, he bested them all, but barely."*

I quickly stood. "Uncle Morningstar? If he's on Safiya and Zafer's trail, then we really don't have much time."

"I agree with you. Their souls are a hot commodity, Dafari. They can tip the scales in either direction."

"So we've been told. That fact is weighing heavily on all of us, especially Elisa."

I saw the empathy plastered on Noreen's face. She knew all too well what we were going through.

"Poor baby. That child has been through so much, lost so much."

"Yes, she has." I paced back and forth before continuing. "Which is why I'm going to New Orleans. I need to recover something that was lost, something that may benefit us in helping to find the souls of our children."

Noreen stood, walking over to me. While she was diminutive in frame, standing at only five-four, even in death, I could tell she was still a force to be reckoned with, a force that I was grateful to have on our side.

Taking my hands in hers, she said, "I don't know what it is you're seeking, and I won't pry, but I can tell it's tearing you up inside, Dafari. You want to find Zafer and Safiya's souls, but you also worry that reclaiming what you lost may come at a high price. Am I warm?"

I looked down at the woman who was closer to me than my own mother. "You've always had the ability to read me, Noreen. I think I've done some things…things that I can't recall. I fear once that Pandora's box is opened, and I learn what I've done…I'm afraid forgiveness for me will not come."

"Forgiveness from whom, your loved ones or from yourself?"

Her question was a valid one. Elisa had already told me that nothing would come between us, and I'm sure that Octavian and Tasmin would be just as forgiving, especially Octavian since I landed in Hell to protect him. I guess the only stumbling block in my quest was me.

"As always, your wise counsel was sorely needed. I thank you, Noreen." I dropped her hands, pulling her into a hug.

"You missed me, didn't you?" she said then hugged me back.

"More than you know."

"I don't have much time left, but tell me, how's my grand-niece holding up?" Noreen asked, disengaging from our hug.

"Tasmin is doing the best she can, considering. With everything going on with her parents and finding out her and Octavian's daughter Attalah is a reaper, she's endured much."

"Tasmin is a tough cookie, but even she has her breaking point. I know both she and Elisa are still...perturbed with me, but will you please let them know that I love them and I'm here for them anytime?"

Placing my hands on Noreen's shoulders, I replied, "That I can definitely do. You have my word. Before you go, can you answer something for me?"

"Anything."

"You appear to be wandering around freely. While you are quite powerful, with souls being stolen, aren't you concerned for your own safety?"

Noreen snickered before responding. "My dear boy, I've got carte blanche here."

"Meaning?"

"Meaning The Powers That Be are so desperate they've enlisted even those they once considered undesirable to assist in this Great War. The coven was recruited to create wards and use protection spells to safeguard vulnerable souls. In return, we, and Akasha, being that she's Duma-Nolan's wife, have been upgraded to the Third Level of Heaven. If this is the closest I'll get to the Garden of Eden, I'll take it. It's a paradise, and we couldn't be safer. The Tree of Life and River of Milk and Honey are magnificent. Of course, my favorite is the River of Wine and Oil." She picked up the empty wine bottle, a grin on her face.

I returned her smile. "I'm glad to hear that you're all safe and I'll be sure to let everyone know." I realized our time was coming to an end, as I felt myself waking up. "I've enjoyed our time together. Will I see you again?"

"Of course you will." She winked at me, then, just like that, she was gone.

I woke up with a start. Elisa was still sleeping soundly. Glancing at the clock, I saw that it was four in the morning. I needed to get up and prepare for New Orleans. Not wanting to disturb her restful slumber, I gently slid from underneath her, resting her head on a pillow. After showering and getting dressed, I kissed my wife on the forehead then stepped through a shadow into The Book Nook. Voices could be heard as I walked down the stairs towards the epicenter of magick.

"Progress is slow, but Jewel appears to finally be on the mend. That concoction you added to that latest intravenous drip seems to have turned the tide in our favor. Excellent work, Rufus. You are a skilled healer in your own right. I am coming to appreciate some…beings of your caliber."

"Might they be magickal beings, Uncle Raphael?" I asked, reaching the bottom of the stairs.

"Nephew. I didn't hear you arrive. You're very stealthy… much like your father."

If he thought that would raise my hackles, he was wrong.

"My stealth has come in quite handy on many an occasion, such as in the heat of battle, or when saving lives, so thank you. And good morning to both of you. How are the Pettifords?"

Jewel was still lying on the cot, golden shimmering fluid from an IV bag flowing into an arm. Her color was much better than it had been the day before. Silas was curled up on the sofa, soft snores coming from his direction.

"Julie ain't woke up yet but she's doin' betta. Sal was up last night and was able ta get some food in 'em." Rufus's penchant for misnaming people never ceased to amaze me.

"Yes, now that Eve no longer has control over him, Silas is gradually regaining his strength," Uncle Raphael added. "He even inquired who I was."

"To which you replied?" I asked.

"Do not be concerned, Nephew. I told the man I was your and Octavian's uncle visiting from up North, and that I'm a doctor. He seemed to accept my simple explanation. Besides, it's not a lie. And to answer your earlier question, yes, my respect for *some* wielders of magick has grown recently. Rufus's assistance," he said, placing a hand on his shoulder, "has been invaluable in treating both of Tasmin's parents."

I nodded. "Our friend has proven to be indispensable. Someone in our care may have perished had Rufus not intervened while we were off battling Eve and her minions."

The little man grinned sheepishly. "Aww shucks, Dayfari, I was glad ta help Tanisha and her baby, Nazali. Y'all was doin' the heavy lifting. Just doin' my small part for the cause and all."

"When it comes to helping others, Rufus, no part is too small," Uncle chimed in. "That said, Nephew, I owe the wit…Tasmin and Elisa my sincerest apologies. I was unceremoniously thrust on all of you by that reprobate brother of mine, and despite my…discourteousness, they did nothing but tend to my aliments and heal my mind and body."

"You're right, Uncle, you most certainly *do* owe the ladies an apology. I'm sure they would appreciate it. Elisa and Tasmin will be here before too long to check on the Pettifords. You can make amends at that time."

"Now that we done makin' nice, I need to get ta café ta get some breakfast for Sal. He's gon' be good and hungry when he wakes again. I'ma head over and whip up some a Rufus's famous oatmeal fa him."

Blocking his path, I said, "Before you go, Rufus, I would like to ask a favor."

"Whatcha need, Dayfari?"

"I have to take a short trip out of town, and Octavian

also has some business to attend to. I would appreciate it if you would watch out for the women while we were away."

"I gotcha, Dayfari," Rufus replied eagerly. "Sure as shootin', I'll keep Tasmania and Elsie safe, ya got my word."

He reached out his small hand for me to shake. I accepted. Rufus's grip was firm and confident.

"Thank you, Rufus. I feel better knowing that they're in your capable hands."

I heard Uncle clearing his throat. Turning to face him, I heard him say, "While I may be at…less than optimal capacity, I will also keep watch over Elisa and Tasmin. It's the very least I can do for them…and Tasmin's parents."

My, how the tide had turned. Uncle Raphael, the Angel of Healing, was the one accustomed to providing healing to humans, albeit from afar. How he must have felt powerless having two witches, the type of humans who had been vilified by higher beings for centuries, provide the same to him, a once all-powerful archangel. I'm sure he felt as if he had a debt to pay, and he did…an enormous one.

"Thank you for offering, Uncle Raphael. Celestial powers notwithstanding, you are still formidable. And with that, gentlemen, I will take my leave."

Chapter 17
DAFARI

I crossed through a shadow into Elisa and my bedroom, noticing she was not there. Heading downstairs to the kitchen, I found Elisa, Tasmin, and Octavian having breakfast at the same kitchen island that I sat at with Noreen in my dream. I walked over to my wife, kissed her cheek.

"Good morning, all."

"Good morrow, Brother. Where have you been?"

I shared with them the details of my visit to the bookstore, updated them on how Jewel and Silas were doing.

"As much as he's not my favorite, I am glad Raphael was there to care for my parents. Who better than the Angel of Healing, right?"

I looked at Tasmin. Something about her was…different. At first, I felt it but then…I saw it. Tasmin was wearing an unbuttoned plaid shirt with a tank top underneath. There, on her neck, were marks that looked very familiar to me; they were passion bites. The bites were very faint, most likely due to her body's ability to heal itself quickly, but visible enough for me to see.

I then studied Octavian, observed his state of dress. Being a stodgy individual, Octavian would usually have his dress shirt buttoned all the way up to his Adam's apple, but today, it was unfastened to just below his collar bones. On his light skin, I scanned the red lesions, some would call them hickeys, on his neck and chest. I also became aware of markings that should not have been there. His protection sigils were visible on this plane? Had his demon blood taken hold of him that much?

I didn't have time to ponder it much further. I needed to clue them in on all Noreen had told me.

"So they're helping to protect souls in Heaven?" Elisa asked, once I was done.

"Yes, my love, and, for their service to the cause, they have been granted access to the Third Level of Heaven. They are all safe."

I felt a sense of relief wash over Elisa at the revelation that her family was being protected.

She said, "We need to let Martha know about Hondo. She'll be glad to know he's with the others."

"I agree," Tasmin vocalized. "I also think we should have that family meeting you talked about sooner rather than later."

Looks of acknowledgement were passed between the women. I was glad to share some good news for once. I realized time was going, and I needed to be on my way to New Orleans. Octavian must have been on the same wavelength because he excused himself, pulling Tasmin to the side.

"You're getting ready to leave," Elisa stated.

Taking her hands in mine, I subtly checked her wrist, confirmed she was wearing the bracelet Tasmin made for her. I didn't need Adour-Nuru trying to take advantage of my leave.

"Yes, but I'll be back before you know it. However, if, for whatever reason, you need me—"

"I know how to contact you." Elisa reached up, pulling on my coat's lapels. "I love you, Husband."

"I love you, Wife."

She kissed me deeply, letting me know how much she did indeed love me.

"You better go, but make sure you come back," she said once we separated. "I need to get to the café." She said that but didn't move while studying me.

I knew what she was doing, especially when her hands cupped both sides of my face. She was locking my face to memory. When she leaned in and sniffed my neck, I knew she was also allowing my scent to flow through her senses. I let her. Anything she needed to calm her nerves about this journey, I'd grant.

I then watched as she picked up her keys and purse before heading for the garage. I turned my attention to the others. Octavian was all over Tasmin, kissing and pawing at her with a ferocity I'd never seen before.

"I hate to interrupt, Brother, but I need to speak with you before I leave."

Octavian eyed me with such scorn I felt as if he wanted to fight me. Luckily, Tasmin intervened.

"I have to go anyway. Elisa's probably tired of waiting," she said, kissing Octavian one last time. "You be careful, brother of mine." She hugged me tightly.

"I will do my best, Sister," I replied, hugging her in return.

Tasmin left us, leaving me staring at my younger brother.

"What?" he inquired.

"I think you know what." I crossed my arms in front of me, raising an eyebrow. The passion marks I observed on both you and Tasmin…"

"What on earth are you prattling on about, man?"

"Look, I'm not here to judge. I have first-hand knowledge of what you're experiencing, but you need to be careful lest you unintentionally harm her," I said, as I was checking the house, making sure it was secure before we left.

Octavian and I walked outside. The air was crisp and cold, and clouds gathered in the sky. The feeling of a storm brewing was thick and palpable. As we stepped off the porch, I heard leaves crunch beneath my feet. Although I didn't feel the cold as humans did, it only felt right to button my wool coat all the way up and put my hands in my pockets. Octavian was quiet, too quiet for him.

"You have something you want to say; it's written all over your face. Speak your peace, little brother."

He shuffled uncomfortably before saying, "I did my best to be gentle with her, but I-I don't know what came over me. I couldn't control myself, felt like I was a novice getting my first taste of a woman's sweetness, the blissful ecstasy of sliding my—"

"If you say stiff cock, I will slug you," I interrupted.

He nodded in acknowledgement before continuing. "Needless to say, I ravished Tasmin. And then there was the voice in my head, it was so powerful...telling me to bite her...and I resisted at first, but...the urge, the need became...overpowering, and I finally gave in...over and over again."

"Octavian, I get it. You are new to the way of the incubus. While you are not full-blooded, I can already sense the power within you. You were given this gift, or curse, depending on how you want to see it, by an extremely powerful, full-blooded incubus, A Fallen at that. Your inner incubus amplifies whatever feelings, emotional and sexual, you already have for Tasmin. It brings out the more...primal side of your being.

There is no telling what other changes you will experience. As my brother's keeper, I would hate to be forced to block you from being with Tasmin the way you prevented me from being with Elisa when I was a tad...out of sorts. I say that to convey that if I, a seasoned half-incubus, can lose control of myself the way I did, I can only imagine what you must be going through. I'll help you as much as I can, but, in the meantime, I suggest you talk to your...maker. Once you get past his riddled jargon, he may prove quite helpful."

"One can only hope."

"My ears were burning. You must have been talking about me."

Octavian and I looked behind us to see my father standing on the porch with a smug expression on his face that I'd seen too many times for my liking.

"I would say that was your narcissism speaking, but in this one instance, you would be correct," I retorted.

"You say narcissism, I say confidence, my seed."

I cringed when he called me that. "What are you doing here, Father?"

He smiled, his pearly whites in full view. "I sensed someone has need of my wise counsel, and you know how much I love being a team player," he said, spreading his hands.

Octavian and I looked at each other then back at Father. Team player he was not...unless it suited his needs. Although I was sure he was just eavesdropping, as he wasn't banned from the outside grounds, Octavian did need him.

"Well, yes, um...Uncle, I would like to speak with you about a matter of...importance," Octavian said, stumbling over his words. "However, I have to make a brief jaunt across the pond, so it will keep until I return."

Father's face held a pensive gaze. "A road trip, say you? I haven't been on one of those in quite some time. I think I'll accompany you, dear nephew."

While father's eagerness disturbed me, it also meant he would be nowhere near Elisa and Tasmin for at least the next day or so.

"I don't want to be an imposition—" Octavian began to protest before Father cut him off.

"It's no trouble at all. I'm ready when you are, but first, let me speak to my one and only child, eh?"

Octavian stepped to the side, affording me and my father a bit of privacy.

"And where are you headed?" He regarded me curiously.

"Who says I'm going anywhere?"

He let out a muted chuckle. "Please, Son. If you were going to your little pet shop, you would have left already, because you are prompt to a fault. My daughter-in-law and the good doctor headed into town some time ago, and my ever-evolving nephew over there is traveling, via otherworldly means, out of the country. If I'm wrong, please let me know."

"First of all, Father, let me correct you. I *do not* sell pets, I *treat* them. Please don't make light of my profession. Second, I see you were doing what you do best, lurking."

He smirked, arrogance oozing from him. "Ah, my dear boy, now it's my turn to correct you. Lurking is something I do *well*. What I do best... I can tell you if you really want to know."

Not wanting to belabor the point, I replied, "That won't be necessary, now or ever." I sighed heavily before continuing. "You'll find out eventually, so I'll just tell you to get you off my back. I'm going to New Orleans. I need to get the memories of my time in Hell back. My hope is those memories can provide some valuable information I can use to locate Safiya and Zafer's souls. Or...you could just tell me what happened. Save me the trouble of taking this trip."

"Now what fun would that be? You had your memories wiped for a reason, Dafari, and believe me when I say some things are best left unremembered."

I began to walk away from him. "Thank you, Father, but since you have nothing constructive to offer—"

"Now, now, one second," he said, holding up his hands. "If you must go on this fool's errand, I suggest you speak to a man named Abdul Haq. He's the owner of an eatery called L'Endroit Caché. It means The Hidden Place. It's on Bourbon Street, but can only be reached by...otherworldly access, hence the name. Think of it while crossing into the shadows. Tell good old Abdul Haq I sent you. And try the gumbo. It's to die for." He turned on his heel before I could thank him, but did a double take, then said, "Do be careful. You are the only child I have."

I was at a loss for words. Father handing me a lead... without asking for something in return, or having an ulterior motive, was foreign to me. Perhaps he did have a motive and I just didn't know it yet. His seemingly genuine concern also confused me, but I didn't have time to dissect it further. I wanted to get to New Orleans and, if possible, find out what I needed to know and be back by tomorrow. Octavian walked back over to me.

"Dafari, are you okay?"

I looked in Father's direction then back at Octavian. "Yes, I'm fine."

"Well then, I hope you find what you're looking for, dear old brother. I pray it's not too painful to bear. You suffered that tortuous horror because of me, and for that, I am eternally grateful."

"And I would do it again in heartbeat, little brother. We should be on our way." I nodded in Father's direction. "Watch your back, will you?"

"You do the same."

My brother and I hugged one another then I stepped through the shadows.

CHAPTER 18
ELISA

"Now...to confirm," Octavian started as he paced in front of us, but it wasn't his normal demeanor. "You ladies are not to go looking for trouble while we're away..."

He'd spent most of the day at the bookstore helping Tasmin and prepping for his trip. Since his departing was not nearly as important as Dafari's, he wasn't in a rush, but still knew it was something he needed to get done. Now, he walked with his hands in his pockets, shoulders a bit more squared than normal. With his sleeves rolled up to the creases of his elbows, and parts of his sigils showing on his arms, he strutted more so than paced.

Normally, his slacks fit his tall, athletic frame nicely, but today, he wore them in a way that suggested he'd had them refitted to compliment his new swagger better. Even his voice was a little rougher around the edges. The five o'clock stubble on his jaw was also new. Brother-in-law was normally very clean cut.

"I know you mean well, Octavian, but that could come off as a bit condescending," I said, then glanced at Tasmin. While she looked at him with annoyance, the underlying sexual tension between the two was so thick, I could feel it. "Now why would we go looking for trouble when it's been landing right in our backyards, so to speak?"

"We also don't go looking for anything," Tasmin added, "...that doesn't need to be found."

From a shadow in the room came a low, throaty chuckle. I wasn't surprised when Azazel came sauntering forward. "Ah... the doctor plays on words," he crooned.

We were in the basement of the bookstore. After I helped Rufus prep the café for tomorrow, I headed over to meet with Tasmin. I hadn't expected to find Azazel casually browsing the Black History section. Apparently, it had been discussed and he was going to accompany Octavian across the pond. Even though Tasmin and I had talked about Azazel helping Octavian adjust to his new powers, I was still on the fence about it being a good idea.

Octavian scowled at his uncle before throwing Tasmin a heated glance over his shoulder. "Well...don't *find* anything until either I or Dafari returns...*please, Poppet*?" The effortless way in which his voice transitioned from authoritative to smooth and seductive by the time he got to 'please, Poppet' was something that even made me uncomfortable with the way it made me want to lower my guard.

Azazel's smirk widened as he looked upon his nephew with obvious pride. Standing wide-legged with his arms folded across his muscular chest, the Fallen stroked his chin with an arrogance unmatched.

"Am I the only one uncomfortable here?" Silas asked, breaking my train of thought.

It was easy to forget others were in the room while this discussion was taking place. My uncle looked a lot better than he had the previous night. His color had all but returned, eyes a bit brighter, and he was standing at full height. I could still tell he was on the mend by the way he sometimes coughed or needed to sit often.

"No, you're not," Raphael chimed in. "I don't know how comfortable I am with all of this. Azazel freely roaming in and out of your lives, all of you trusting him—"

Cutting in, I clarified. "To a point...we just trust him to a point. Let's keep things in perspective here."

Tasmin snickered under her breath.

Azazel chuckled. "Good one, *tart maker*."

The way he mumbled *tart maker* made me think it was definitely an insult.

"Yes, but even that is questionable, and now Octavian is going on a trip with him?" Raphael questioned.

Octavian scoffed. "You say that as if it's an excursion. There will be no leisure time."

"Either way," said Silas, "with all that has happened, let's just say, my nerves are a little jumpy, and I'm not so sure how I feel with both you and Dafari being gone at the same time."

The basement door came flying open, and we saw Rufus making a noisy entrance down the stairs. "Tasmania and Elsie gonna be in good hands. I heard'chall before I got the door ta open," he explained. "Octovian and Dayfari done asked good 'ol Rufus to keep an eye out," the short, jolly man said, but there was a seriousness in his tone that said that he meant business. He was carrying fresh towels, more tea, sandwiches and soup on a tray for Silas.

Talking about the brothers being gone reminded me that it had been six hours since Dafari left, and I hadn't heard a peep from him yet. I hoped he was fine and that everything was going according to plan. I tried not to worry, but it was hard. On top of that, tomorrow would be day three, and Attalah said she would return with more information then. I was practically beside myself hoping for news of Zafer and Safiya.

"Yes, Rufus, I know you will, no doubt, keep your word and make sure the ladies stay safe," Octavian said as he moved around the room to get closer to Tasmin. "Uncle and

I should probably get going. The quicker I get this done, the sooner I can get back." When he looked down at Tasmin, something in her shifted and she gave him her full attention. "May I speak with you privately for a moment?" he asked, and before I could advise Tasmin to tread lightly, they disappeared up the stairs.

"I'ma get on back to the café and finish cleaning for the night. Just wanted to bring dinner and such and check on Julie over here. She still resting good, so I'll be back later." And with that, the fairy man was gone with the snap of his finger.

"I'm going to the bathroom," Silas said then jogged up the stairs.

Azazel's honeyed laugh brought my attention back to him. I hated that he knew something about my children I didn't. "What did you find out about the kids? You've been running off every time Dafari or I want to ask about them, under the guise of finding out more information. Well?"

"*Well,* what?" he asked, feigning ignorance. Dressed in all black, the man made the simplest attire look debonair.

"Did you find out anything?"

"More or less," he said, regarding me with his normal intrusive gaze.

"Do you know where they are?"

"I can't say that I do…However," he said, raising his voice an octave to stop my angry comeback, I was sure, "your son, my grandson, is quite the troublemaker…"

"Why does it seem like that pleases you, Brother?' Raphael asked.

Azazel turned with his usual flair, clasped his hands behind his back, and then moved about the room. "Why wouldn't it? He, wherever he and his sister are, turned the moon to blood and then my esteemed grandson tried to eclipse the sun with said moon…"

"What?" Raphael and I yelled at the same time.

"Is he insane?" the archangel then bellowed!

Azazel tilted his head as if in thought. "Good question. Let me get back to you on that."

Raphael moved to Azazel's direct line of sight. "Is he trying to start the apocalypse?"

"How is he even able to do that?" I questioned, my heart floating somewhere in the bottom of my stomach.

"Power, my dear daughter-in-law. *Power* like no one has ever seen," Azazel bragged, his eyes glowing red.

"And you still refuse to tell me and Dafari where they are?"

"As I said earlier, I can't say that I know where they are, and not sure it would be safe for any of us if you, or any of you, knew. That boy and his sister could change the world, and on their terms. They found this out very early in their afterlives."

"Then help me find them," I pleaded. "I need to know my children are safe and not out there somewhere being hunted down like rabid animals! I know you're getting some kind of sick pleasure out of all this, but I am their mother—"

"Which makes you not only vulnerable, but a target as well. You know this. Both sides already want you and Tasmin, dead or alive, but imagine how much harder they will come after you if they had even an inkling you knew where your children were! I will not put my grandchildren in anymore danger, and I will not put my son in a position to have to choose between saving his wife or his children."

"That sounds all well and noble of you, Azazel, but I know there is more to this. There is something in it for you. You don't expect me to believe you actually give a damn about me or Tasmin."

"*Oh, but I do*," he said in a singsong voice, the bass of it carried on the air and goosebumps rose on my flesh. "Your

THE RECKONING & THE REAPER

womb carried all that power... And Tasmin's...well...you've met Attalah, right? My grandniece is truly something else, isn't she?"

"You've established a relationship with Attalah as well?" I asked. I was about to get ready to say something else when Raphael cut me off.

"Your wording worries me, Brother. Elisa is right, there is something in this for you. No matter that both of us are now Fallen, remember I can still read you—"

"—and I you," Azazel cut in, squaring up with his brother. "You're terrified of being here on Earth, not knowing the extent of your powers. You're so eager to help the witches because you don't know you can survive this plane on your own."

"I will not lie about that. I am unnerved, but..." Raphael circled his brother, and I felt the energy in the room shift. "...there is something unspoken in your words. What do you know that you're not telling us?"

Azazel snarled as he glared at his brother. Even though Raphael was a few inches taller, Azazel's power made it impossible to tell the difference. "It would just make your day if I was withholding something, wouldn't it? It would take the attention off you? How convenient that you fell in Salix Point, no? Could this be some elaborate scheme to get back in Father's good graces? Gain the witches trust along with Dafari and Octavian's, and then hand all of them over to Him? I mean don't throw stones while living in glass houses and all that. I know as much as I've told. I'm many things, but I am not a liar."

"Then look me in the eyes and honestly tell me that you don't know where Zafer and Safiya are?" I snapped.

Turning my direction, Azazel moved closer to me, looking at me head on. "I cannot say... that I do," he repeated pointedly.

Tasmin opened the basement door. As she briskly made her way down the stairs, Azazel caught a passing shadow and disappeared.

"Ugh," I screamed through gritted teeth. "He is insufferable!"

"What's happened?" Tasmin asked, the wistful smile she had been carrying faded away.

"Azazel is hiding something," Raphael answered.

"Water gets things wet. Tell me something I don't know," she responded. "Daddy will be back down shortly. He wanted to grab a few books to help pass the time. Octavian's gone."

"His wording about your and Tasmin's wombs carrying all that power alarms me, but it's bugging me to no end that there is no clear reason why." Raphael's brows furrowed as he kept talking.

Exiting the stairs, Tasmin said, "Excuse me?"

I gave her a quick rundown of our exchange with Azazel.

Raphael was shaking his head now, pacing and reminding us of Octavian when he was on a tangent as well. "Quick question, do either of you watch the news? Keep up with current events?"

"Of course," I answered. "Why do you ask?"

The angel of medicine was quiet a long time and then he groaned as if aggravated. "I can't think properly. My mind is like its own database of knowledge normally, but I can't get my thoughts to slow down. It's starting to make me wish I could quiet my mind if only for a second. It's like a spinning vortex of all my thoughts being narrated by…me, but…" He took a deep breath, then looked at us. "They're intrusive… almost obsessive…However, is there something going on with women as a collective right now? Are you under attack in some way?"

THE RECKONING & THE REAPER

"If you're talking about politicians trying to ban abortion, then yeah," Tasmin quipped.

Studying her now, he asked, "What do you mean?"

"It's pretty self-explanatory. Politicians want to ban abortions no matter the reason."

The incredulous look on the archangel's face would have been funny, if the situation wasn't so serious. "Under whose authority?"

I answered, "Under God's apparently."

Raphael waved a dismissive hand. "Elisa and Tasmin, be serious."

"We are," we responded in unison.

"My Father?" he asked, slapping both hands against his chest. The angel stared at us for so long, I wondered if he thought we were daft. "No, that can't be right," he then said absentmindedly. "That would cause too much chaos. He wouldn't dare betray Her again that way…would he?"

Tasmin and I looked at one another, confusion in both our eyes. "Raphael, are you okay?" she asked.

"I-I-I need paper and a pencil…" he fussed, moving his hands around. "I need to get these thoughts out my head. Nothing is making sense…"

Moving quickly, Tasmin moved to a corner that housed boxes. She reached inside and came out with a ream of copy paper, and after rambling through the box a few more minutes, she pulled out two pencils and two pens.

"Give me a few hours to get things down on paper and I can better explain everything," he said once taking the items from Tasmin. The man rushed to a corner, pulled an old square table toward him, grabbed a chair then sat down to write.

Tasmin and I headed out, and after ensuring Silas we'd be back in the morning, he headed back downstairs while

Tasmin locked up the bookstore. We left soon after, making our way back to my home.

"What did you make of all that?" she asked me after we were on our way.

"I honestly have no idea. I think being on this plane has thrown him out of whack in some way," I said. "It's weird. It's like…I can still feel his powers, but he doesn't know how to ground it here, it seems."

"Yeah, and on top of that, I think he knows more than he's telling us, but unlike Azazel, I don't think he's intentionally withholding anything."

"I don't follow," I said quickly glancing at her then back at the road.

"You know how he said he can't get his thoughts to quiet?"

I nodded.

"Well, because of that, he can't remember what he hasn't told us."

"Like memory loss?"

"Hmm…not really. More like dissociative amnesia. Only he can remember his name, people, places, and things, but because of the trauma of being violently thrown from the heavens, he can't remember important information."

"Oh, that makes sense…"

"Yeah, but he knows there is important information that he's forgotten."

"This is all so much…"

"Tell me about it," she agreed then winced as she reached to press the touch screen on the dash to adjust the heat in the car.

"You okay?" I asked. "You're wincing like you're in pain."

"I'm not in pain…technically." Cousin laughed sheepishly then moved a stray loc behind her ear. "Just really feeling…last night…and it's not a bad thing. Also…if you're not tired when we get home, I'd like to pick your brain about a few things…"

I glanced at her neck before asking, "Would it have something to do with those marks on your neck?"

For a moment, I couldn't believe what I was seeing. Tasmin Pettiford's cheeks flushed so red, I would have thought she was gushing like a giddy school girl. "Good grief," she rushed out. "I feel so vulnerable…"

"What do you mean?" I asked, even though I'd already assumed what she meant.

"Last night with Octavian was an experience…and I enjoyed it so much, I feel guilty about it. If that makes any sense at all."

I chuckled lightly. "It makes perfect sense to me; a woman married to the son of a full-blooded incubus. Sometimes I come away from our intimate time as high as a kite, and it's an all-natural high."

"See? And this is why I want to talk to you. I know I can heal myself, but the bites are healing very slowly."

"Probably because Octavian's powers in that area are very new. Think of it this way; he's a newbie, a virgin at being an incubus if you will. Just like he was your first and only, you are his first and only. He's never been with a woman the way he was with you last night. His budding incubus power is overwhelming him probably. It's going to take a while for him to learn how to kiss the wound and make it all better. Trust me. His brother has left me covered in bites before."

From my periphery, I saw Tasmin gawking at me. *"Every…where?"*

I nodded with a gleeful smile. "Hmmhmmm…everywhere." I laughed. "I can run you an herbal bath once we get home. It will help ease the soreness and help to lessen the flashbacks."

"Oh goodness, Elisa, tell me it's not going to always affect me like this?"

"I wish I could, Cousin." I laughed. "Just like he will have to learn to control it, you must learn to handle it."

She sighed heavily, laying her head back. "Handle it? I was barely able to stand afterwards. It took us a while to get up, even longer to dress and get downstairs. I felt high out of my mind! Handle it? How do you handle something like that?"

"Once you learn what his incubus likes, he has to give you permission to control it. Now that will be harder to do the more his incubus and angelic side blend."

"Huh?"

"Once the incubus gives you permission to control it, you have but so long before his angelic side latches on and they start working in tandem. These are all the things I learned with Dafari…over time. But because he was born that way, once he gave me permission to control his incubus…let's just say…his angelic side is just as commanding as the incubus. The good thing about this is, you and Octavian get to learn together. I was thrown in the waters headfirst. I know you remember how out of sorts I was way back then when Dafari and I were first intimate. You couldn't tell me shit from shinola!"

We laughed then she said, "True… I remember!"

"Are you nervous about tomorrow?" I asked.

"More than you know. When Octavian asked to speak to me privately, one of the things we discussed was what I would do if Attalah showed up while he was away. He wants me to keep her here no matter what I have to do. Part of me just wants to hold my daughter and never let her go, but… she's so different. I feel as if I need to get to know her all over again. I just feel like we're running out of time."

I couldn't argue with her there. The more I thought

about my children, the more I realized they were not the same children anymore. Just as Dafari and I had changed as their parents, I knew they had too. Still, all I wanted… needed was a chance to see them again. Speak with them… I was desperate and prayed that wouldn't be used against me in the future.

CHAPTER 19
RAPHAEL & LILITH

"Raphael, where are you?"

Lilith was frantic with worry. She had not heard from Raphael for days. In fact, the last time they had been in contact was shortly before the start of Earth's new year. Something must have happened, but what?

"Please, Raphael, I need to know you're alright."

As she paced back and forth in the Garden of Eden, she had all but given up hope until she heard, *"I am here, Lilith."*

"Thank goodness, Raphael. Where have you been? I was worried sick."

"My apologies," he said, walking upstairs to the bookstore, leaving Silas to spend some time alone with Jewel, *"but I wasn't…myself, and was unable to contact you."*

Lilith sat by the River of Wine and Oil, dipping her chalice in it then taking a sip of the wine she collected. *"Out of sorts? What happened to you, Raphael? And where are you now?"*

"You didn't know?"

"Know what?" she asked, her thought almost coming out as a yell.

Raphael made himself comfortable in a seat by one of the fireplaces before continuing. *"He knows, Lilith. He knows that I coupled my nephews with the witches, and because of it, He ordered my brothers and sisters to beat me pitilessly. Then they…they…stripped me of my wings, tore them from my back even as I cried out in pain. To add insult to numerous injuries, I was tossed to the earth plane, as if I was nothing more than a lowly Fallen. I guess He never truly forgave me for not fully carrying out Azazel's punishment as ordered."*

Lilith dropped her chalice, clapping a hand over her mouth, a combination of shock and terror gripping her at the same time. *"So much for a forgiving God,"* she spat angrily. *"Raphael, I am so sorry. How did He find out? We were the only ones who knew of your plan, and I definitely did not tell anyone."*

"That I do not know. My fear is that He will discover your involvement and will come after you next."

"Let him," she replied defiantly. *"What more can He do to me, Raphael? I was already punished mercilessly for the simple act of not bowing down to a man. While the Seventh Level of Heaven is lovely, a veritable utopia, this is the least of what I deserved in reparations."* She paused reflectively for several long seconds. *"That said, I do take your concerns seriously. I will be careful. You said you were on the earth plane; where exactly?"*

"I am with my nephews and their mates. I was found on the first day of the new year by Azazel, believe it or not." He chuckled sardonically. *"Surprisingly, he brought me to the home of Dafari and his wife Elisa. I was amnestic and severely injured, wounded in mind and body; I would even go so far as to say on the verge of death had it not been for Tasmin and Elisa. Despite my…deplorable behavior toward them, they nursed me back to health the best they could. I am recovering…slowly…which is why I'm finally able to connect with you."*

Lilith couldn't believe what she was hearing. *"Perhaps*

Azazel helped you because you spared him the punishment that should have been doled out to him...although, I can't see him being that noble. Regardless, at least he got you somewhere safe. And on that same note, I've been in contact with Elisa and Tasmin's family members."

Raphael gasped. *"Lilith, you don't mean—"*

"Yes," she quickly cut in. *"The same family members who were slain on His orders. Noreen Chadwick, Amabelle Nall, Duma-Nolan and Akasha Hunte. They, along with Hondo Singleton, the husband of the coven witch who betrayed Noreen Chadwick, have been elevated to the Third Level of Heaven; a reward of sorts for helping to protect vulnerable souls. I was able to connect with them because where they reside on the Third Level is a mirror image of the Garden of Eden. They're good people, Raphael. They never should have been murdered to begin with."*

Raphael sighed, rubbed his palms down his face. *"You'll get no argument from me. I'm starting to see the error in having...blind loyalty."*

Chuckling, Lilith chided, *"And it only took you centuries to realize that. Look, Raphael, I need to get to earth to see you."*

"But how—"

"I don't know yet," she said, cutting him off. *"I'll think of something. But first, I need to speak with Noreen Chadwick and the others."*

"Lilith, please be careful. I don't want to see you once again end up on the other side of the Third Level of Heaven, only to be tortured and tormented unceasingly by other angels."

Lilith shuttered as she thought back to her time there, a chill running through her. *"Nor do I. I should go. I have a lot of planning to do."*

"Wait, please," Raphael said. *"There are things going on*

down here that you should be aware of. Tasmin and Elisa told me that politicians, men in particular, but some women as well, are attempting to prevent women from having control over their own bodies, and…"

"And what?" she demanded impatiently.

"They are allegedly doing all this in His name."

CHAPTER 20
ATTALAH

I was being chased through the streets of the underworld, a place that sat between the veil and the shadows. It was a realm that no human knew about and only those of us who weren't afraid to walk in between worlds frequented. Sometimes it was a place of safety and refuge. At other times, it was a place so dangerous, only the bravest of beings visited.

I was only here to drop something of importance off to my cousins; however, upon my arrival, Granduncle was waiting for me. He'd been tracking me for days as I moved around, desperately searching for Zafer and Safiya.

I shoved a being with wings and taloned feet out of the way as I barreled through the silk road that lent all those looking for redemption a place to hide. My granduncle was after me because I'd abandoned my post. I did so for the sake of family, but Uncle Izrail didn't care about any of that, even though he was family. He was a gotdamn tyrant of the first order. He carried out his Father's order without question.

My family was in a bad way. Heaven and Hell were after them and there was nothing I could do to stop it. However, I could tip the scales in their favor, and that was going to cost me.

"Attalah," his voice roared behind me.

As if time had stopped, the world around me disappeared. I was now surrounded by Level three Messengers with levels one and two waiting in the wings. He had not come to ask my cooperation nicely, that was clear.

Throwing my cape off, I whipped around to face my handler. I was caught off guard to find him in his true form. It was a frightening sight on a good day, but in this realm, it was far worse…a much more malevolent aura surrounded him here. Not one of the four faces he possessed was easy to look at. The number of eyes making up his body put fear in my heart, and even though only eight of his wings were out, the massive span caused the already darkened realm to cast shadows where there should have been none.

"You must return to your post," he demanded.

Trying to catch my breath, I said, "I can't do that! Not until I find—"

"That is not your assignment, Attalah!"

"My family is always going to be my assignment!"

"You have been compromised."

"Have I?"

"You cannot efficiently do this job because of your biasness."

Just as he said those words, the Messengers stalked closer, cutting off all my escape routes.

"I'm not going back," I protested, squaring off with my granduncle as we circled one another like combatants.

Uncle Izrail's eyes turned to ice as he took me in. I didn't like the way he looked me over. Lowering all four of his heads, lips pressed into tight grimaces. It was almost a look of disappointment as his eyes pulled down in the center. He was reading me and determining if I was being truthful, and he had the ability to do such a thing, which was probably why he acquiesced to me having free will.

"Where are they, Attalah?" he asked, awareness now in his tone.

Fist balled at my sides, I stood defiantly. "I don't know!"

It was hard to lie to a supernatural being who could literally see right through me. Good thing I wasn't lying. After briefly coming across them two days ago, I had no idea where they had gone.

One of his heads swayed hypnotically, as if it was a cobra dancing to a musician's flutes, the slits in its eyes flipped sideways, and instantly I knew it was scanning my aura for hints of deception.

Once he had found whatever it was he had looked for, his facial features relaxed and he lifted all four of his chins. "Where... *were* they?" he then asked.

My breath caught and suddenly my heart beat to a staccato rhythm. I remained silent. Fear danced around my body like fireworks.

"Answer.me." The harshness of his demand almost made my knees buckle.

"I-I don't—"

Before the lie could leave my mouth, my ears rang loudly, palms burned to the point I knew fire was coming next. My stomach knotted, forcing bile to my throat, and I gagged as I crumbled to the ground.

"Mercy...please," I begged, shame having no place where this kind of pain resided.

"Where.were.they?"

From the ground, I gawked up at his otherworldly form. Shaking my head, I got ready to lie again only to have my head start pounding incessantly. The pain was maddening. I screamed out while arching backwards, feeling the punishment for lying to him course through my veins like poison.

"Please," I screamed through blurry vision. "Please..."

Kneeling before me, the angel of death used an elongated, crooked and gnarled finger to gently sweep the loose strings of my kinky curls away from my forehead. I saw the sweat glistening on my face through a set of his eyes. "Free yourself of your own torture and tell me the truth," he said, voice now a monotone that suggested he had all the time in the world to torment me. *"Where.were.they?"*

Tears spilled from my eyes as I fought to keep the truth in. "I…do-don't…kn-know…"

A scream erupted from somewhere deep within me. Fire raced through my veins as my blood ran hot. Pain exploded behind my eyelids forcing my teeth to ground together. He could have stopped it if he wanted to, but he wouldn't.

Zafer and Safiya had long gone from Mount Hermon. Granduncle Azazel had instructed them to leave that location swiftly.

"Are you out of your ever-loving mind?" he had yelled at Zafer upon learning what he attempted to do. "Your arrogance is going to get you caught or worse, get your sister caught and your parents killed. What do you think happens to them if you'd accomplished what you set out to do?"

"I wanted to send a message," Zafer snapped back.

Granduncle stormed to stand face-to-face with him. Zafer didn't back down. While he had an insurmountable amount of respect for Granduncle Azazel's authority, he had a heart of steel. Even in the face of danger, Zafer stood tall. Seething with anger, Granduncle Azazel spat, "You aren't thinking. You're allowing your anger to lead you blindly. That is a problem, Grandson."

"I-I didn't know he was going to go that far," Safiya had cried from the corner. "If I had, I would have tried to stop him. His arrogance knows no bounds."

She was in pain more often than not since Zafer's attempt to break a seal and bring on the apocalypse. Dressed in a long black skirt and a white top, she always did her best to make herself as incognito as possible.

Zafer scoffed as he paced away from his grandfather. "It

has nothing to do with arrogance. Why are we sitting idle while they threaten our very existence?" His thick locs angrily swayed against his broad back and shoulders as he walked in an angry circle. The white mark across his right eye and forehead only adding to his menacing appearance. "Why can't we see our parents?"

"Timing, Grandson. Timing and patience!"

"My patience is thin, and time is no longer on our side, Grandpops!" Zafer's voice held a hard edge.

The glare he sent Zafer would have made the most seasoned of demons cower, but not his grandson. However, he also knew his grandfather wasn't in the mood to be tested or pushed any further beyond his limit. The silent conversation happening between grandfather and grandson made the tension in the small cave all the more suffocating. Zafer was the first to turn away. He retreated to a far corner of the cave, anger still riding him in waves.

Granduncle Azazel's eyes were softer when he turned to Safiya. "Based on her aura, the pain she feels is because of you," he said to Zafer.

Zafer rolled his golden eyes and gave something of a grunt, but he couldn't hide the worry in his eyes when it came to his sister. "How did I cause this?"

"She can feel all the pain, angst, and anguish you try to hide, and I mean that in every sense of the words." Snapping his gaze my way, Granduncle motioned for me. "I cannot stay here long as my marker is strong in this realm. They can share powers and that leads me to believe he is now also sharing his emotions with her. Unintentionally. How much can you safely syphon from her before it starts to affect you negatively?"

"Quite a bit," I said, kneeling next to Safiya.

"Do it, and then they must leave this location. Too many still in the Valleys who are desperately seeking redemption and will turn on us in a heartbeat."

As the memories passed in and out of my psyche, Granduncle Izrail syphoned every bit of information he could from me. I felt powerless as pain riddled my body.

"Mount Hermon," I screamed.

Anything to stop the pain. Instantly, my body went still. My breathing was hard and ragged, but the pain subsided in waves.

Granduncle stood tall. "Azazel helped them then? He knows where they are?"

I knew as soon as he heard Mount Hermon, that would be his next logical conclusion.

"My brother...forever on the wrong side of right," he then snarled. "And as for you—"

Incessant barking and snarling rent the air, cutting off his rant. Dogs, abandoned hellhounds, and even wolves came barreling from the woods. They attacked in formation, the oversized wolves, dogs and hellhounds going after the Messengers with a ferocity I'd never seen. They aggressively went for throats, arms, and legs, their jagged fangs ripping into the dead flesh of the demons. In the shadows of the alleyways, between a castle-like tavern and a succubae-house, stood a hooded feminine figure.

A few seconds later, the heavens split, and an angelic being's angry white eyes bore down on me then whipped around to face Granduncle Izrail.

Get up, Safiya screamed in my head.

I didn't waste any time. I knew she was using her magick to control the animals, but she was playing with fire. Granduncle Izrail could snatch her up in her weakened state. I had to wonder what her pain levels were and if she and Zafer had figured out a way to counter his emotional and mental anguish latching on to her. She stood statue-still, only her glowing eyes from beneath her cloaked hood could be seen along with her delicate hands and curved red nails. I didn't have time to make a fuss about it though. As soon as I got to my feet, I ran south, toward the feminine being who had split the skies; Grandaunt Lilith.

She was colossal in her true form, standing the same height as the Empire State building. Her normally waist-length locs now cascaded down to her calves. At the end of each loc was a snake-like face with poisonous fangs. Most people thought her locs of hair were snakes when in reality, she had captured the souls of those who had tried to cause harm to her in some way. She'd found a way to make her enemies her footstools. They did her bidding whether they wanted to or not. Just like now, as I ran in her direction, using two sections of her hair like lassos, she lashed out at Granduncle Izrail. Long tendrils of hissing locs wrapped around his wrists and legs, yanking him forward.

That was the only distraction I needed. I remembered the exact place I crossed over into this realm, but I was too weak to project the place I wanted to land.

I need to get back to Salix Pointe, I shot Safiya telepathically. ***I'm too weak to project, Cousin…***

My breaths came out in short spurts. Chest was on fire and my body moved like sludge was weighing me down even though I was running at full speed.

I can only project the wooded area surrounding the town, she said back. ***You will have to do the rest!***

Before me, near a pasture was the wooded area of the shadows I'd crossed over, I saw a sliver of a tear in the atmosphere. The closer I got, the wider the tear became, revealing the woods just outside my Aunt Elisa's home. With every bit of strength I had left, I barreled through, leaving the fight between my grandaunt and granduncle behind me.

Chapter 21
OCTAVIAN

"This is exactly the area I would expect you to dwell," Uncle drawled as soon as we touched down in my flat. "A placed called... Bloomsbury."

The snark in his voice made clear he meant that as an insult. Even though Bloomsbury was a high culture place to live in central London, Uncle probably found it pretentious. Intellectuals, creative beings, and students alike flocked to the area to live and work. It was also home to some of London's greatest universities and museums. I stayed in the luxury flats called The Peabody near Russell Square, which some considered the most famous square in Bloomsbury.

My place looked exactly the way I'd left it. Clean and neat with almost everything in its place, which worked out well for me since I didn't plan to be here long. My loft was an open space that boasted of exposed brick walls and overhead beams. Many of the American students studying in the area chose these flats because they most reminded them of lofts back in the U.S.

There were several books and notebooks on demon mythology lying on the bench of the breakfast nook where the bay window overlooked the park down below. Stainless steel appliances and stained concrete flooring lent a hand to the modern, industrialized feel of the place. My king-sized platform bed was made, but a coffee-colored blanket lay tossed about near the edge of it. The night I felt Tasmin's aura was the night I left London, and my flat looked as if it was frozen in time because of it.

Envelopes, sales flyers, and the like were piled under the mail slot in the door. I moved around, packing up things most dear to me. Some books that I couldn't leave behind, notes, journals, two laptops which held all my important lecture documents, and small trinkets and artifacts I'd collected over the years.

"It's one of the best areas for an intellectual to live. The museums and bookshops alone are worth the hefty price I pay to call this place home," I retorted, moving about quickly, grabbing a duffel from my closet and tossing it on my bed. I started tossing things inside. Something told me I didn't need to be away from Salix Pointe for long.

Uncle scanned my flat with a look of disdain. "Yeah, well...to each their own," he mumbled then scoffed. "Anyway, as I was saying...You took your first pleasure bite from Tasmin, who also happens to be your first love...You have pure dopamine and euphoria running through your system. Your nose is wide open, and right now, you're in your most vulnerable state."

"What does that mean?" I asked, stopping to study him.

"It means...if any male, human or otherwise, even looks at Tasmin the wrong way, it's liable to set you off. You'll fight to the death, something you wouldn't do under normal situations, and that is a dangerous thing, for you and your doctor."

I grunted as my only response. My mind was racing, trying to process all he was saying. "But what if you're wrong? I am mostly angel. What if none of these things happen?"

"We took this journey through the shadows..."

"Yes."

"How do you feel?"

I hadn't really stopped to think about it. We had traversed the shadows and I felt no worse for wear. "I actually feel…a bit recharged now that you mention it. That isn't normal."

"Correct."

"That could be because I was with you—"

"But it isn't. You're far more angel than demon—you acknowledged that yourself—but now that you've fed your incubus, that small bit of demon DNA flowing through your blood is now a raging inferno. Even things in the shadows know when it's best to move out the way. An incubus is all about pleasure, yes, but it is still a demon. A thing that goes bump in the night. A very dangerous predator when it is in this state. There is no *what if they don't happen*, Octavian, but *when. When will it happen?* That should be the question. Which reminds me, I need to teach you how to move through the shadows, without me. You'll be able to better travel about when need be."

The idea of transporting through the shadows didn't appeal to me. Although I felt no discontent after going through them with Demon Daddy to get here, I didn't want, nor did I need, to make it a habit.

"I don't know about that. I can still get through the veil just fine," I said tensely, zipping the duffel bag on my bed.

"Yes, but what about when the demon side is too strong? How do you think you'll fair behind the veil when your incubus is in control, and trust me, during your most intimate moments isn't the only time it can show up. Not that it ever goes away."

Snatching up a few books, I said, "You speak about it like it's a parasite."

"I talk about it that way because it's a part of you now—more so than ever since you've fed it. Just like your angelic part will take over when you need protecting, so will your incubus," he spat emphatically.

It was at that moment, I not only saw but felt the seriousness in which Uncle Azazel was speaking to me. His normal sarcastic flare for delivering insults was no longer there.

"This is serious, Octavian. For the first time, you've fed a side of yourself that has been lying dormant since your inception. It is hungry and the incubus is very greedy. It will latch on to your baser nature and demand to be satisfied. The need will become incessant and unless you know how to control it, it will control you."

As he talked, I felt the changes he mentioned in my body. I'd always been able to control my sexual urges. Sure, I had liaisons here and there, but I'd always been in control of my person. Sex was not something that had ever ruled me.

"What are you saying, Uncle? That I'll be unable to control myself like I'm some sort of bloody fiend?" I asked, disturbed at the very thought.

"Here's the thing," he said, sliding his left hand in the pocket of his slacks while he moved around the room. "Right now, you're one dream invasion from being strung out. So it's a good thing you got away from Tasmin. Tonight would have been rather chaotic for the both of you otherwise."

"Chaotic?"

"Yes, you're in no condition to protect her without hurting her yourself. Sure, your guard is up, but only because you're thinking about feeding and fucking. Notice I didn't say fighting because in this state, fighting is the last thing on your mind. It's why you're so full of energy right now. Why you're coated with a sheen of sweat and your clothes probably feel a bit too restrictive…"

I hated the way that he was so clearly reading me. It made me feel exposed.

"You are exposed. You're probably at your rawest—"

"I can and will always protect Tamsin. So what if my incubus is the one to do it? She'll still be protected."

"Who will defend her from you, Nephew? Yes, you'll guard her because you want to get her away to seclusion so you can do as you wish with her. And because she has experienced you this way, because she is in love with you, she will not deny you. She will be just as anxious and willing as you. So posit this, will you? You would never hurt her intentionally, but your incubus' very nature is to seek pleasure at all costs. You're a fledgling who is coming into his incubus at an accelerated speed. What Dafari learned naturally over time, you will have to learn at a rapid pace. You don't know what you don't know…And what you don't know could hurt the good doctor."

I got ready to protest but he held up a manicured hand to stop me. "I know you're a professor and are accustomed to leading the conversation on all things mythological; however, I am…who I am. Who better to give you this crash course in the way of the incubus other than the king of incubi himself? Please, Octavian, be slow to speak now and quick to listen. Something is coming for Salix Pointe and your witches. The last thing Tasmin would need right now is her lover being out of control."

Uncle Azazel's words broke through my defenses. The risk of hurting Tasmin made me do more than take what he was saying under consideration. I had to be on top of things from here on out.

Still, I was a bit confused by the caring nature in which Uncle's words were being delivered.

"There is a difference between a battle bite and pleasure bite, same as there is for a battle bulk and a pleasure bulk. What I want you to worry about is the pleasure bulk because if you do it while inside your woman and do not properly prep her, you can ruin her body in ways she won't recover." As he talked, he asked permission to enter my mind, and when I opened up, he projected images that showed me what can happen when an incubus was out of control. The images were disturbing and made me regret giving him access. "I have banished and extricated plenty of incubi and succubae for losing control. And by banished and extricated, I mean thrown in a lake of fire or outright killed." Scenes flashed by of Uncle Azazel doing exactly as he described. "The incubus is a strong force. You can create any paradise your lover dreams of. You can also create their own personal hell." Uncle waved a hand and the scenes disappeared.

I thought back to my first time with Tasmin. That pleasure bite took me to heights unknown and now being told that it was possible this new part of me could hurt her to the point of damaging or even killing her? I felt anger and apprehension where excitement had once been.

"Why did you activate this...phenomena within me, knowing it would have this effect?" I asked, already feeling the stress of carrying this extra weight around.

Uncle stopped his pacing, giving me his full attention. "My only intention in that moment...was to save you, not only from your mother, but also from yourself. I had no real inclination that a touch from me would ignite your incubus blood. How could I? I'd been imprisoned for a long time and while I learned the way of this new world fairly quickly, there was no way for me to know that specifically."

Frowning, I thought about that night as I walked over to my desk. I scribbled down my brother's address in Salix Pointe. I planned to leave it with the concierge so my mail could be sent there. Uncle had stepped in to keep my mother from gutting me in the middle of a battle that saw me and my brother going toe-to-toe with our parents. If I were to remember correctly, he was there for his own nefarious reasons.

"That makes no sense, Uncle Azazel. You-you were there, in the middle of the battle, gloating about not being the bad guy they'd painted you to be! You were only trying to save yourself and further your own agenda!"

"Yes, and I will never deny that, but in *that* moment, my only agenda was to save you. Also, we shouldn't pussyfoot around here any longer. It's best we get moving."

Silence enveloped us as my uncle moved to the area where my desk was before he disappeared into my bathroom and left me with my thoughts and confusion. What did he mean he only wanted to save me? It was something I would have to ponder later.

While he was doing whatever in the privy, I finished packing up the things I was going to take with me. Uncle had thrown me for a loop. I'd never known him to be a caring man. What was I supposed to do with all the knowledge he'd given me? It was safe to say if I had known any of this beforehand, I'd have done everything in my power to keep this new part of me at bay. But according to him, that would have only lasted for so long. It was bound to happen whether I happily participated in its awakening or not.

A few minutes later, my bags had been tossed through the shadows, and under Uncle's careful instructions, I was able to project them to the guest room Tasmin and I shared at Dafari's.

"There is another incubus in Salix Pointe," I told him as we prepared to head back through the shadows.

"I'm aware," came his curt response as we stepped out into the cold, dank air.

That should have been my first clue that something was amiss. When we'd crossed over, the weather had been warmer. It wasn't the way I was used to traveling, and I knew it would take some getting used to. The Shadows was a scary place, where things grabbed and yanked at you. Demons tried to latch and who knew what else was there.

It was dark. No sun or moon shone. The huge boulders decorating the sides of the pothole riddled streets moved. Yellow jaundiced eyes leered at us. Dead trees with elongated gnarled limbs appeared to reach for us. The shadows was not a place I wished to dwell for extended periods of time.

Keeping my wits about me, I said, "He's coming after Elisa and, might I add, very aggressively."

Uncle stopped before we went further. Perhaps he could sense something was off, too. "Then it seems my son had better get a handle on that."

Uncle's answer annoyed me. Dafari was always looking out for everyone else, and I often wondered if any of us were repaying him in kind. My brother wasn't known to fly off the handle, yes, but it seems Adour-Nuru had rattled him. The way he all but demanded Elisa ward her café to keep the incubus away attested to that.

"These are your ilk. You can control them, no? Is there nothing you can do to put him in his place?" I asked.

Uncle stopped walking. His eyes darted left and right before he took an audible breath. The hairs on the back of my neck rose, and even as the normal beings for this place moved about, I felt something else in the air.

Steely, cold eyes studied me. "Put a full-blooded incubus in his place while he is on the hunt? I think the fuck not. My son had better pull his head out of his ass and do what comes naturally to him; defend his territory."

"Elisa is not a place or thing. She's a woman, who happens to be a powerful witch, yes, but she was put off her paces by whatever it was he did to her. He wants her in his bed for nothing more than thrills—"

"I assure you, if the incubus has set his sights on Elisa,

then he doesn't just desire her sexually, he is also looking to breed. To establish a home base. To lay down roots."

A mirthless chuckle from me made Uncle look my way. "But he knows Elisa and Dafari just tied the knot."

"And? That makes the chase even more appealing to him. Imagine getting the wife of one of the most notable figures in Salix Pointe whose father happens to be your king, in his bed…willingly. It is a conquest, and the incubus is looking to conquer."

My breathing intensified as the wind whipped up. Rain that felt like ice-cold water fell in huge droplets. Trees swayed violently and the howling of the air around us put me on alert. Something in my periphery caught my attention. My eyes narrowed to adjust to the mounting darkening of the skies.

Uncle nodded toward the looming figures in the shadows. With a sense of urgency he told me, "We need to leave. Izrail has infiltrated the shadows."

Just as the words left his mouth, dark shadows casted the world around us into near total darkness. In dutiful fashion, Uncle Azazel bulked, his transformation somewhere between human and Olympian. My body readied itself, hot blood rushing through me in a way that alarmed and excited me. I ripped my trench and shirt off, tossing them haphazardly to the left. The sigils on the right side of my upper body rolled and coiled underneath my skin. My wings unfurled at the same time as my uncle's.

"Izrail is one of the fiercest fighters of us brothers and his powers are not to be taken lightly. He's methodical and an ideologue to boot. He's brought along his Messengers from levels one and two, which says he is no longer in a talking mood," he yelled above the wind and rain.

"And the Level three Messengers were conversation

starters?" I asked sarcastically, remembering how ferocious the beasts had been in battle.

A fast-moving flash of lightning struck one of the dead trees, setting it ablaze. Dark, rumbling clouds the size of a city block came bolting toward us at the speed of light. The smell of smoke caught my senses. To my left, my uncle moved his hands in wild but formulaic circles. With each wave of his hands, the winds whipped harder around us. Using the wind to carry the fire and its smoke, Uncle Azazel slammed it against the rolling cloud, tossing it about as the blaze danced like a hurricane.

Calling my bec-de-corbins to me, I swung underhanded, catching a Messenger just under its meaty chin as it tried to sneak in behind me. The Messenger dropped to its knees as I yanked the raven's beak of the war hammer free. The spike of the other one caught another Messenger dead center of its head. As soon as I got rid of those two, four more breached the shadows.

"We can't beat him when he's standing between two worlds, especially not with this kind of anger," Uncle yelled. "He can manipulate the shadows this way and multiply his Messengers many times over, especially from the shadows he creates. We have to get back into your flat. It's the only way to ensure we don't cross into a world of his making."

Uncle Azazel then slammed his meaty fist into the chest of a Messenger coming from the left of him, coming away with a slimy, blackened heart. As we fought and moved back toward my flat, I prayed my brother, Elisa and Tasmin were faring much better than I was at the moment.

CHAPTER 22
DAFARI

Although it was early in the morning, Bourbon Street was already bustling with natives and tourists alike. As I walked the street, the sounds of jazz, the blues, Zydeco, bounce, and traditional rhythm and blues could be heard blaring from numerous establishments. I hadn't been back to New Orleans since I had visited my family's mausoleum back in November of 1932. The pain of their loss kept me from returning. But now, I had a reason, a purpose for my visit, and I couldn't leave until my mission was fulfilled.

To that end, I started my day visiting their resting place. While I had my Elisa back, albeit in this time, I still mourned the loss of the Elisa I lost all those years ago. I also missed Zafer and Safiya. I missed watching them become who they could have been had the fateful events leading up to Tasmin and Attalah's deaths, Octavian's retribution, and my eventual incarceration not occurred. I knelt, said a prayer for those lying in our family crypt; Elisa, Zafer, Safiya, Tasmin, and Attalah. Next, I said a prayer asking for guidance and a successful outcome to my journey.

With that done, I decided it was time to make my way to L'Endroit Caché. As much as I didn't trust my father, my gut was telling me that, for once, he was offering up something useful. And yet, I still questioned it. Why? Why would he?

While I knew I should have just been grateful and left it at that, I couldn't let it go. What I could do, for the sake of my children's souls, was put my misgivings on the backburner...for now.

Arriving back on Bourbon Street, I walked into an alley between two buildings. Traversing a shadow, I did as Father instructed and thought of L'Endroit Caché. Once I crossed over, everything looked and felt the same, including the cloudless blue sky and cool winter crispness. However, I now stood in front of a building that was not there before. The building itself was all brick in construction, the darkly stained accoya wood entryway double doors giving the structure a sophisticated feel to it. I tugged on one of the steel handles then stepped inside the bustling eatery. I was immediately greeted with, "Welcome to L'Endroit Caché, The Hidden Place. Can I get ya a table, booth, or a seat at the bar?"

"Actually, I'm looking for Abdul Haq," I replied.

"Who may I say is askin'?"

"Dafari. Dafari Battle."

The roughly six-foot tall man regarded me carefully. I did the same. Although he welcomed me at the door, the fellow with the café au lait complexion; low cut, curly salt and pepper hair; mustache and goatee; and piercing brown eyes appeared to be more than a greeter. The custom-designed, three-piece cashmere maroon pinstripe suit fit his muscular frame to a tee. His black silk shirt, solid gold cufflinks and pinky ring said he was someone of importance.

"Azazel sent me," I quickly added.

His unreadable expression slowly turned to a smile, then he extended his hand to me, which I accepted. "I knew it. You look too much like him to not be his kid. Aside from ya colorin', you're his spittin' image. I'm Abdul Haq. Come with me." Abdul Haq motioned to a young Black man who quickly made his way to the front of the restaurant. "Handle the door for me."

"Sure thing, boss," the youth, who looked to be no more than eighteen eagerly replied.

Abdul Haq began to walk towards the main dining area. As I followed him, I took note of the décor. Round and square oak tables were placed in the middle of the room. Oak dining chairs with upholstered silk slip seats sat around the tables. Booths comprised of the same wood and upholstery lined the exposed brick outer wall on one side of the room, while couches, loveseats, and comfortable chairs lined the other. Although the place had darker hues of reds and purples as a color scheme, it still had a warm, homey feel to it. Classic, mellow New Orleans jazz played in the background.

At the rear of the building was a sizeable dance floor, DJ booth, and a large, rectangular bar area with swivel, high-back barstools. Adbul Haq pulled out a barstool for me then walked around to the bar's swinging door.

The well-dressed man stared at me hard for a few seconds before turning around, grabbing a bottle from the massive selection on the shelves. When he walked back over, he had two Glencairn glasses in his hands.

"Nothing but the best bourbon for the son of Azazel," he said, handing me a glass.

I took a sniff before sipping it. It was indeed the best. "How did you know I liked bourbon?"

"Because yo' daddy likes it. Took a chance and figured like father, like son."

Why this man would make an assumption like that was beyond me, but I decided to let it slide. I was, however, curious about the relationship between Abdul Haq and my father.

"How do you two know each other?" I asked before taking another sip of my drink.

Letting out a hearty laugh, Abdul Haq replied, "Now that's a story right there. I'll tell ya all about it, but first, lemme get cha somethin' to eat. Got some fresh gumbo cookin'. Lemme get cha a bowl."

I was going to refuse, but then I remembered Father saying I should try it. Despite that, as much as I appreciated Abdul Haq's New Orleans hospitality, I was more interested in hearing about the connection between him and Father. Thinking about it, aside from what he showed me, I didn't really know much about my father, and I think he liked it that way. I felt as if he prided himself on being mysterious and somewhat aloof. At times, I found it quite unnerving. I didn't have long to ponder my thoughts, as Abdul Haq had returned, carrying a bowl with steam coming from it. As he placed it in front of me, the smell of chicken and andouille sausage overtook my olfactory sense. Abdul Haq handed me a spoon then waited for me to partake of the simmering dish. While, as a supernatural being, I didn't require human sustenance, I did enjoy a good meal. I scooped up a spoonful of gumbo, placing it in my mouth. I savored the blend of seasonings and spices.

"This…is quite good," I said then took another spoonful.

Slapping his hand on the bar, he grinned widely. "I knew you'd like it." Picking up his drink, he took a healthy swig before continuing. "That's yo' daddy's recipe."

I almost choked on the food in my mouth. I coughed, cleared my throat then gulped down the rest of my bourbon. "Excuse me?"

"You heard right. Azazel is quite a master in the kitchen."

No wonder Father suggested it. I envisioned him being a master of many things, manipulation and subterfuge among them, but the culinary arts…definitely not on the list.

"How do you two know each other?"

"It's like this," Abdul Haq said, refilling both our glasses. "Yo' daddy did me a huge solid a very long time ago. He got me out of pretty sticky situation."

"What kind of situation, if you don't mind me asking?"

"Don't mind at all. Have you ever heard of a Gray-Walker?"

Until recently, I was unfamiliar with that term, but after Ilene Lovett revealed, under duress, that Doc Benu was a Gray-Walker, a being who was neither good nor bad, but instead walked the middle, I learned that Father was among their ranks. It makes sense since I never really know what side he's on.

"Yes, I have," I replied.

"Well, I am one. A very old one, although I look good for my age," he said then chuckled, reminding me of Father. He paused, his demeanor becoming serious. "There have been times throughout history were Gray-Walkers have been targeted by those Above and those Below, where attempts were made to force us to align with one side or the other. Each time, a few chose to pledge allegiance to the Light or the Dark, with many more of us declining, opting to remain neutral. This one particular time when we did refuse, retaliation was swift. A good number of us were slaughtered. The rest of us had to go into hiding.

And this is where yo' father comes in. Ya see, Azazel has a thing about bullies; he's not fond of them at all. When he found me, I was squatting in one of his New Orleans properties. He had been away for some time, and I needed somewhere to lay low and get myself together. When Azazel busted me, he could have thrown me out, but he didn't."

"Why was that?" I had never known Father to be charitable, which is why I found Abdul Haq's tale intriguing and wanted to know more.

"Because when I told him my story, he said he knew what it was like to have someone attempt to control you, and, when you don't comply, be subjected to their harsh retribution."

That definitely sounded like my father. I knew he still harbored much ill will because of the punishment he received from the One Most High.

"He told me I could stay at his place," Abdul Haq continued, "but with one caveat; I had to pay it forward. He said he didn't care how I did it, but it *had* to be done in order for us to have a binding agreement."

I finished the rest of my bourbon, tapped the glass for a refill. "And what did you come up with?"

Abdul Haq poured more of the brownish liquid into my glass. "You're lookin' at it. The Hidden Place is just that; it's a safe place for Gray-Walkers hidden from those who seek to control us, those of us who want to be left in peace, ya understand what I'm sayin'?"

I understood all too well what he was saying. Since Elisa and Tasmin had come into their powers, none of us had any peace. We had either been defending others or fighting for our own lives with barely a respite, so I truly appreciated where he was coming from.

I nodded in agreement. "Peace is something we take for granted…until we don't have it anymore." I paused before asking, "You said this place was hidden from those who seek to control you. How is that possible?"

Abdul Haq chuckled. "Azazel knows some powerful people. He knew a spellcaster, someone who could cloak the place so only those sent here in good faith can locate it. Every so often, a descendant of that spellcaster reinforces the cloaking spell. Way he tells it, he and that family have an arrangement of some kind. I didn't ask and he wouldn't tell.

Regardless, this place has been protected for a very long time, and I hope to keep it that way."

I couldn't believe he was talking about the same being who refused to tell me and Elisa where the souls of our children, his grandchildren, were. The generousness Abdul Haq seemed to be attributing to my father was foreign to me.

I looked at the Gray-Walker curiously. "It sounds like you and my father are...friends."

Abdul Haq raised an eyebrow, taking my now-empty bowl and placing it in a plastic bin behind the bar. "I guess you could say we are."

"I never knew Father to have any friends...then again I never got to know him when I was growing up." I didn't know why I was talking so freely to this man, but I found it easy to do...that disturbed me.

"Hmph," Abdul Haq said, wiping down the bar. "I think I'm yo' daddy's *only* friend," he said followed by a light chuckle. "He really doesn't let anybody get close from what I've observed, not even the ones he cares about. 'Tween you and me, I think he's still in his feelins about his and ya mama's marriage bustin' up...and the fact that she wouldn't let him see you."

I swirled my drink, looking into the glass. "I wouldn't know. Neither of them ever discusses their previous relationship, except to make derogatory remarks about each other. I'm surprised he opened up to you. He's very...elusive."

Abdul Haq nodded a few times. "You'll get no argument from me. Honestly, he is a hard one to figure out, but I've known him for so long, and have picked up on things that he's said over the years. It wasn't that difficult to put two and two together. Whether he's told you or not, he does love you...and, believe it or not, he's very fond of that brother of yours, too."

"I do find that hard to believe." I looked at Father's... friend, raising an eyebrow.

Smirking, he replied, "Full disclosure; my name, Abdul Haq, means servant of truth, so I'ma always tell you like it is, whether or not you want to hear it, or believe it."

While I found the entire conversation fascinating, I didn't have time to contemplate the emotional complexities of my father. I was in search of information and the sooner I acquired it, the better. "While this has been...enlightening, I did have a specific reason for seeking you out."

"Oh, I figured as much," he said, then took a long sip of his bourbon. "Azazel doesn't send just anybody to see me. There must have been a good reason. Tell me whatcha need."

"What I need," I began, taking a deep inhale, "is to retrieve something that was lost."

Abdul Haq, leaning on the bar, asked, "Care to be more specific?"

No, not really, I thought, but I needed his help and knew beggars couldn't be choosers. "I require the assistance of someone who can help me recover some lost memories."

"Oh, is that all?" was his nonchalant response as he pulled a pad and pen from beneath the bar. He scribbled something on the paper, ripped it from the pad, then handed it to me.

"Kiojah. Seven Sisters Intuitive Readings & African Magick Shoppe," I said, reading the words on the piece of paper.

"Um hmm. It's a family business that's been passed down from generation to generation. Kiojah's the owner. She's only twenty-five, but don't let the young age fool ya. If anybody can help you, she can. Head north on Bourbon Street. Ya can't miss it."

I finished the last of my drink before standing. "Thank

you, Abdul Haq. It's been a pleasure," I said, extending my hand to him.

"Likewise," he said, his grip on my hand firm. "I hope ya find whatcha lookin' for. Don't be a stranger now, ya hear? And next time, bring ya brother."

"I will do that and thank you again."

I exited the same way I came, through the shadows back into the alley where I started. As I had spent quite some time chatting with Abdul Haq, Bourbon Street was much livelier than when I first arrived in New Orleans, with more pedestrians and vehicles out and about. Although there was still a chill in the air, there was no lack of revelers carrying long plastic yard cups that I was certain contained alcohol. It was a festive time indeed.

CHAPTER 23
DAFARI

As Abdul Haq instructed, I walked north along Bourbon Street until I came upon a large brick building, the words *Seven Sisters Intuitive Readings & African Magick Shoppe* in acrylic purple letters atop the building. I stopped directly in front of it, hesitation wrapping itself around me like tight bindings, preventing me from entering. A mix of apprehension and trepidation had taken hold of me. What was I so afraid of? If what Tasmin saw when our minds linked was any indication, I had good reason to be fearful. Nonetheless, my consternation was irrelevant. I needed to face my fears, find out what happened when I was in Hell, find out what happened with Attalah. I pulled on the door, bells ringing to alert someone to my presence. Walking inside, I saw a shop filled will crystals, incense, jewelry, books, card decks, oils, and various other wares typical of this type of store. The scent of sage wafted through the air.

"Can I help you?" I heard a light voice off to my left.

A young woman with a bronze skin tone; agate-colored eyes; small nose with a diamond stud in her left nostril; heart-shaped lips; and long, curly, auburn hair set in braids cascading down her back came to stand in front of me. Dressed in dark denim blue jeans and a black hoodie that said 'Normal est surestimé', which means 'Normal is overrated', her attire was completed by gold door-knocker earrings, and thigh-high lace-up boots. I didn't know what to make of the woman who appeared to be about five feet, eleven inches tall.

"Can I help you?" she repeated.

I composed myself then replied, "I'm sorry. I'm looking for Kiojah."

"I'm Kiojah," she said, crossing her arms in front of her, her gaze steely. "And you are?"

"My name is Dafari Battle. I was told by Abdul Haq that you could possibly help me."

Her gaze softened at the mention of Abdul Haq's name. "He's a good guy. I get a lot of referrals from him." She walked up front, locking the entrance door, and turning the sign to 'Closed'. Coming back in my direction, she commanded, "Follow me," as she headed towards the rear of the store.

She led me through a door to a room that reminded me more of therapist's office than that of an intuitive reader. The room was painted in a buff color. A boysenberry-colored leather chaise lounge sat off to my left, while a modern Ford desk in a mahogany shade was to my right, a black leather ergonomic office chair behind the desk. Two upholstered swivel barrel chairs in the same shade of boysenberry were placed in front of the desk. On the wall behind the desk were two degrees from Howard University; one a Bachelor's in Psychology, the other a Ph.D. in Psychology with a Neuropsychology Specialization.

When I turned around, I noticed an altar covered with a white altar cloth against the wall closest to the office door. On it sat a tall, white pillar candle; blue violet flowers in a glass vase; a Mason jar with a clear liquid in it labelled 'moonshine'; water in a glass bowl; a clear quartz pendulum; an ancestral oracle deck with Adinkra symbols on them; and various crystals, including clear quartz, selenite, amethyst, black tourmaline, tiger's eye, pyrite, and turquoise. What really caught my interest was a black and white framed photo of a woman who looked very much like Kiojah. She looked oddly familiar to me.

Closing the office door, Kiojah said, "Have a seat, Mr. Battle." She motioned towards the chaise lounge, taking a seat in one of the swivel chairs.

"Dafari's fine," I replied, sitting on the chair as she requested.

She smiled, before saying. "Okay, Dafari. I'm Kiojah Nyathera Williamson, and it's a pleasure to meet you."

"It's a pleasure meeting you, as well. Your names are very…unique."

She chuckled lightly before speaking. "I can thank my parents for that. You see, I had to be resuscitated when I was born. The way I heard it, my umbilical cord was wrapped around my neck for quite some time. The doctors didn't think I'd make it, but here I am. My first name means miracle, my middle name means she survived."

"That's quite a tale."

"Yes, considering overall Black maternal and fetal outcomes are not great, it's a wonder I'm alive to tell it. But enough about my origin story. Before I find out why you're here, let me tell you a bit more about my family and the shop. I'm the seventh daughter in a long line of seventh daughters, all of whom owned this shop at one time or another. Ownership leads all the way back to my great-great-grandmother, the original proprietress."

That explained the store's name, I presumed. I turned my head, pointed toward the ancestral altar. "Was that her?" I asked, regarding the woman in the picture.

Kiojah nodded. "Yes, that was great-great-grandmother Deva. She helped a lot of people in her day. That said, how can help you, Dafari?"

I found it quite easy to state the reason for my visit, considering Kiojah's vast educational background. "I've experienced amnesia for a specific time in my life. Up until recently, I was perfectly fine not knowing the events of that time, but now...circumstances dictate that I need to know what happened during those years...even if I don't want to."

Kiojah reached back, taking a pad and pen off her desk, writing as she talked. "First of all, where were you living at the time?"

"Here, in New Orleans."

"Okay, how long ago did you experience this amnesia?"

I suddenly became uncomfortable. I felt as if Kiojah was psychoanalyzing me, putting her degrees to good use. How was I to explain that my self-imposed amnesia occurred back in 1932, and that I had my recollections from the time I arrived in Hell in 1855 up until the day I left wiped from memory? "Mine is a difficult story to tell. You might think I'm off my rocker—"

As if she was reading my mind, Kiojah interrupted me, saying, "Look, Dafari, if Abdul Haq sent you my way, I'd expect something in the realm of the...supernatural. You'd be surprised how much I've seen and heard in my twenty-five years. Trust me when I say whatever you tell me won't faze me. So, again, I ask you, when did this amnesia occur?"

"I believe it was mid-1932."

She looked at me, stone-faced, her expression unreadable. "And what was the time frame you forgot?"

"It was from 1855 up until my amnesia occurred, a total of seventy-seven years."

Her expression unchanged, Kiojah scribbled something on her pad then stood up to grab her laptop from the desk.

She sat back down, then, without a word, began typing furiously on the keyboard.

"Um hmm." She rose from her chair, sitting next to me on the chaise. "Just as I thought; it appears you saw my great-great-grandmother back in 1932."

"That explains the familiarity I felt when I saw her picture, but…how do you know this?" I asked, understandably baffled.

"Great-great-grandmother Deva kept meticulous records of everyone who visited her. The person's name, the date, the reason why they came to her, service provided, and how much they paid; everything was written in journals. Once the digital age took over, my mom computerized all that information and I've been keeping up with it ever since."

She turned the screen so I could view it. Clear as day was my name along with the date I came to the shop; the reason for my visit, simply listed as 'memory removal'; the service she provided – spell number seven; and the fee amount. She also had a column labelled 'Successful', with either the words 'Yes' or 'No' in the corresponding row. 'Yes' appeared in mine. I didn't need confirmation; I wouldn't be here now if the spell had not been successful.

"What is spell number seven?" I inquired.

"It's a forgetting spell," Kiojah responded. She regarded me with caution. "What did you do that was so bad you needed to forget?"

"That, Kiojah, is what I'm trying to find out. Can you help me?"

The young woman stood up, placed her laptop back on the desk then sat back in the swivel chair. "Of course I can. For every spell she performed, Great-great-grandmother Deva had a counter spell, just in case her client had buyer's remorse. Question is do you *really* want to do this?"

THE RECKONING & THE REAPER

I sighed, running my palms down my face. "While I am dreading what I might see, this is something that *must* be done. The fate of my family depends on it."

"Okay, then," Kiojah stated, slapping her hands on her thighs. "It's settled; we'll get this done. My shop closes at ten tonight. In the meantime, I'll get my supplies together for the ritual and will meet you at Congo Square at midnight. What I need you to do is think long and hard about what it is you want to manifest. That's going to be important for tonight." She stood, walking out of the office then towards the front door. "I suggest you get some rest; I have a feeling tonight is going to be pretty intense." She unlocked the door, opening it for me. "See you later."

I was just about to walk out when a thought hit me. "What about payment?" I asked.

"We'll settle up after the deed is done. Fair enough?"

"Fair enough."

I thanked her, assuring her that I would meet her at the designated place and time, knowing that tonight's encounter would change everything as I knew it.

I DID AS KIOJAH ASKED, GETTING SOME REST PRIOR TO our meeting. Wanting to have a clear head for tonight's ritual, I decided to walk to Congo Square, which was located in the Tremé area, at the edge of the French quarter. Taking a leisurely stroll, I reflected on the Square's storied history.

Via Louisiana's Noire Codes enacted in 1724, enslaved Blacks were given Sunday off as a day of rest. However, there was no designated location for them to legally congregate, despite them doing so in remote and public locales. That was until 1817, when the mayor of New Orleans issued a city ordinance forbidding the enslaved from gathering anywhere, save for Congo Square, also known as Place des Nègres, Place Publique, and Circus Square. It became the go-to spot for congregants to sell and trade their wares, sing, dance, and play music. It also provided a venue where the enslaved could conduct voodoo and hoodoo rituals.

In the 1960s, the area where Congo Square was located became known as Louis Armstrong Park, named for the famous jazz musician. Today, some of the traditions of yesteryear carried over, with drumming circles, dancing, and other musical performances being the standard Sunday fare. Voodoo and hoodoo practitioners still considered Congo Square a spiritual conduit, performing rituals there on a regular basis.

I arrived just before midnight, noting that Kiojah was already there. As I approached her and we exchanged greetings, she pointed to a folding chair situated in the gray brick innermost circle located in the center of the Square.

"Have a seat, Dafari." She then handed me a piece of paper, which I could tell had come from a brown paper bag. "Use this petition paper to write down what it is you wish to manifest. Write it three times, as three is the number of manifestation. I'll finish setting up."

Earlier, I thought about what I wanted, and needed, to manifest during this ritual. *I wish to remember all that I have purposely forgotten during my time in Hell* was what I wrote three times on the petition paper. Once I finished that, I watched as Kiojah prepared the space for the work to follow. She started by lighting an incense smug stick.

"This is a mix of white sage and Palo Santo. White sage is used to dispel all energy, while Palo Santo only gets rid of negative energy, leaving the good."

She walked around her workspace in a clockwise direction, waving the smudge stick in the air. She then cleansed all the materials she planned to use during the ritual. Taking my petition paper, she moved it back and forth through the smoke. Finally, she waved the still-burning stick around me and, lastly, herself. She handed the petition paper back to me and began to place her items, starting with three candles, which she used to form a triangle on the outermost bricks of the circle.

"These three candles have already been dressed and blessed. High John the Conqueror and Crown of Glory for victory over any obstacle, and Spiritual Cleansing to clear away old energies and remove negative thoughts and feelings." She then placed four yellow candles among the others. "These will aid us in having success with your vision quest." Standing in front of me, Kiojah said, "Last chance to change your mind. After this, there's no turning back."

For me, from the moment I arrived in New Orleans I knew there was no turning back. Don't get me wrong, the thought of reliving my time in Hell terrified me...but not knowing where the souls of my children were, and that Heaven and Hell wanted to possess them, terrified me even more.

"Please, let's get on with it."

"As you wish," she replied. "Let's get started." Kiojah walked clockwise, lighting each candle starting with the three named candles; she then lit the four yellow ones. "Close your eyes and take three deep breaths."

As I took the final deep inhalation, I felt something powdery hit my face. I breathed in some of it, which caused me to cough profusely. I opened my eyes, only to see something that made me rub my eyes a few times. I had been drugged, most likely with a hallucinogen of some sort; perhaps a mix of dimethyltryptamine and salvia divinorum, based on what I was experiencing. I also assumed there was some magick thrown in for good measure. Standing in front of me was not one woman, but seven. They were all identical to Kiojah, but were dressed in clothing from different eras. Each one took a position between the candles with the Kiojah I knew standing front and center.

"I call on Archangel Michael and Our Lady Guadalupe for protection during this journey," I heard in seven distinct voices. Then they began to recite Psalm 23 in unison. "The Lord is my shepherd, I shall not want."

Kiojah didn't get much further before I saw her eyes turn white and my world went dark…

"Octavian, what have you done?" I yelled.

I watched as the plantation and those who were unfortunate enough to be in the vicinity were ablaze with holy fire, the smells of burning cotton and flesh permeating the air. Those lucky enough to survive were running around like chickens with their heads cut off. I gathered as many enslaved survivors as I could find, freeing them from their hellacious bondage; steered them in the right direction leading north. I had one more life to save, that of my brother, Octavian. He violated supernatural order and for that he would have to be punished, sent to Hell for his crimes. Not that it mattered because Octavian would never survive where they would send him.

First, he'd be sent to the 2nd Level of Heaven, a dark place where angels who had committed severe crimes were sent to await sentencing. Then he would serve out his sentence in the 7th Level of Hell, where they sent those who committed violent offenses. Furthermore, that level contained three sub-levels, the Outer, Inner, and Middle Levels. Octavian would be sent to the Outer Level, where those who committed violence against people and property were held. In addition to years of *hard labor, he would be guarded by centaurs who indiscriminately shot at prisoners at will with arrows. I could not allow that to happen. As he was in a near-catatonic state, I took him home, removing him from the scene of the crime, but not before placing my supernatural marker over the devastated area. As planned, I was held at fault for Octavian's affront, my sentence being seven years of hard labor in Hell.*

I thought I had gotten away with protecting my baby brother, but I thought wrong...I had only been there a few days when I saw someone I never expected to see...my beloved niece, Attalah.

I quickly ran over to her. My hand on her shoulder, I turned her to face me. Tears were streaming down her lovely face. "Attalah? What are you doing here?"

"Uncle Dafari," she cried as she quickly embraced me, burying her tear-stained face in my chest. "I don't know. One minute I was in Heaven, the next I was yanked down here. I've been here for a day, maybe two, I can't be sure."

My shock at seeing Attalah in the one place she should have never been quickly turned to anger. Why would Attalah, of all people, be dragged down to Hell, from Heaven no less? In her nineteen years on the earthly plane, she unselfishly fought for the rights of others, much to her own detriment. Hell, that's what got her and Tasmin killed. This...this atrocity just added insult to injury.

"Don't worry, Attalah, I'll get to the bottom of this."

"No, my dear progeny, we'll *get to the bottom of this."*

Attalah and I turned around to see my father, his stance one of authority. His blood red three-piece suit, black silk shirt and leather loafers, and crimson tie with a solid gold tie tack said he meant business.

"Father, what—"

"Because of my position, I was given notice of a rela-

tive's...arrival," he replied, cutting me off. "When I heard which relative, I demanded a meeting with the Tribunal of Three, as, by all accounts, she is an innocent child."

"Uncle Dafari, who is he?" Attalah asked through her sniffles.

"That, Attalah, is my father...your granduncle, Azazel."

"It's a pleasure to meet you, Attalah," Father said, his tone smooth and soothing.

"It-it's...nice to meet you, too, Sir," she responded apprehensively.

"Granduncle will do, my dear."

I looked at my father dubiously. "Why are you doing this? You don't even know Attalah."

Father folded his hands, index fingers pointed upward, chin resting on those fingers. "True enough, and while I am relatively confined to the depths of Hell, I do have aboveground sources. Believe it or not, I've been keeping an eye on all of you. I've been made aware that my grandniece here is a good girl. Same with my grandson and granddaughter, Zafer and Safiya. Bottom line is she does not belong here."

"You'll get no argument from me, Father, but you've been watching us? Why?"

"That, my offspring, is a topic for another time. Both of you, come with me," he commanded.

We followed him to a small room. Within the space was a black granite stone table with three matching chairs. Seconds later, a door behind the table opened, the putrid smell of sulfur wafting into the room before we even saw them. In walked three of Hell's lead councilmembers called the Nameless Ones.

The first, who took the seat on the left, was a creature with the body of an ogre and the head of a hellhound, its entire body red in appearance, save for a streak of black fur *extending from the top of its head to the nape of its neck. Its long, claw-like toenails clicked on the concrete ground before it took its seat.*

The next, with the head and wings of a gargoyle and the body of a lycanthrope, had a gray skin tone with pure black horns extending from its head. It took its place in the seat on the right.

As the third and final member walked in, I took note of its svelte, feminine human frame with three hydra's heads. Each head had three eyes, the third in the location of a human's third eye. As she took her seat, the door behind them closed, as did the one behind us.

"Why have you demanded this meeting, All Sin?" the hydra human asked, as each of her heads looked at the three of us, her mouths speaking in unison.

Although I knew that term 'All Sin' was given to Father by those Above for the deeds he carried out as a Watcher, I had never heard anyone call him that to his face. While I bristled for him, he held firm, his posture one of defiance.

*"I called this meeting to find out why my grandniece, Attalah Jerrod, an innocent, one who is as pure as the driven snow, was brought down here. I'd like an explanation...*now."

The hydra human's three heads focused solely on my father. "Because of your station, we are indulging you, Azazel, but be mindful of your tone," she hissed.

"I'll be mindful of mine when you're mindful of yours," he replied in a manner only he could get away with. "What is the reason behind my grandniece's detainment?"

"It's simple, Azazel. Your grandniece, the one known as Attalah Jerrod, is being charged with sins of the father."

"What the fuck *are you talking about?" Father asked, cool as a cucumber.*

"Let me explain. You see, we," she began, one set of eyes on us, the others on her counterparts, *"performed our own investigation, and it turns out that your son was* not *the perpetrator of the crime for which he was tried and convicted. It was, in fact, his brother, your nephew, who committed that transgression. As such, they both must be held accountable for their duplicity."*

Glancing in my direction, Father stated, *"That cannot be true. I was told my son's marker was found at the scene."*

The hydra heads refocused on Father, Attalah, and me. *"Oh, it was. However, upon further inquiry, it was discovered that your nephew burned the plantation, along with the guilty…and the innocent, in retaliation for the molestation and murder of his wife and child. Your son here, as the older, protective sibling, took the blame to protect his angelic brother. While it was an admirable act, he interfered with supernatural law, and a price must be paid…a severe one,"* she sneered.

"Dafari, Son, tell them they're wrong." For the first time ever, I heard worry in my father's voice.

Lowering my head to avoid his gaze, I sighed heavily. *"I…I cannot, Father. It's as she said. I covered the region with my marker in an attempt to cover for Octavian."* I raised my head, standing tall, looking from the Nameless Ones to my father. *"And I would do it again if it meant preventing him from having to endure punishment in Hell."*

I thought I would see disappointment in his eyes, but none was there. Instead, I saw pity…and pride.

The hydra-headed female chuckled lightly, applauding slowly and facetiously as she spoke. *"Your bravado is commendable, young one, but, clearly, you fail to comprehend the consequences of your actions. Let me spell it out for you; because you chose to deceive both those Above and us Below, and your brother willingly went along with the deception, the souls of your children have become forfeit. As Attalah Jerrod has already died, her soul is ours to do what we will. Dafari Battle, as for your children Zafer and Safiya, once they leave the earth plane, their souls* will *belong to us."*

"No," I said, voice low. "Not my children. They did nothing wrong, nor has Attalah. There must be another way."

"There is *no other way, son of Azazel. You violated primordial law and must now face the repercussions of your actions."*

"Perhaps an equitable trade can be made," Father said, stepping forward. "My soul for those of my grandchildren and grandniece. You must admit, it would be a boon for you to have someone of my caliber in your servitude, especially since I serve…no one," he smugly stated.

"Intriguing thought," the leader of the committee said.

She then turned a head towards each of her colleagues, keeping the middle one on us. They appeared to be communicating telepathically. Their conference seemed to take forever, but she eventually spoke.

"Sorry, Azazel, but we must respectfully decline your not-so generous offer. While it might be advantageous to have you in our servitude, your soul is too tainted, and you are too… unpredictable. You said it yourself; you serve no one. How long before you decide to become disobedient and rebel against us? We'd be making a fool's deal. No, as much as we appreciate your bargaining attempt, it is denied.*"*

*"*I *will do it," I stated. "I will take the punishment for my children and my niece, whatever it may be."*

Her left and right heads again regarded the ogre hound and the gargoyle lycanthrope. This time, it took them nowhere near as long to confer before she returned her attention back to us.

"These are our terms. Son of Azazel, you will serve out your incarceration with us. In addition, you will assume the

role of Hell's overseer for a period as yet to be determined. As for Attalah Jerrod, her soul will be released…however, because her father has yet to face any retribution for his actions, she will not be allowed to return to Heaven. It only seems fair."

"If I may," Father broke in. "I would like to make young Attalah my ward…make sure her soul doesn't fall into the wrong hands, if that pleases the council."

She once again consulted her peers before replying. "We are amenable to that, All Sin. Attalah Jerrod is yours. Now, back to you, Dafari Battle. Do you agree to our terms?"

I looked at Father, who gave me a nod. "I accept the terms as stated."

"Then step forward," the three-headed woman ordered. "A handshake will seal this unbreakable contract."

I stepped forward, extending my hand to her already outstretched one.

"Our business is now concluded," she said, her three voices reverberating throughout the room. "The Tribunal has spoken."

With that, the lead councilmember stood, followed by the other two, triggering the doors on both sides of the room to open. They departed just as stealthily as they arrived.

"Thank you, Uncle," Attalah said, hugging me tightly.

I held her close, kissed her on top of her head before speaking. "There is no need for thanks, my dear sweet niece. Your lot in life was not smooth and ended tragically. I refuse to let your afterlife be filled with turbulence and strife. This is a burden you will not carry." I looked over her shoulder at Father. "Attalah, please allow me a few moments to speak with my father."

She nodded, walking through the rear door of the chamber.

When I was sure she was out of earshot, I spoke. "Father,

I know you and Attalah must leave soon, but before you do, why?"

"Why what, oh, son of mine?"

"Why would you offer yourself in exchange for the children's souls, children with whom you've never had any interactions?"

He flashed a smirk. "Why would I, indeed." He walked over to me, placing his hands on my shoulders. "Simply stated, through no fault of my own, I was unable to be there for you most of your life. Now, I can at least look out for your and Octavian's offspring...and no one can stop me."

I didn't know what to make of that last part, but considering our dire predicament, I saw Father's timely assistance as a blessing.

"Thank you, Father. Now please, get Attalah out of this place."

"I will, as I will also continue to have my above-ground sources look out for my grandchildren." Without another word, he disappeared, leaving me to face my own bleak fate.

THE FIRST YEAR WAS DIFFICULT, TO SAY THE LEAST. WHILE I was half-demon, I was not a malevolent being, my angel side balancing me out. But, as I had a duty to uphold for the sake of my family, I had to embrace the role of Hell's overseer, doling out whatever punishment suited the perpetrator's crime.

I found my role had fully taken hold the day a familiar face was presented to me. The man was already shackled at the wrists and ankles, the chains secured to four pillars. Jebediah Thorton was a local plantation owner and slaver. He was well-known for his particular brand of cruelty, violating the female enslaved while forcing their mates to watch. Then he would beat them both mercilessly. Ironically, he was also one of the bastards who took part in Tasmin and Attalah's lynching. Like so many of his ilk, even in death, he displayed a particular brand of arrogance. This was why I took such perverse pleasure in meting out his comeuppance.

I emerged from a shadow, my barbed whip in hand. Upon seeing me and my weapon, Thorton's arrogant expression was replaced with one showing fear. I walked over to him slowly, savoring the terror oozing from his every pore. Once I was face-to-face with him, I silently stared down at him for a long time, watched as beads of sweat dripped off his brow. Here stood one of the sons-of-bitches responsible for my family's turmoil and anguish, and I had him in my clutches.

When I tired of looking at his wretched face, I bent my head down, uttering words that caused the man's coloring to turn from alcoholic yellow to a ghostly white.

"My name is Dafari Battle, brother-in-law of Tasmin Jerrod and Uncle of Attalah Jerrod. You were one of the men responsible for their lynchings. I want you to remember that as my whip rips the flesh from your body."

Nothing more needed to be said. I allowed the claws from one hand to extend, dug my nails into his shirt, ripping it off his back. Hearing his muted whimpers only heightened my desire to make him suffer, hurt him the way he hurt countless others, including Tasmin and Attalah. With the first swing of my whip, Thorton's cries rent the air, shrill and...oh, so beautiful. While he deserved each and every laceration-causing gash I inflicted upon him, I still could not believe my own cruelty. The vengeful look in my eyes, the sneer that crossed my lips. I enjoyed torturing him as much as he enjoyed torturing those who were enslaved. I was indeed Hell's overseer. I wanted vengeful justice, and eye for an eye, the punishment, indeed, befitting his crimes.

And so it went. For seventy-seven long years, I conscientiously played my part to the letter, always in fear that, despite a deal-sealing handshake, the council would renege on the contract and would once again seek out the souls of my son, daughter, and niece. When my sentence in Hell was finally over, and I returned to the earth plane, I had…nothing. My wife and children were no longer of the world I once knew. Life held no meaning for me. All I wanted to do was…forget.

I came back to the present with a start.

"Dafari, can you hear me? Are you okay?" Kiojah had her hands on my shoulders, shaking me vigorously.

I filled my lungs several times before responding. "Ye-yes, I'm fine."

Her face showed relief. "Thank goodness. You scared me there for a while. I didn't know if I'd be able to get you back."

"How long was I out?" I stood, stretching my legs.

"About five hours," Kiojah said, as she began packing items on a rolling cart. "Did you find what you were looking for?"

"I…did."

She watched me for several long seconds. "It seemed pretty…intense. Are you *sure* you're okay?"

After what I saw, I'd never be okay again, but I didn't need to transfer any of my guilt to Kiojah. "Yes, it was intense, and I'll recover…in time."

"Okay, if you say so. I'm headed back to the shop. We can settle up there."

I helped Kiojah load her cart into her car then she drove us back to her shop. We kept the conversation light, as I had no desire to further discuss what I had experienced. Once we reached the shop, I paid her for her services, including a hefty tip, for which she seemed most grateful. The last thing she did was hand me her business card, telling me to get in touch with her if I needed to talk. After thanking her for all her help, I walked back out into the chilly night air, taking the first shadow I saw. I realized I'd have quite a story to share once I arrived back home. My time in New Orleans had been quite enlightening.

CHAPTER 24
TINASHE

Tinashe wasn't sure what she was looking at. The man before her was something out of a romance novel. Skin so dark it had to have been kissed by the suns of Africa. Shoulder-length locs swayed around his broad shoulders. Immaculately dressed in designer threads she couldn't name, he was the epitome of tall, dark, and handsome. He bore the countenance of a man of importance, his eyes flashing like beryl gemstones. That was how she knew something wasn't quite right.

"Who are you?" she asked.

"Who do you want me to be? It's your dream," he responded, voice dripping with honey and a smile that put her at ease and made the hairs on the back of her neck stand at the same time.

"I have that effect on people," he spat with arrogance.

It may have been her dream, but instinctively she knew he shouldn't have been there. He wasn't the man of her dreams. The man from her dreams didn't make her want to run and hide. This man scared her…

He took his time strolling toward her. His left hand was in his pocket while the right hand lay over his heart as he spoke. The gold ring on his left pinky finger had a crest on it she couldn't make out.

The darkness around her seemed to scream with anguish.

Tinashe didn't say a word as she looked around then signed the cross over herself. The man's eyes stopped swirling different colors and then turned to abysses of pitch blackness.

He rolled his eyes as if annoyed. "Oh please. You really think that is going to work? As diluted with evil and watered down as all religions have become, you really think *that*, of all things, is going to work? Going after those who have lost faith in the church and religion itself is my favorite pastime." He chuckled evilly. "When the time comes, the Church will pay severely for driving away people in droves. And to blame it on me? I know I'm always busy, but to blame me for your so-called religious leaders not only leading people astray but also driving them away from...well *Him*? I'm so offended." The smile on his face was now so sinister, Tinashe's knees threatened to give out. "Anyway, If I wanted to harm you, I'd go after your daughter. That would hurt you far worse than anything I could do to you physically, huh?"

Fear slammed into her so hard, she struggled to breathe. This was definitely not the man of her dreams. "I don't know who or what the fuck you are, but if you go toward my daughter, even in her dreams, I will—"

The man laughed manically at first and then it trailed off into a mere annoyed, but smug, chuckle. "Give me a break. You'll do what? You still can't even name who I am? How can you do anything to an evil you can't name?"

Tinashe swallowed, looking around. It was only then she realized she was...standing in the middle of a five-point star. The stone and marble floor of the raised platform where she stood was cold under her feet. Her nightgown clung to her body. She was sweating bullets and her stomach felt hollow. Strange symbols and letters glowed and swirled on the stone walls. The lit torches around the chambers rose higher. Above her head, a swirling mass of blackness greeted her. However, it was only when she looked down that she realized snakes were slithering beneath the platform. Bile rose in her throat as fear fisted her heart.

"Oh God," she cried. "Oh God…Oh God…"

"You can call Him, but He won't answer. Not down here anyway."

Hot tears flowed down Tinashe's cheeks. What had she done to deserve to wake up in Hell? Had she died in her sleep? What would happen to Nazila?

"Thought we'd already established that dead you are not. I just need you to deliver a message for me. Think you can do that?"

Her gut knotted so badly, it hurt. She started praying, something she hadn't done a lot of lately.

"Lu…ci…fer," she stuttered.

His smirk morphed into a grin that showed jagged fangs and she almost fainted where she stood. "That's a good girl. Say my name, but this time with feeling."

Pray, her mind screamed, but in the voice of her grandmother. *Pray without cease!*

She went to grab at the pendant around her neck. Inside was a small, palm-size vial was holy oil. Something that their grandmother had given all of babies in the family upon their births. She still wore hers at all times. But instinct told her to stand as still as possible as the man circled her.

What was that prayer her grandmother had taught them?
The Lord's Prayer?
No that wasn't it…
She was so scared she couldn't think straight!

"Mommy?" she heard, and she didn't know if it was all in her head or if the entity before her was playing mind games. *"Mommy…help me, Mommy!"*

"Leave her alone," Tinashe screamed.

"Tell me about the Witches and their little coven."

"You're the gotdamned Devil. You should already know,"

she snarled, her anger mounting at the thought of her child being harmed.

Talking with his hands, he paced. "That's...not how this works and my patience isn't what it used to be. Not with what I need to do."

Tinashe watched in horror as the man grew in size. His clothes ripped from his upper body as black wings unfurled from his back. His teeth got longer, deadlier.

"Mommmmyyy! Where are you?" Nazila cried.

"Nazila," Tinashe screamed. "Where is she?" She tried to lash out but suddenly, she couldn't move. It was as if some invisible force had her wrists and ankles locked to the platform.

She didn't know what to do! Her dream lover had told her he would protect them, but where was he? She tried hard to conjure him up, call him to her.

"Grandma said pray, Mommy! Pray now, Mommy!"

His distorted laughter reverberated like surround sound. "Most humans couldn't utter a decent prayer if they wanted to. There aren't many True Believers anymore. Those masquerading as Christians say prayers at night, and by morning, they are creating laws to oppress others, wishing death and calamity on anyone who doesn't believe what they believe, and then they call on God. Tell me, Tinashe...if you and the people oppressing you are praying to the same God, who is he going to answer? So, yes, *prayyyy, Mommy*...It's not going to help," he shouted.

Tinashe's ears rang and made it hard for her to focus. Her heart was trying to claw its way out her chest. She didn't care what he said, she came from a family that had always walked the walk. Even when she became disenchanted with the Church, she kept the teachings her elders had taught them close to her heart. She hadn't stepped foot in a church in years, but she remembered how to pray fervently, just as her grandparents had taught her.

"Father God…Mother God… Spirit and Mother Earth, I humbly ask for your guidance and protection right now," spilled from her lips like she hadn't forgotten it at all. Her grandmother would've been proud.

Instantly, she felt the invisible shackles release her and she fell to her knees, a prayer in her mind and heart as she grabbed at the pendant around her neck. "I call on archangels Michael and Gabriel to watch over and protect my daughter, Nazila…"

The snakes beneath her hissed loudly as the grounds under the platform quaked. Shock and fear were warring inside her, and at that moment she wasn't even sure what she was looking at. She put the pendant to her lips then kissed it before twisting off the small cap. Placing her pointing finger atop it, she turned it over then quickly anointed her head with the oil as she backed away.

"Picking on defenseless women and children…is so… well I would say it's beneath you, but that would be a lie, now wouldn't it, Dear Brother?" This man's voice was low and melodic, almost as if it was rocking her to sleep.

Through hazy vision, Tinashe saw another man. He was dressed just as impeccably, was just as undeniably attractive with golden eyes and long, wavy hair. Her dream lover was here? Protecting her? She felt her womb quiver.

It appeared as if Tinashe was floating on air as she felt her head spin. Her eyelids got heavy, and she could barely keep her eyes open. Her dream lover also grew in size as he circled Lucifer.

"But you just may be out of your league here, Morningstar. The dreamworld is my realm and you've made your second mistake. Your first was going after my grandchildren," he snarled then charged at the Devil.

Tinashe woke with a start, her eyes wild as she shot up in bed, looking around frantically.

"Nazila," she screamed, throwing the covers.

As soon as her feet touched the floor, she took off running toward her daughter's room to find her baby girl still sleeping just as soundly as she had been before. She had never thanked Mother God and Father God the way she had in that moment. She thanked the Great Spirit and Mother Earth again as tears of relief rolled down her cheeks. The dream felt so real. She could have sworn her daughter was in imminent danger, but there she was in her bed and safe.

Rushing to the front room, Tinashe snatched open the prayer closet where her alter sat. After what she and her daughter had experienced a few weeks ago, she knew evil was real. She just didn't know if her dream was. She grabbed the Holy Oil and the book of prayers her grandmother had left her. She then went back to Nazila's room and crawled into bed with her. Anointing Nazila's head with oil, she said another prayer and tried to catch her breath while telling herself it was just a dream.

It had to be, right?

Right?

CHAPTER 25
ELISA

"Elisa!"

Tasmin's frightened screams jolted me awake. I hadn't heard that kind of panic from her in a long time. I shot up in bed, having fallen asleep worried about Dafari and Octavian. I still hadn't heard from my husband. Now, I raced from my room heading to the stairs just in time to see Tasmin bolting out the front door, the back of her thin housecoat flying behind her like a superhero's cape.

"Tamsin," I screamed, fear and anxiety taking root in my gut. "What's wrong?" I asked, now running behind her, down the stairs and out the front door.

"It's Attalah!"

Shoeless, I sprinted to catch up with her, my head whipped left and right as my eyes scanned the layout of my front yard, trying to spot my niece. "What? Where?"

"In the woods—" Tasmin pulled up short just as a figure stumbled from the edge of the woods to the east of my home, directly in Tasmin's line of vision, then collapsed.

"Attalah… Attalah," Tasmin cried, rushing to kneel next to her fallen child.

I got to them seconds later, falling to my knees on the other side of my niece. "She's burning up," I said when I took her hand in mine.

As Tasmin sat back on her haunches, she cradled her

daughter's head on her lap. "Please be okay. Please be okay," she whispered, frantically. Cousin looked up at me with red, watery eyes. "Help me carry her inside."

Nodding, I hoisted up my niece's legs while Tasmin did the same to her upper body and we, almost clumsily, carried her into the house. After placing her on the couch, I moved quickly to close the front door then headed to the bathroom to grab a wash pail to fill with hot water. Rushing back to the front room, I was shocked to find Attalah sitting up.

"Tasmin," I yelled, not seeing her in the front room anymore.

"I'm here, I just wanted to grab—" She had rounded the corner with bags of herbs and essential oils but stopped midsentence when she saw her daughter was awake. "Attalah, you probably shouldn't be sitting up. We don't know the extent of your injuries."

"I'm fine, Mommy," Attalah said on bated breaths. "Just need a moment, thank you, and a spot of hot tea would help me get along much better." Her accent made me think of Octavian.

It was always the running joke amongst us that she was born in America and yet had an English accent. Something we chalked up to her father being a celestial.

"You are not fine. You just collapsed coming out of the woods," Tasmin spat, rushing to her side.

"And you look as if you're about to pass out," I added.

Attalah's clothes were dirty, caked with mud and whatever else she had crawled through to get here. Her hair was in a bushy ponytail while tired, heavy eyes watched us.

"Yeah, well, trying to escape Uncle Izrail will do that to a girl," she quipped, almost jokingly so.

"What?" Concern clouded Tasmin's eyes.

"I was in, what some of us call, the Exchange. It's a world between worlds. Beings from the veil and the shadows can cross. The bloody thing is like a labyrinth of dark alleyways, abandoned buildings, and plenty of roads to nowhere. A place that's everywhere and nowhere all at once. I was there looking for Safiya and Zafer."

"You found them?" I asked.

"It's complicated."

"So you didn't find them?"

She got ready to say something then stopped. I had to wonder if she was hiding something from me.

Wincing, she removed her shirt, revealing welts and bruises. "Technically, Safiya found me. She saved me from Izrail's wrath."

"How is she and where was Zafer?"

Attalah shrugged. "No idea. I had to get out of there. Uncle was going to imprison me, I'm sure. Luckily for me, Aunt Lilith showed up. I left them fighting so I could get back here." She stopped talking then glanced around. "Where's Daddy?" she asked. "And Uncle Dafari?"

"They're away and should be back soon." Tasmin put the herbs and oils to the side. "What does this mean? Are you here to stay?"

"I've completely abandoned my post, Mommy. I'm a wanted woman. Uncle Izrail more than likely wants my head. I have no choice but to stay."

A knock on the door put me on high alert. All three of us jumped to our feet, readying for battle if we had to. Who in hell would be here at this time of morning? Walking to the window, I cautiously peaked out to see it was the Merry Widows and Rufus.

As soon as I opened the door, the jolly man smiled. Rufus was fully dressed as if he was ready to start the day. "Good morning, Elsie!"

"Good morning, Elisa," the Merry Widows said in unison, all three of the women dressed in white kaftans with their staffs by their side. While they all were smiling, there was a seriousness in their eyes that told me this was more than a social call.

"Good morning, all of you. Wh-what are you doing here?" I had to ask.

"Well, good ole Rufus here just doing his due dillymagence in keeping you and Tasmania safe," the fairy man said, casting his gaze around as if he was searching for something.

Instinctively, I knew he meant due diligence.

"And we," started Martha, "…felt trouble in the air. The sisters and I have been trying to stay away to give y'all a little space, but…all of us were awakened at 3:33 this morning…"

Nodding, Mary Ann said, "Our spirits wouldn't let us sleep."

"Guts told us y'all needed us," Cara Lee added.

"On top of that, Archangels Michael and Gabriel paid us a little visit. Someone here in Salix Pointe called upon them for protection of a child, and according to them, they battled demons on the main road leading to Salix Pointe."

"What?" I asked, eyes wide.

"I take it those wide eyes mean it wasn't you or Tasmin who called them?" Cara Lee asked.

"No!"

"Wasn't good ole Rufus here either, 'case ya was wondering," the fairy man quipped.

"Who is it, Elisa?" Tasmin yelled from the front room.

Sighing, I didn't know how we would explain Attalah, but figured with all that had happened, explaining that Death was sitting in my front room shouldn't have come as a surprise, but I knew it would. Because Death was my niece, Tasmin's daughter.

"May we come in?" Mary Ann asked. "I don't feel right comfortable out here in the open like this."

"I'ma just stay on out here," Rufus said. "Summin' freaky going on 'round the way…"

"You're sensing something?" I asked the man.

"Can't put my fanger on it just yet, but summin's a'coming. Trouble I 'spect."

Taking a deep breath, I stepped to the side and let the Widows walk in. After assuring Rufus was okay to stay outside, I walked in just as the Merry Widows looked curiously from Tasmin to Attalah then back to Tasmin again. The resemblance between mother and daughter couldn't be missed.

"Yes, we're related. She's my daughter," Tasmin said, shocking even me that she would reveal that outright. "You can ask all the questions you want later, but right now; I need this time to talk to my child. You're free to stay otherwise."

I wanted to shoot Tasmin a telepathic message about what the Widows had told me, but she was already on an emotional rollercoaster with Attalah coming back, and she had barely escaped Izrail. The archangels being summoned for protection could wait.

"Did Izrail follow you? Does he know you're here?" I asked, not wanting Attalah to forget what she was saying.

Shaking her head. "That's not even the most pressing matter at the moment. I've been away, gathering information from my underground sources. I needed those three days and what I found is disturbing. Morningstar has been unusually quiet so far, right?"

Tasmin and I nodded as she blended herbs and oils. "Keep talking," she told my niece.

"According to what I've gathered it's because…six seals have already been broken."

"What?" all three Widows asked at the same time.

Tasmin stopped mixing and Attalah had my full attention.

"Already been broken?" I repeated.

"Yes, that's why the world feels like it's upside down." Standing, Attalah walked in circles as she talked. "There has always been this theory amongst the religious humans that the seals have to be broken and then Gabriel will blow his horn and thus signals the Second Coming."

Martha said, "We're in the south, and in the Black community in this part of the world the elders would always say 'we in the last days'."

"Guess Mama was always right when she said it," Cara Lee added.

"We are in the last days. Your mother was correct. The first seal is said to bring false prophets," Attalah said.

"We have plenty of those," Tasmin quipped.

"The second seal is war."

"Check that off the list," said Mary Ann. "We have wars and rumors of wars."

Holding her head and frowning as if in pain, Attalah kept talking. "Third seal is famine."

Tasmin said, "Homelessness and food deserts are all around. There are places all over the world where people are starving. And with all going on with the food and food sources…the dead cows, chickens and bird flu, the scarcity of eggs and the like, there is proof."

"The fourth seal, pestilence."

I started counting viruses out on my fingers, trying to remember all of the ones we'd heard about within the last decade. "Ebola, SARS, H1N1, MERS, Zika…"

"The fifth seal, The Great Tribulation…"

"This the one Mama'nem used to say only the True Believers would be persecuted. Them folk calling themselves Christians now got nothing to worry about because they don't serve the Most High. Just themselves. They aren't True Believers," Martha bemoaned, a look on her face that said she was disgusted. "True Believers will be hunted down for trying to tell the Church that the Word as they know it is false."

"The true gospel ain't even been preached yet," said Cara Lee.

Attalah walked to the other side of the room, her breathing slow and sometimes uneven. I glanced at Tasmin and watched as she wrang her hands. She was worried but knew how headstrong her daughter was. Attalah couldn't be stopped once she was on a tangent, similar to her father.

"The sixth seal, heavenly signs."

"Climate change, earthquakes that completely decimate the areas they hit, devastating floods, volcanic lightning, fire rainbows…stars falling from the sky…"

"It is the seventh seal that we should be worried about. It's…" Attalah stopped, took a deep breath then stumbled. Tasmin moved toward her, but Attalah held up a hand to stop her. "The seven thunders will come before the seven trumpets and since…all of the seals have been broken, minus the seventh…we are closer to the battle between Heaven and Hell than ever. Zafer and Safiya together can absolutely stop the devastation the seven trumpet plagues will undoubtably cause, and if they can stop that, they can stop the Second Coming, which is what Heaven is trying to prevent."

My heart beat so rapidly in my chest, it felt as if it was hard to breathe. My children? I'd birthed children so powerful that they could change the course of the world? I needed Dafari to get back home and fast. The more I learned about who and what our children were, the more my heart longed to have them with me.

"You okay, Elisa?" Martha asked me, her eyes showing the same concern her voice held.

"No, Martha, honestly I'm not. I'm kind of freaking out.

I know my children are grown, but still, they're my babies and our time was cut short so many lives ago. Now…I have to worry about them being snatched away from us again? I don't know how much more of this I can take!"

"I'd like to tell you that everything is going to be okay, but the truth is, we don't know that," Tasmin said, walking over to me at the same time as the Widows stood and did the same.

Martha laid a comforting hand on my back. "But what we do know is that we will be here every step of the way. Know that."

"Sure will," said Cara Lee and Mary Ann in unison.

It took me a few moments, but I pulled myself together. I couldn't break down now.

"I hate to tell you all this, but that's not all. Women being under attack is by design," she told us, still pacing like her father and uncles when they were in the middle of talking about something important.

"What do you mean?" I asked.

"Matthew chapter twenty-four, verse nineteen speaks about how these times would be dreadful for pregnant women and nursing mothers."

Tasmin said, "The fight against abortions lends to that."

"Eve has been silent. It registered in the Exchange when she was dragged back to Hell. Any and every supernatural being in the place felt it. As soon as he got hands on her, the torture began. And then just as suddenly, nothing."

"Maybe Lucifer is still torturing her, but more privately now?" Tasmin suggested.

Attalah was already shaking her head. "No, Mommy. If he was, we'd know. The Devil torturing his mistress can always be felt in The Exchange."

Martha answered, "According to southern Black superstitions, if it's raining and the sun is shining, it means the Devil is beating his wife."

"And there is some truth to that," Attalah agreed. "That would be how humans would know, but for us…the female supernatural beings…we'd feel it, too."

"May we ask how Eve came to be the Devil's mistress?" Cara Lee asked.

"She ate from the fruit of the tree. That was all it took. No matter how much good she did, no matter how much she tried to prove she wasn't like Lilith, Hell is where she lifted her eyes."

"That makes no sense," said Mary Ann, brows furrowing in confusion. "The texts say it was Lilith who rebelled. It was her who refused to be made second class to her husband."

"She is also who they depict as threatening the most evil acts against women and children," Tasmin said.

"Yes, but she rests in on the Seventh Level of Heaven. How did she not end up in Hell?" I asked.

"I don't have the answer to that, Aunt Elisa. It would be something you have to ask her. Attalah stumbled toward the group. It was clear she needed rest. Looking at her mother, she said, "I think I'll take you up on that offer to rest now."

CHAPTER 26
TASMIN

"Come on, baby," I said, walking over to Attalah. Then, taking her by the hand, I led her upstairs.

I first stopped at Octavian and my room, Attalah trailing behind me. She needed fresh clothes, the ones she was wearing caked with mud and who knows what else. Raiding Octavian's closet, I grabbed some of his workout gear, a sweatshirt and a matching pair of sweatpants, throwing them over my shoulder. Although she was several inches taller than I was, looking at her body structure, I knew she could easily wear the same size underwear that I did.

I fished out a sports bra and a new pair of matching boyshorts from my underwear drawer, as well as a pair of socks from my sock drawer, handing the items to her. I noticed the obvious tremor in her hands when she took them from me. I also observed how quiet she was, which was not like my daughter at all. Whatever trauma she had endured at the hands Izrail was clearly taking its toll on her; not only could I see it, I felt it. My heart ached for her. Luckily for us, Dafari and Elisa had plenty of spare bedrooms. I settled on the one right next door to the room Octavian and I were staying in; I wanted to keep my baby close.

Seconds after we walked inside, Elisa raced up the hall to join us. "Here you go," she said handing me small muslin bag with an herbal mixture of lavender blossoms, rose petals and buds; elder, chamomile and calendula flowers; and peppermint, spearmint, rosemary, and lemon balm leaves. She also handed me a plastic garbage bag, I assumed for Attalah's clothing. She stood in front of Attalah, gave her a quick hug. As she was leaving, she held my hands in hers, giving them a supportive squeeze, a look of understanding passing between us. Then Elisa departed, closing the door behind her.

Once inside the bathroom, I turned on the water in the bathtub, checked the temperature to make sure it wasn't too hot. Attalah leaned against the sink, her silence tearing at my soul. I wanted...no, I *needed* her to talk, get her feelings out. But I had to remember, this wasn't about me, it was about Attalah, and all that had happened to her. My job was to be her mother, to listen, and provide whatever support she needed.

After the tub was full, I turned the water off, dropping the muslin herbal bag in the water. Facing my daughter, I lifted her head with my index finger, saying, "I'll give you some time to yourself, but I'll be sitting right outside that door if you need me."

As I was about to walk out, I heard a resounding, "No!"

Turning back to Attalah, the pleading in her eyes told me I was exactly where I needed to be. Closing the door, I sat down on the stool in front of the vanity mirror. Attalah began to strip off her soiled attire. I held the trash bag open for her, allowing her to toss her garment inside. Once she had stripped naked, I tied the bag shut tight, then placed it near the bathroom door.

While Attalah was undressing, I looked away to give her some semblance of privacy. But as she climbed into the tub, I couldn't help but stifle the gasp that threatened to escape my mouth when I noticed the bruises and abrasions all over her back, legs, and arms. It immediately infuriated me. I was just about sick of Octavian and Dafari's supernatural family members. If I didn't have sense enough to know it would be a suicide mission, I'd try to kick Izrail's butt myself.

I needed to do something, comfort my child in some way. Checking the linen closet, I found a fresh bar of African black soap, used for its antibacterial, exfoliating, and deep cleansing properties. Elisa always kept some in the bathrooms in case they had unexpected guests, which seemed to be the rule, as opposed to the exception, nowadays. Removing the plastic wrap from the soap, I located a medium-sized metal basin and a plastic tumbler under the sink. After I filled the basin with water, I carried it, along with the soap and cup, to the tub.

Kneeling down, so as not to startle her, I slowly reached out to Attalah, who was lying back, eyes closed. I gently unfastened the tie around her ponytail, allowing her loose curls to fall free. Suddenly, Attalah dropped beneath the water, her entire body submerged. Had I not known my daughter, I would have panicked, but I knew exactly what she was doing. When she was a child, I would sometimes wash her hair while she was in the tub. Prior to me lathering her tresses, she would duck below the water, wetting her hair. It became a ritual of sorts.

Once she'd resurface, I'd use the soap to lather up her hair, then would gently massage her scalp. I did the same with her now. As I did, I felt her starting to relax, her emotions becoming more centered. She still hadn't spoken, but I knew that would come, in time…her time. I dipped the cup in the basin, using the water to rinse the soap from her thick coils, repeating until her hair was soap-free. After that task was completed, I wrapped a hair towel around her head.

Attalah took the soap, washing her skin, allowing me to gingerly cleanse the back of her neck and back. Her bathing complete, Attalah dried off with the towel I handed her. I helped her apply a mixture of shea, coconut, and almond butters to her skin, then she put on the clothes laid out for her. When she removed her hair towel, I took note of how her damp locks fell to her shoulders, framing her pretty face. She sat on the stool in front of the vanity while I applied the same mixture to her hair and scalp.

Finishing that, I led Attalah to the bedroom, pulled back the fluffy down comforter on the California king-sized bed. She climbed in, then I followed suit, placing a pillow on my lap. Attalah laid her head down, and only then did she allow herself to release all that she had been holding in. As her silent tears fell in earnest, I felt the emotional weight lift off of her. I wanted to cry with her but would not allow myself to. I needed to remain strong for my baby.

"I was so scared that I wasn't going to make it back like I promised," she said, still crying.

I truly understood her fear, as Attalah and I had the shared experience of being denigrated, demeaned, and murdered together. The same fear she experienced back then was the same fear I felt within her now. I hated it, and anyone, who made my child feel that way.

"He practically tortured me. All to find out where Safiya and Zafer were. I tried to hold out, lie to protect them, but the pain was so bad, worse than it had ever been when I had lied before. He made it much...much...worse."

Like her father's accent, Attalah had also inherited Octavian's trait of being unable to lie. When they did, they immediately experienced headaches, burning palms, and ringing of the ears.

"I fear he would have taken his wrath out on me further had it not been for Aunt Lilith's timely intervention. Auntie attacked him while Safiya projected the location for me to land in the woods on Uncle Dafari and Aunt Elisa's property."

"Octavian and Dafari's jacked up family is *really* getting on my last good nerve," I said behind gritted teeth.

Sure, our families flat out lied to us about who, and what, Elisa and I were, but the more time I had to mull it over, the more I understood the method to their combined madness. They desired to keep us safe from harm, earthly and otherworldly. But some of these...beings...they were just...cruel.

I composed myself. I wanted to get more information about Zafer and Safiya. "Baby, you said Safiya helped you get to the woods on the property. Why couldn't she come with you? And where's Zafer?"

"It would be too risky. The Exchange is full of bounty hunters as is. Trying to cross over would bring them all out. Zafer has a bit of a...reputation, too. Them crossing the shadows without Uncle Azazel or someone else just as powerful could be deadly for them."

As if on cue, there was a knock at the bedroom door. I instantly knew it was Elisa.

"Come in," I said.

When she entered, I noticed her expertly carrying a tray. Closing the door behind her, she walked to the other side of the bed. Sitting down to join us, she placed the tray between her and Attalah. On it was a small tea pot, cup on a saucer, and a covered dish.

Attalah sat up slowly, eyes scanning the tray. While Elisa poured her a cup of tea, Attalah lifted the lid from the dish. For the first time since her arrival, her eyes lit up, a weak smile crossing her face. "Auntie, are these what I think they are?"

"If you're thinking your favorite, blueberry scones, then yes," Elisa replied, smiling back at her niece. "Vanilla chai tea with honey. Careful, it's hot." She handed Attalah the cup.

"Thank you, Aunt Elisa. I never thought I be able to

enjoy any of these again." She breathed in the aroma of the tea then sipped it slowly. Picking up one of the scones, she bit into it, savoring the taste, a look of euphoria on her face.

Putting down her tea and scone, she sighed heavily before reiterating what she had told me up to this point. "Auntie, I'm so sorry I couldn't get more information on where they're hiding now." Her eyes cast downward, a look of disappointment clouding her face.

"Nonsense," Elisa said, wrapping her arm around Attalah's shoulders. "You're my niece, a formidable warrior in her own right, not unlike your mom and aunt here," she said, causing Attalah to smile. "Remember, we've seen you in action, and while you're a force to be reckoned with, he's one of *them*. I can only imagine how powerful he must be. Do not blame yourself. I'm still worried about Zafer and Safiya, but you've given us more information than we've had previously, and for that, I'm grateful. I just wish we could get to them. I know if Zafer was here with me and his father, we could get a handle on him."

"I don't know about that, Auntie; he seemed quite unhinged when I last saw him. Just like I told Mommy, he has a reputation, and while many in The Exchange fear him, the bounty on his head is still worth a whole lot, especially with Heaven and Hell being after him. Although, he did ask Uncle Azazel about why he and Safiya couldn't see you and Uncle Dafari."

"And his response was?" I asked.

"He said something about timing and patience."

Elisa scoffed, anger lacing her features. "To hell with timing and patience," she stated plainly. "Time's up, and my patience has run out with Azazel and the rest of them. As soon as he and Octavian get back, I'm demanding answers. No talking in circles, no riddles; I'll only accept straight answers. I don't care how much he tries to proclaim us not knowing the whereabouts of my children is for our own safety."

"Cousin," I said, putting a hand on hers, "I'm going to play devil's advocate here, no pun intended. You and Dafari have tried the direct approach with Demon Daddy several times already. How's that worked so far?"

Elisa took in a deep inhale, letting it out hard. "It hasn't. It just makes him double down even more and infuriates us."

"That's what I thought. So, instead of going to him, I say we now focus on the one person…Celestial who was with your children last…well, at least one of them…Lilith."

"I might be able to help with that," Attalah eagerly replied. "If Safiya is still with Aunt Lilith, I could attempt to reach out to her telepathically, then she can get word to Aunt Lilith."

"That sounds like a plan," I said. "The sooner we can get some *straight* answers regarding Safiya and Zafer, the better."

"Mommy, why do you and Aunt Elisa dislike Granduncle Azazel so much?"

Elisa and I glanced at each other before she said, "Let us count the reasons. He's shady, always has a hidden agenda, is self-serving—"

"Not to mention he's the reason your father is going through all his recent…changes," I cut in.

"*He's* the reason Daddy has demon in him? Granduncle never mentioned that little tidbit."

"Why would he?" Elisa retorted. Your granduncle is duplicitous as the day is long. He can't be trusted as far as I can throw him."

"Baby girl, there's so much you don't know. Octavian's transformation occurred the night your paternal grandparents tried to kill your aunt and me."

"What?" Attalah exclaimed. "Grandfather Michael and

THE RECKONING & THE REAPER

Grandmother Eset? But why? Why would they try to kill you?"

Elisa and I quickly filled Attalah in on the sorted details of Elisa and my contentious relationship with Michael and Eset, trying our best not to leave anything out.

"It was also during that battle that we found out they were responsible for the deaths of my parents; Tasmin and my grandmother, Mama Nall; and Tasmin's Aunt Noreen, supposedly on His orders," Elisa concluded bitterly.

"I-I can't believe it," Attalah said in disbelief. "They've all been so good to me. Granduncle advocated for me in Hell, even offering himself up in my place. He protected me from harm, and secured my spot in the Reaper Academy. And my grandparents...they were livid when word got to them that I would not be allowed to return to Heaven. They went to bat for me, alas, to no avail, but at least they tried."

Elisa's face held a confused expression; it matched the one I had on mine. "Attalah, we still don't know how and why you ended up in Hell, and now you're telling us that you weren't allowed to go back to Heaven? What is really going on?"

Attalah gazed from Elisa to me. "Auntie, Mommy, I want to tell you, *really* I do, but...I think we should wait to see if Uncle Dafari got his memories back. The story should really come from him. However, if he's not able to retrieve that lost time, I will share everything with you, I promise."

"Fair enough," I replied. "But, baby girl," I continued, "you need to know that our experiences with your supernatural relatives have been very different from yours, so you can understand if we don't share your exuberance when it comes to them. Your grandparents despise us and killed our family members, and as for your granduncle...well, he's done a lot of sketchy things."

Attalah sighed, running her palms down her face. "This

is…I don't even know what to say. Here I was thinking I was going to be the one sharing big news with you but instead… I've discovered so much. It-it's a lot to process."

I hugged my daughter, placing her head on my shoulder. "I know it is, sweetheart, but we'll deal with it…as a family. You're home now and you're safe. Believe me when I say if *anyone* on or *anything* comes at you, they'll have to get through me."

"You mean get through *us*," Elisa chimed in.

As we shared a group hug, I thought about how in the supernatural world, Attalah may have been Death herself; but to me, she was, and will always be my little girl. Back in 1855, I couldn't protect my daughter, but this time, I swore to myself, on my very life, that I was going to do everything in my power to protect her now.

Chapter 27
AZAZEL

Octavian and I decided to traverse a circuitous route through the shadows in hopes of outrunning Izrail and returning to my nephew's flat, but to no avail. Try as we might, we were outnumbered by my brother's minions, top level Messengers, that he was creating at a rapid rate.

"Nephew," I yelled, after eviscerating one of the Messengers, my claws ripping through its abdomen like the sharpest knife through freshly baked bread, "we'll never make it back to your flat. We need to regroup, and I know just the place to do that."

Octavian had just dispatched two more Messengers, his deft aerial maneuvers allowing him to end up behind them, his bec-de-corbins slicing through their necks, easily decapitating them. I couldn't help but notice Octavian's wings, the once pure white feathers now intermingling with quite a few black ones. They were nowhere near the equal mixture of black and white feathers like Dafari's, but still enough to be concerning.

Even more concerning was the lack of protection sigils that should have been visible in this realm but were not. My nephew was changing in ways not even I could imagine, and that worried me. But I couldn't focus on that at the moment.

I needed to keep my head in the game, lest we become overrun by my hideous brother and his lackeys.

"Where to, Uncle?" Octavian landed at my side.

"Follow me and think of The Hidden Place. It will provide us with safe refuge for a bit while we reassess our battle strategy."

Simply nodding, Octavian quickly followed me through the shadows, as we appropriately re-clothed ourselves along the way. In no time, we arrived in New Orleans, the door to The Hidden Place in front of us. While the air was cool, the day was bright and sunny. I had a feeling that would soon change. I pulled on the wooden door's handle, allowing Octavian to enter ahead of me.

"Welcome to The Hidden Place. Would you like a table, booth, or a seat at the bar?" an attractive young woman asked. I sensed she was a Gray-Walker, one of many who worked here.

"My good woman, I would love nothing more than to patronize this fine establishment… and partake in your company. However, I desperately need to speak with Abdul Haq. Is he here?"

The woman blushed, cheeks turning two shades darker. "He's in his office. I can go get him—"

I raised a hand, gently cutting her off. "No need, my dear. I know where it is," I said, walking around her.

"Okay, but he doesn't allow strangers back there," she countered.

I turned around, strolling back over to her, lifting her chin with my index finger. "Ah, my delicate flower, I am *no* stranger. Abdul Haq and I go way back. He and I are old friends. Excuse my rudeness, I am Azazel."

Her eyes widened, mouth dropping open at the same time. "Azazel, *the* Azazel? Oh, my gosh, I didn't know. I'm so sorry, please forgive me."

If time had been on our side, I would have allowed her to show me just how sorry she truly was. But alas, it wasn't meant to be...at the moment. "There's nothing to forgive," I said, giving her a quick onceover. "However, perhaps one day, you can make it up to me for your faux pas...properly." I smiled down at her, purposely showing a hint of fang, the aroma of her arousal strong. I turned on my heel, knowing full well she was watching.

"Dare I even ask what that was about?" Octavian queried.

"You can ask. Doesn't mean I'll answer."

Reaching the office door, I opened it, walking in. Abdul Haq was sitting at his desk, adding number to a spreadsheet on his computer.

"Now I know you didn't just walk up in here without knockin'", he said, not looking in our direction. "If I told ya once, I told ya a million times, knock—" He stopped mid-sentence when he turned around to see me standing in the doorway. "Well, I'll be damned."

"If that's what you choose, I'm sure I can arrange it," I replied in jest, walking further into the office.

Abdul Haq stood once I reached his desk. After we shared a brother's handshake, he said, "It's been a while."

"Too long, my friend." I stepped to the side. "Abdul Haq, this is my nephew, Octavian Jerrod."

"Dafari's brother." He smiled as he walked over to him, shaking his hand. "It's a pleasure to meet cha. Now that introductions are out of the way, what brings you two here?

"Let's just say the shit is about to hit the fan," I stated matter-of-factly.

Shaking his head, Abdul Haq folded his arms in front of him. "Now what fresh hell have you brought to my doorstep, man?"

Although he was well aware of who I was, what I was,

and the power I possessed, the man who had become a friend was one of the few people who wasn't afraid to speak his mind. I respected him for that.

"The fresh hell you're referring to is named Izrail, my brother. He's a bit perturbed with me at the moment. I guess no good deed goes unpunished," I said with a smirk.

Raising an eyebrow, he gazed at me with suspicion. "Your idea of a good deed doesn't always vibe with that of others."

Beside me, Octavian chuckled low in his throat. "I see the man knows you well, Uncle."

"Your uncle is known for gettin' in some shit that ain't got nothin' to do with him." Abdul Haq paused. "However, not mindin' his business is what saved me and many others, so what can I do to help?"

"All I require from you is safe haven for a short time... and some of your best bourbon."

He laughed heartily before saying, "Nothing but the best for you, my friend. Make yourselves comfortable. I'll be right back."

Octavian and I sat in two leather lounge chairs before either of us spoke.

"While this is nice and all, Uncle, shouldn't we be focusing on getting back home?"

"My dear nephew, we will return shortly. Since our path to your flat was cut off, we need to find a new path back to Salix Pointe. It should be a bit easier now that we're back on familiar turf. No worries, Octavian. We'll get you home in time to see Attalah. My grandniece is returning today, is she not?"

"Allegedly," he replied with skepticism. "That is the hope."

"And hope springs eternal."

Before another word could be spoken, Abdul Haq

returned, not only with the bourbon, but with a familiar face in tow.

Octavian was the first to his feet. "Dafari, what are you doing here?"

"I could, and will, ask you the same question, Brother," he said, giving Octavian a firm hug. "My answer is simple. I was on my way back to Salix Pointe but decided to stop in and thank Abdul Haq for all his help."

"I take it your quest was successful," I said, more as a statement than a question.

"You would be correct, Father. Now, why are you two here?"

"We came seeking shelter after Uncle Azazel caused some trouble with Uncle Izrail. He and his Messengers attacked us while we were crossing back into the shadows from my flat."

Abdul Haq passed out shots of bourbon, keeping one for himself. "I already know you three won't be here for too long with all that's goin' on. To luck and safe travels," he said, raising his glass. We all joined him, then swigged the libation.

"Dafari, Octavian, we must go. Time waits for no one. My friend," I began, turning to Abdul Haq, "thank you for your timely assistance." I was about to walk out of his office but stopped before saying. "Prepare yourself; the final battle is coming."

With that, my son, nephew, and I departed The Hidden Place, unaware of the chaos ensuing outside. Blue skies had turned dark, storm clouds replacing fluffy white ones. Dafari, Octavian, and I ran from the alley to the shadows' Bourbon Street.

As appearing out of nowhere, Izrail appeared, his eight wings flapping, causing windy currents on the now-desolate street. The three of us battle bulked, standing back-to-back-to-back, ready to defend our position.

"Azazel, did you really think you could outrun me? I have eyes everywhere."

I chuckled wryly before saying, "That's an understatement. And before you say anything further, you walked right into that one."

"I find your humor...amusing. You helping Zafer and Safiya, not so much."

"Well, we'll never see eye to eye...to eye...you get the picture."

I guess he was no longer in a talking mood. Instantly, we were surrounded by top level Messengers. Izrail watched as Octavian, Dafari, and I were attacked from all sides. Dafari had his dark matter sword in one hand, and one of his Mabo throwing knives in the other, cutting down Messengers with a ferocity that made me proud.

Not to be outdone, Octavian was slicing and dicing Izrail's minions with his sword, but I noticed it was no longer pure white light. It now alternated between light and dark energies. He called one of his bec de corbins to his free hand, stabbing a Messenger in the skull, shattering it. A Messenger made the fatal mistake of coming directly at me. It lost its heart in the process. While holding it by the neck, I pulled the heart from its chest, shoving it down its throat for dramatic effect. Messengers were coming from all sides. While Octavian was dispatching one, another attacked him from his blind spot, knocking him to the ground.

"Octavian," Dafari and I yelled in unison.

I sprang into action, positioning myself behind the attacking Messenger, summarily snapping its neck. Dafari grabbed Octavian's hand, helping him to his feet. At first, I thought my eyes were playing tricks on me, but soon realized they were not. It was brief, but while their hands were clasped, an aura that flashed between light and dark surrounded them. Then they separated, as if they were shocked by electricity.

"What was that?" Octavian queried.

"No clue, but we don't have time to figure it out," Dafari shot back. "We need to get out of here. The question is how."

As if by divine intervention, Dafari's question was answered. I heard her before I saw her. *"Hello Azazel,"* my sister said in that lilting voice of hers.

"Ah, Lilith, from one black sheep to another, it's good to hear your voice."

"At least Octavian was only partially correct about you and that title. I won't have to fight you for it, since you're willing to share," she said then chuckled lightly. *"Izrail, on the other hand..."*

"Yes, he's got his knickers in a knot because I helped Safiya and Zafer."

"And it's good that you did. They are both safe, as is Attalah. Safiya is here with me, while our hotheaded nephew is with someone whose calming influence is keeping him at bay...for now. As for Attalah, she's back home with her mother."

"I knew I could count on you, Sister."

"Oh, I'm not done yet, brother dear. I've brought some high-powered help of my own to get Dafari and Octavian out of this sticky wicket you've gotten into."

She finally revealed herself, her form massive. Appearing on the other side of us opposite Izrail, she looked like the warrior she truly was. Dressed in royal purple leather battle gear and carrying her lavender energy sword and solid gold shield, her long tendrils hissed and swayed. She was regal in her stance.

"Aunt Lilith?" uttered Dafari.

"Hello, nephews. I wish we could be seeing each other

under better circumstances, but there will be time for that later. On that, you have my word."

"Lilith, why do you keep interfering in affairs that are not your concern?" Izrail questioned.

"Not my concern? My grandniece and grandnephew *are* my concern," she spat angrily. "They are my ***family***, Izrail. Outcast or not, I will defend those I care about, ***always***."

"I see you're just like our brother here, on the wrong side of right."

She smirked before saying, "Your definition of right is matter of opinion, one I ***do not*** share."

"Nor do I, Izrail. I tire of this banter."

"Why is that, Azazel? Is it because you cannot match wits with me?"

I chuckled loudly. "***Please***, Izrail. Let's not get beside ourselves here. Not only can I go toe-to-toe with you in any battle of the mind, I'm also better looking that you… much…much better looking."

My words pissed him off. Just when I thought the skies couldn't get any darker, they did.

Octavian touched my shoulder, spun me around to look at him. "Uncle, why must you antagonize him like that?"

"My dear nephew, have you met me? Besides, while he's focused on me that will give you and Dafari time to escape. Lilith and I have a plan. All you two need to do is follow our lead."

Dafari eyed me questioningly. "You're not coming?"

"Someone had to stay behind to keep ole thousand eyes occupied," I said with a chortle.

"Father we are ***not*** leaving you here."

"You can and you ***will***," I snarled.

"Nephews, we've got this. Attalah has returned, and—"

"My daughter's back?" Octavian asked, looking up at

Lilith. "Dafari, we must head back immediately." His voice held urgency.

"Well, what are you waiting for?" I shouted. "Go! You heard Lilith. Besides, Tasmin, Elisa, and Attalah need you."

Dafari hesitated for a moment. "The least I can do is leave you with some additional backup," he said, and within seconds, his dogs Dorcas and Mimzi appeared before us.

"Ah, my favorite bitches. Dorcas, Mimzi, go do your worst," I said with a sneer. They ran off, chasing down and mangling Messengers at will.

When I looked up, Dafari and Octavian extended their hands to me. After we said our silent goodbyes, they both ran toward the alley.

That was when Lilith entered the fray. Her locs jutted forward, wrapping around a distracted Izrail's limbs. "Coven, now," she yelled.

Suddenly, I saw the ones I recognized as Noreen Chadwick, Mama Nall, as well as three others, appear next to Lilith. They began to chant as one voice, heard above the din of the battle. "We call on our almighty Ancestors far and wide, impeaching you to bridge the great divide. We request safe passage for the brothers two, so they may return to their loved ones, tried and true. Protect them from all manner of strife and harm, surrounding them in your protective balm."

A blinding white light so bright even I had to shield my eyes appeared like a portal. My son and nephew ran into it, and then...they vanished. That left me free to fight at will, and I had a fist with my brother's name on it.

CHAPTER 28
OCTAVIAN

"Brother," Dafari called, grabbing my forearm, forcing me to turn in his direction. The urgency in his voice the only thing stopping me from admonishing him for standing in the way of me reuniting with my daughter. "Something you should know before we go inside."

Sensing his declaration had to do with him regaining his memories, I put my anger to the side and gave him my full attention. "What is it, Dafari?" I asked.

"We're the reason Attalah's soul ended up in Hell."

Caught off guard, I frowned. "What…do you mean?"

We had just stepped beyond the light, into the backyard of my brother's home, and I didn't think anxious could properly describe how eager I was to see my daughter. However, clearly seeing the conflict on his face, I knew his answer wouldn't be one I wanted to hear. I listened intently as Dafari told me about his journey to get his memories restored…and my heart dropped to the bottom of my stomach when I heard why my baby girl had ended up in Hell…and also why his children, my niece and nephew, were now being hunted down.

Where adrenaline had me on a natural battle high minutes before, now I felt as if the rug had been pulled from underneath me. They knew. Both sides had always known it wasn't Dafari who had set the plantation ablaze, and for our duplicity back then, our children…and Elisa suffered.

How could I face Tasmin and Attalah now?

"I know it's hard to hear and even harder to digest, but we mustn't allow shame to cloud our judgements from here on out," Dafari said, making me wonder if I had asked the question out loud. "No," he said, answering me with something akin to regret in his tone. "Your mind is wide open. I suggest you calm down before seeing the women. You know how powerful Elisa's telepathy is, especially when emotions are high. She'll already be anxious to know what I found out and how it can help our children. Tasmin will no doubt be in her own bag of emotions… Your daughter's back, and who knows what kind of baggage she's carrying. Do you understand what I am getting at, Octavian?" As he asked that last question, he slapped a hand on my shoulder.

All sorts of things ran through my mind, like how would Tasmin and Attalah react to that news? I thought they'd suffered the worst possible outcome when they'd been murdered, when, in reality, they were still suffering because of my momentary lapse of judgement. For many years after the incident, the fact that I'd killed innocents haunted me. As time passed, I learned to cope with the tragedy, utilizing my work as a professor and other jobs to help keep my mind at ease.

Looking at my brother now, I saw that he, too, was at war internally. He was questioning his own morality. Dafari had always prided himself on being a man of integrity. Even knowing that some of the people and beings he'd tortured in Hell more than likely deserved it, what he'd done while locked away was in direct conflict with who he was topside. Waves of grief wafted from him, and I knew it was my turn to be there for my brother. I knew I had to put my feelings to the side for the moment and for once be the one Dafari could lean on.

I gave a curt nod, showing I understood.

"I know there is a lot going on," he said, "but—"

"Dafari," Elisa yelled, cutting off whatever it was he was about to say.

Sissy came rushing down the front steps and didn't stop until she was in my brother's arms, kissing and hugging him as if he had just come home from a war. I backed away to give them space and privacy. Just as I was about to head to the house, I looked up to see Tasmin and Attalah at the door.

My eyes burned with unshed tears as my vision blurred. My daughter was here, in the flesh. Dressed in my sweats with the matching shirt, she looked the same as she had that fateful night. She hadn't aged a bit, and the way her face lit up when she realized it was me made my heart beat faster. She leapt off the porch and ran straight to me.

"Daddy! You're back," she exclaimed, wrapping her arms around me same as I did her.

"I am," I said as joy, grief, pain, relief, and acceptance settled within me.

I didn't know what any of this meant for the future, but right now, I was thankful. Especially to my brother who had paid the ultimate sacrifice. Tasmin watched us from the door. A mixture of elation and fear on her face.

Pulling away from the father-daughter hug, I cupped Attalah's face and looked her over. "Are you well? Did you get hurt?" I asked in rapid succession.

She giggled in a way that brought back memories of her playing in the yard as children. "In my line of work, I'm always hurt in some way, but Mommy and Aunt Elisa have been taking care of me."

Mentioning Elisa made me remember she and Dafari were near us. I glanced in their direction, seeing that they were having their own intimate moment. Elisa's aura was off. Her grief like a cloak. She felt desperate and the way she scanned his face and eyes for any positive sign almost broke my heart.

Morning was brighter than I expected considering the storm we'd left behind. Flocks of small black birds were flying in formation overhead as they headed toward the town. The sky was a beautiful shade of blue with white, fluffy clouds floating. The wind gave off a gentle breeze and the sun was sitting just above the canopy of the dense forest behind the house. The brightness of the day was in stark contrast to the sullen mood.

"Ah…why don't we head inside?" I said to Attalah. "That way I can properly greet your mother as well?"

As the two of us made haste getting to the steps of the porch where Tasmin waited, she smiled at me and everything that had happened over the past few hours seemed to dissipate. I pulled her into my embrace while keeping an arm around our daughter. For mere moments, I stood there, relishing in the love of my family.

It was quickly broken up by the sight of the Widows rounding the corner as they came to the door with Martha in the lead.

Leaning in, Tasmin told me, "They already know Attalah is our daughter."

It was good to know we wouldn't have to tiptoe around the subject.

"Good morning, Octavian," Martha greeted, but it wasn't necessarily cheery. There was a worrisome frown on her face that put my nerves on end.

"Top of the morning to you, ladies," I replied, keeping my arm around Tasmin as she moved to my right side and Attalah on my left.

Rufus came trotting out of the wooded area. "Octovian

and Dayfari! Y'all got here just in time. Shole did! Julie done woke up and she demanding to see Tasmania and Elsie. She 'bout swung on Rafiki when she opened her eyes and saw'im." Rufus laughed heartily then, his stomach moving up and down. "Ole Sal had to grab her and calm her down. She sho' was feisty, that one."

"Which is why," Martha cut in, voice raised an octave, "we need to get inside and discuss what the ladies and I talked about earlier. I understand y'all got a lot going on with family matters right now, but we are in trouble here. Salix Pointe's safety and existence are on the line. And when two archangels come to visit us in the middle of the night, telling us that they had been summoned here—and by none of us—something's wrong."

"Who else would be powerful enough to summon actual archangels?" asked Attalah, whipping her head from me to Dafari. "I mean, I know humans can pray and put in requests, but…to have their ear directly?"

"Ain't no telling who dat could be in this ole town," Rufus said, standing next to the front door as if guarding it. "Lotta folk here got summin' extra going on with'em."

"Whoever it is, must be from a very powerful bloodline," Martha noted. "They did something that not many in Christianity do; called on the feminine and masculine of the Most High, while also calling on Mother Earth and…the Great Spirit."

"My word…" Attalah exclaimed, standing to her full height. "It's rare that people do that. They don't know the power in acknowledging the Mother." She paced and I couldn't help but smile, seeing bits of me still in her. "Christianity in its current form does not acknowledge the Mother at all. They only acknowledge the Father...which has caused...some division in the Heavens. Now that I think about it, that's probably why Aunt Lilith had been given free rein to come and go as she pleases! If that means what I think it means...she has been in communication with the Mother. Her Mother." My daughter stopped, tapping her chin thoughtfully. "Widows, if I may call you all that, did my granduncles say anything else before they left?"

"It was odd," she said. "While Gabriel took a seat and allowed us to make him tea, Michael went out to the backyard for 'bout ten minutes. Once he came back in, they left."

"And that was it?" Dafari asked.

The Widows nodded.

"I wish I could say we had time to sit around and discuss it, but with all that Attalah revealed, compounded with whatever Dafari has learned, there isn't enough time to dwell on one solitary thing," Elisa said.

"I agree with Elisa," Tasmin added. "I think we need to strategize. We know the final battle is coming and events are being put in place to kick off the endgame. We need to be prepared."

"And we will be, Poppet," I told her, feeling her body tense as she said the words. "Dafari and I learned a lot on our reconnaissance missions, him especially, and even though I only went to close out personal affairs back home, I now know more about Uncle Izrail and how his strategist mind works."

"We will definitely need to know all of that before going into battle," Dafari said, tapping his wife's thigh to let her know he wanted to move. Elisa stood, and he walked to the middle of the room. "Widows, we hope you will understand that we need a few private moments with our loved ones to discuss some personal matters after we disclose this information."

The sisters all nodded as they looked at one another before Martha turned back to Dafari and said, "That's absolutely fine with us."

Now giving Rufus his attention, he asked, "Is that okay with you as well?"

"Well shucks, Dayfari, this yo' home. I'ma guest. Whatsoever you wanna do is fine by ole Rufus heah," the jolly man replied, even bopping up on the tip of his toes and poking his chest out.

No matter what the man said, we all saw that he was touched by Dafari's thoughtfulness. It was an unexpected and touching moment in the middle of all the chaos.

Dafari gave the man a respectful nod then turned to Elisa and dropped his head before taking deep breaths. Once he composed himself, he looked over at her. "I wanted to do this in private, with just us, before revealing it to the coven at large, but…I can't lie and say I'm not happy everyone is here. Well, almost everyone," he clarified, referencing the Pettifords, and possibly Uncle Raphael's, absences. "I know what you told me before I left, about loving me regardless, and it's one of the things I held on to while completing the journey. However, I have to admit that parts of me are…unnerved that what you hear will—"

"Dafari," Elisa said softly, as she rushed up to him. "I don't care." A look of confusion crossed his features before understanding set in. "I don't care what you did or why you did it. I care that you came back to me. I care that we get to do love all over again. I care that our children are out there somewhere, fighting for their lives, and they need us. What you did to survive in Hell was mind over matter, and I understand that. I have to in order for us to work through the trauma individually and collectively as a family."

Dafari's eyes danced over hers, but it was easy to see he was still unsure. "I'm praying with everything that you mean that..."

He then started the story of his time in Hell. During the parts about Attalah, I made sure to wrap my arms around Tasmin tighter as I felt her whole body stiffen. It was almost like hugging a stone statue. Attalah moved to stand next to her mother, also wrapping a supportive arm around her.

I didn't know what the Widows were actually thinking, but if their faces were to be read correctly, shock and dismay were registering at the top of the list. The deeper he got into the story, the more tears rained down Elisa's face, and when he got to the part, revealing that the reason he had to agree to do all those things was because both sides knew that he didn't start the blaze, Elisa's watery eyes settled on me, but where I expected to find blame...I only found...understanding. I thought for sure she would be angry once more. Tasmin eased off my lap, turning to look at me. My nerves frazzled when Attalah looked at me with unease.

"I think it's safe to say, that by now, Tasmin and I have no room for anger at anything you two have done to protect yourselves and our family," Elisa, wrapping her arms around Dafari.

"Elisa's right," Tasmin said, kneeling so she wouldn't have to keep looking down at me. "So much has happened—too much sometimes—but I can't in good faith hold *anything* that happened back then against you or Dafari." When she reached up and lovingly stroked my chin, I felt my whole body relax.

I didn't realize how much her understanding would mean to me right now. Standing, I pulled my woman into my embrace, needing to hold her close. I didn't bother looking at the Widows or Rufus. I had already suspected they would need more time to process it all. When I looked back over at my brother and Elisa, I saw they were locked in an intimate embrace. A few seconds later, Elisa excused the pair as they headed to their quarters upstairs for more privacy.

Our daughter walked over to lay a hand on my shoulder. "Daddy…I am Death. I have done and seen things that…" Attalah stopped talking while shaking her head. "I'll just say…life as a reaper has taught me some things. I had to grow up quickly. The Academy was no joke, and sometimes in order to get ahead, I had to make my own backroom deals. Having bad ass parents while being the niece of Hell's enforcer *and* being the granddaughter of two of Heaven's top generals did me no damn favors, that's for sure. And I still have so much to tell you, things I've already told Mommy. I said all that to say, neither of you will get any judgements from me, especially not you, Daddy."

When she wrapped her arms around her mother and me, I couldn't hold back the tears that finally released. I had my wife and daughter back, and absolutely no one and nothing would take them away from me again.

CHAPTER 29
DAFARI

It had been several hours since Octavian and I had returned from our battle in the shadows with Uncle Izrail, and there was still no word from my father. I was still reeling from his selfless act of forcing Octavian and me to escape in order for us to get back to our family. Father was not known for his beneficence; there always seemed to be strings attached. And yet, centuries ago, he took Attalah under his guardianship, and she adores him. He also has relationships with my children, the extent to which is still unknown to us.

This side of him, a being who's shown unselfish benevolence, was foreign to me. He was foreign to me, although much of our estrangement during my childhood was through no fault of our own.

I had to admit, I was starting to worry. Although Father was a savage warrior in battle, Uncle Izrail was in a league all his own, literally the Angel of Death. His endgame was to cause…death. And what a boon it would be for him to snag the one notoriously known as All Sin.

There were some on both sides who would eagerly celebrate the demise of the Fallen Azazel with unmatched zeal, as father had committed many, many unholy acts. But now… Uncle Izrail said Father was on the wrong side of right. Like Aunt Lilith, I wholeheartedly disagreed with his assessment.

If protecting Zafer and Safiya was wrong, there was no amount of right that would keep me from saving them.

Tasmin and Elisa, along with Rufus acting as security, had departed for the bookstore, the reunion with Tasmin's mother Jewel long overdue. The women's intention was to see how Jewel was doing physically, and, if she was well enough, bring her back to what I now thought of as ground zero.

Add to the mix Uncle Raphael, Silas, the Widows, and Rufus, and our home was overflowing with visitors, once again being turned into a war room in preparation for yet another battle. Case in point, the Widows were in the living room, locked in conversation, as they formulated a plan of action.

Octavian, on the other hand, spent his time getting reacquainted with Attalah. Father and daughter not only talked but found themselves in the gym sparing. While my brother was an exceptional fighter trained by two of the most seasoned high-archs, Mother and Uncle Michael, I had to admit that my niece was no slouch. Attalah kept her father on his toes, showing us how she earned her place as Death.

"What troubles you, Brother?" I heard from behind me as I stood looking outside one of the windows in my office.

I turned around, watched as Octavian walked over to the bar, pouring himself three fingers of bourbon. I couldn't say I blamed him for the drinking. The atomic bomb I dropped on him was an enormous burden to bear. While we had found forgiveness from our mates, I still could not find it within myself. I could only imagine how Octavian was feeling.

"Believe it or not, I was thinking about Father; wondering if he escaped from Uncle Izrail's clutches."

Octavian sipped his drink before taking the seat in front of my desk. "I, too, was thinking about that and Uncle's unusually helpful actions as of late. I don't know what to make of them or him, for that matter."

Sitting in my executive office chair, I swung my legs on top of my desk, crossing my arms over my chest. "Nor do I. While I would like to give him the benefit of the doubt, you and I both know that my father is the king of quid pro quo. However, to hear Abdul Haq tell it, Father is quite generous."

I reiterated the story of how Abdul Haq and my father met, to which Octavian's face held a puzzled expression. "Uncle Azazel just...gifted that man an entire establishment, no strings attached, save for paying it forward? Brother, color me surprised, to say the least."

"That makes two of us. Despite our skepticism, regardless of what we believe, he did help us escape from Uncle Izrail, affording us the time to get back home to our loved ones, and for that I do feel some sort of indebtedness to him."

Octavian sighed heavily, his brow wrinkling. "As do I. When we were across the pond, we discussed my metamorphosis, and why he caused the chain reaction that occurred within me."

"And?" I asked, tilting my head to the side in curiosity.

"Uncle said, and I quote, 'My only intention at that moment was to save you, not only from your mother, but also from yourself.' He also stressed how I needed to control my incubus nature, lest it control me and I harm Tasmin in the process. He actually schooled me on the changes I'm experiencing in a, dare I say, thoughtful manner. It was quite surreal."

"On that point, he and I agree. You *must* learn to take hold of your incubus before it does so to you. You already know I will aid you as much as you allow me to."

"Thank you, Dafari. As Uncle told me, when it comes to this process, I must be slow to speak and quick to listen."

We both sat in silence for a few moments, contemplating

that statement. That was until there was a knock at the door, with Elisa peeking her head in. "We're back," she said as she stepped inside.

"Is Jewel with you?" Octavian queried.

"Yes, everyone's here."

"Wonderful," I replied sardonically.

Elisa giggled as she sauntered over to me, kissing my lips. "I know you meant that in the best way possible. I'm going to get lunch started. I'll let you know when it's ready."

I smirked at her, my hand running down her backside as she walked away. "Thank you, my love."

Elisa winked at me then left my office. Once she closed the door, Octavian spoke. "Dafari, you were quite adamant about me and Tasmin finding our own accommodations. This must be sticking in your gullet having extra interlopers in your home."

I huffed. "That, little brother, is an understatement." I rose from my chair, grabbing Octavian's drink as I meandered to the bar. After refilling his glass, I poured one for myself. Retaking my seat, I took a sip of bourbon, continuing my thought. "While I understand the mindset that there's safety in numbers, I don't particularly appreciate the added guests."

"That's what you get for having such an opulent abode," Octavian retorted then chuckled.

"Touché, little brother, touché," I said, raising my glass to him. "I will say with all these family members in house, I am looking forward to bringing my children home."

Octavian extended his glass in my direction, to which I eagerly clinked with my own. He swigged the last of his drink then stood. "One last thing. During that melee earlier, when you helped me up—"

"That strange jolt of energy that passed between us," I interrupted. "I've been thinking about that as well. It's only ever happened once before when we were children, but it wasn't that strong, not like now."

Octavian rubbed his chin thoughtfully. "And even that time was brief. Perhaps if we try to recreate the occurrence, except this time we don't let go," he replied, always the scholar.

"Are you sure you want to do that?" I raised an eyebrow, staring at him questioningly.

"Don't tell me you're not just as curious as I am, Brother."

I had to admit, I *was* curious. In spite of my misgivings, I stood, walking to stand next to my brother, who turned to face me. Wordlessly, he reached his hand out to me. I, in turn, extended one of mine, grasping his, and…nothing. No energy jolt, no feeling of being shocked by static electricity a million times over.

I released Octavian's hand. "Well, that was anticlimactic."

"Agreed," he said. "Oh well, no time to dwell on it at the moment," he said matter-of-factly. "I would like to spend a few moments alone with my love and my daughter before lunch." He left without saying another word.

By the time Elisa had mentally reached out to me and I made my way to the dining room, mostly everyone had already taken seats. I took mine at the head of the table next to my wife. Octavian, Tasmin, and Attalah were the last to arrive. Flanked on one side by his woman and his daughter on the other, he was holding one of their hands in his. Knowing my brother, if he could keep them tethered to his side at all times, he would. Considering all they'd been through, I couldn't say I blamed him. Octavian's cleaving to Tasmin and Attalah spoke to his need to protect them at all costs…and his fear of losing them again.

"And when Julie hauled off and slugged ole Rafiki, I just 'bout died, I tell ya," Rufus said with a hearty laugh, slamming his hand on the table, reiterating what he had told me and Octavian earlier that day. Everyone laughed with him, amused at what had taken place.

"Yes, well," Uncle Raphael begin, himself chuckling, "a reaction like that was to be expected, especially after finding a stranger standing over you. You're quite strong, Jewel. I see where your daughter gets it from."

Jewel blushed, herself finding amusement in the tale. "Thank you for that, Raphael, although I do apologize. I'm definitely not used to being on the other side of healing, but I'm grateful to have had the Angel of Healing himself, Rufus, and, of course, my gifted daughter nursing me back to health."

"We're both grateful," Silas chimed in, squeezing his wife's hand.

"Always happy ta help, Sal," Rufus replied jovially, then took a hearty bite of the shredded barbeque pork sandwich he was holding.

"What Rufus said." Uncle appeared to be enjoying his meal, lingering on the forkful of baked beans he had placed in his mouth.

"I'm still getting over the shock that my baby has a baby of her own," Jewel remarked, looking over at Tasmin and Attalah. "And I get that she's from another time, but in some way, it still feels like Attalah's—"

"Our granddaughter," Silas finished. "She looks so much like you, Tazzy. It's uncanny."

Tasmin regarded her parents thoughtfully. "Mom, Dad, I know it's a lot to process, especially after your ordeal with Eve. I promise you, once things get a bit more settled, you'll both have time to get to know Attalah better."

"I would very much like that," Attalah said. "I never had the opportunity to know my maternal grandparents back then, and I didn't meet my paternal grandparents until, well, after I died."

The room suddenly became quiet, as if no one wanted to address the enormous elephant in the room, that elephant being my mother and stepfather, and their distain towards the women we loved.

Martha, obviously playing neutral party, broke the silence. "Now that Attalah is back and we know what we're up against, more or less, we must focus our efforts on the battle that's coming."

"We have our full coven once again, which means we have a lot of power and many resources at our disposal," said Martha.

"We also have Noreen and the others," I added.

The rest of lunch was a somber affair. After helping Elisa clean up, I escorted her to our bedroom so she could rest for a bit. I knew the lunchtime conversation weighed on her heavily. Once she dozed off, I took a quick shower then retreated to my sanctuary for a few moments of solitude. The room was dark, save for the light from the double-sided fireplace built between the living room and my sanctuary.

Sitting in the middle of the moss island, I allowed my mind to reflect on my father, Aunt Lilith, and their battle with Uncle Izrail. I could only hope they were victorious. My thoughts then drifted to Safiya and Zafer. Why was Father keeping their whereabouts a secret? He knew firsthand what it was like to be separated from his child. Couldn't he see how much this was tearing at my and Elisa's souls? Perhaps he did, and just didn't give a damn. Lastly, I focused on the events that led to my stint in Hell. Try as I might, I couldn't let go of the guilt I felt. I was attempting to dismiss the thought when I heard a knock on the door.

"Come," I said.

Elisa slowly entered. I noticed she was wearing a silk

golden yellow, knee-length nightgown with a matching robe. How late was it that she was already dressed for bed?

"You've been in here for a few hours," she replied, as I remembered my mind was open to her. "I didn't want to disturb you, but I needed to make sure you were okay."

I rose from where I was sitting, motioning with my hand for her to come to me. Barefoot, Elisa crossed the bridge leading from one side of the room to the other. Standing in front of me, I smelled the peppermint soap on her skin, as well as the almond and coconut oil mixture in her hair. Her chocolate skin glistened in the firelight.

"I'm sorry. Time got away from me. We haven't had much time to ourselves as of late, have we?" I already knew the answer to my own question.

"No, we haven't." She closed the gap between us, placing her hands on my bare chest. Looking me squarely in the eyes, she stated, "Honey, your thoughts are so dark. Talk to me."

I sighed deeply before responding. "In retrospect, I-I wonder if I should have done things differently back then. I still would not have allowed Octavian to take the blame, but perhaps if I—"

"You can't go back and change the past, Dafari, so there's no use dwelling on it. What's done is done."

Gazing into her big brown eyes, I saw the wisdom of a woman who had experienced so much pain, a great deal of it caused by me. "You're right, my love. However, I will say this; had Octavian consulted with me first, had allowed me to enact vengeance in his stead, I am sure things would have turned out differently…much differently."

"Oh?" Elisa's eyebrows furrowed, curiosity lacing her countenance. "Do tell."

Placing my hands around her waist, I rested them on the roundness of her backside. "You said my thoughts were dark. Are you sure you want to know?"

"I could just read your thoughts," she countered, a smirk on her beautiful face.

"That you could, Wife." I paused before continuing. "Had cooler heads prevailed, I would have discovered the identity of each and every person at Tasmin and Attalah's lynching, whether they were active participants or interested observers. Then, when the time was right, I would seek out the guilty, one by one, and deliver the same punishment that was dealt to Tasmin and Attalah, my true form being the last image seen before I took his or her miserable life. Who knows? Since I would have been doling out divine retribution, I may have avoided consequences for my actions altogether. Even if it did lead to some form of penance, I would have gladly taken it in defense of my family." I knew my eyes had turned red, my emotions high at the moment. "Does that frighten you?"

Elisa was my wife, the person who knew me better than anyone. If I couldn't share my innermost thoughts and feelings with her, no matter how dark they were, who could I share them with? She reached up, touching a hand to my face, her thumb brushing across my lips. "Do I look frightened?" was her response.

Sucking her thumb into my mouth, I nicked the pad of the finger, my fangs having elongated slightly. She flinched but did not recoil as I tasted her honeysuckle-tinged blood. I took the thumb out of my mouth, kissing it, sealing the small puncture wound.

"Let's go to bed," she said on a breathy whisper.

"Let's not," I articulated assertively. I barely had time to observe the confused look on her face before I disappeared into a shadow, reappearing hastily with bedding in hand.

Elisa watched as I spread out a sheet and some pillows, placing another sheet and comforter to the side. Crossing her arms over her ample bosom, she tilted her head. "Dafari Battle, you are not suggesting—"

"I'm not suggesting anything."

I stood in front of her, sliding her robe off her shoulders, letting it drop to the floor. I did the same with her gown, slipping the straps down. She stood before me with nothing but her lace panties on, honeysuckle fragrance oozing from her pores. I leaned my head down, kissing her with the ferocity of a man starved for his woman. She moaned into my mouth, letting me know how much she craved what I was offering. So much had happened in our world recently that Elisa and I hadn't had time to enjoy each other the way we were used to. But tonight, uninvited guests or not, I was going to make the time.

Grabbing her thick mane, I gently tugged on it, exposing her neck. My tongue ran along one of her external jugular veins before I sank my fangs in, slowly savoring her warm lifeblood. I slid my hand behind her lace barrier, felt the slickness between her folds. As I gently stroked her bud, I brought her to her first climax, her body shuttering as the wave overtook her. I closed the wounds in her neck before lying her down on the sheet-covered moss island, ripping the lace from her body.

My wife needed to be catered to, and I was here to serve. Kissing her lips, I trailed lower, my hands fondling her breasts, while my mouth sucked on her hard nipples. Placing light kisses down her abdomen, I stopped, giving her pleasure bites to each femoral vein. Spreading her legs, I dug in, tasting her sweetness. As an incubus, I could do things mere human men could only dream of. Elongating my tongue, I found one of the many spots I knew well, stroking it over and over again. Elisa's back arched as her flood gates opened, her juices flowing freely.

Raising my head, I asked, "What do you want Elisa?"

"I want you. *All* of you, now," she demanded.

That was all I needed to hear. I quickly removed my silk sleep pants, tossing them behind me. Placing her legs on my shoulders, I entered her, savoring how her silky walls hugged my penis.

Elisa hissed then said, "More."

She wanted to fuck, and I was not going to deny her, her passionate screams giving me all the encouragement I needed. As I pierced one popliteal vein behind her knee, her walls spasmed, as I once again took her over the edge. And so it went for several hours, fucking and sucking, until Elisa was close to being spent. I sat up on my haunches as she turned around, her back to me. Stroking my manhood a few times, Elisa took control, placing me inside her. I held onto her waist while she pushed back on me hard, the pressure rising in my sac. At the moment she was about to take me down, I tilted her head, my fangs sinking into the one unexplored vein on the other side of her neck. She cried out as one final orgasm took hold of her, her essence saturating my thighs. Only then did I allow myself to release.

Morning arrived to find us basking in the afterglow of our passionate night together. Elisa's head lay comfortably on my chest, one of her thick thighs sprawled across my waist, a sheet covering both of us. As I ran my fingers up and down her back, she began to stir.

"Good morning," she said, her voice groggy.

I rolled on to my side, my body becoming flush with hers. "Good morning, my love. Someone slept well. First time in weeks."

She giggled before saying, "You gave me good reason." Her eyes opened slowly, a slick grin on her face. "You didn't get enough last night?" she queried, feeling my need for her rise to the occasion.

"Now, Elisa, you know I can never get enough of you."

I was about to show her better than I could tell her until I heard a brief knock at the door before Tasmin swung it open.

"There you are. We were...oh, never mind, it can wait," she said before quickly shutting the door behind her. "Oh my gosh," my keen ears heard her say. I also heard her snickers as she walked away.

Elisa covered her face in embarrassment.

"Remind me to put a lock on that door," I muttered.

"Maybe we should get up and go see what she wanted."

Elisa started to remove her leg from around my waist, but my grip on her was firm. "We will do no such thing," I declared as I slid inside her. "Like Tasmin said, it can wait."

CHAPTER 29.5
URIEL & ZAFER

Archangel Uriel and his grandnephew Zafer walked along Broadway in Manhattan's Financial District. Lilith had entrusted her brother, in his role as the Angel of Wisdom and Enlightenment, to help Zafer turn his negative thoughts into positive ones. They knew Zafer needed to be reined in quickly, lest he bring death and destruction upon them all. Snow was lightly falling, a cold, biting wind whipping through the air. The crowded street made passing other pedestrians almost impossible. However, Uriel found a break in the crowd, quickly crossing over to the cobblestone traffic median that housed Wall Street's Charging Bull statue.

"Why did you bring me here, Granduncle Uriel?" Zafer queried, communicating with Uriel telepathically.

"Why do you *think I brought you here, Grandnephew?"* Uriel asked.

"I have no idea." Zafer's voice held annoyance.

"Well, let me enlighten you. This statue of a charging bull," Uriel began, walking over to the statue and patting it so as to look like a tourist, *"reminds me of you, Zafer. You charge in, led by your anger, wreaking havoc without a thought to the consequences of your actions. It's that unresolved anger that can get you, and perhaps your sister, killed,*

and almost did. Not to mention the countless humans who were almost affected because of your uncontrolled rage."

Zafer's face held a puzzled expression. *"What do you mean?"*

"You attempted to send the sun and the moon on a collision course. Do you realize what could have happened?" Uriel didn't give him a chance to respond. *"Your actions, had you been successful, could have led to catastrophic consequences for the planet on which we stand. Negative environmental changes, which already plague the Earth, would have become worse. And the loss of life...I dare not think about how massive that could have been."*

"I didn't think—"

"That's right, Zafer, you didn't think. Instead, you let your emotions take hold. You need to start using your brain; let your head, as opposed to your heart, lead you. Hear me; if the wrong side gets a hold of your powers, and by extension Safiya's, they can be used to destroy this world as we know it. Not that you didn't already try that yourself, albeit for attention like a petulant child. You, and you alone, Zafer, are responsible for almost getting yourself and Safiya killed by Morningstar."

"I swear, I never meant for Safiya to get hurt. I only wanted to send a message to those attempting to harm us." His tone held remorse.

Uriel ran his palms down his face. *"That's just it, dear grandnephew; your* message *could have affected innocents. Hell, it* did *affect an innocent, your own sister!"* Uriel took a deep breath before continuing. *"Tell me, Zafer, what, or who, angers you so?"*

Zafar shrugged. *"Like I said, those who attempt to harm us."*

The six-four high archangel crossed his arms in front of him. *"And?"*

Zafer shuffled uncomfortably. *"And...Grandpops Azazel."*

"What about him?" Uriel's curiosity was piqued.

"Safiya and I want to see our parents, but Grandpops appears to be blocking that from happening, and we don't know why. The only reason he gave was timing and patience."

Uriel rubbed his chin in contemplation. *"I don't know what to make of that, Grandnephew. Azazel has a reason, I'm sure. Whether it's a good one...knowing him the way I do, doubtful."* Uriel moved closer to Zafer, looking him in the eyes. *"I appreciate your honesty...so far, but I feel as if you're holding something back. Is there anything else you need to tell me, Zafer?"*

"Yes, but..."

"It's okay," Uriel encouraged, placing a hand on Zafer's shoulder.

"I...I'm so angry at my father. He told us he'd only be gone for seven years, but never returned. He left my mother destitute, with no means of support. She had to become a washerwoman just to survive," Zafer spat with disdain. *"It broke her. I hated seeing her like that."* Zafer balled his fist at his side, water lining his eyes. *"He abandoned her...he abandoned us."*

"Good. Now we're getting somewhere."

Chapter 30
ELISA

Three days later, Dafari and I were in one of the walk-in pantries in the back of my café. The pantry was smartly put together. Shelves of spices, sugar, flour, yeast, and other baking supplies were neatly organized throughout. Faint hints of coffee and tea wafted on the air, along with the aroma of freshly baked breads.

The day had been long and strenuous. Between on-the-spot interviews, going through applications, running the café, baking goods, clearing out online orders—even with Rufus' help, I was overwhelmed. I closed my mind. I didn't want to accidentally overhear anyone's thoughts, and because I was so emotional, I didn't want to risk accidentally allowing my own to be read.

The Coven been training nonstop. Tasmin, Octavian, and Attalah were spending a lot of family time together; time Dafari and I were careful not to interrupt. Dafari had been sending Rufus on what they called fact-finding missions. He and Octavian wanted to know every magickal being in Salix Pointe, what they were, how long they'd been here, and what powers they possessed.

Raphael was still journaling, using reams upon reams of paper to do so. As he paid close attention to world news, he went on random rants about unseasonal heavy rainfall, the worst droughts some areas have ever seen, floodwaters and mudslides. On top of that, strange things were happening like an eye of fire in the middle of the ocean blamed on a gas leak from an oil rig, but we knew it was a portal of some sort. We just didn't know which side had done it or what they were conjuring up.

When the weather had remained dark and gloomy for days with heavy rainfall at night and dense, almost blinding fog in the morning, Attalah told us to prepare.

"Granduncle Izrail is coming," she said as we all stood on the porch of mine and Dafari's home, looking at storm clouds roll in. "This is a signature calling card of his. He tampers with the weather. It makes it easier for him to create his illusive worlds…"

"Where is your mind, dear wife?" Dafari asked as he slid the last of the muffin pans onto the oversized shelves on the left of the wall, bringing me out of my thoughts.

Giving him my full attention, I took in his appearance. I was in love with the way the black sweater and black slacks complimented his fit body. The powerful outline of his shoulders and chest strained against the expensive fabric. Hair back in a ponytail, his dark skin glowed with the faint hints of his power. The incubus in him was out in full force. Everything he did was seduction. From the way his stance emphasized the force of his thighs to the way his eyes openly studied me from head-to-toe.

Having his golden gaze sweep over me critically and casually beam with approval every time was enough to make any woman putty in his hands. I always had to fight the overwhelming urge to go to him and have him do with me what he pleased. Alas, that couldn't happen, at least not right now anyway.

Between seeing his pet patients, he had been back and forth all day, checking on me, and now he was helping me wash and put away dishes as the day came to an end.

After taking a seat on a random box, I answered, "All over the place to be honest. The cafe closes in forty-five minutes, and I am anxious to get back home. I just feel like that is where we need to be."

As Dafari's picked up the last of the pots and pans, his brows pulled into an affronted frown. "I won't lie, I have that same anxious feeling. Still haven't heard anything from my father…I'm starting to worry." There was a critical tone in his voice, one that suggested he was also starting to think the worst. "Normally, I'd welcome his absence, but this doesn't feel right. Something's off."

"Have you tried reaching out to him again?"

"Yes," he answered, placing the items where they were supposed to be before turning back to me. "I've gotten no response. One of the only things stopping me from going to look for him is the fact I know he can take care of himself… and I don't want to be far away just in case… Zafer and Safiya show up here. I don't want them to feel…let down again if they show up and I'm not here to greet them. I've disappointed them enough, I'm sure."

I didn't like that he thought of our children and felt an overwhelming sense of guilt. I wanted to take his mind off them for a while, lest we both end up in the pantry weeping and mourning.

Changing the subject, I asked, "Why didn't you tell me your mother was Eset? Well, outside of the obvious reasons anyway?"

Adjusting the waist of his slacks, my husband strutted over to me. The bottom of his dress shoes clacked against the hardwood floor. The noise seemed abnormally loud, and suddenly a wave of dizziness hit me. I struggled to get my wits about me for a few short seconds. It was easy to play it off since I was already sitting, but the nausea almost made me want to topple over.

"It was easier that way." His voice lacked inflection, which told me this was a question he was prepared to answer. One he had been waiting on. "How do I explain that the goddess of healing and magick...hates my wife because of... well, magick?" Studying my husband now, I saw the resignation on his face. "Octavian and I have...this is something we have gone back and forth on for centuries."

I went to reach for his hand, but he moved away from me. Started pacing like the men in his family were known to do when their thoughts were running deep.

"She, my mother...the bringer of magick...protector of women...hates my wife and a woman whom I love like she is a blood related sister because they are witches. She resembles that which she hates."

The aura around my husband flashed bright and then dark. His incubus and his archangel were present, both in conflict because of the conversation. I watched as he rolled his shoulders, twisting his head from side to side to stave off the emotions of the moment I assumed.

With his back to me, I saw each slow inhale and exhale he took. Tasmin and I had yet to discuss our husbands' mother. Before Michael had addressed her by name, the magnitude of who and what she was had been lost on us. It was something that we should have been able to sit down and discuss at length, but there hadn't been time.

As soon as the thought crossed my mind, a power surge that felt like white-hot fire raced through my veins. Golden-white, static-like electricity snapped and crackled all over my body. As time slowed down, I heard Dafari ask if I was okay, but his voice was distant, almost as if it was fading away.

Background noises aggressively shoved their way to the forefront of my mind. Other sounds—two distinct voices could be heard. I couldn't quite make out what they were saying, but I knew who the voices belonged to. Michael and

Eset. They were in the middle of an intense disagreement with Michael snatching up his sword and abruptly storming away from his wife.

What was happening? How was I able to see and hear my in-laws? Why was I seeing them?

Time seemed to move at a snail's pace now...Eset picked up a black matter sword and sheathed it in the scabbard on her back. It wasn't her normal weapon of choice. How I instinctively knew that was beyond me. I felt as if I was floating in and out of consciousness. When Eset pulled on knee-high combat boots, I took in the black catsuit she wore. She was dressed for comfort and speed, adorned in clothes that she could easily fight in.

What in the world was going on? How was I able to see her this way?

"Elisa?" Dafari yelled my name, but I couldn't stop staring straight ahead. "Elisa!"

Like we were on opposite sides of a mirror, I watched Eset, watch me. If I hadn't been used to the paranormal things happening, I probably would have lost my mind when the warrior locked eyes on me and held me in place. Staring into her ink black orbs was like staring into an abyss, and she held me in that trance until she materialized in front of me.

Both Dafari and I quickly scrambled away, my husband taking a defensive stance in front of me, bulking quickly. "What do you want?" he demanded of his mother.

"Don't be alarmed," she said in a low, composed voice. "I come in peace, and we"— she said pointing from me to back to herself "—you, me, and Tasmin— need to talk."

CHAPTER 31
TASMIN

"Oh…my…gosh, baby. Don't stop," I whispered.

"Like that, Poppet?" Octavian asked.

"Yes, just..like…that."

I was in the middle of our bed, eyes closed, lying prone while my love worked out the knots in my neck and back. Between cataloguing the magickal beings in Salix Pointe with the information Rufus had gathered so far, and training with Octavian and Attalah, I was mentally and physically wiped. I took in the smell of lemon-scented candle burning on the nightstand, my body relaxing under Octavian's firm, yet gentle touch.

"A girl can get used to this," I said then giggled.

"You have but to ask." Octavian leaned down kissing between my shoulder blades.

As he continued to massage my sore muscles, I heard Elisa trying to contact me telepathically.

I knew she and Dafari should have been on their way home from café, so if she was calling, there must have been a reason. I rolled onto my side before sitting up to focus on answering her.

Hey, Elisa. I thought you and Dafari would be on your way home by now.

We would have, but we had an…unexpected visitor, she

replied. *Also, tell Octavian to open a link to me as well. I don't want to have to repeat this.*

I tapped Octavian, letting him know Elisa needed permission to drop into his head. She paused a bit too long for my liking. *Who was the visitor?* I queried.

Elisa let out a hard breath before saying, *Eset.*

Come again.

Eset, mother of my husband and Octavian dropped in just as we were about to pack it in for the day. And get this; she's coming back to the house with us.

Sissy, our mother is coming here? Octavian asked in disbelief.

Yes, Octavian. Here's the kicker; Eset told Dafari and me that she, Tasmin, and I need to talk.

She said what? I questioned, quickly redressing myself.

You heard me, Elisa replied. *Eset said the three of us need to talk.*

Did she now? And what, pray tell, could we possibly have to talk about?

No clue, but I guess we'll find out soon enough. One last thing before I hang up. She wants to have this meeting without the guys.

Absolutely not. I won't stand for it, bellowed Octavian.

You sound like Dafari, Elisa voiced. *He's not buying her 'I come in peace' spiel.*

Nor am I, Octavian uttered defiantly. *And neither should you two.*

Oh, you already know that I trust your mother as much as I believe the moon is made of green cheese. I am curious to hear what she has to say, though.

So am I, Elisa expressed.

Ladies, I don't care how curious either of you are. If this meeting is going to happen, I will not leave you two unguarded.

Octavian, if it'll make you and Dafari feel better, we can have Martha there as a neutral party. Michael trusted her; hopefully, Eset will, too.

It's not the ideal situation, but I'll consider it. However, I think I can put things on an even playing field a bit more. Poppet, if you'll indulge me, I need to run a quick errand.

We're about to head out. I'll mention Martha sitting in to Dafari," Elisa said. *"See you soon.* With that, she cut her mental connection to us.

I turned my full attention to Octavian, my eyes squinting as if trying to read his mind. "Baby, what's this errand?"

He smirked, taking my hand as we walked towards Attalah's bedroom. "Let's just say my mother will more than likely be on her best behavior if I can convince someone to join us."

"Who, Michael?"

His nose scrunched up as if he smelled something rotten. "Heaven's no. He's probably the very last person we need there. I don't want to get your hopes up, my love. Just trust me, yes?"

Touching his cheek affectionately, I replied, "You know I do…always."

He leaned down, kissed my lips. "And I, you. While I'm gone, I suggest taking Attalah with you, at least for the first few moments. Mother is extremely fond of her, and their… reunion can buy me the time I need to secure our…surprise guest."

I looked up at him, my hands resting on his chest. "Octavian Jerrod, I love how your mind works. It's one of the many things that drew me to you in the first place."

"That…and Uncle Raphael's machinations," he replied with a sexy chuckle, pulling my body flush with his. "Regardless of his scheme, it's what brought us together…and I wouldn't change a thing."

"Neither would I."

Our eyes locked for a few long seconds, a mutual understanding passing between us. Octavian kissed me once more before stepping through the veil. After he departed, I grabbed Attalah from her room, quickly filling her in on what Elisa conveyed and her father's plan. She eagerly jumped on board, expressing that while she loved her grandmother, my safety, as her mother, and Elisa's, as her aunt, was more important.

I found Martha in the kitchen, drinking some tea and eating a leftover breakfast muffin. After I reiterated everything to her, she, too, was ready to do her part, including making tea and heating some muffins for our 'guests', as well as going to her room to fetch The Book of Prognostication and her satchel. With the tea and muffins ready, Attalah, Martha and I settled in the living room, awaiting Elisa, Dafari, and Eset's imminent arrival. While we waited, I reflected on how relieved I was that my parents were out with Rufus and Raphael having dinner. While they previously had a chance to tear into Michael with a few choice words, they had yet to chew out Eset. That day would eventually come; I was just glad it wasn't tonight.

Before too long, Dafari, followed by Elisa and Eset, walked into the room. Eset's attire, along with the sword on her back, suggested she was more ready for a battle, as opposed to a peaceful discussion. I stood up from the couch, my eyes intently on her.

"Mother, you already know Tasmin. This is Martha, the leader of the coven."

Both women nodded at each other in acknowledgement. Eset's features soften when her eyes panned over to Attalah.

"Granddaughter," she said warmly, spreading her arms. In my head, I rolled my eyes and sucked my teeth, refraining from carrying out the actions.

Attalah walked over to Eset, embracing her. "Hello, Grandmother."

Eset gently pushed Attalah away, arm's distance apart. "Let me look at you. I heard about your battle with Izrail. Are you okay?"

"I'm fine, Grandmother. Mommy and Aunt Elisa took excellent care of me."

"I'm...sure they did. As I told Dafari and Elisa," she continued, addressing me and Martha, "I come in peace. I would like to speak with Elisa and Tasmin...in private."

"That's not happening, Mother," Dafari stated firmly as he protectively stood in front of Elisa. "You may confer with them, but only if Martha is allowed to stay. I'm sure you can understand why."

Eset's jaw was set hard, as she contemplated her options. "It appears I have no choice. What I need to say cannot wait any longer. However, I do feel outnumbered with three witches here and all."

"And that's why I brought someone to even out those odds," I heard Octavian say, as he walked into the living room.

Following close behind him was a tall, beautiful woman. With skin the color of sienna, waist-length burgundy red locs, chestnut brown eyes, and round lips, she was breathtaking. Her garb, which fit her tall, muscular yet feminine frame to a tee, was similar to Eset's, except hers was royal purple in color.

"This is what you call evening the odds?" Eset questioned with disdain.

Octavian stared at her hard, his eyes thin slits. "It's her or nothing, Mother. Her presence here is non-negotiable."

Crossing her arms in front of her, she replied, "Once again, it appears you've left me with no choice. She can stay."

"I knew you'd see it my way," Octavian remarked smugly, his eyes flashing a hint of red. He then introduced us to the regal woman standing before us. "Tasmin, Elisa, Martha, this is my aunt, Lilith."

Attalah was the first to speak. "Grandaunt Lilith," she said, as the two walked towards each other then hugged.

"I'm so glad to see that you're safe," Lilith replied, holding on to Attalah as if for dear life.

"Zafer and Safiya, are they—"

"They're fine," she said, cutting Attalah off. "At the moment, Safiya is in a safe location, and your volatile cousin Zafer is with Uriel. He needs to get a handle on his emotions. It took some convincing and maneuvering, but…I couldn't bear the thought of you two having to fight in any way to get your children back. Elisa, you have suffered over and over and over again. Not this time. You both," she continued still looking at Elisa and Dafari, "will be able to see them soon."

The solace on their faces said it all. I felt the overwhelming sense of relief that had washed over them.

"Thank you," Elisa said, tears welling up in her eyes. "Thank you…Oh my Lord…thank you…"

"Yes, Aunt Lilith, we are in your debt," Dafari voiced, holding his wife who looked as if she was about to collapse from the relief of it all.

After she took the few short steps to stand in front of them, Lilith held Dafari and Elisa's hands in hers. "There is no need to thank me. You lost them in such a traumatic way, the least I can do is make sure you never suffer that way in this life again. I went to get them to make sure of it. No fights to get to them. No other obstacles. This is what we do for each other, as a *family*." She briefly shifted her sight to Eset then back to the couple in front of her. "Now, I suggest we get down to brass tacks. Nephews, Niece, if you'll excuse us."

"We will be in my office if you need anything," Dafari said to us as he, Octavian, and Attalah departed.

We were all still standing when Martha asked, "Before we get started, may I offer anyone some chamomile honey tea and a muffin?"

Lilith nodded. "I will take you up on your gracious offer, Coven Elder. I can't remember the last time I savored human delicacies."

"Martha is fine," she said with a warm smile as she poured Lilith a hot cup of the brew. She passed her the cup and small plate with a muffin.

All of us, except for Eset, accepted the tea and muffin, then we took our seats; Lilith and Martha on the recliners, Eset on the couch, and Elisa and I on the loveseat.

A tense silence settled in the room for several minutes before Lilith broke the ice. "Elisa, I've heard so much about you and your marvelous baking. I'm glad to finally meet you in person, and this muffin is to die for."

Even with her dark skin, I could tell Elisa was blushing. "Thank you, Lilith. That is high praise coming from someone who, I'm sure, has sampled treats from all over the world."

Lilith chuckled lightly. "That I have." Turning to me she said, "It's a pleasure to finally *see* you, as well." I heard the mirth in her tone. Her emphasis on the word *see* let me know she was making reference her officiating over Octavian and my vow ceremony on the 7th Level of Heaven. I felt naked, exposed…pun intended.

I noted the curious gazes from both Eset and Martha as I responded. "It…it's great to finally meet you."

Eset audibly cleared her throat, obviously wanting our attention. "Tasmin, Elisa, I wanted to speak with you because I feel we...need to get a few things straight. Certain... developments have come to light that have forced me to view our interactions with fresh eyes."

"Do tell," Lilith said, pouring herself another cup of tea.

Eset sent her a death stare but continued. "I was recently made aware of Raphael's part in pairing both of you with my sons. For centuries, I had always wondered why Octavian and Dafari would forsake all the heavenly beings they could have partnered with to instead couple with common witches—"

"Excuse me for interrupting, Eset, "Martha chimed in, "but Elisa and Tasmin are anything but common. They are two of *the* most powerful witches on earth. Why else would He go after them and their bloodline?"

"Agreed, Martha. They definitely are *not* common. However, they are witches, and, as you know, His law prohibits witchcraft, so for my sons to become involved with their kind goes against everything we, and my sons, were taught."

"You were also taught not to cavort with demons, but you did that, didn't you, dear sister-in-law?" With her quick wit and sharp tongue, she reminded me of Azazel, but in the best way possible.

I didn't know what family drama was going on between Lilith and Eset, but my gut was telling me it was due to Eset's involvement with Lilith's brothers, first Azazel, then, after her divorce, Michael. Even saying it in my head sounded scandalous.

"Yes, well, we're not here to discuss my relationship, or lack thereof, with my ex-husband. As I started to say, Raphael, acting in his role as the Angel of Love, brought you together. As a high archangel, his power is immense. Dafari and Octavian's will was no match for Raphael's...might."

"Apparently, you only heard part of the story. While Raphael did provide the catalyst, had there not been mutual attraction at play, his plan would never have worked. Ergo, Octavian and Dafari we genuinely enamored with Tasmin and Elisa, and, clearly, the feelings were mutual."

Once again, there was a dead pause. It seemed as if Eset didn't want to believe that her sons chose to be with us of their own volition.

Elisa was on the same wavelength as me when she asked, "Eset, why do you hate us so much? Dafari told me you were the goddess of healing and magick. Tasmin and I are healers and practitioners of magick, just like you."

"Yes, that is true. And I don't...hate the two of you."

My mouth twisted into a scowl. "You could have fooled me being that you tried to kill us. And don't you think you're being a bit hypocritical? You're the goddess of healing and *magick*. How does that even work considering He outlawed magick? Sounds like you're walking a very thin line to me."

"You have a very smart mouth, Tasmin," Eset shot back.

Not to be outdone, I countered, "Funny, according to your own husband, Elisa and I have a mouth like you. I guess that's something else we have in common. Go figure."

When I mentioned Michael, I felt the oddest wave of emotions coming from Eset, a combination of anger and remorse that I found strange. But I didn't have time to dwell on it. Besides, it wasn't my business.

Lilith chuckled before saying, "She's got you there, Eset, but I'll just sit here and continue to sip my tea."

"Hmph. Despite both of our initial misgivings," Eset said, looking from Elisa to me, "after fighting by your sides in battle, you two seemed to have won over my husband."

I sat back on the loveseat, crossed my arms in front of me. "That's nice and all, but that doesn't negate the fact that both of you tried to kill us, and Michael killed members of our family. We know they were killed because Michael was ordered to do so. So, let me ask you this; were you trying to kill us on His directive, or because we're with your sons? Or maybe it was a combination of both."

Eset slowly gazed at Elisa then at me, her eyes eventually becoming downcast. "If I must be completely honest… although I was acting on His edict, I-I did not want Octavian and Dafari to be with witches."

"Which is ironic, Eset, since you are the quintessential witch. But you stifled that part of your being long ago, all to appease Him, even to the point of hating that side of yourself and others like you," Lilith chastised.

"I admit that I suppressed my magick and renounced my lineage, but I was made to believe that all magick was inherently evil, something that must be quashed at all costs."

"I guess that quashing included Michael killing my parents, grandmother, and Noreen Chadwick," Elisa spat. I could tell she was fighting back tears that threatened to fall. I squeezed her hand supportively as she proceeded with her thought. "Except, Eset, they weren't evil. They were good people who performed good works…all…the…time. This blind loyalty you and Michael have…I just don't get it."

"Nor do I," Lilith spoke, bitterness in her tone. "You used to stand up for your convictions. Your marriage to Azazel spoke to that…until you divorced him because he wouldn't conform to your standards of what you wanted him to be. You knew who…and what…he was from the outset, and yet, when it came down to it, you caved to convention, His will; tossed to the wayside someone who loved you and would have done anything for you…and still would to this day. Unlike you, his love was unconditional. What has your absolute obedience gotten you, Sister-in-Law? Please, enlighten me."

Standing up abruptly, Eset moved to stand in front of Lilith. "For your information, *Sister-in-Law*, not that it's any of your business, but Azazel and I have long since made amends. He and I..." And just that quickly, she stopped speaking, returning to her seat.

Lilith tilted her head to the side, a slight smirk on her face. "You two what, Eset? Don't stop now. Unburden yourself. Woman, thou are loosed!"

Despite Lilith's prodding, Eset remained silent. I could tell she was hiding something big, a secret concerning her and Azazel that she didn't want us to know about, but, clearly, Lilith already did.

In her role as coven leader, Martha attempted to steer the discussion back to why Eset called for the meeting in the first place.

"Eset, from what I'm gathering, are you saying that you no longer believe that all magick is evil?"

"Yes, Martha, that is *exactly* what I'm saying. I realize magick is neither good nor evil, it just exists. It's only when that magick in the hands of practitioners that it can be molded, shaped into something that can help or harm."

Martha nodded in approval. "Well said, Eset. If that is how you really feel, then it's time I share this with you." Standing, Martha pulled a small, black velvet bag and a book from the big satchel she was carrying. She then placed the bag and The Book of Prognostication on the coffee table.

"Let me start off by saying that what I'm about to share with you has been kept in confidence for over two decades, even from my sisters. I was sworn to secrecy by Noreen and Amabelle not to reveal what I'm about to disclose unless Tasmin and Elisa ever came into their magick. Even with clipping their magick and trying to keep them safe, they knew it was a possibility that they could still realize their powers."

Elisa, thinking the same thing I was, asked, "Is this what you wanted to talk to us about a while back?"

"Yes, but with all that was going on, there was never a right time. Also, for the life of me, I couldn't figure out what significance they held," Martha said, opening the velvet bag, pouring three smooth, flat crystals, each formed into a pendant and attached to a gold chain, into her hand.

Lilith and Eset walked over to the table to study the stones.

"I was instructed by Noreen and Amabelle to guard these no matter what. While they hoped your powers never manifested, if they did, I was to present you with these at a time I thought was appropriate. I had all but forgotten about them until something in my soul tugged at me and I found them in my desk. After I fetched them, The Book of Prognostication did that glowing thing."

She placed the necklaces on the table one at a time. As she did, I noticed a symbol etched in gold on each stone. Instinctively, I reached for a crystal with various shades of purple, including lavender, lilac, and violet.

"This is lepidolite, and the Adinkra symbol is Nyame Dua, which translates to God's tree or God's altar. It represents God's presence and protection."

"Correct, Tasmin. I assume you chose lepidolite because empaths are drawn to it."

We all looked at Elisa, waiting for her to make a selection. She chose quickly, saying, "I recognize this crystal; it's pink petalite."

Martha nodded. "That's right, Elisa. It attracts telepaths."

"Mate Maisie, I've kept what I've heard, is the Adinkra symbol. It means receptivity to learning and education," Elisa said, running her fingers over the emblem.

"Some things you never forget," I said, more to Elisa than

the other women, remembering all the things we had studied over the decades.

Looking at the third crystal, a stone with a red-orange color, I took note of the engraved throne, which was not an Adinkra symbol.

Eset examined the stone, rubbed her index finger along the etched emblem on the front of the carnelian crystal. "This throne is my symbol," she said, addressing the room. "How did they come to possess this?"

"I have no idea," Martha replied with a shrug. "But maybe this prophecy can give us a clue." She picked up The Book of Prognostication, turning to a page she had bookmarked. "As the final battle nears, three must unite to bring an end to Salix Pointe's terror and fear. Two of the sheroes are bonded by blood, magick, and love, while the other is a fierce general to The One Up Above. She who wields cosmic powers views the two with contempt and derision but will fall on her sword to cease the division. An olive branch extended though the witches were the ones aggrieved, the warrior with wings of white will humble herself and receive. Time is of the essence, malevolence already showing its evil hand, but in the end these fearless women will come together, as a unit they will stand. With Salix Pointe's fate, and that of the entire world, on the line, their will, their force, and their strength they will combine."

"Oh, hell no," Elisa exclaimed, springing to her feet.

She was more than likely thinking the same thing I was. We already had to work with Eset in some way, but now that it was a prophecy, it meant we really had no choice in the matter.

"Say it ain't so," I replied, just as surprised as she was.

The gazes on Eset and Lilith's faces spoke to their confusion. They looked just as puzzled as Elisa and me.

"Martha, when did this prophecy reveal itself to you?" Eset asked.

"The book glowed a few days ago, right after I found the necklaces."

"What could it all mean?" Lilith asked.

"I have no idea, but one thing I do know," Eset began, looking from me to Elisa, "we have no choice but to figure it out…together."

CHAPTER 32
ESET

"Not to change the subject out of the blue," Elisa said, giving me her full attention. "However, my husband...your son is worried about his father. He hasn't heard from him in about three or so days. Have you, by chance, heard anything?" she asked, studying my eyes in a way I hadn't seen before.

She and Tasmin were still leery of me, but at least they were willing to hear me out. It was more than I deserved truthfully. My time on the Second Level of Heaven had not been a punishment I was familiar with. Physical pain aside, it almost broke me mentally. I had to face my indiscretions and the way I carelessly mothered my oldest son in his youth. I had to sit with the pain of the rejection he felt then and now.

As a hooded angel with eyes of fire and the face of three burning suns tortured me—mind, body and soul— I had to stew in the hollowness, pain, anger, and abandonment my son felt when he thought of his father. Then I was left to wallow in his mother wound. The injury deep and all consuming. I'd have rather the angel peeled back layer-by-layer of my skin than to ever feel that agony again. Even now, I was angry with myself. I owed both my sons an apology, but I owed Dafari so much more.

"No...no... I haven't—" Clearing my throat, I composed

my breathing— "heard from him as of late. Who knows what a being like Azazel is up to…"

"He was injured badly after the fight with Izrail. Something he didn't want Dafari or anyone else to know. With everything else happening, he didn't want to distract any of you. Perhaps he has gone somewhere to heal and regroup," said Lilith. "That would explain his absence."

As if there was a direct line to his ears from our mouths, the being who had been missing for at least seventy-two hours strutted in from the shadows, catching the room at large off guard. So much so that Martha, Elisa and Tasmin took defensive stances, readying for battle. I braced as well, but quickly stood down realizing it was…him.

"Well look at what the cat dragged in," joked Lilith, eyes wide with amusement.

"When my ears start ringing, I know I'm being discussed in a contemptuous manner," Azazel crooned calmly, his voice edged with curiosity. His eyes scanned the whole room, stopping on me the longest as if challenging me— daring me to look away.

I lifted my chin, meeting my ex-husband's icy gaze head on. Dressed in black from his shirt to his booted feet, hair pulled back into a serious ponytail, the owner of all sins looked like the general he once was.

My body betrayed me as it had done in times past, coming alive at the sight of him. It reminded me of the things…secrets that went unspoken between us.

"Good of you to rejoin the living, Brother," Lilith said, clearly surprised to see him.

"You have no idea," was his only response. His eyes were still on me. "What brought you off your perch back down here with us…sinners?"

"I came to extend an olive branch to Elisa and Tasmin,"

she muttered hastily. "Why are you here? Where have you been?"

"Not that it's any of your concern...I come bearing intelligence from my underworld sources..." His voice trailed off as he turned to face me fully.

The tensing of his jaw told of his deep frustrations; his golden gaze filled with questions—one demanding an immediate answer. His eyes clung to mine, asking and receiving his answer with not so much as a word from me. The betrayal that flickered in them confused me. The sudden icy contempt though? That was all too familiar. However, when the smugness returned to his eyes, I knew he was hiding something, too.

Seething with restrained anger, I tried to keep my voice steady. "Please spare me your judgements!"

I expected Azazel to have some sort of comeback, he always did. I was prepared to have a war of words with him that would probably leave our sons trying to pull us apart. However, what I didn't expect was for him to stare at me so long that the silence between us loomed like a threatening storm. Suddenly, I felt vulnerable and that angered me. I promised myself I would never allow him to get underneath my skin again, but the hostility in his golden eyes clawed at me like the sharpest of talons.

"Azazel," Lilith said smoothly, her voice like a calming balm. "Why don't you take a walk outside? Attalah is here and...soon Safiya and Zafer will be as well..."

Her tone was gentle and coaxing, and without another word, Azazel stepped into a shadow and was gone. Lilith turned to me, and while there was no judgement in her eyes, they did question what was going on.

"What was that about?" she asked.

Shaking my head, I ran aggravated hands up and down my face as I walked in a small circle. It was only when I stopped and my eyes landed on Martha, Tasmin, and Elisa that I remembered they were still in the room. All three regarded me with quiet curiosity.

"I'm going to tell all of you something that isn't to leave this room…"

"Please do and fill me in while you're at it." The firm voice with no vestige of emotion belonged to a very angry Michael, who had ripped his way through the veil and marched to stand before me.

Our eyes collided, his commanding that I give him an explanation. "There is nothing to fill in," I defended then sighed. "I was going to reveal my condition to the women."

I'd hoped that explanation would be enough for him, but my husband didn't take his eyes from mine. His muscular arms were bare, protection sigils glowed bright. He was powerful, his chest broad and defined. Tall and athletic, I saw our son in him.

"What condition?" Tamsin and Elisa asked at the same time.

Martha wanted to know, "Are you ill?"

"That's not what I'm talking about, and you know it," Michael spat, still holding me hostage with his fiery, black gaze. "Why was he in your space? What was the energy I felt from the brief connection? Why are fear and panic knotted inside your gut right now? And you're carrying so denying what you're feeling is futile. I can feel…every single emotion you do. Talk to me!"

I searched anxiously for a way to explain things to my husband. I'd been trying to find the words for far too long, allowing thoughts…mere thoughts to go entirely too far. Panic like I hadn't known in eons welled in my throat, but I could not bring myself to admit fault in front of company.

"Fine," Michael snapped, turning away from me. "Since

you won't tell me, I'll ask him." Then, before I could even protest, he was gone, back through the veil.

Suddenly, there was a commotion outside. Bright flashes of light crashed to earth, one after the other. Octavian and Dafari could be heard questioning what was going on. The ladies and I rushed outside just in time to see Michael and Azazel squaring off while Gabriel, Uriel, and Raphael watched on. It didn't matter where the brothers were, and even with Raphael being casted down, they would always show up for one another.

"Attalah, come with me," Lilith commanded with urgency. "We need to make a quick run. The only way we'll be able to stop this is with a bit of unconventional reinforcements. We'll be right back." And before we could next blink, she and my granddaughter were gone.

My sons had rushed outside, Octavian body blocking Michael and Dafari doing the same to Azazel, both questioning their fathers' madness. Martha, Tasmin and Elisa all stood next to me on the porch, their shocked expressions saying everything they couldn't.

"Martha, I think you should go find your sisters and the others. Tell them we need all hands on deck now," I heard Elisa say.

"You may want to add Rufus if you can find him. We may need all the extra magickal help we can get," Tasmin added smartly.

"You got that right," Martha said, then headed on her way.

"Father, please! What in bloody hell is going on?" Octavian demanded.

"Stop this at once," Dafari's rough voice boomed as he faced off with Azazel.

Raphael's distinguished features were contorted into a conflicted frown. The Angel of Healing moved Dafari away from his father and then did the same to Octavian before speaking to the two archangels who were readying for battle. "Brothers, I implore both of you to think about doing this in a more cultivated manner and setting. Your sons are before you!"

"I agree," said Gabriel, but he kept his distance.

The disdain in his eyes while watching Azazel not lost on me. While all the brothers were close, they still each had their own, separate relationships with one another. Gabriel and Michael had a closer relationship. So when he casted his despondent gaze in my direction, I automatically knew what he was thinking.

"No. He will answer me here and now. What have you done to my wife that she would have that kind of reaction upon seeing you?" Michael asked, the slight edge to his voice made it hard to bite back his disgust.

Azazel's dark eyebrows slanted in a frown. As he and Michael continued to circle one another like opponents, he sneered in my direction before turning red, glowing eyes back to his brother. "Ask…your wife," he replied coolly. "Ask her why her body reacted the way it did." His mouth then took on a derisive grin.

Facing his brother, Michael spat out his next words through clenched teeth and a hard-set mouth. "You are a disgrace to our kind, to our brotherhood!"

Azazel's face grew incredulous! "Me? I'm the disgrace? I didn't crawl between your wife's legs. You broke the covenant of the brotherhood long before I did!"

"She chose me!"

I could tell the words socked Azazel in the gut, but like the masterful manipulator he was, he only grinned while the demon in him fought to take over the fight. I knew him. Sometimes better than he knew himself. At times I mused that was what had kept us together so long. He wasn't a hard man to love. Just a complicated one. One who wore his convictions…and his love on his sleeve. One just had to break down all the walls he'd put in place to get to know the true being; the man, the demon, the myth…the lover.

And it was because I knew him so well that I was acutely aware of when his gloves came off. He was going in like a bare-knuckle brawl. That became abundantly clear when he turned tense, calculating eyes in my direction. "She chose you, you say…I say *ask her* why her body still comes alive when we are in close quarters, Brother. Ask your duplicitous wife," he ended on a threatening growl.

My husband took deep breaths. He and his brother being at odds had always troubled him. Michael was also stubborn and often at conflict with himself in regard to His orders. He was becoming more jaded by the day, hurt and confused because he couldn't make sense of where the world was headed. Michael had found me in a hopelessness that I had a hard time fighting my way out of. He saved me from myself. Helped me get through my pain. Never judging me. Always allowing me to…just exist. That was the kind of man he was. Always able to see to the core of who I was underneath all the hurt and pain.

"Have you no shame, Brother?"

"Why must I wear the shame you feel?" Azazel bellowed, marching to face his brother head on!

Dafari and Octavian moved in, but Uriel stopped them. "No," he spat firmly. His voice holding no ill intent. "Let this happen. It is the only way we move on and continue to work as a cohesive unit!"

I stared on horrified of what was playing out in front of the whole family.

"You are ashamed. Not me! I accept who I am! The good. The bad. The ugly. *The.down.right.despecible!* The unmentionable! I own who and what I am, Brother! Can you say the same and not feel disgust for being a coward afterwards? You and none of the others will continue to use your shame to burden me!" By the time Azazel was done raging at his brother, he shoved Michael so hard, he went flying backward, landing hard against the trunk of the thick oak tree in the yard. The sound his body made as it crashed to the ground sickening.

When Michael stealthily got back to his feet and charged Azazel, I raced from the porch into the yard, only to have Gabriel step in front of me. "This isn't your fight, Eset."

"You can't be seriously telling me you all are going to let this continue," I cried, squaring up with him.

Dafari and Octavian tried to go after their fathers again to no avail. They were blocked by their uncles. I'd seen these kind of squabbles before, but normally between other high-archs.

A black bolt of energy came flying from the palms of Michael's hands, landing square in the middle of Azazel's chest. Seconds later, Michael tackled his brother to the ground. Both archangels pummeling the other as if they were in a fight for their lives.

I stumbled backward, Gabriel swiftly moving me out of the way. "You're in no condition to get in the middle of this!"

I had no time for his brand of sexism. I had to deal with it enough on the heavenly plane. I would not stand for it when my husband and his brother were literally trying to rip one another apart! Seething with anger, I pushed my brother-in-law backward, catching him by surprise. He was more than likely more shocked that I'd put hands on him than anything. The piercing dark gaze and his hard-set jaw attested to that.

"I am a warrior angel! Same class as the rest of you! My condition has no bearings on whether I chose to fight or not." The last part came out angrier than I'd intended, but I didn't have time to dwell on it.

"I do not care," Gabriel snarled, preventing me from getting between the men again.

I screamed internally while wanting to all but punch the angel before me in the mouth, and he knew damn well I could. Which was probably why he stood defensively in front of me.

Time stood still. The fight between my husband and his brother resembled a deadly category-5 hurricane battling a supercell tornado. Both brothers giving just as good as they received. The grunts and groans of pain and power exchanges were enough to send birds flying and creatures skittering about in the wooded area around my son's home.

"This is insane!" Dafari roared, trying to maneuver his way around Uriel.

"It is the way of our brotherhood!" he yelled at Dafari in return.

Uriel kept him at bay when he made another attempt to get to his father. "And it has been a long time coming. I know this isn't something you and your brother would like to see, but it has to happen. It *needs* to happen!"

The sky darkened, birds took flight, and the earth shook. The fighting between Michael and Azazel ceased when we all were tumbling to the ground.

"I think now would be a good time to call a truce?" Raphael said as he extended a hand to help Azazel to his feet while Gabriel did the same to Michael.

Uriel started, "I actually think that would be best. At least until we figure out how—" He stopped, looking toward the distance at something unseen.

I casted my gaze in the same direction and my heart started pounding rapidly against my chest. I heard a gasp so intense that it sounded like it was hard for the person to breathe.

"Safi...Safiya," Elisa screamed as she beat a hasty pace down the front steps. The woman was so shaken, she fell down the last few stairs, but got back up and sprinted toward Lilith.

All but forgetting about his father and uncle, Dafari took off after his wife, racing toward their daughter.

CHAPTER 33
OCTAVIAN

Something was wrong. That was painfully obvious as Lilith started waving her hands frantically, yelling words that couldn't be heard over the thunder and the wind. The trees lining the yard seemed to quake with trembling that had nothing to do with the rumble overhead as the leaves and branches swayed back and forth angrily.

"Run! Run! Go back!" Aunt Lilith shouted, getting closer and waving her hands wildly as she, Safiya, and Attalah ran at breakneck speed back in our direction.

Like the Red Sea, the trees parted and out came a legion of demons—Sirens, vampires, were-demons, Shifters on ground and on the backs of winged beasts with skeletal faces — and they moved fast!

"Spread out," Father yelled then called his dark matter sword to him. "And be mindful of the Shifters! They can become any manner of animal or demon at will!"

Uncle Gabriel sprinted in the opposite direction, taking flight as winged riders came from the other side. Uncle Uriel was right behind him, tackling a beast midflight, ripping its wings from its back then twisting the horse's neck so far around that it was backwards.

On the ground, Uncle Raphael was on the back of a were-demon. With its unhinged jaws in his clutches, the medicine man used brute force to rip the animal's jaws from its face. The beast fell limp, collapsing to the ground. It was safe to say, he still had his supernatural strength.

Before I could react, a Shifter attacked me from behind. Its meaty hands gripped my neck, trying to lift me from the ground. I swung my body to the left, jamming my elbow into its midsection forcing it to release me.

Immediately it launched my way again. I sidestepped it, slammed its head down into the dirt, then punched at the base of its neck. Hearing its spine crack, I smiled wickedly. My palms itched and burned. Head rang as if someone had placed a bell inside my skull, but the angrier I became, the more euphoria rushed through my veins.

I heard my brother's angry growl and knew he had gone full battle bulk based on the shiver that ran through me. His power flux induced mine, and his adrenaline had spiked to the point that he was fighting like it was life or death—and technically it was, but this was different. He kept Elisa in his line of vision. When she moved, he moved. If she pivoted right, so did he. When a were-demon went airborne to get to Elisa, Dafari grabbed its hindlegs, slamming it back down to the ground.

"Dorcas! Mimzi!" he bellowed.

Seconds later, the hellhounds came bounding from the shadows, tearing into demons like wild, rabid animals.

The winds picked up, causing the trees to violently snap in half then uproot.

Out of my peripheral I saw Elisa slide through Dafari's legs, grab a vampire by its manhood just as fire engulfed her entire fist. She twisted and yank down causing the vamp to howl in pain. When the being swiped at her, she ducked her head, laid her palm flat to the ground and I watched as roots of fallen trees slam through the vampire's heart. Its ashes landed at her feet.

Loud sirens went off, coming from the heart of the town.

THE RECKONING & THE REAPER

In the distance, I noticed a funnel cloud touching down. Standing still, I took note of how wide and dense the cloud seemed to be.

Tasmin rushed to my side, hands jutting out to stop a female rider from crashing into me. She sent the being and its horse flying across the yard.

"Get away from him," she then snarled as another Shifter jumped on my back.

Tasmin slammed her hands together and it went hurling, crashing into the same tree Uncle had thrown my father against earlier. She was pissed. The whites of her eyes red with fury, mouth set in a hard scowl.

She and I were now surrounded, not able to see what was going on with the others, but we still heard the fight. More and more Shifters, were-demons, and even vampires came rushing from the dense forest.

In a Matrix-like move, my woman dodged a flaming spear thrown by a vamp, crouched low, then hopped back up, extending her hands forward. The spear redirected and slammed right into the chest cavity of the vamp, incinerating it on impact.

Even while going hand to hand with a were-demon, my manhood thumped with the need to sink deep into her and see if she could take that anger out on me. I was no better than a man who couldn't control himself. A dark voice in the back of my mind laughed manically.

"Octavian," Tasmin yelled, locs whipping in the wind. "Those are tornado sirens coming from the town," she yelled. "That means they've touched down somewhere close."

My eyes were on the funnel cloud. Shock made me recoil when a second...and then a third...and a fourth funnel cloud touched down on the ground. From where I stood, I could clearly see, they had Salix Pointe surrounded.

"Poppet, I don't think those are tornadoes in the sense

you think they are," I yelled, over the now howling winds. "Look," I said, pointing toward them. "They are not moving. It is as if they're waiting to be commanded to attack!"

The severed head of a horse and its rider came tumbling from the left of us. I looked to see Uncle Azazel using the body of the dead horse to beat another Shifter. His face was twisted with rage as he then grabbed a vamp, yanked her head to the side then sank his fangs so deep, he ripped out her whole throat.

My father was next to him, his sword beheading were-demons, vampires and Shifters alike. When Uncle went left, Father went right. His foot slammed into the chest of a hooded figure, sending it to the ground in a hard thud just before he shoved his sword down its throat.

My mother let out a sharp yelp of fear that sent my father racing in her direction. As I dodged dark energy charges from vamps, I saw Sirens were slashing at Mother, going for her stomach, but she was wearing a breastplate of righteousness. It had contoured to her upper body in such a way that even when their poisoned talons sliced across it, they could not injure her.

Mother was with child? Confusion swept through me and knocked me off my game. A hard kick sent me stumbling forward to the ground. Landing on my back, I saw a vamp get blasted by white light from my aunt's palm in my defense.

"Guard your six, Nephew," Aunt Lilith yelled, yanking me back to my feet, and then she was gone, running toward Mother who was still battling Sirens.

My aunt's locs hissed while attacking, elongating to accommodate their defense of their master. While Aunt Lilith drew symbols in the air, her locs whipped left and right, eviscerating any enemy in their paths.

Attalah was hot on her heels, her scythe working overtime. She sliced and diced her way through were-demons, slicing one's stomach open as it flew at her.

I hadn't seen Safiya fighting but judging by the blood and gore decorating her clothes, my niece had been kicking arse. Running to the middle of the melee, she took a deep breath and let out an angry yell. Demonic bodies went scattering, the force of her scream jettisoning them out of her path. She was beautiful in her father's image. Battle bulked to three times her normal size; her appearance was menacing. Jagged fangs lowered inch by deadly inch. Her already long, black nails took on an even deadlier curve. Braids extended down to her backside. Her blood red eyes sunk into an oversized skull, and in her hands were rope darts— long inches of ropes with Mabo throwing knives similar to her father's. She expertly used her weapons as if they were extensions of her hands. She tossed one forward, her aim precise as it impaled a winged rider in its right eye. Safiya yanked it from the back of its horse.

"Dorcas, Mimzi," she called to the hellhounds.

They came charging, jaws locking into the demon, head shaking aggressively from side-to-side as they tore it limb from limb.

The momentary distraction gave another winged rider the opening to snatch up Tasmin. Seeing red, I felt my body go into full battle mode. Instantly my wings unfurled. With a hard snap, I took to the skies, circled under then around the beast until I was in its direct line of vision. Bec-de-corbin in hand, I brought it down hard, directly in the center of the rider's head. He and his horse went plummeting to the ground. Swan-diving, my wings expanded and grabbed Tasmin, yanking her from the air just as her body almost slammed into the ground.

Taking flight on a low pattern, I shot through the forest, dodging tree branches while holding Tasmin protectively against my chest. My shirt was now gone, ripping away from my body as soon as I bulked. The cold and rainy wind pelted against my bare skin like Cat o'nine tails.

Taking a sharp right, I dipped in and out of the trees in a maze, forcing the wind chasing me to have to re-strategize its follow pattern. I flew just above the canopy, trying to see if the supercells had moved.

They had.

They were now closer to the town, inching forward in an intimidation tactic I could only assume. What better way to frighten your opponent than to take your time moving in, forcing us to wait for a fight we weren't even sure we could win.

Just then, a set of red glowing eyes appeared in the shadows of the dense foliage. As the being came closer, the intense anger in his eyes magnified. When he finally broke through the trees, it was like staring at a younger, angrier version of my brother. My nephew's long locs hung down to his waist, and while his dark skin was smooth and blemish free, the white scar decorating his right eye was startling. It went all the way up to his scalp and disappeared into one long loc, which had turned snow white.

As he emerged from the shadows, his warrior's body moved with easy grace. The shadow of his beard made the similarity in looks to his father even more uncanny. He, too, was just as powerfully built as the rest of us. He looked tough, mean, and sinewy. While he had always been a little cocksure of himself, his aura was different. Already bulked to battle proportions, Zafer was malicious in his attacks, easily ripping the wings and limbs from demon bodies.

He was a majestic, but terrifying being. Eyes blazing with a blood red glow, fangs fully extended. The angrier he got, the longer the wings on the backs of his arms and shoulders became. Grabbing one winged rider by its jaw, he forced its deformed mouth open, shoved his hand down its throat and came away with entrails.

Safiya and Attalah came running from his left, with my daughter yanking a handful of wings from Zafer's back. She tossed them in Safiya's direction who then shot white hot tendrils of energy from her palms, sending the feathers chasing after demonic entities. Zafer's wings sliced through the vampires, paralyzing some while completely ripping through others. Attalah yelled for her scythe, and I watched her behead the paralyzed beings.

I was so focused on trying to assess the situation that when something that felt like pure electricity slammed squarely in the middle of my back, I went crashing down through the trees. Thick branches cut, scraped, and slammed into arms, back, legs, and thighs.

I tightened my hold on Tasmin, ducking my head into my wings and gritting my teeth. Blood rushed to my ears, my heart pumping into overdrive. Nutrient rich blood raced throughout my body, strengthening its ability to protect me as my fight or flight instincts kicked in. Now I could sustain any surface wound and not bleed to death. All functions of my body that didn't weren't needed for my survival shut down, instantly transforming me into my true form.

I crashed into the front yard of my brother's home, landing on my back to take the brunt of the fall. As soon as we touched land, I unfurled, allowing Tasmin to get up first then I sprang to my feet. A look of fear and awe in my woman's eyes, she jumped backward, almost confusing me with her reaction.

"Get down, Mommy," Attalah yelled as she raced forward, tackling a battle bulked vampire who had aimed his poisoned filled talons at Tasmin's back.

With a rage untethered by fear, I ran with supernatural speed, slamming into the undead being full force. As his screech of pain rent the air, I punched my fist into his chest, slamming through bone to snatch his heart. His limp body hit the ground.

Not taking time to savor the victory, I turned to search for Tasmin and Attalah just in time to see an angry Tasmin jut her hand toward a thick tree branch that was among the flying debris. Slapping both her hands together, she then shoved them forward, knocking down every demon that had surrounded Attalah.

Rushing to stand back-to-back with our daughter who had gotten to her feet, Tasmin was fluid in her motions, reminding me that she was indeed back to her full, reawakened self. While she used her hands to throw everything, including a kitchen sink, at incoming demons, she turned her head to the left, her eyes searching for something. As if she and Mother Earth were one, a big oak tree went sailing in the wind. Tasmin's mind locked on to it, then sent it in a wicked spiraled throw, sending vamps scattering like bowling pins.

I want her. Right now, echoed in my head, followed by a lecherous chuckle.

I was no better than Uncle Azazel. My incubus outright guffawed at that. I ran toward my family.

Utter and complete chaos surrounded us but as I looked at my wife and daughter, a sense of reverence overtook me. Both took defensive stances, Tasmin not hesitating to use her powers to protect them both, while Attalah used her scythe with an agility that showed her skill as a reaper.

My moment of solace was interrupted, and as lightning danced across the dark clouds, the outline of a horseman appeared in each funnel.

I felt time and my heart stop. In the middle of our family drama, Heaven and Hell had decided there was no time like the present to kick off the beginning of Armageddon.

CHAPTER 34
TASMIN

My eyes tracked in the direction Octavian was looking. What they landed on caused me to stare in horror, seeing something that I had only read about in books, but instantly knew who the beings were. Roaring through the sky were four horses, all engulfed in flames matching the color of its coat, four distinct riders on their backs...The Four Horsemen of the Apocalypse.

Catching my attention first was the brown-skinned Horseman of Conquest. Sitting atop her white horse, her golden crown, bow, and neck-to-toe armor lit up the dark, foreboding sky. Her thick braids swayed behind her with each stride of her equine companion. To her left was the completely bald Horseman of War. His red skin tone would have made it appear that he and his horse were one, save for his dark gray armor. He held his massive black energy sword high, ready for battle.

On the other side of War, the emaciated Horseman of Famine held the reins of his black horse in one hand, his spear with balanced scales on top in the other. Black armor protected his sallow-skinned body. Last, but certainly not least, was a pale horse, its rider a fiery skeleton with a feminine frame dressed in silver armor and carrying a flaming scythe, one twice as big as Attalah's...the Horseman of Death.

We watched as they separated, flying in different directions, cutting the rest of the family off from us. Death trained on Attalah. Octavian, protective as ever, swooped in, landing to her right, while I stood firmly to her left. I needed to keep my head in the game because our lives depended on it. But my thoughts were distracted by Octavian's...evolution.

Months ago, when I was unceremoniously introduced to his celestial form, I thought it was one of the scariest things I had ever seen. A being of pure light energy with an oversized lion's head, seven eyes, and massive white wings. It was enough to make anyone run for the hills...and I did. But now, looking at the man I loved...his angelic self was far less frightful in comparison to whatever he had become.

Octavian's hybrid appearance caught me completely off guard, his anatomy seeming to be in a constant state of flux, shifting from light to dark. His seven-eyed lion's head alternated with that of a demon; three horns, two on either side of his head, one smack dab in the middle, and huge jagged fangs protruding from his mouth.

His angelic body reflected that of a human, while his demonic one...razor sharp talons replaced his well-manicured fingernails; his incubus' skin leather-like as opposed to his butter-smooth human skin. Even his wings, which were considerably larger with his incubus' emergence, had changed considerably, now having an equal mix of white and black feathers. His change was frightening and at the same time...fascinating.

"Baby, are you okay?" I asked, quickly eyeing the numerous cuts and scraps on his body.

"I will heal, my love. Right now we need to focus on Izrail's minion."

Death's horse had landed a few feet away, while its rider glared at us...at least I think she was. It was hard to tell when she had nothing but flaming eye sockets. The horse whinnied then rapped one of its front hooves on the ground several times, as if preparing to charge.

"Attalah Jerrod, I have a bone to pick with you," came from Death, pointing her scythe in Attalah's direction.

Had the situation been less dire, I would have found that statement amusing considering Death was a burning bag of bones.

"You have deserted your post and must suffer the consequences for your actions."

Our daughter stepped forward defiantly. "I had very good reasons for what I did, and I would do it again it if meant saving the people I love. You know what that's like, don't you, Death? You always do anything your daddy requests of you, whether it's right or wrong."

"Her daddy?" I asked of Octavian.

"Yes, Poppet, Death is the daughter of Uncle Morningstar and Sin."

"So Death is—"

"My cousin," Octavian and Attalah said in unison.

"Gee, great." Just when I thought the supernatural family tree couldn't get any more messed up.

"Let's get this over with, dear cousin," Attalah said, positioning herself, preparing for battle, her scythe held in front of her.

Octavian quickly jumped in front of her, blocking her way. "Have you lost your mind?" he demanded, his form still shifting between angel and demon. However, I noticed the angrier he got, the more his incubus side took hold.

Attalah tilted her head to the side, stared at Octavian curiously for a few seconds before saying, "Daddy, you really need to get a handle on your emotions. Look, I appreciate your paternal need to keep me safe, but have you forgotten that I am a Reaper? I…am…Death."

"You may be Death, but that," he said pointing sharply in the Horseman's direction, "is a bigger Death. As leader of the Horsemen, her father has bestowed upon her immeasurable power. And like you said, she will do anything Uncle Morningstar asks of her. That includes killing you. I will not allow that to happen. I watched you die once; I will not do it again."

Attalah's resolve was very much like mine. That resolve, hers and mine, is what got us killed in 1855.

I mimicked Octavian, standing in front of our daughter. "Baby girl, if what your father says is true, and I'm sure it is, while I have all faith in you as a warrior, it sounds like your powers and Death's are not…equal, like this is going to be an unfair fight."

"Daddy, I am so sorry for the trauma you endured after Mommy and I were killed. I can't begin to imagine what you went through. But I am not your little girl anymore. I have powers of my own, some you haven't even seen yet." Attalah then took my hands in hers. "Mommy, you and I are cut from the same cloth, so I know you understand where I'm coming from. I must do this myself. I can do this."

Death cleared her throat, shifting on her horse impatiently. "I have my orders. Attalah, you can surrender yourself peacefully to me now or…not. Choose."

Squeezing my only child's hand reassuringly, I said, "Do what you have to do. Octavian and I will be right here, right, Babe?" I looked at Octavian pleadingly.

He was breathing hard, his emotions on complete overdrive. "Everything within me wants to pick you up, take you through the shadows and keep you there, away from harm… but I realize you are no longer the same young woman who died before me all those years ago. I will…step aside and let you handle this, but, like your mother said, we will be right here."

THE RECKONING & THE REAPER

I grabbed Octavian's forearm, gently nudging him to back away. Once he did, Death leapt from her horse, commanding it to back up. She then raised her scythe above her head, whirling it three times in a circular clockwise direction. Suddenly, a ring of flames surrounded her and Attalah.

Stepping further into the circle, Death continued, "You should have known it would come to this, Cousin."

Attalah, taking a battle stance replied, "Yes, well, I knew Granduncle Morningstar would have his knickers in a knot after I abandoned my post."

"You know you can't win. Give up now and save yourself...and your parents the embarrassment." Death gazed in Octavian and my direction.

"I know no such thing. Now, are we going to fight, or are you going to continue to run that fire ring you call a mouth?"

I smiled inwardly. My daughter was well-versed in the art of sarcasm. She was baiting Death, and it worked. Death let out a roar, charging Attalah. She deftly moved out of the way, and while Death was off balance, landed a sharp blow to the back of her head with the snath end of her scythe, knocking her to the ground. Quickly recovering, Death stood up, twirled her scythe like a majorette's baton, moved along the periphery of the fire ring.

Running into the center of the circle at same time, their scythes met. There they stood, eye-to-eye, each warrior pushing back on the other, until they both relented, backing up slightly. Death swung for Attalah's face, which she avoided by ducking. Attalah then aimed for Death's chest, her weapon deflecting off the snath of Death's weapon.

They battled hard, one fighting for her life, the other, her father's approval. Death feinted an overhead strike, causing Attalah to react. When Attalah brought her scythe up over her head, Death changed course, bringing her weapon around, the blade end scoring Attalah's ribs. She sprang backwards, one hand reaching to cover her now-bleeding wound. Instinctively, Octavian and I started to run towards her, but she immediately threw up a hand, stopping us in our tracks.

"Stay back," she commanded. "I've got this."

I wanted to have faith in Attalah, but I wasn't so sure. I grabbed Octavian's hand, holding it tightly. I told myself it was to keep him from interfering, but deep down, I knew it was to prevent me from doing the same.

"I could have skewered you, Cousin, but I still want to give you the opportunity to submit."

Attalah's eyes became thin slits, determination written on her face. "Never," she proclaimed.

"Oh, well, I tried."

Death didn't give Attalah a chance to respond, instead rapidly slashing and stabbing with her scythe, Attalah having to go on the defensive. Death would strike, Attalah would block or parry, doing her best to ignore the pain I knew she was feeling. Unfortunately, Death's offensive moves forced Attalah backwards, closer to the ring of fire. She looked back, saw how close she was to getting scotched.

Fear was a great motivator, and, although I was sure she'd never admit it out loud, Attalah was scared witless. I was guessing she had a much-needed epinephrine boost, because she leapt into the air, maneuvering herself to land behind her cousin. Dropping to the ground in one swift motion, she swung one leg in a semi-circle, kicking Death's feet from under her, causing her to land hard.

Not wasting any time, while Death was down, Attalah rapidly drew something into the soft, damp earth with the blade end of her scythe. Slamming her hand down over the drawing, she shouted, "Ancestors far and near, my entreaty I ask that you hear. From the earth this watery shrub will grow, aiding me to defeat my foe."

After she recited those words, I instantly knew what Attalah was up to. I prayed her plan would work. Springing to their feet at the same time, Attalah and Death squared up, positioning themselves for the next round. Within seconds, numerous plants sprouted up within the blazing arena, surrounding the combatants. Eyeing the red flowers, I realized they were scarlet swamp hibiscus. While the plant was indigenous to the Southeastern United States, it usually didn't grow in cold temperatures. However, Attalah's magick and the recent copious rains changed those conditions in her favor.

"Well isn't this a cute parlor trick," Death remarked, then chuckled. A pretty flower garden, Cousin?"

Attalah, still in a defensive posture, smirked. "They're not just for the aesthetics, Cousin." Aggressively waving her scythe back and forth, she drove Death to defend herself. But Attalah wasn't attacking to fight, she was doing it to distract. "You see, my dear Death," she spoke while swinging her weapon, "this land is currently saturated with water, thanks to Granduncle Izrail. Omi!" Attalah yelled.

Too late, Death realized what was happening. When Attalah spoke the Yoruba word for water, copious amounts of the fluid shot out from the flowers' stigma, soaking the adversaries. The water had no effect on Attalah, but Death on the other hand...

"While I can't kill you, I can weaken you." Attalah watched as the life fluid doused the daughter of Morningstar, extinguishing her flames, silver armor her only layer of protection.

"How can this be?" Death asked in astonishment.

"It's like this," Attalah started, still showering Death, "Your strength and damn-near invulnerability derive from your supernatural flames, and normal water has no effect on you, but water infused with magick...that's something different altogether. My spell, magick. My ancestors who I called upon, magick. And let's not forget this land we stand on. Magick runs through it, under it, and around it. We are surrounded by magick, Cousin. Now, we can continue fighting, but since you're not at full strength, I think we both know how this will end."

"Father will not be pleased," Death spat, and within seconds, she, her steed, and the ring of fire were gone.

Octavian and I rushed to Attalah, first hugging her then giving her a onceover. I checked her wound, healing it completely.

"Baby girl, are you okay?" I asked, hugging her again.

"Yes, Mommy, I'm fine and thankful to our Ancestors… and for my Reaper teachings."

"So that's how you knew what do in order to neutralize Death," I replied, in awe of my child.

"Yes, we learned all about the Four Horsemen and their vulnerabilities at the Reaper Academy. Morningstar expected blind loyalty from everyone, never thinking that information would be used against them."

"That's one Horseman down, but Death is correct," Octavian spoke, gravity in his tone. "Both uncles, Morningstar and Izrail will be furious. Izrail is already smarting from Attalah's escape from his clutches. Now that she's defeated the Horseman of Death, his best warrior, with inside information…he will continue to seek retribution for your betrayal, and he's worse than all his Horsemen put together. So is Morningstar."

I took in Octavian words, knowing that this was but one small victory in a seemingly insurmountable war. As if we didn't already have enough to deal with. While Attalah tussled with Death, the rest of the conflict shifted to the back of Dafari and Elisa's property, the sounds of combat ringing through the air. The three of us ran in the direction of the fray. What we saw stopped us in our tracks. Beings from both Heaven and Hell were locked in battle, the carnage massive.

Azazel was surrounded by battle angels who had split the skies and came charging right for him. Sometimes, it was easy to forget that there was still a hefty bounty on his head as well. Black charges of power pulsated from his palms as he shot them at his opponents. Chakrams in hand, he countered moves then went on counterattacks. His round, discus-like blades injuring angels and demons fatally.

Octavian was the first to speak. "All Hell has definitely broken loose."

The wind had kicked up several notches, and a cold, hard rain had begun to fall, no doubt Izrail's doing. I quickly surveyed the scene, taking note of where family and friends were. The Merry Widows, along with my parents and Rafael, were fighting a new contingent from Hell consisting of hellhounds, imps, and ifrits. As for the Celestials, Eset, Michael, Lilith, Gabriel, and Uriel were locked in battle with the three remaining Horsemen, as well as several of Izrail's angel forces. It reminded me of a WWE free-for-all, with angelic beings fighting each other, as well as their enemies from Hell.

My eyes scanned the area, spotting Dafari and Elisa. Sirens were going after Elisa just as hard as they went after Eset, trying to slice at her stomach. Dafari was fighting with a vigor unmatched. His angelic form was nowhere in sight. Full demonology had taken residence. Dafari's body had grown massive in size, protecting Elisa. Hand-to-hand combat met magick in its purest form as she grabbed hold of a lightning bolt when it touched land. She then launched it toward a group of battle angels, electrocuting them where they stood.

"We need to get in there," I said. "Attalah, you know how to weaken the other Horsemen. Get that information to the others. The high-archs should already know how to battle their kin."

"What about you?" Octavian queried.

Eyeing my niece and nephew, I watched as Safiya and Zafer worked in tandem, he using his brute strength to tear an attacker to pieces with his bare hands, his sister feeding off his sheer will to dispatch an ifrit with her magick. Dafari and Elisa were cut off and couldn't get to them, but I could.

I stood back-to-back with my nephew and niece, while Dorcas and Mimzi positioned themselves directly in front of Safiya as she called out to the town's animals.

"Guys we have to get rid of this wave of attackers," I yelled.

"Already on it, Auntie," said Safiya, then began shouting over the roar of the howling winds. "Fierce creatures of Salix Pointe, of thee I humbly implore. I beseech you to use your massive fighting spirits, so that order may be restored. Respectfully I ask that you hear my plea, and join with us to set this town free!"

In the distance came barks and howls. Out through a grove of trees charged a band of coyotes, skulk of red foxes, and clutter of bobcats. They encircled us three times then spread out, claws and teeth tearing into the first thing they could get their paws on, making short work of the hellhounds and imps.

"Safiya," I called at the top of my lungs, the sounds of battle and harsh weather making speaking at normal volume almost impossible, "the ifrits can only be defeated by magick. I know you can tap into Zafer's powers, but what about your mom's?"

"I-I don't know," she said, still controlling the animals she called on for help. "I've never attempted it before, but tell me what you need, and I'll try."

"See if you can control this rainwater in any way. If you

can, form some waterspouts." I then turned to Zafer. "Nephew, we need Michael now."

He simply nodded then flew off. I watched as Safiya concentrated, holding off the ifrits as best I could with fire balls, while Dorcas and Mimzi fought off everything else. Safiya's look of determination turned to a smile when several funnels of water formed in front of her.

"Great job, Safiya," I remarked encouragingly. "Now hold them steady."

Zafer landed near us just in time to slice and dice an arrow-wielding angel with his wings, blood and guts splattering everywhere. The perverse look of satisfaction on my nephew's face disturbed me.

Michael glided to a stop between me and Safiya. "We need holy water and hell fire," I yelled, drawing rocks and toppled trees towards me.

Michael quickly infused Safiya's water creations, and my debris then hurried off to rejoin the aerial assault.

"Douse the ifrits, Safiya," I commanded.

Working together, my niece drenched the ifrits closest to her while I hit the ones near me with everything I had, the fiery debris effectively destroying them all.

Although it was probably temporary, the high-archs, along with Lilith and Attalah, had made the remaining three Horsemen retreat back to the funnel clouds. On the ground, the coven and Rafael had defeated whatever hellhounds and ifrits remained.

Octavian and Zafer…both appeared to be in what could only be described as a berserker-type rage, slaughtering any angel who had been foolish enough to stick around. They even worked together, Zafer holding the final attacker while Octavian used his jagged talons to snatch its organs from its body. What caught my eye was the look of horror on both Eset and Michael's faces, remembering they had not seen

Octavian in battle form since, well, since they tried to kill me and Elisa. If we all lived through this, I was sure Octavian and his parents would be having a serious discussion.

"Both sides are retreating," Safiya shouted.

Scanning the area, I realized she was right. All that was left around us was the carnage of the dead, body parts, and other fallen debris.

"Everyone okay?" Martha asked as we assembled.

Various yesses came from our ragtag band of warriors.

"They're more still coming!" Attalah pointed at the skies. "Do not get comfortable. The second wave will be harder to defeat."

"We really should get to more sacred ground," I heard Uriel say this time. "The Horsemen will be back and this time I suspect Izrail and Morningstar will lead the charge."

"Heaven and Hell working together?" I heard Martha ask.

"Why are you so surprised? Its rider's name was Death and Hades follows close behind. Of course they work together," Azazel snarled as he stalked toward the forest.

"Father," Dafari called. "Where are you going?"

"To regroup," was all he said as he disappeared into the trees.

CHAPTER 35
AZAZEL

My wounds from the fight with Michael and the ensuing battle smarted in the worst way. While I knew they would take time to heal, I took it upon myself to fix the rest of my appearance. Walking deeper into the forest, I smoothed down my hair, placing it once again into a neat ponytail. Materializing clothing befitting my station, I was now dressed in an haute couture black suit, with a blood red silk shirt, and expensive Italian loafers.

Although my facial scars were still visible, I cloaked them from public view. I didn't want the person I was going to visit to see them. I made haste getting to my destination, knowing time was not on my side.

One minute Michael and I were trying to tear one another apart, the next we were fighting side by side to protect those we loved. Being thrown into battle in the middle of a family quarrel wasn't how I saw my day going, but alas…

Thanks to my ex-wife, my brother and I probably hated one another more than ever. The affair on the astral plane had only happened a few times here and there. She would call out to me in her dreams, and even with all the bad blood between us, I would oblige. It was in my nature to come when she summoned me. It had been something that only she and I had known about…until now.

It stopped shortly after Eset and Michael attempted to kill the witches the night of the Halloween jubilee at the home of the insipid mayor and his vapid wife. And that was only because Eset had to be punished for failing to kill the witches. I couldn't front and say I hadn't worried about her during that time. Sometimes she would call out to me for any kind of relief from her torture, but I couldn't help her where she was and neither could Michael.

Then Eve had reared her ugly head and she, along with her minion Madame Marie Delphine Laurie, had been wreaking havoc all over Salix Pointe. Eset and Michael had been at odds after he decided that it was in their best interest to work with Tasmin and Elisa to defeat the madame and her mistress.

The contention between them had gotten worse after he voiced his respect and admiration for them after he fought with them side-by-side against Eve. For some reason, she still had a severe hatred for Elisa and Tasmin.

"First my sons, now my husband," she said, as I wined and dined her at the top of the Eiffel Tower in her dream. It was right after she had been released from the Second Level of Heaven. Ironically, it was one of her favorite places to visit when we were together. "What is so special about them?"

"Perhaps you should ask your sons," I suggested, standing up from my chair, walking to stand in front of her. "In the meantime, Eset," I began, holding out my hand to her, "I'm sure you didn't request my presence to talk about the witches, Dafari, Octavian, and definitely not Michael."

She took my hand, and as she stood, I stepped back slightly, taking in her rich chocolate skin, long braids, and the way her dress hugged every delectable curve of her toned body.

"I'm sorry, Azazel. No, that is not why I called out to you. Actually, I don't really know why I reached out. It's just

that...Michael and I...we haven't been in synch for some time, and...I just need—"

I placed a finger over her lips. "Say no more."

I took her mouth, tasted the sweet red wine she had imbibed a few minutes before. My fingers traced lightly down her spine, eliciting a moan from her. I pushed the limit further, sliding my hands down to her full, round derriere, pulled her body flush with mine.

I broke our passionate kiss long enough to ask, "Eset, are you sure this is what you want...what you need?"

Her only response was to wrap her arms around my neck, kissing me as deeply as I had kissed her. I reached over, knocking everything off the table. Before picking her up to place her on it, with just a thought, I shed our clothing. Her body was so...so...ready. Sitting her on the table, I slid inside her. Her tight wetness was familiar; it felt like...home.

And so it went; Eset summoning me, and me answering her call. I happily fulfilled her every need, her every desire. I was my ex-wife's dream side piece.

I had to wonder how long she had known she was with child, his child. I didn't know why, but I felt betrayed. Ironic since I was technically having sex with a married woman, even if it was in the dream world. Add that to my other... indulgences and it would seem I was being hypocritical.

That was neither here nor there. My disloyal ex be damned, I had somewhere I needed to be and ever precious cargo to protect. Heaven and Hell weren't the only ones with an agenda.

CHAPTER 36
ELISA

The coven and the celestials had retreated to the basement of the bookstore, regrouping. The town had been torn to shreds it seemed. The storm had knocked out power, uprooted trees, and damaged many of the buildings around town. The winds had been so strong it had tossed vehicles and small dwellings all over the place. While Rufus was upstairs trying to whip up mugs of tea, I couldn't stop hugging my children.

My injuries…the bumps and bruises from the battle weakened me, but from somewhere, I found the strength to stand strong in front of my children. My babies were grown, but still my babies, and I hadn't seen them in lifetimes. It took a few minutes for me to pull myself together. I was so overwhelmed with emotions that I could barely find my words. As carnage lay all around us, I could only focus on the fact that my children were here.

"He found me. He followed me," she said breathlessly as she paced. "Out of all my lifetimes, Lucifer has never been able to trace me, but now?" Lilith was stressed as she paced the floor. "I'd safely hidden Safiya away in the least likely place anyone or anything would look for her."

"Which was?" Eset asked, her breathing erratic.

"Purgatory."

"Say what?" came from a still very angry Dafari.

I wanted to tell him that my womb felt as if it was on fire but wasn't sure if it was because of nerves or internal injury.

"Yes. I figured if I hid her amongst other souls looking for redemption only for a short time, who would be the wiser, especially with all going on, but he found me. That two-faced, slithering bastard found me!" Lilith's eyes were wide as saucers and for the first time, I saw apprehension and maybe fear.

Tasmin casted a gaze in my direction. *Why does she seem so terrified?* She shot to me mentally.

Other than the obvious, I don't know, but should we be concerned? What does this mean?

Tasmin shook her head, giving me a slight shrug.

"The Coven...on the other side," Lilith cried, looking from me to Tasmin. "They're gone and we don't know where." Turning to her celestial siblings, she said, "Heaven is in turmoil. There is a literal war."

Tasmin walked over to Lilith, laying a hand on her shoulder. "What do you mean?"

"They are no longer on the Third Level of Heaven. Their sanctuary has been ripped apart, torn asunder and they're gone!"

Eset's face contorted and when she swayed on her feet, Michael hoisted her up. "How did you get Safiya if—"

Safiya stood next to me, squeezing my hand on one side while Dafari flanked both of us. "When the fighting started, some of the souls hid me amongst their bosoms. Some were family from other lives they said. As soon as Grandaunt Lilith and Attalah came through the veil, they shoved us back through it. By then I saw creatures and beings I'd never lain eyes on before and I've seen some shit, okay?"

"Granduncle Uriel had already told me to stay in the shadows of the trees. I'd been with him for some time by then, walking the streets of New York until he felt Granduncle Michael and Grandpops about to go at it. I watched the fight from shadows, but couldn't intervene," Zafer stated, his voice so low the bass of it thundered around the room. "Granduncle Uriel put some kind of prayer circle around me. I wasn't able to break it until the demons breached the veil."

"Demons breaching the veil is unheard of!" Attalah said, frowning. "Even I, as a reaper, have to go through certain protocols to bring souls into Heaven."

Lilith said, "Morningstar and Izrail have to be working together now."

"Is that what Azazel meant when he said Hades was coming behind Death?" Silas asked.

Jewel looked from her husband then back to Lilith. "Hades meaning Hell?"

"Yes," answered Raphael as he started bringing boxes of papers he'd written to the middle of the floor. "Will someone help me with these boxes, please?"

Silas and Jewel immediately jumped to the task.

Martha walked around the room drawing Adinkra symbols on the walls along with her sisters. They were in a zone and had been since we all got here. They hadn't said much, only mumbling prayers and spells.

"Does that mean...the Devil—quite literally—is going to show up?" Jewel asked as Silas took the box she was holding and placed it on the floor next to Raphael.

"Going to show up?" Raphael repeated. "If I know the man, the beast—he's already here. He's been here. Do you really think Morningstar has been sitting on his hands? Because I can assure you, he hasn't. He's more like Azazel than any of us care to admit."

Eset said, "Both are cunning and crafty and move pieces into place like skillful chess masters. Before the rest of us abandoned our posts, Michael and Gabriel had been tracing Morningstar's movements across the globe. That so-called oil spill was his first move. He opened a literal portal of Hell. A direct challenge and threat to our Father. But he also went after Zafer and Safiya—almost capturing her. A direct threat to us." She moved over to the window, tugging the curtain aside.

Sliding his hands in the pockets of his jeans, Silas frowned. "I'd like to hear more about Lucifer already being here…" He looked from Eset to Uncle Raphael. "Do you mean as in Salix Pointe?"

"Izrail is bringing the battle to Salix Pointe, a place which holds the epicenter of magick. That is confirmation alone that he not only knows we have Zafer and Safiya, but that he is also aware Morningstar is here as well," Raphael replied, thumbing through pages and pages of his handwritten words.

I turned to my daughter, needing to clarify a few things. "You know I'm happy to have you, your brother, and your cousin back home—all of our family, but…I have to say I'm confused by some of the things that have come to the light. How is that you all are already so well-acquainted?" I asked.

Lilith waved both her hands in the form of arch, and before us played a memory. A much younger Raphael knelt in a corner, drawing on a wall in a cave. "Long ago Raphael told me of his plan, and since our father had already betrayed me and my image, he didn't have to say much to convince me to help him. I've always been his accomplice in this. It registered with us as soon as all three children were conceived. He and I made a pact right then that their souls would never be recorded in the Book of Life. They couldn't because then his plan would have been exposed much sooner."

Raphael joined Lilith. Standing next to her, he too made shapes in the air and another memory formed. It showed Lilith standing in front of a tree, pulling at gold, white, and silver tendrils that looked like strings of fine thread. "I made sure that the familial line would always be the tie that bound us together. It's something that has never been done. I was able to intricately thread our soul ties, making sure that no matter where their souls landed upon death, we would all feel it first. It took a while to get the others on board, and Gabriel still thinks what I'm doing is betrayal."

"Clearly, he's changed his mind," said Silas, a bit sarcastically.

"I haven't. What my brother has done is the ultimate betrayal and he knows it. Just like he knew I would refuse to help him if he asked. He is our father's son." Gabriel's eyes were cold as he spoke. "As far as the children, once I got to know them, there was no way I could stand by and watch them suffer more than they already had."

"Raphael, may I ask how you were so sure your plan would work?" Mary Ann asked.

"I didn't think it would work at first, but when Dafari and Octavian first met the ladies, we all felt it. It was like a jolt to our hearts. We knew instantly that they had found the loves of their lives...however many lives there were to be."

"Raphael is an outstanding strategist. His ability to quickly assess a situation, develop a plan of action, and effectively implement it is remarkable. It's why even I was able to see his vision after I took the blinders off." As Uriel talked, he moved to stand on the opposite side of Lilith. "Things have been unbalanced for so long that many of us have forgotten..."

"*Her.*" Lilith stated plainly. "Say it. We've forgotten Her, and she is pissed. She has all right to be."

"Not all of us have forgotten Her," Michael snapped. "She abandoned us."

Lilith was across the room in seconds. "You don't know that! You're basing it all—"

Gabriel stepped in between the two, eyes ablaze with irritation. "We're not doing this here. We've had enough family squabbles today and I have had my limit!"

While Lilith looked fit to be tied, Eset stared at Michael as if she was now disappointed in him. Tasmin and I shared a look. She was just as confused as I was.

"Do you know what they are trying to do down here?" Raphael asked, looking pointedly at all his siblings. "They are forcing women to give birth even when they have no desire to be mothers. They are making it so that even if a woman's body rejects a pregnancy, she can still be persecuted."

"And prosecuted," Tasmin added.

The Angel of Healing flipped through the pages of paper in his hand as he walked to stand next to Uriel. "See here," he said pointing. "I've written down some of the ways in which what is going on in the heavens correlates with what is happening on earth. Our Mother has been erased from all biblical texts here."

"Yes, I know the history," Uriel said with urgency, hurrying Raphael along.

"Yes, but we were told that it was to protect Her and the power she possesses. We were told the reason Mother chose to walk away was so that man would never know the full extent of—"

"Pause," came Zafer's commanding voice. "You telling me there is a female equivalent to the Man Upstairs?"

"Of course there is," said every archangel in the room.

"Genesis chapter one attests to this," then said Uriel.

"But Raphael just said any mention of Her has been erased," Tasmin interjected.

Raphael nodded, flipping through more pages. "She has been, but that doesn't mean she isn't there... What many don't know is that Genesis chapter one details the courtship between the two. After all the creations including the animals, He said let *us* make man in *our* image. After *our* likeness. Not once did He say let me create man after my image, but in the rewritten text, in the very next verse, it's written as if he contradicts himself."

Pacing now, Uriel clasped his hands behind his back. "Yes, it says and then God created man in his image, as if he alone has the power to create life. Doesn't make sense, does it? This is what happens when your lot gets power hungry, they rewrite the scripture to fit whatever narrative they need."

"And because most people don't even read the Bible and just go off of what's been quoted to them, they never think to question the inconsistencies," Lilith added. "Look at me... I've been pretty much erased from the scriptures. I'm only mentioned once and not by name. They call me a monster. Say that I was a demon for refusing to bow to Adam. I was his equal! Why must I submit?" The last part came out on a harsh edge, showing her emotions were taking over.

"And then came Eve," said Eset, hand covering her stomach in the way pregnant women sometimes did when standing still.

Tasmin and I were so focused on the conversation that neither of us noticed Dafari and Octavian watching their mother.

Tasmin scoffed. "Another one of your family members who tried to kill us…"

"She's misunderstood," Lilith quipped, surprising everyone with her statement.

The room fell silent as all eyes turned to her.

"Misunderstood," Eset repeated, one brow raised. "Are you well, dear Sister-in-Law?"

Sighing, Lilith rubbed her head…before storming off upstairs.

"Let her go," said Uriel when Gabriel and Raphael called after her. "You know this is a sensitive, touchy subject for her."

"Mother, are you with child?" Octavian asked out the blue, catching me off guard.

He'd been so quiet, I almost forgot he was in the room.

"We will discuss that later, Son," Michael responded tensely. "Now is not the time."

"It's a simple yes or no, Father. The Sirens kept going for her womb while we battled. Is she or is she not with child?"

Michael got ready to say something, but Eset stopped him. "It's okay. They will find out sooner or later anyway," she replied softly, looking from one son to the other. "I am.".

"Is it my father's or Michael's?" Dafari asked.

The incredulous look that overtook Michael's features almost made me recoil. With the speed of light, he was face-to-face with Dafari. "I don't give a damn what is happening between your mother and I, don't you ever call the paternity of a child she is carrying into question."

Zafer bristled and moved to stand next to his father. Dafari didn't back down, but it was Octavian who spoke up. "Is it not a fair question? You and Uncle were damn near ripping the other's heads off before—"

"I.Do.Not.Care!" thundered Michael, now whipping around to face his son, his eyes now blazing furnaces. Head so close to Octavian's it looked as if he was about to headbutt him.

Attalah and Safiya pulled Tasmin and I back in an effort to protect us, I supposed, but I was too shocked to even say anything. Gabriel, Uriel and Raphael moved in, forming a semi-circle around the trio with Zafer bringing up the rear.

"That is your mother, and you will, at all times, respect her. She did what she did, but that is between she and I. Do not dare ever fix your mouths to think you can call her to task for what goes on behind our closed doors! You want to speak with her about the way she treats you as your mother? Fine," he snapped, looking from Octavian to Dafari. "But that is the only line either of you are to ever cross in my presence or even when I'm not around. Hold your damn tongues! Do I make myself clear?"

The tension around the room was so thick, it would be felt as the hives raised on my skin, cut with a knife, and tasted on the back of my tongue. Michael was enraged. While neither Dafari nor Octavian responded verbally, they also didn't back away from his fury.

"Dafari. Octavian. Why don't you two take a leave until cooler heads prevail," came from the shadows. Azazel stepped through, the fury in his eyes only matched by the blaze in Michael's. "You may not like his delivery, but Michael is correct. You two have no right to speak to your mother in such a way. Tasmin…Elisa…take your husbands to the café until they cool off. Perhaps the battle has made them take leave of their senses, but just for the record, it is Michael's child she carries, eh? Thank God for small favors and all that," he finished on a familiar sarcastic note.

Neither Dafari nor Octavian said anything else. They turned and headed up the stairs.

CHAPTER 37
DAFARI

"So you guys have been battling for this place since Halloween?" Zafer asked, his eyes serious, but I could tell he was trying to cut the tension.

We'd been at the café for at least thirty minutes, and while the bookstore was still standing, the café had suffered great damage. We'd picked up debris, overturned tables and chairs, and swept up broken glass. All of us moving by rote, anxious about when the next wave would reveal itself.

Neither Octavian nor I wanted to address what had just happened in the basement of The Book Nook. Both of us feeling a twinge of guilt about the whole thing. It was a difficult position to be in, but just as Uncle had stated in so many words, their business was none of our concern.

"We had no idea how much magick this place held before finding out we were witches," Elisa said. "Your aunt didn't even live here before then." She picked up a trash bag and then sighed as she looked around at the damage to her café. "I'm going to take this to the back and check to see what the damage to the pantry and storage looks like."

As she turned and headed to the back, I felt the anxiety riding her like waves. I knew seeing her café in such disrepair saddened her.

"Morningstar and Izrail have chased us all through the

Exchange," Safiya said, bringing my attention back to the conversation at hand.

Zafer stood on the east wall, legs spread shoulder width apart, arms folded across his chest. "My connections do a good job of helping us to hide, but the Exchange is a lawless land."

"Your connections?" I questioned my son, something about the way he said it piquing my interest.

"I think it would be best if we discussed that at another time," he said coolly. "Just know, I did and do what needs to be done to keep my sister and I well-protected."

Octavian and I glanced at one another before turning back to Zafer. He didn't look away. There was no cowardness in my son, and the father in me was proud of that. Still…in the back of my mind, I wondered what he had gotten up to in our time apart. I took note of the bottom row of gold teeth, the watch, the ring, his style of dress and way he carried himself. He had "the streets" written all over him. Another thing we would discuss was the white scar that decorated his right eye.

"Attalah, is there anything about Izrail that can help us when he decides to show up?" Tasmin asked.

"He's jingoistic that's for sure," my niece said as she moved around, helping Elisa grab ingredients. "He is belligerent in his pursuit of ensuring his father's edicts are upheld. Being under his command left no room for error. The fact that I have free will chaps his arse."

"Does he have any weaknesses?" Octavian asked.

"To be completely honest with you, Daddy…I don't think so."

"You'd be better asking Grandpops," Zafer cut in. "He tends to keep his ear to the streets. And he would know his brother better than we would."

"Oh, my gosh, how did you get in here?" from Elisa made the hairs on the back of my neck stand.

I didn't know who she was talking to, but I didn't wait to find out. Zafer took off before I could. The broom dropped to the floor as I ran through the double doors, Octavian hot on my heels. Tasmin, Safiya, and Attalah were right behind us.

"Mama, who is this guy?" Zafer asked, his tone lethal, as he was extremely protective of his mother.

"Someone who knows he has no business being in here," I replied, walking past my son. "You heard my wife. How the hell did you get in here, Daystar?"

Adour-Nuru smiled, inspecting his nails before turning his attention back to Elisa. "He called you Mama. You look way too young to have a son this old. And the ebony beauty...I'm guessing she's your daughter?"

"Take your eyes off my wife *and* my daughter, Daystar, now. You need to leave, before I throw you out."

"I'd like to see you try, half-breed," he retorted with a guffaw. "I'll leave after I get what I came here for," he replied, his red-eyed gaze fixed on Elisa.

Quick as a flash, Tasmin, Zafer, Safiya, and Attalah placed themselves in front of Elisa, while Octavian situated himself at my side.

Adour-Nuru looked from Octavian to me. "What's the matter, Dr. Battle, can't fight on your own? Need your brother and your family to even out the odds?"

I know I shouldn't have, but I let my anger get the better of me as I leapt forward at the incubus, both of us crashing into pantry wall. As I momentarily knocked the wind out of him, I turned my attention back to my wife.

The fear in her eyes strengthened my resolve and pissed me off further. The last thing I wanted to do was damage my wife's life blood any further, but Adour-Nuru Citlali Daystar needed to be dealt with, once and for all.

"Elisa, get out of here, now!" I bellowed, more forcefully than I should have, but she was a distraction, and I needed to focus.

"But Dafari—"

"Go, now! Safiya, Zafer, take your mother to the bookstore."

"What about you, Papa?" My daughter asked, worry in her tone.

"I'll follow along as soon as I can."

"Come on, Mama, let's go," Safiya said, grabbing Elisa's hand, pulling her toward the front door.

Adour-Nuru tried to stand in an attempt to follow them, but I clocked him squarely in the jaw, knocking him back a few inches. The momentary distraction gave my wife and daughter more than enough time to run out the café.

I noticed my son had not left. "Zafer, what are you still doing here? I told you to go with your mother."

"Sorry, Pops, I ain't going nowhere. You might need my help."

As much as I hated to admit it, I didn't have time to argue with my son right now. Daystar, who had quickly recovered, grabbed me by my coat lapels, tossing me across the room.

I landed awkwardly on my back, but quickly jumped to my feet. Daystar grinned lecherously as he rushed me, and I ran for him, dragging him out the back door so I could have more room to inflict damage.

Once there, Daystar partially battle bulked then swung his arms, tossing me like a ragdoll. I landed hard near the green dumpster.

"Ah, the fight we've all been waiting for. Let me get my popcorn," I heard off to the side.

"Father? Why are you here?" I asked, wondering when he'd left the bookstore.

"As the Incubus-in-Chief...Head-Incubus-in-Charge... whatever, I sensed something was off in my world. Clearly, I was right."

As he was speaking, Octavian, Tasmin, Zafer, and Attalah burst through the back door. Tasmin had fireballs in her hands, Attalah had materialized her scythe, and my son...he had battle bulked, his poison-filled wings on full display. Octavian and I followed suit, as did Adour-Nuru, his true form almost twice as large as mine.

Regardless, I was going to take this fight as far as I had to in order to protect Elisa. There was no way I going to allow him to get his slimy claws on my wife. I charged at him headlong, but this time he parried, his fist connecting with my jaw. It felt as if I had been hit with a brick. From the corner of my eye, I could see Octavian and Zafer rushing toward my opponent.

"No," Father yelled. "Same as the fight between me and Michael needed to happen, so must this one. It's a matter of honor and respect. Dafari must do this on his own."

I watched my brother and son reluctantly back off, flanking Tasmin and Attalah. Needing some sort of edge, I materialized my dark matter sword in one hand, a Mabo throwing knife in the other. Unfortunately, Adour-Nuru also had a sword, one that was larger than mine. With one hand, he swung it in a semi-circular arc, bringing it down with the intention of splitting my skull.

Luckily, my reflexes were quick. I heard audible gasps as I brought my sword up defensively, blocking his strike. Daystar then wrapped his other hand around the hilt, doubling the amount of force, pushing the sword lower, forcing me to drop to one knee. So focused was Daystar on splitting me in two, he allowed his guard to drop for a second.

Turning my Mabo throwing knife to the side with the single blade, I swiped it horizontally, slicing through his sinewy abdominal muscles, forcing him to jump back, visibly in pain. But instead of relenting, my drawing first blood only seemed to egg him on.

"Nice one, son of Azazel, my king." His smile was taunting as he bowed to my father, who only glared at him, eyes fire red.

My gut told me Father wanted a piece of Adour-Nuru in the worst way, but knew, in all fairness to incubus law, he could not intervene. Looking at the deep, bleeding wound I created, Adour-Nuru let out a loud battle cry, one that I was sure could be heard for blocks. This time, it was he who lunged first, his blade moving in arcs, first left, then right, the sequence repeating.

I had to rid myself of my knife to hold on to my sword. He swung, I parried. And so it went until he finally switched it up, catching me off guard. I felt the blade pierce my side, hot fire running through me. I fell to the ground.

"Dafari," Tasmin and Octavian shouted in unison mixed in with Attalah's cry of, "Uncle".

Surprisingly, the loudest of all was Zafer, with, "Pops," coming through loud and clear. "We have to help him," he bellowed, trying to get to me.

His grandfather stepped through a shadow, blocking his path, a single word leaving his lips. "No."

Blood leaking heavily from my laceration, I stumbled as I tried to rise. My eyes met with Daystar's, the sneer that crossed his lips angering me. His words enraged me even more.

"I'll be sure to tell Elisa you fought valiantly...as I take her to my bed." He raised his sword above his head. I tried to lift mine, but the pain was unimaginable.

"Brother, get up," Octavian shouted.

"Come on, Pops. You can't let this popinjay beat you," my son chimed in.

"Hmmmm, popinjay. Old world, but…I like that," Father mused, still preventing Zafar from interfering.

Attalah swore as she encouraged me. My beloved niece… she always had faith in me.

"Dafari, you've got this. Elisa needs you to win!"

Tasmin's mention of my wife, the woman for whom I would die a thousand deaths…the sound of her name did something to me. While I knew she wasn't physically in the vicinity, her strength, her will, and her heart were here with me. I stood slowly, every movement, each breath excruciating, but as I focused on Elisa, thought about all the years I spent in Salix Pointe, patiently waiting for her to reawaken, to reunite with her…Adour-Nuru was just another obstacle that needed to be overcome.

As he brought down his sword, mine rose to meet his, dark matter sparks flying through the air. Simultaneously, I called a Mabo throwing knife to my free hand. I dropped to one knee, allowing him to think he had once again gotten the upper hand. Daystar shifted his stance a bit sideways, allowing the opening I needed to quickly slice through his Achilles tendon. He cried out in pain, his footing becoming unsteady.

He took to the air; my guess was to avoid a ground fight now that he had lost the advantage. What a coward. An extra burst of adrenaline kicked in and within seconds I had caught up to him, despite his greater wingspan. Grabbing one of Adour-Nuru's legs, I swung him around in circles until I had just enough momentum to hurl him the way an athlete would toss a hammer in the hammer throw. He hit the cobblestones hard, cracking several in the process. The wind knocked out of him, he struggled to get up. I landed in front of him, sword pointing in his direction.

"Ready to yield?" I asked.

"Never," he boldly replied, breathing hard. "I will *never* yield to the likes of you. You are not worthy of a woman such as Elisa."

I chuckled then said, "Believe me when I say Elisa wouldn't on her worst day choose you. She was, and will always be *my* heart, *my* soulmate, *my* wife. Never will she be yours. Not in this lifetime, not in any lifetime."

"Well said, Son," Father uttered, pride in his voice.

The combination of my words and his king's adoration infuriated Adour-Nuru. He vaulted towards me, sword aimed to skewer me, but his gait was hampered by the wound I had inflicted. As his body propelled forward, I maneuvered myself behind him, wrapping an arm around his neck, my sword placed against his now-exposed throat.

"Hear me, Adour-Nuru Citlali Daystar, you *will* stay away from my wife, Elisa Hunte-Battle, and every other member of my family. Do…you…understand?" He nodded. "Say it," I demanded.

"Y-Yes, I…understand," he replied on labored breaths.

"Now," I continued, "say it to him." I pointed in my father's direction.

Any promise made by an incubus to his king was binding. If broken, an incubus' life would be forfeited.

"My liege…I will…stay…away from…Elisa Hunte-Battle…and… all family… members of Dafari…Battle," he reiterated. "My word…is my bond."

Father looked at the beaten demon, a hint of fang showing as he spoke. "I will hold you to that. Now, leave my presence, peasant." He waved him off with a hand.

Adour-Nuru didn't say another word; when I released

him, he simply disappeared into a shadow. Once he was gone, a sense of calm wafted over me, along with the pain of the wound in my side.

Tasmin was the first to reach me, her instinct being to heal my wound. Octavian held me steady while she provided her healing touch. I was grateful for her timely intervention.

"How do you feel now, Dafari?" she asked.

"Much...better. Thank you, Sister."

I needed to get to the bookstore. While Tasmin's touch healed my physical wound, I needed Elisa to give me the healing only she could provide.

CHAPTER 38
OCTAVIAN

Laying a hand on Dafari's shoulder, Uncle Azazel stopped his son's retreat into the shadows. No doubt Dafari had been about to go after Elisa. His battle fangs had retracted and in their place were now bicuspids of another kind. He flashed a violent red glare in his father's direction, to which Azazel was unmoved.

The wind blew leaves across the wet pavement as a light sprinkle of rain started to fall. Any other time, the cool breeze would have created a relaxing atmosphere, but the noxious odor that carried on the air was offensive as was evident by the way Tasmin, Attalah, and Zafer all frowned and covered their noses.

"Deny your baser nature and listen to what I'm about to tell you," Uncle commanded, looking between Dafari and me. "That was a distraction."

"I don't follow," I said, not sure I understood Uncle's declaration.

"You're not making sense, old man," snarled Dafari who stilled looked as if he was seriously considering snuffing his father.

The demon was hungry, and not for food. Uncle Azazel was standing in the way of Dafari's absolute need to be in Elisa's presence.

He whirled around to stand face-to-face with his son. "Are you issuing me a direct challenge...Son?"

Dafari, not backing down, squared his shoulders. "You are standing between me and—"

"I am...asking you to think about what I just revealed to you! Adour-Nuru challenging you now, right as we're about go up against the enemy of our enemy, who is not our friend?" This could quite possibly be the start of Armageddon, and now he wants to fight my son whose wife is the mother of the children both Heaven and Hell are after? Does that not ring as chaotic and out of order to you?" Uncle spat, each word spoken clear and precise.

Tasmin, Attalah and Zafer had stopped talking amongst themselves. Tasmin then shot me a glance that conveyed she was now tuned in to the conversation.

"Put your demon to rest for a moment and use the logical part of your brain, Son. One of my subjects challenges my son, which is also a direct challenge to my throne! Because you are my heir, had you been defeated, Adour-Nuru would be next in line to take my seat!"

"Wait," Tasmin said, walking forward to stand next to me. "Wouldn't Zafer be next in line as Dafari's son and heir?"

"The rules of Hell work a bit differently, Doctor. Sure, the rights to the throne are often passed down that way, and if this were any other time, with any other family, that would be the case. However, Dafari is not a full-blooded demon, and there have been times when direct challenges to a throne have occurred. Not many have been foolish enough to try it, as those of us who rule parts of Hell often kill any being foolish enough to even allow the thought to cross their retched minds."

Attalah's loud gasp drew our attention as she moved forward, eyes wide as if she had just had a light bulb go off. "You're not suggesting..."

Uncle's voice took on a deadly tone when he responded. "Only a demon with a death wish would try such a thing. Adour-Nuru is seasoned. He knows a move like this has severe repercussions. He is one of the most well-versed incubi I've ever come across. Only one being would have convinced a man of such high intelligence to make such a foolhardy move. A clever barrister like Adour-Nuru would need to know with certainty that win, lose, or draw he would walk away with a victory."

"The victory in this case being that he went up against the king of incubi's son… and lived to tell about it," Zafer spat, his delivery making it sound as if the words tasted foul on his tongue. "I knew you should have killed that muthafu—"

"But how would he have secured such a deal? Who would have given it to him?" I asked, cutting off what was sure to be a profane-laced sentence from my nephew.

"Only one being is cold and calculating enough to use one of my own to make that move…"

I saw the moment the severity of what Uncle Azazel was saying sunk in for Dafari as it hit me at the exact same time. Dafari's red eyes slowly faded to a dull, bruised red with rays of golds splashed in the background, making it appear as if his demon had been eclipsed by his angel side.

"I'm listening," he growled.

"You're not talking about *Him* are you?" I asked Uncle Azazel, referring to his father.

"No, Octavian, I'm not," he replied angrily. In his hands appeared his Chakrams, blazing with the Blood of the One True Son and hell fire. "The only reason I allowed this fight to take place was to test my theory, and I was correct. Morningstar has issued a direct challenge to me, and he's shown his hand by using one of my own to betray me. ***Strike three, you*** *motherfucker*," he then snarled, a black current of force encircling him as he bulked to proportions unseen.

Growing at least eight feet in height with a massive body bulk, my uncle's war cry rent the air and stilled the night. Instantly animals scurried. Deer came charging from the trees, birds took flight, critters screamed and screeched as they ran for cover.

I grabbed Tasmin, yanking her back just as a hard flick of Uncle's wrist sent one of his Chakrams charging into the ground, splitting it open. Like a heat-seeking missile, the Chakram blasted through the ground as Hell fire vomited up. With pure hatred in his eyes, Uncle's wings snapped open, blacking out the moon as he flew up in a spiral pattern then abruptly switched to swan dive head first into the pit. But just as quick and violent as the earth had opened, it snapped close, locking Uncle Azazel inside.

"Father," Dafari yelled just as Zafer grabbed him, to keep him from trying go after Azazel.

From around the corner, I heard running and saw Elisa, Safiya, my parents, aunt, and uncles along with the Widows, Silas and Jewel.

"What happened?" asked Lilith as she came to halt next to me and Tasmin.

"I think Grandpops just went kamikaze on Hell," Zafer shouted over the roaring of the winds.

Thunder slammed against the earth as violent lightning strikes lit up the sky.

"The second wave is coming," yelled Attalah, pointing toward the heavens to the jet-black battle angels with oversized goat heads, eyes that leaked blood, and massive wingspans.

"Fall back!" Father yelled and we all went scrambling for cover.

My wings unfurled and I grabbed Tasmin, running for cover.

Silas and Jewel ran back toward the bookstore as a host of angels that looked like floating, eye-covered wheels chased them.

"Ophanim," Mother yelled! "Aim for the eyes!"

Bec-de-corbins in hand, I swung it at the Ophanim, knocking a handful out of the air while Tasmin shot white light energy from her palms.

The Widows formed a triangle pattern, using their staffs to defend themselves against the onslaught of angels attacking them from all sides, while my father and uncles had taken to the skies with their fight. There was no mistaking, the 7th Battalion, second wave, had arrived.

Chapter 39
ELISA

And the fight, once again, was on! Gusts of wind aggressively propelled me, Dafari, Tasmin and Octavian into the street. I let out a muted grunt, tucking and rolling so I could quickly get back to my feet. I felt debris and gravel cut into my palms.

None of us had time to think about it as we scrambled back to our feet. The rustle of the trees and swaying fog in front of us had captured our attention. A sea of bodies, shadowed in eerie gray fog, stood just beyond the shadows of the dense forest and surrounding area. I could make out glowing red eyes and the low din emanating from them. But there were other things mixed in. Some with eyes as black as tar and others with white, clouded over pupils like zombies.

"The funnel clouds are back," Dafari yelled!

"And it doesn't look like they're alone," Tasmin said just as Octavian yanked her out of the path of an oncoming black energy strike. They went crashing, rolling down a ditch to avoid contact.

Turning my head in Dafari's direction, I saw four frighteningly massive funnel clouds. Each had to be miles wide, practically caging Salix Pointe between them. They looked like solid-gray masses of violently swirling wind, getting ready to tear through the town. As the lightning flashed and thunder roared, four figures of destruction sitting atop larger-than-life thoroughbreds was enough to make my heart slam against my chest.

The sight was so jarring that I almost forgot about the things hiding in the fog. Until they started coming toward us, their jerky movements catching my eye.

"Dafari," I screamed, vigorously tapping on his shoulder to get his attention.

His gaze snapped ahead. "They have us surrounded!"

The stench wafting from them lit up the area. The smell almost so unbearable, my eyes watered, and nose hairs felt as if they were burning.

"There are too many of them! What are they?"

"A horde of Gray-Walkers mixed with a collective of tainted souls…and to keep things simple, the walking dead," he replied.

"Yeah, but since they can be controlled by either side, who sent them?"

"That answer is yet to be seen, although at this point, it doesn't matter."

Red, glowing orbs stared at us from the shadows of the trees, the road, yards of surrounding houses… More alarmingly, they were steadily closing in on us.

Dafari instantly bulked in height and size, the increase making him an imposing and commanding sight. I felt the ground beneath me vibrate. My body came alive with electricity.

"We have to—"

Demonic screeching rent the air, cutting off whatever he was about to say. It was so loud that both of us grabbed our ears and ducked our heads as if that alone would stop the assault. My vision locked in on the ground as it seemed to vibrate. Masses of rats with yellowing eyes and misshapen mouths were running right at us.

My husband looked skyward then left and right, his dark

matter sword materializing in his hand. "I can't take to the skies because it may be too dangerous with the battle angels. We're going to have to fight our way out to clear a path," he yelled.

Lowering my hands to my side, I felt my palms burn. Snapping my fingers, I watched as balls of energy formed over my palm, blasting through the throng of creatures. Popping and crackling flesh along with balls of fur splattered around, spewing sulfuric ash in its wake.

I stumbled backwards, catching sight of my husband as he ran forward. Quick moving shadows attacked him with fervor. The Gray-Walkers and souls were wild and careless in their onslaught. Sharp talon like claws ripped at his arms, back, and face. Souls with sallow skin, cloudy eyes, and serrated fangs leapt through the air at him only to be incinerated upon impact when his sword sliced through them. I almost lost the contents of my stomach when he spit in the face of one and I watched his sunken skull-like face melt.

Frowning, I cried, "Ew, Dafari!"

Giving a quick smirk over his shoulders, he crooned. "I am my father's son," before he grabbed the hilt of his sword like it was a football and launched it down the middle of the horde.

When the heavy metal sailed through the air, flames engulfed it, killing the creatures in its path. As the sword doubled back to land in his grip, he flung his Mabo throwing knives one after the other. The spider motifs on the wing, crown, and spur cut into dead flesh while moving in a boomerang pattern.

Demonic rats were coming faster than I could send fire blasts after them, and they looked hungry. Tiny sharp mangled teeth were visible as they scurried and scattered.

"Mother Earth, I humbly beseech your protection. Send the things that seek to harm me in another direction…"

My palms shot white-light explosions toward the mischief, exploding them on impact as the earth shook. Cracks in its surface widened enough for the small critters to fall toward fire pit that opened below them. Billowing clouds of smoke forced me back.

No longer worried about the rats, I charged in the direction of my husband. Stopping long enough to touch the earth, fisting grass and dirt. "Blessings to the guardians and protectors of the earth," I said. "From the north, south, east and west, I call on you to clear away all enemies at my request." My fingers burned as flames lit the tips. "Flashes of lightning take charge in my defense!"

Bolts of electrical discharge danced through the sky then crashed to the ground, clearing Dafari's path of Gray-Walkers, souls, and zombies alike.

Growling and holding the hilt of his sword with both hands, Dafari swung upward, slicing through decayed limbs and heads.

I dropped the earth in my palm back to the ground then waved my hands in a slow rhythm until the torrential rain followed the pattern. "Rush of the water and howls of the wind, clear my path so that evil may exscind…"

The rain and the wind shifted, slamming against the horde and the collective alike. Bodies went flying in the opposite direction. Roots of the tree crawled up from the ground to shackle the Gray-Walkers' ankles and wrists, ripping them apart with ease. And still they kept coming!

"Come on," Dafari ordered, taking my hand and pulling me forward.

Trees uprooted, shingles from the roofs of buildings flipped off, and hard bits of wood and roofing material through the air. Flaming arrows whizzed over our heads, slamming into dead bodies and Gray-Walkers. They incinerated on impact while the souls desperately tried to retreat.

"Get down," Dafari yelled, closing his arms around me to pull me to the ground. We landed awkwardly on our sides.

"You two okay?"

Peeking from behind some of the fallen logs, my eyes landed on my husband's mother. The wind didn't seem to sway her, and the heavy rain had no effect on her aim or precision. The breastplate she wore contoured to her upper body while also shielding her abdomen.

Standing tall and statuesque like the warrior she was, the woman's movements as she advanced were poetry in motion. Like the most skilled of archers, Eset was quick as she walked forward, releasing arrow after arrow. Like it was a dance, she moved left and right, lining up her targets, shooting down Gray-Walkers, souls and zombies, giving us time to run for cover.

CHAPTER 40
DAFARI

As we all ran, looking for a hiding place, I noticed Zafer stood in plain sight. Even though it was bitterly cold and rainy, Zafer had shed his jacket and shirt, his black leathery wings on full display. I didn't know what my son was. On more than one occasion we had been told he was unhinged and based on his actions now? I was starting to believe it.

Astonished, Elisa and I watched as his eyes went from golden to red, his arms stretched to the heavens. The rain suddenly turned to thick red droplets. Fire shot up from the ground as pillars of smoke and sulfuric ash released from the cracks in the earth.

A pale horse and its rider came trudging across the skies, splitting the clouds as it bore down on my son. Energy radiated throughout my body. It was hard to stay focused on the task at hand when my son was in mortal danger.

Uncle Izrail's true form was so frightening that it was said to cause instant death to any mere human who laid eyes upon it. Seeing him that way showed why the Most High often sent him to unleash his wrath.

As he and his nightmare steed stepped through the veil, he snarled, "You must have a death wish, upstart. Are you trying to make acquiring your soul easy?"

Zafer said not a word in return. Only grinned in such a way that it put me on high alert.

Aunt Lilith then materialized in front of him, lavender energy sword and gold shield saying she didn't come to play. "No, Izrail, he's not. In fact, neither Zafer nor Safiya's souls are up for grabs." Her long tresses hissed and snapped as if in agreement.

Izrail looked at us with his many eyes before saying, "We shall see."

With a wave of his flaming sword, the clouds spread, a wave of Level four Messengers raining down on us. Aunt Lilith, along with Uncles Uriel and Gabriel took to the skies, surrounding Uncle Izrail. Uncle Michael joined them, but not before saying something to Mother, who stayed on the ground.

The Messengers came at us hard, forcing Octavian and I in separate directions as we dived for cover. Tiny black orbs of energy chased us as if they had been specially coded to seek us out. When a beefy body slammed into mine, I knew the fight was on.

My dark matter sword came whizzing through the air, landing against my palm just in time for me to swing and cut a Messenger's head clean from its body.

Octavian was quick on his feet, calling his bec-de-corbins to him before flinging them at Messengers. "Guard your six, Brother," he then yelled before having to pivot to keep a Messenger from blindsiding him.

"Go! Go! Go," I heard Elisa shouting.

I looked up to see her running with our daughter as Messengers chased them across the street.

Rufus quickly threw up a golden arc as his body began to glow. The squat man had rushed from the bookstore, a determined look on his face as he pushed the arc toward a wave of Messengers. As soon as it touched them, they fell to ash.

Mother, Attalah, and Uncle Raphael were in hand-to-hand combat, easily putting the Messengers down. It suddenly occurred to me that these weren't that difficult to dispatch…it was almost too easy. Then I realized why; the next wave sent by Uncle Izrail was a horde of Level three Messengers.

"Weapons and brute force only," Attalah yelled. "Remember, Level three Messengers are immune to magick."

Adjusting our ranks, we broke into five groups of three, two on the inside and three surrounding them. Mother, Octavian, and I; Zafer, Safiya, and Attalah; and Tasmin, Elisa, and Uncle Raphael made up the outer defenders. If any Messengers somehow broke through our first line, our inner units, consisting of The Merry Widows, along with Jewel, Silas, and Rufus fought them handily. Looking skyward, the battle against Uncle Izrail waged on. While Aunt Lilith and my uncles were holding their own, I had a feeling that He had diminished their powers, while increasing those of Uncle Izrail.

Seeing that his ground forces were losing, Uncle Izrail called out the big guns, Levels one and two Messengers, the worst of the worst. Our group would have to fight our hardest to beat them, and we had already been fighting for some time without pause. I was sure fatigue would set in soon. I worried most for the Widows. While they were seasoned warriors, they were up in age.

Knowing that we were stronger when we shifted into our otherworldly forms, Octavian, Zafer, Safiya, and I battle bulked, firmly standing as the outermost layer of defense. We once again shifted our positions, with the Widows remaining in the center, and the others forming a middle circle.

"Throw everything you have at them," Mother called out.

My brother and I did our best to slow the onslaught; along with our various weapons, thrashing, biting, ripping, and tearing apart the Messengers helped to diminish their numbers. We were a destructive force. But it wasn't enough. Those in the still advancing mob that got past us attacked hard, weakening our already battle-weary team. I saw it in slow motion. Mary Ann was the first to go down, a Messenger picking her up and slamming her to the ground. Next came Cara Lee and Martha, the black orbs attacking their bodies causing them to grab at their hearts and fall to the ground.

"Rufus, get the Widows to the bookstore now," I yelled.

"On it, Dayfari!" The fairy picked up the fallen Widows, creating a portal.

I wasn't sure how badly they were hurt, but I wasn't taking any chances. If they needed healing, I didn't want to wait. "Tasmin, go with them. Return as soon as you can."

She acknowledged me, rushing to follow Rufus. We were five defenders down and fading fast. Observing our plight, Uncle Michael left the air fight, landing next to Mother. Even with his help, one by one, we were overrun with Silas and Jewel going down next. Rufus quickly picked up the wounded from the battlefield, taking them to be healed by Tasmin.

"Our numbers have dwindled too much. We need to retreat," said the Angel of Protection. "Get back to the bookstore!"

Heeding Michael's words, those of us remaining did our best to flee. As I was running across the backyard, I heard a bloodcurdling roar of pain. It was Octavian. From the corner of my eye, I saw that he had sustained a large shoulder wound. I needed to get him.

"I'm coming, Brother. Hang on!"

Two Level one Messengers attacked me simultaneously. I latched on to the wings of the first, whipping it around, causing it to knock down the other. I then ripped its wings, along with its spine, from its back, leaving the Messenger helpless. The second was easier to subdue, still in a daze after being hit by its counterpart. Grabbing it up by the throat, I dug my talons in, ripping it out. I dropped the Messenger and its voice box onto the cold, hard ground.

By the time I reached Octavian, he had just finished off a Messenger, despite his severely wounded limb. He was struggling to breathe, his wound gushing blood. I put one hand over it to stave the flow.

"I have to get you to the bookstore. Hold on to me."

Octavian grabbed my extended free hand. When he did, something familiar occurred. I felt the same energy jolt, volts of static electricity running though my entire body as it had before. We tried to release each other, to no avail. I watched as my brother's wound began to heal, the hole in his shoulder closing rapidly. Then, our bodies appeared to be…merging.

The electricity coursing through my body was invigorating, and I wondered if Octavian felt the same. I watched as our arms, legs, and torsos became one, our body doubling in size. Turning my head, I viewed our doubled wingspan, large black and white feathers with shiny silver tips.

My brother and I had trained together from the time we were children, knew each other's style forward and backward. I just hoped that translated well now. With a mere thought, our sword appeared in our hands, except now, the hilt no longer contained a single blade, but two, one light, the other dark.

Octavian and I leapt in the air, our wings quickly carrying us to Aunt Lilith, Uncle Gabriel, and Uncle Uriel. We didn't give them a chance to ask questions, but instead focused on Uncle Izrail.

"Ah, my sorely misguided nephews, if you only understood the gravity of the situation. Zafer and Safiya's souls hold more weight than either of you can ever imagine. They are a combination of some of the best...and worst beings in the universe. Angel, demon, Sybil, Nephilim. The power contained within just one of their souls is immeasurable, let alone both. Whichever side controls them could rule indefinitely. We want them...and we will have them."

"Those are my children!" I snapped. "They are not weapons in Heaven and Hell's battle for superiority. You will not have them!"

We didn't wait for a response. Lifting our sword, we swung on him, his horse rearing up to avoid our blade. Uncle Izrail grabbed the horse's reins, steading it.

"Nephews, if you continue this course of action, this fight may be your last."

"So be it."

Energy and flames flew outward as our swords met. Uncle performed a maneuver, turning like a centrifuge, forcing us to back away from him. When he stopped, his sword let out an intense flaming blast that hit us squarely in the chest. Although it hurt like hell, it didn't take us out. Our upgraded form had some perks.

Capitalizing on that, we took the fight to Uncle, slashing our weapon in the manner of an expert swordsman. While he was distracted with our swordplay, Octavian materialized one of his bec-de-corbins, arcing it in a slashing motion, cutting diagonally across Uncle's chest, severely wounding him. As he began to plummet towards earth, his trusty steed was there to break his fall.

Uncle Izrail was dazed. The injury he had sustained doing more damage than even he realized. Seeing Uncle in his true form was creepy enough, but when his eyes started oozing dark blood-like ichor, I knew we had turned the tide.

Like a predator hunting wounded prey, we closed in, taking the fight to our uncle with vigor. Going airborne we sent tactical charges from the tip of the blade that dragged the angel across the yard. We came back down to the ground fast, striking while the iron was hot.

Those still on the impromptu battlefield gave us a wide berth. Even injured the Angel of Death was formidable. Dodging strikes even while stumbling, trying to get away from us. One of the things Tasmin and Elisa had done while we were in the cafe was take some of Zafer's feathers and put the poison on the tips of our weapons. After seeing how Attalah and Safiya had used his feathers to attack the vampires, Elisa and Tasmin wondered if the poison would have the same effect on all otherworldly beings.

Uncle Izrail was struggling to stay on his feet as Octavian and I stalked him. While the poison didn't outright kill the angel, it had weakened him.

We smelled blood in the water just as another wave of swift moving winged wheels of light that interlocked in groups of four—all covered in angry black eyes— flew at us, slicing and cutting into the monster we'd shifted into.

We got knocked back so hard it was as if it had thrown us across a football field. We crashed hard, landing in a way that would have surely killed us if we weren't supernatural beings.

Adrenaline still high, Octavian and I began to detach from one another; slowly but surely our bodies once again becoming two separate entities. After the process was complete, we both stood there for a few seconds. I felt a bit dazed, but no worse for wear. I looked up just in time to see all manner of angels and other heavenly creatures grabbing Uncle Izrail, throwing him into a burning chariot, and then riding like Hell was on their asses back to the heavens.

I saw something like a blur speed past me. Zafer was running pell-mell at Uncle Izrail. He was moving so fast it was almost as if he was floating on air.

What was he doing? Elisa called to him and so did

Mother to no avail. My boy was closing in. As soon as he was within swinging distance, he took to the air, landing on the back of the chariot.

With a mouth full of elongated fangs that now dripped with a clear-like substance that I could safely assume was poison, I watched my son sink his teeth into in the neck of Izrail's middle head. Uncle Izrail thrashed wildly about, trying to throw Zafer off, but he only sunk his fangs in deeper.

"What is he doing?" thundered Michael.

Uncle Raphael came running to stand next to his brother. "He truly is insane!"

Screaming, hissing, and fighting for his life, Uncle Izrail couldn't contend with Zafer. Thick, dark red blood poured down his neck, and before our very eyes, we watched on in horror as my son took over Uncle Izrail's body.

The angels and heavenly beings manning the chariot stood shocked and dazed, not sure what to do next. Uncle Izrail's body writhed and thrashed around. I could only assume his angel side was at war with the entity possessing his body. While Zafer's dark, wicked laughter raised the hairs on the back of my neck, Uncle Izrail was decimating angels and other heavenly beings against his will.

The angels manning the chariot of fire abandoned it, running in fear. Warrior angels dispersed, taking cover, but no matter where they ran, the Angel of Death's eyes followed them. Try as they might to get away, they couldn't move fast enough. The town emptied of angels and demons alike as Zafer used his granduncle's body to bulldoze through those on the ground. He was pure motion, his fury causing Uncle's body to look even more frightening than it had before.

Capillaries burst in eyes and temples. Thick, blood-red ichor filled all his eyes. Two of his heads fell back as black smoke erupted from the mouths. The sound making the rest of us grab our ears to stop the onslaught of ringing it caused. Uncle Izrail's body jerked midair then vibrated. The angel's wings flapped wildly while his hands clawed at his eyes, ripping them out as blackness drizzled down. A heavy blast of black light then propelled Zafer's body forward while Uncle Izrail's body dropped limply to the ground. In his hand was a bloody, oversized heart that he aggressively bit into, sucking the life force out of it until it turned to a hardened black stone. He then tossed it aside like it was nothing.

Looking at my son, I wondered just what kind of monster we'd created. His body naturally produced a poison that could maim and kill archs of the highest order? He could also kill them?

My gaze found Elisa's to find that she, too, had her eyes on Zafer. I couldn't read her. Didn't know what she was thinking and that was a first. As Elisa ran to my side, Attalah and Safiya went to Zafer. Our children were beyond the supernatural. I didn't quite know exactly what they were, but as I looked at them standing side-by-side, I felt fear I'd never known.

I had to take deep breaths to calm my center. Mangled bodies and body parts belonging to animals and fallen angels alike littered the town. Heaven had retreated, my father had disappeared into the belly of Hell. And my son…was something that couldn't be explained.

CHAPTER 41
AZAZEL

Messengers, hellhounds, and other demonic beasts lay scattered around my feet. The rancid smell of sulfur and rotting flesh made even me want to vomit. I was drenched in entrails, blood, guts and gore. The wails of anguish and torture rent the air as I looked around. While my family was a part of the raging war topside, I had been in Hell cleaning house.

Not another one of my kind would betray me without consequences so severe they would wish for death. Neither would I allow Morningstar to think his attempt at a coupe would go unanswered. Adour-Nuru was in hiding and that had better be where he stayed if he wanted to continue to draw breath. I trusted no one, which was why I ended up in Lucifer's chambers to find that it was empty. Not even his princes were guarding his lair.

"Where are you, you slimy bastard?" I murmured, walking around Morningstar's chambers.

The snakes were gone, the imps, vampire bats, the tortured souls…none of the creatures and demons on any level of Hell were present. All the thrones sat empty, which told me that whatever he had planned was more sinister and more calculating than even I had suspected.

Closing my eyes, I thought back to the moments after the battle with Eve, when the witches had been tending to the little one, Nazila. Forcing Tasmin and Elisa into a deep sleep so that I could steal some of the essence from their wombs had been fortuitous at best. I knew it would come in handy, just didn't know when…until now.

My eyes narrowed to enraged slits. Fury roared through me as I snapped my fingers and outstretched my hands. Like flaming arrows, black ice shot forward, freezing everything in its path. Malevolent beings that had been hiding ran and screeched for cover as the ice encroached every level of Hell. I would have my revenge one way or the other.

Storming out, I sent word to my grandchildren that I would need them sooner rather than later. I folded myself into a shadow, coming out on the other side of the Zambezi River. As the mighty river crashed over a basalt rock ledge, I took in my surroundings. A dazzling cloud of mist floated just above the falls, creating an ambience that she loved. I'd carved out her own piece of Heaven for her, a place to keep her and her daughter safe until the fight was over.

Sitting on the edge of the bed next to her, I stroked the hair from her face. Her kinky natural hair forming a halo around her head. As she and her daughter had hidden away in her prayer closet, afraid of all the chaos they heard outside, I put them into a deep slumber, not wanting to frighten the child while I escorted them to safety. Neither would remember their time here, and that was for the best. At least for now anyway.

I palmed her stomach, feeling the life force beat in a steady rhythm. She was with child. *My* child.

All my hard work had paid off. From reconnecting with my son to having my grandchildren and grandniece in on my plan, everything had fallen into place.

"Good of you to rejoin the living, Brother…" Lilith's voice had replayed in my head, causing a smirk to adorn my face.

After the fight with Izrail outside of Abdul-Haq's place, my injuries had been so severe that rest was required. For three days, I'd lain in this same tomb-like cave, hanging on to life by a thread, and on the third day, I rose.

A maniacal chuckle erupted from me and reverberated about the small space. Gently scooping the woman up in my arms along with her sleeping child, I took my time getting them back to Salix Pointe. Even with the battle that had taken place, I knew that was the safest place for my unborn child's mother and her daughter.

Tinashe stirred when I laid her on her bed. Eyes fluttering open, she watched me curiously. "Are you coming back?" she asked, sleepiness giving her voice the same sexy undertones it carried while she was in the throes of passion.

"Don't I always?" I asked, cupping her chin.

"I don't want to be here alone…just in case Lucifer comes back, especially in my dreams."

"No worries, my pretty. The thief comes only to steal and kill and destroy. I have come that you may have life, abundantly. Rest now. For we have a long journey ahead."

EPILOGUE
OCTAVIAN

Three days after battle…

After the anxiety of battle had worn off, we finally got around to discussing the wrongs that had befallen our family. For those first forty-eight hours we were on high alert, not sure if Heaven or Hell were going to send reinforcements. Tasmin and I didn't want to let Attalah out of our sights for fear we would lose her again. Dafari and Elisa spent those two days getting reacquainted with Zafer and Safiya, but it had been hard to do when we were all worried about what was going to happen next.

While my parents, aunt, and uncles had gone off to see what they could find out about what was going on in Heaven and Hell, we sat around the dinner table, enjoying a dinner of roasted duck, collard greens, yellow rice, and homemade cornbread, I could tell that even with the down time, we were still paranoid. The conversation jumped from one subject to the other. All of us trying to make sense of the events that had occurred during the battle.

"Back then, I didn't think about how my actions would push you over the edge. It was selfish, and I didn't know it would be the last straw. I'm so sorry," Safiya said to Elisa, pushing her empty plate to the side. "I know I keep saying that, but I don't think I can say it enough."

My niece was dressed in a plain long black skirt, a white blouse, and simple sneakers. Her natural kinks were styled in pencil-thin braids that stopped at her neck. The lobes of her ears were donned with gold hoop earrings and studs. Gold bangles decorated her wrists. Four of her long curved, black painted nails had small hoop earrings dangling from the tips as well. Around her neck was a lace choker with a crescent moon shaped pendant along with a small cat. If nothing else, she looked every bit of the eccentric witch she was.

"I know, baby, I know. It's okay. I meant what I said last night. It's over now. It's all over. That part of our lives is done. You're back with us. We can only move forward now. We have a chance to start over."

Zafer and Safiya exchanged quick glances then they both turned to Attalah. A silent message passed between the three that seemed to go unnoticed by everyone else, including my brother.

"For a long time I was pissed at you and Uncle Octavian, but as time passed and I got to experience life on the other side, I started to understand the method to your madness. Zafer and I had to do a lot of things to survive. I would do anything to protect my brother, and he would do the same for me."

"She's right, Mama," Zafer said, sitting across from his parents and sister.

Dressed in all white, something about him still unsettled me. Maybe it was seeing him completely decimate an arch of the highest order like it was nothing or maybe it was just because he and his sister had changed drastically because of the position they were placed in. Either way, my nephew was someone—something—I'd have to keep my eyes on.

"Ain't nothing I wouldn't do for her, and I've proven it many times over," he continued. "I'm not going to lie, Pops, before my talk with Uncle Uriel, I really had every intention of ripping you and Uncle O a new one, but after seeing the way both sides were coming after our family, I realized that there was a very real possibility that I wouldn't get to see or spend time with any of you again. I really don't want to waste time living in the past anymore. I get why you did what you did, Pops. Of course, I wish you would have thought it through, but Uncle O didn't really give you time to." Cutting a quick glance my way, he said, "No offense, Unk, but you didn't. I'm not saying that to make you feel bad or nothing. Just stating facts."

Giving him a head nod, I said, "I know, Nephew, and I respect it."

He and I had already talked man-to-man and gotten things squared away. My nephew may have been a little—a lot— off his rocker, but he was intelligent to boot. There was no need to continue to rehash the past, especially with everything that had already happened.

Still, when he turned his golden eyes to me, a shiver chilled me to the bone. Red flashed behind his eyes and, as his inner demon locked gazes with mine, the sinister way his eyes smiled raised my hackles.

"You okay?" Tasmin asked, lowering her voice so only I could hear. Leaning in closer to me, she glanced at Zafer who smiled wide for her before turning back to his mother. I looked at Dafari to see he, too, was watching his son. It was our turn to exchange meaningful glances. His asking me if I felt the same thing he did. Mine showing that I had.

"Yes, Poppet," I finally said, giving her my full attention. "Still a bit tense about everything."

Smiling, she nodded, then turned her attention to Attalah, who had been unusually quiet. Why did I feel like our children were hiding something from us?

"For those first few years, Zafer was a menace. He hated

everything and everyone...and he proved it many times over." Safiya chuckled but I could tell that she and her brother had stories, tales of their experiences on the other side that we would never know about.

Tasmin said, "And judging by what happened with Izrail, he just may still be a menace."

Our nephew smiled wickedly. The gold on his bottom row of teeth peeking out. "I just may be, Auntie," he agreed casually. "Heaven and Hell want to come after me and my sister's souls—come after my family, then they'd better know what they're doing," The arrogance dripping from his words told us that he was very much aware that he was the ultimate weapon.

Zafer relished in his power, unfazed by the repercussions that could come along with it. He'd killed the Angel of Death. Sucked the life from his still beating heart and left his body dead on the streets of Salix Pointe.

Dafari and Elisa were losing sleep over it. They'd just gotten their children back and already had to worry about the possibility of losing them again.

Not only had his actions sent angels running back to Heaven, he'd also sent the Horsemen running back from which they came. Instinctively we all knew that neither Heaven nor Hell were going to let that go.

FINALLY BACK FROM THEIR RECONNAISSANCE MISSION the next day, my parents were still on shaky ground, but they were working it out. The fight between them in the days following the battle had put some things in perspective.

While Father was still severely upset about Mother's astral

plane affair with Demon Daddy, when she mentioned the times that he would come home, smelling like the female angels from Solomon's temple, his bark had a little less bite.

"I'm only going to take so much of your brow beating before I call you on your own crap, Michael! How many times did I turn a blind eye to you staying out with Gabriel and Solomon? What about the trips with David to Bathsheba's lair where she and her girls were all too eager to help you and your brothers "rest" after battle? Coming home smelling like cinnamon, myrrh, balsam oils? *Don't piss me off,*" she had snapped at him, causing Aunt Lilith to stare on with an amused smirk.

"I...that's not the same, Eset," Father defended, glancing from me to Dafari then back to Mother.

"Please explain to me what's not the same about it?" Mother demanded, eyes turning pure white with rage.

"I had no connection to those women. No history...and they...I didn't get to know them the way man does woman. I mean...I may have read some poetry or even—"

"Stop talking," Uncle Gabriel said, his eyes on Mother as her breathing deepened and her body slowly bulked. "You're not doing yourself any favors, man."

"That's for sure," agreed Uncle Uriel, who looked as if he was ready to run from the front room where we had all been congregating.

Uncle Raphael, the most chaste of the group of brothers, chuckled while shaking his head. "I knew this was coming."

Father backed down, biting his tongue as he stormed out of Dafari's home. We hadn't heard him say anything else about the affair since.

As Tasmin and I lay in bed that night, sleep escaped us. The lovemaking had been salacious, but once the high came down, our minds were back on the battle and what would happen next.

"Where do we go from here?" she asked.

"Honestly, Poppet, I don't know. Things have been too quiet. Uncle Azazel has all but disappeared, and quite frankly, I'm tired, my love." Pulling her flush on top of me as we lay in the guest room of my brother's home, I covered her in my wings. "I'd like for just one lifetime where we could live peacefully and die of old age while still in love. I'd like our family to have at least one lifetime where we don't suffer, where we don't have to fight to live. I'd like a life where we can just exist."

She didn't say anything as her head lay on my chest, locs spilling around us. Both of us were naked in the afterglow of our love. Did she know her scent was killing me softly? Was she aware that she was trailing an energy signature that said her body was now ready to procreate? The sweet smell of raw, unprocessed nectar hit me full on. We hadn't even discussed having children this lifetime. I wasn't sure if it was something I even wanted. The risk of losing another child or children created a hollowness inside of me that I didn't like, which took my mind back to the secret Dafari had revealed to me.

Elisa was with child. They didn't know when it had happened, and she hadn't confirmed it by normal human standards, but he could hear the faint heartbeat of the embryo as it nestled in the safety of her womb. It explained why he had been so vicious in battle when it came to protecting her. They hadn't revealed it to the family or coven at large yet, and I was sworn to secrecy until Elisa wanted to reveal it to Tasmin.

"Why are you so quiet? Did I say the wrong thing?" I asked when she had been silent for longer than a minute.

"No...I'm just imagining us having the life you just

described. It would be wonderful." Sighing, she popped her head up and looked at me. "A girl can dream, even for a little while anyway."

We lay that way, dreaming, hoping, wishing, praying...I didn't know how to admit outright that I was terrified of what was to come. Not because I was afraid to fight, but because I was afraid of losing her and Attalah all over again. Even the possibility of it made my heart ache.

"Tasmin?"

"Yes?"

"I have loved you many lifetimes and I don't want to know what it is to not be able to love you again and again and again...and again."

Sitting up to straddle my lap, she gazed down at me with warm eyes. Even after the battle and all we'd just endured, the love her eyes exuded calmed me. She made me feel everything was going to be all right even though I knew better.

"You've marked me, Octavian, and I don't just mean because your incubus likes to bite." She smiled. I grinned, eyes flashing red then back to black. "I want to do as many more lifetimes with you as I can, while I can, whenever I can."

Staring up at her, I felt my heart skip a beat. "Marry me. Tomorrow."

Giggling she asked, "What?"

"Marry me. Tomorrow. Soon as day breaks. Marry me...again."

WHILE I WANTED HER TO MARRY ME THE VERY NEXT day, Elisa wouldn't hear of it. After she and Tasmin warded the land around the property, she wanted to at least be able to bake a cake and put together a small menu. She also wanted to decorate and generally make a big deal of her cousin getting married again.

It took three days to plan the small wedding. While Dafari helped to acquire the documents needed to recognize our wedding as legal from the human standpoint, I begged for help from Rufus and David Herschel to help set up decorations.

Elisa immediately jumped in the kitchen to start baking a cake and preparing a small menu. Neither set of our parents were invited much to their dismay. It was a unilateral decision on my part, but with the coven from the other side missing and all the bad blood that still needed to be discussed where my parents were concerned, I knew it was for the best.

While Aunt Lilith wasn't invited to the wedding, she did gift Tasmin a dress of beautiful silk. That was the gist of what I knew about the garment as I hadn't laid eyes on it yet. Isiah Taylor, Salix Pointe's resident seventh-generation tailor, was able to get me fitted for a suit of my choosing. Even with the damage to his store in town, his basement, where he had what he called a back-up shop, looked like a replica of the store upstairs.

I forewent the tux—I wasn't a traditional man in any sense of the word— opting for a cream-colored silk-linen suit with long trousers and a collarless button front, long sleeve shirt. The expensive thread felt good against my skin. I presented as the archangel I was.

By the day of the wedding, Rufus and David constructed a beautiful archway in Dafari's backyard that transported us to a different time and space. It looked as if fairy lights were strung throughout the hanging lavender vines while a tunnel of greenery and orchid lilies led to a replica of the Tree of Life where I stood along with Dafari and Zafer acting as my best men.

Low hanging lights combined with the sun setting in the background casted a beautiful ambience over the land. My brother and nephew matched my style of dress while Attalah, Safiya, and Elisa wore sleek lilac gowns made of the finest silk. In the women's hands were boutonnieres made of white roses and ranunculus. They were all smiles as they waited for my woman to make her way down the rose-covered walkway.

Barefoot just like the rest of us, Tasmin was stunning. She wore a simple lavender silk gown with thin straps that hung ever so gently to her fit and feminine frame. Her locs fell beautifully around her shoulders. The delicate fabric against her brown skin made my mouth water as we stood across from one another. She was beauty personified. Minimal makeup enhanced her natural features and made me want to hurry this ceremony along.

Elisa was already sniffling, tears raining down her cheeks as she watched her best friend who happened to be her cousin saunter down the aisle.

And for a short time, we pretended we were a normal family, Tasmin and I exchanging vows once more to solidify our love in this lifetime.

Smiling up at me with watery eyes, she said, "Ours is a love that's been tested on so many levels, and we've experienced so many changes; some good, some bad, and some downright horrific. We've epitomized the phrase in sickness and in health. Through it all there's been one constant, the love we have for each other. It's unwavering, never-ending, and unbreakable. Octavian Jerrod, I once again pledge to be your loving wife, being faithful to you for as long as I exist on this earth. My heart and my soul are yours, and nothing or no one will ever change that."

I barely paid attention to Dafari putting the blue hexagon sapphire in twenty-four karat rose gold ring in my palm. Not wanting to leave to go to a jeweler, I petitioned my Aunt Lilith in helping me to find the perfect natural stone for my love.

Taking a deep breath, I began my vows. "Because of you, I know what it means to love unconditionally. I give you my word that from this day forward, as your love anchors me, my heart will always be a place you can find shelter. In my arms you will always find a home. Tasmin, I take you as you are, loving who you are now and who you are yet to become. You fill me with a fervent, burning passion that is often hard to contain. I promise to grow as you grow, laugh with you, cry with you, fight by your side until this lifetime ends and we meet again in another."

And when Rufus asked me if I took Tasmin as my wife, yes was my answer before the fairy man could finish the question.

As the days and nights went on, the rest of the coven recovered while my parents, aunt, and uncles all continued on their fact-finding missions. Tasmin and Elisa took the time to add rings of salt around the house, pulling out all their southern hoodoo roots to add to the protective measures. Our lives had been turned upside down. Sure, we had lived to fight another day, but the world had been turned on its axis.

Bizarre weather patterns had people watching the skies. Rumors of a new world order had taken over social media. States were trying to limit the information the public had access to by banning all social media sites, censoring what news stations could report, and limiting what printed media could publish.

Chickens were dying at an alarming rate. Locusts were attacking crops. Fish were dying as oceans, rivers, and springs turned red with what some were saying were chemicals, but we knew it was blood. On one coast, rising sea levels were sinking Florida at an alarming rate. On the other, California was seeing unprecedented rainfall, snow and, of all things, tornadoes.

Lilith's voice held thinly veiled anger as she slowly made her way around the room seven days after the battle. "My sources above told me that Izrail had this place surrounded and he'd also been given command of the whole 7th Battalion."

Brows furrowing with confusion, I said, "The 7th Battalion? Father, aren't you and Uncle Gabriel the generals of that army?"

"Not after we abandoned posts," he replied. "That's why they kept attacking, even after we no longer commanded it."

"Izrail had also been given control of my horn," Uncle Gabriel revealed. "He'd planned to blow it at any time."

Gasps were heard around the room. The Widows, Silas, and Jewel were still on the mend, but were healing nicely. No one was happier about that than Tasmin and Elisa. It started to occur to me that they cared more for the Widows more than they let on, and they did all they could to be sure that the elder coven members were taken care of.

"You've been casted out?" Uncle Raphael asked. "All of you?"

"Worse," said Aunt Lilith. "They're rebelling." At this, she smirked.

"His hand is against us now," Father added.

"Why is rebelling worse than being tossed out?" Tasmin asked.

"Because...those who are tossed out, almost always, always go crawling back. He rejected them. They didn't choose to leave. They crave His forgiveness. His acceptance." Lilith moved to the middle of the room as she talked. "Those who rebel, however? Their willingness to abandon their posts is seen as a rejection of Him…They chose to leave."

"And took their wings with them," Eset said, causing Aunt Lilith and the other high-archs around the room to chuckle.

Clearly it was an inside joke between the lot, one they didn't bother to let the rest of us in on as they moved the conversation steadily along until there was an incessant knocking at the door. Assuming it was the children coming back from their undercover trip to the Exchange, I hurried to the door, eager to hear what they had learned.

"Good afternoon, Octavian. I would lie and say it's good to see you, but why bother?" I heard as soon as I opened the door.

Before it could register who the dark-skinned, regally dressed man was in front of me, he used a gale force of wind to blow me away from the door. I went crashing through the foyer, down the hallway. I heard the team scrambling. My wife coming around the corner first, fist balled and ready for a fight only to be held in place by Uncle Morningstar's powers.

When Elisa and Dafari came running, they suffered the same fate as Tasmin and I. Dafari was knocked backwards while Elisa was forcibly held in place. All the archangels rushed to our aid. We'd been waiting on Morningstar to lead with a sneak attack, and he walked right up to the house and knocked on the door.

"I would suggest all of you rethink this," Lucifer taunted loudly, waving a hand, causing a black swirling hole to open behind him as he backed away from the door, down the steps and into the yard. His voice sounded as if all of the demons in Hell were talking through him. "I only came to talk, but I can always unleash literal Hell on this small town, killing everything in my wake, including innocents. Choose wisely…"

Dafari and I were on our feet now, guarding Tasmin and Elisa while urging the elder coven members, Silas and Jewel to stay back.

Once Lucifer saw he had our attention, he continued. "Perhaps we can be of assistance to one another? Would any of you happen to know the whereabouts of Azazel?"

"Where's Eve?" Aunt Lilith asked, completely ignoring his question.

"Dead," he answered plainly.

"What?" she screamed!

"I killed her."

"What do you mean, you killed her?" Lilith asked, her voice shaking with quiet rage.

"I meant what I said. I killed her. She was no longer of use to me."

Lilith scoffed as she descended the steps one-by-one. "She—she was no longer of use to you? Do you hear yourself?"

"Yes, and I, too, happen to love the sound of my voice." Lucifer's voice dripped with a honeyed cadence that gave me goosebumps and made me recoil at the same time.

"She was more than just some vessel for you to use and bend to your will and then discard! She was a human being!"

"At one point in time, sure, but I wouldn't even compare her to an animal these days."

Lilith was crying now. A gasp of disbelief escaped her lips; she shook her head and looked around. "I am so tired of all the false narratives! Didn't she suffer enough?"

"Spare me the theatrics, woman. You're crying over a bitch who wouldn't care if you lived or died. Have you no sense of self-worth left? She would have sooner slit your throat—"

"She was what you made her," Lilith screamed, her voice carrying on the wind, sending small creatures and fowl of the sky scattering for safer environments. The ends of her locs rose from her shoulders, swaying and hissing violently at Morningstar. "Tell the truth for once in your miserable lifetime!" She advanced on him slowly, her breaths coming out heavy and ragged.

Lucifer only smirked and he took his time stepping backwards. If Zafer was arrogant then his granduncle was haughty.

"And what version of the truth will be enough to quell your misguided anger, Dear?" he then crooned.

The word 'dear' came out so condescendingly that all the women sucked their teeth as they looked on. Eset stood with her arms folded across her chest while the widows stood like sentries, holding their staffs firmly at their sides. The uncles all had their weapons at the ready, poised to attack when the time came.

"Tell them the full truth! Tell them what really happened in the Garden of Eden. Tell them how Eve came to be the Mistress of Hell! The truth! I was casted out because I saw you for who you really were. It's why you hated me so much that you went—"

"Careful now, Lily-girl. You don't want to go making false allegations now, do you?"

"Oh, go to Hell, Adam!" Lilith seethed through clenched teeth, throwing a blast of white light at the man that he easily sidestepped as they slowly circled one another.

The malevolent smirk slowly disappeared from Morningstar's face.

A stunned chorus of, "Adam?" rang out.

Surely Lilith must have misspoken? The Widows eyes widened while Jewel gasped loudly. Eset stood to her full height, staring on as if she, too, had just learned something new.

"You drove her crazy... Coming to her in the Garden as a serpent."

"Removing his hands from his pockets, Morningstar grinned wide and wickedly, showing glistening fangs and red eyes. "Your righteous indignation is laughable at best. She knew what she was doing."

"She was so innocent!"

He scoffed. "Like hell she was. She wanted to taste it. I could see it in her eyes."

"She didn't know good from evil, but you did. So gullible that she didn't even question how it was that you would even know about the Tree of Life. Switching from one face to the other, convincing her to partake from the fruit of the tree."

"That she had already been instructed not to eat…"

"Just to switch back to your other face so you could pretend to still be just as ignorant as she? How dare you show your face and say you killed her so carelessly!"

"Oh please, she was just as eager a participant as I! She wanted it, and I gave it to her…raw no chaser. Are you still jealous, Lily-girl? Want me to show you what it is to know a man again?"

Aunt Lilith scoffed disgustedly. "When Hell freezes over!"

The being chuckled. "Well…remember you said it…"

His fangs lengthened as Aunt Lilith ran headlong at him, her locs attacking before she could. Adam, better known as Lucifer Morningstar, grinned devilishly, his locs taking on the form of snakes now. Aunt Lilith threw a white light charge that he easily deflected. She then called her sword to her, its power radiating through the atmosphere.

She skillfully sliced at her ex-husband, fighting like her very life depended on it. There was something about the way Adam wasn't outright attacking that was odd to me. And that's when I saw it, as Adam bulked, his lower body had turned into the massive form of a snake. His upper half still human, and while Aunt Lilith was distracted by rage and anger, his tail whipped her off her feet, slamming her backwards to the ground so hard her sword went flying out her grasp. Before any of us knew what was happening or could react, he had dragged her through the black hole, sealing it shut behind them.

EPILOGUE
DAFARI

Three weeks later...

Like so many of the businesses in Salix Pointe, my veterinary practice also needed repairs. Luckily for me, the damage was not extensive, which allowed David Herschel and his crew were able to complete the reconstruction quickly. I had been able to return to work within several weeks. I was glad to settle back into a routine, as ruminating on the fate of Aunt Lilith had started to become obsessive. All of us constantly wondered where she was, and if we'd ever see her again. While we, as Celestials, searched diligently for her, we were unsuccessful.

"Hello, Son," I heard behind me as I put a rabbit back in a cage, breaking me out of my thoughts.

Imagine my surprise when I turned around to see my mother standing there. Clothed in a long, red, flowing frock that stopped at the ankles with gold strappy sandals on her feet, Mother was appropriately dressed for Salix Pointe's springtime weather. Because an angel's pregnancy was considerably longer than that of a human woman, she didn't look as if was with child.

"Mother. To what I owe the pleasure of your visit?" I walked from the pet holding area to my office, Mother following close behind. I pulled back an office chair, encouraging her to sit before taking the seat behind my deck.

"Do I need a reason to visit my eldest son?" Her face held a slight smile.

I eyed her with curiosity. "No, you do not. However, you've never darkened the door to my home, let alone my office, until we had to go to war, so excuse my suspicion."

She nodded before responding. "True enough. I hope to change that. I've had a lot of time to think over the last few weeks. Dafari, I made a lot of mistakes raising you, many of them unconsciously…but that's no excuse. I failed as a mother, for that, I am so sorry. I'm here because wanted to… I was hoping that…I was wondering if you could ever forgive me, Son."

I gazed at the woman whom I got my rich, dark complexion from, saw the genuine remorse in her eyes. I knew exactly how she felt, asking for forgiveness from someone you love. I had to do it several times.

I rose from my chair, walking around my desk. Taking her hand in mine, I said, "I know it took a lot for you to say that. I've been where you are, Mother, so I appreciate you for the gesture. And, yes, I forgive you."

She stood, a look of relief washing across her face. Mother pulled me into an embrace, something she hadn't done in eons. I had to admit, it was nice.

Once she released me from her hold, I asked, "How are you feeling?"

"I am well. My pregnancy is progressing nicely."

When she mentioned the pregnancy, I thought about my own pregnant wife. I wanted to share the news, as it could have been something they has in common, but it wasn't my story to share.

"How are things with Michael?"

I noticed the pause before she responded.

"We are still working through things, but our relationship is better. Having our dirty laundry aired out in front of an audience has forced us to face our issues head on, before they escalate further."

"Michael loves you and you him. You two will get through this, and I'm sure you'll be stronger for it."

"Our love is strong. It's the trust that needs reinforcing. But that will come…in time." She sighed deeply. "I should go, but before I do, I still need to make amends with Elisa and Tasmin. As prophecy would have it, we will be intertwined in each other's lives having to work together. I would rather do so with no more bad blood between us. Please tell them to expect a visit from me soon."

My ears perked up when she said that. Mother was truly on an apology tour.

"I will let them know. And Mother?"

"Yes, my son?"

"I'm glad we had this talk. Don't be a stranger."

She touched my face before saying, "I won't, I promise. I'll see you soon."

Taking a step back, Mother walked through a shadow, ending our conversation.

I HAD STEPPED THROUGH THE SHADOWS INTO OUR kitchen. "Hello, my beautiful wife," I said, wrapping my arms around Elisa's waist from behind, noticing a bit of added girth from her pregnancy.

"Hello, my handsome husband." She turned around, kissed me like she hadn't just seen me a few hours ago.

We kissed like teenagers for a long time before I asked, "Do you hear that?"

"Hear what?" Elisa's brow furrowed, a confused gaze on her face.

"Exactly. No visitors interrupting us, the house all to ourselves."

Elisa giggled. "It is nice, isn't it? Don't get me wrong, I miss Tasmin and Octavian, but I do appreciate our privacy."

My brother and his blushing bride had moved out shortly after their nuptials. Their presence was missed, but now, with a child on the way, I cherished every solitary moment I shared with Elisa.

"As do I." I became quiet for a moment.

"Dafari, what is it?"

I took her hand, walking her to the living room. After we settled on the loveseat I replied. "I had a visit from mother today."

Elisa's eyes widened. "Eset? What did she want?"

I filled Elisa in, telling her how Mother wanted to apologize for her past misdeeds, told her I how had forgiven her.

"She also said she needs to see you and Tasmin. She wants to make amends."

I could tell how surprised Elisa was. "Wow, I didn't expect this. I never thought your mother would be the one to cross that bridge first."

"Nor I, but it appears Mother is taking the words in The Book of Prognostication very seriously, and since the three of you are destined to work together eventually, she wants to clear the air."

"I'm all for that," Elisa said. "Did she say when?"

"No, all she said was soon. Truth be told, I'm actually looking forward to you and Mother getting along, especially with you carrying our child." I reached over, placing my hand on her abdomen. "Our son or daughter could stand to have grandparents, especially since Zafer and Safiya never had that luxury growing up."

Elisa sat back, placing her head on my shoulder. "I think I'm ready to tell everyone."

"Are you sure?" I asked, taking her hand in mine.

"Yes, I'm sure. After everything that's happened, we need some good news."

Elisa was right. We'd all suffered so many tragedies. Sharing our news could be what everyone needed to lift their spirits.

Later that night, I sat in my sanctuary, thinking about my wife and the new life she would bring into the world. Elisa already had a glow about her. The fact that she even wanted to be a mother again after all she'd been through amazed me. With all the stress she had been under, I wanted this pregnancy to be as uneventful as possible.

To that end, I planned to talk to Zafer and Safiya. They had only been with us a short time, and, although they were adults, I didn't want them to feel alienated because of the baby. We still needed to bond as a family, and I would do everything possible to make that happen.

I worried less about Safiya more than I did Zafer. Safiya had the temperament of her mother...fiery yes, but also with a level-headed calmness. My son, on the other hand, was a loose cannon, one who had savagely murdered a high-ranking archangel...and relished in it. To this day, he showed no remorse for his actions.

Granted, Izrail was gunning for him and his sister, but still...even I was fearful of his immense powers. My son was a force to be reckoned with, and I would hate to be on the wrong side of his anger. I still wanted to know how Safiya and Zafer survived, what they did to survive...or did I really want to know? Regardless, I loved my children, and would be there for them...no matter what.

OUTRO
ZAFER

His grandfather's plan was coming together nicely. There were still some kinks that needed to be worked out, but Zafer didn't care. As a black energy portal transported him to a frozen over Hell, he was ecstatic.

He landed just outside the Devil's lair…or what once had been his lair. The beast had all but disappeared, which was smart. When his grandfather had told him, his sister, and their cousin of his plan, they thought it to be farfetched. However, all the hard work had actually paid off.

As soon as his hands touched the huge, stone-like doors to push them open, he felt a power surge so strong, his manhood threaten to erupt from the rush of it all. The black marble floor gleamed underneath his feet and shone as if it had been polished recently.

Hell was indeed empty. His grandfather had cleaned house. What was left of it anyway.

"Ah, my dear grandson. Took you long enough," greeted him as he walked further into the chambers.

His smile widened when he saw his grandfather, Azazel. "You were quiet for so long, we got a little afraid you'd forgotten about us."

Azazel's grin matched his grandson's as he walked forward

from the shadows to hug Zafer. Giving the younger man a warrior's embrace, he said, "Not hardly. I had some important matters to attend." Pulling away, Azazel studied the being before him. Dressed similar to Azazel, in a black suit that had been tailored to fit him, the brand-new red bottom dress shoes he had on made Zafer appear more businessman than demon. "How're your sister and Attalah? Are they ready?"

Nodding, Zafer walked around, wiping his nose with the back of his hand. The high was potent and he hoped his grandfather had something feminine and female waiting for him. He was going to need a willing and ready woman, and soon.

Azazel chuckled proudly while pointing to the high back stone-like throne. "That comes after, but first...take your place, Grandson, as the new king of Hell."

What felt like a magnetic force pulled him toward the chair. He could practically feel centuries of knowledge just waiting for him to partake. Removing his suit jacket and then the collarless dress shirt, he handed the garments to his grandfather. He felt his body bulk in ways he never had before, tendons and muscles seemingly adjusting to his new position by instinct.

As soon as Zafer sat down, instant pain made him grit his teeth, which was hard to do when his fangs were ever-lengthening. Sigils began to swirl in the air as the platform the chair sat atop rose slowly. Saliva built in his mouth as he tried to keep from slobbering because of the intensity of it all. Every instinct he owned coiled his gut.

The sensation of power was so strong that ecstasy wasn't the right word to describe what he felt. History, images, knowledge that no mere human would ever possess beat against the recesses of his mine. If he had been a computer, his hard drive would overload from how fast his mind was processing the information. An elicit moan that turned into an animalistic growl escaped him.

Zafer's head slammed back against the chair, and before his mind's eye, he could see it all. The beginning of creation. The rise and fall of nations. The past, present, and future. He saw the inevitable fall of first world countries. Those who were last shall become first. And so it went until he was so filled with dark energy that he had to stand.

He was dazed. Beside himself with power…and lust. Sometimes it was easy to forget he was part incubus. He took deep ragged breaths, trying to not embarrass himself in front of his grandfather, but he needed to feed. His demon blood rushed through him like molten lava.

"That's right, Grandson, take it all in," Azazel encouraged him.

Turning blood red eyes to his grandfather, he crooned, "It's too much…too soon…need to feed."

Azazel's smile widened, and when he snapped his fingers, from the shadows seven succubus of various hues and shades of brown walked forward. From the darkest of skin to lighter shades of brown, his grandson had his pick of the litter. And all seven were willing, ready, and more than able.

He knew now was not the time to try to talk anymore business. He would let his grandson satisfy his baser nature, and then he would return to discuss the power move they'd just made. As the pleasurable feminine moans began to circle the chambers, Azazel stepped back through the shadows.

He would have his revenge yet.

ALSO BY NOELLE VELLA

The Witches of Salix Pointe Series

The Witches of Salix Pointe

The Witches of Salix Pointe 2: Something Wicked This Way Comes

A Weekend Affair

A Weekend Affair: The Best Way to Get Over One Man is to Get on Top of Another

A Weekend Affair 2: Back to Reality

ABOUT THE NOELLE VELLA

The writing team of Noelle Vella is two talented authors, hoping to make their mark on the literary scene. Both authors began writing at an early age, and they continue to write novels, short stories, and poetry. The authors of Noelle Vella are hard at work on their next novel in the series. During their downtime, they enjoy spending time with their families. Their email address is NoelleVella@gmail.com.